Rick Moritz spent twenty-one years working for the Burlington Northern Railroad in western Nebraska and northern Colorado, during one of the biggest "boom" expansions in American western history.

The author's second career comprised twenty years as a student and professor of history and communication, and the process of identity development as it is affected by a sense of place.

Rick and his wife, Jill, live in Santa Fe, New Mexico.

Deadhead Home is dedicated to my wife of a hundred years (give or take), Jill. I cannot imagine a partner more encouraging or supportive. And patient. Really patient.

Rick Moritz

DEADHEAD HOME

AUSTIN MACAULEY PUBLISHERS™

LONDON * CAMBRIDGE * NEW YORK * SHARJAH

Ordering Information
Quantity sales: Special discounts are available on quantity purchases by corporations, associations, and others. For details, contact the publisher at the address below.

Publisher's Cataloging-in-Publication data
Moritz, Rick
Deadhead Home

ISBN 9781647508371 (Paperback)
ISBN 9781647508388 (ePub e-book)

Library of Congress Control Number: 2021915883

www.austinmacauley.com/us

First Published (2021)
Austin Macauley Publishers LLC
40 Wall Street, 33rd Floor, Suite 3302
New York, NY 10005
USA

mail-usa@austinmacauley.com
+1 (646) 5125767

I have a team of people who regularly assure me I can do whatever I set my mind to. I am grateful beyond description to my sons, Ben and Tom, and their wives (the daughters we never had) Kristina and Saba.

Forward

Crawford Hill.

It sounds innocent enough, doesn't it?

And like the Great American West, it's as obvious as its topography, as inscrutable as its potential—one that empowers as well as constrains.

The Burlington Northern Railroad is challenged around the clock, 24/7/365, with powering loaded coal trains, fresh from the bottomless mines that honeycomb the Powder River Basin in Wyoming, up and over Crawford Hill in northwestern Nebraska, and onward south and east to insatiable power plants from Texas to Chicago.

Now here's the trick—we're talking an 18,000-ton-load, divided into over one hundred separate coal cars, from Crawford, at 3,678 feet in elevation, to and past the next major siding at Belmont, looming (for the High Plains of northwest Nebraska, anyway) at 4,419 feet. And although this push appears doable considering Crawford and Belmont are eleven miles apart, the climb (and therefore descent) is concentrated at the legendary Horseshoe, a massive one-turn train-track switchback so acute, the engineer on the train's leading locomotive, ascending, can wave at his conductor as he rides the caboose, descending.

Now to confound the situation, let's overlay the physical challenges with the pure magic that is the transport of massive unit-trains. Each coal car rides on eight steel wheels, and each wheel meets and turns on a shared metal surface with one of two iron rails, and the wheel and rail meet in a space only three quarters of an inch long and five-eighths of an inch wide. Getting one truly massive train moving demands not only the three or four diesel locomotives pulling from the lead, said train requires the additional push a set of "helper" locomotives can provide. These additional units are essential, and three helper train crews—one engineer and one brakeman per crew—are permanently stationed at Crawford, available to be called on duty around the clock to assure there is time and opportunity for the loaded train to pull into the Crawford train yard, stop, part the cars in the middle, switch two or three locomotives into the train, put it all back together, and proceed up the Hill.

These tasks are further complicated by the hours-of-service rules the Federal Railway Administration enforces to assure the safety of train crews and the public alike. A train crew must have at least eight hours off from the minute they stopped working last (their *tie-up time*) to the minute they resume duty (their *call-time*). Once called, a crew can be required to work as many as twelve hours straight. At the end of twelve, the crew is officially out of time, and must cease and desist work where ever that train may find itself—the crew is, in effect, "dead." And because they were made to work twelve hours, they must now have ten hours, not eight, before they are once again considered rested for duty.

If a train "dies," that is, its crew is out of time, a new and fully rested crew must be transported to the dead train before that train can proceed along its route. Depending on the planning and execution of train travel between stations by train dispatchers (challenged to play a three-dimensional chess-game with hundreds of trains-as-pieces, and moving them about in unique patterns on a confining board), the supply of rested enginemen and trainmen at major terminals along the way, plus the variables of weather, geography, and pure dumb luck, the relief of a train crew out of time can be accomplished in as little as a few minutes or as much as several hours. This is because in a normal circumstance (and normality is a condition claimed by company spokesman more often than it actually occurs) a train dispatcher sees in advance that his train and its crew, due to unforeseen traffic, or mechanical problems, or cars derailing—or plain bad luck—won't get to the opposite terminal to tie-up within twelve hours. Commonly, a new and rested crew is called on duty to "deadhead" to the point which the train, out of time, sits and waits for relief. By "deadheading," a crewman understands that she or he will travel for some length of time and miles with nothing else to do save sit in a taxi van and ride. And again, commonly, this news is greeted by most crewman positively, as getting money for doing nothing is cake, and getting to do it "on a ride" is frosting on that cake.

I provide this information to give context, to share my sense of place, in appreciation of a part of the American West that in ways both subtle and sublime still exists, at least for those brave and fool-hearty and impatient and optimistic and impulsive and judgmental and forgiving souls, exploring and discovering and giving and taking and standing-tall-proclaiming and hiding-re-inventing—but most in pursuit of a dream defying rational expectation, and most content to behold a vision whose scope and range draws them relentlessly forward, never back.

I'm not saying life in the West is the best life (though it is), that true and organic connection to the natural world is most completely and providentially achieved here (yes, that too), or that your life is somehow minimalized, hell, marginalized as it is constrained by Eastern populations and practices (and again, just sayin').

I am saying that here an incident is an anecdote, an anecdote a story, a story soon mythical, and myth a legend. And this is because of the stage on which these stories play out, that stage that is the West. A fifty-degree temperature swing in a single day; red-rock canyons giving way to snow-covered peaks; eighty-, one hundred-, even a hundred-and-twenty-mile views, beginning in one state and terminating in another; sunrises and sunsets so spectacular as to freeze you in place, render you mute, transcend your understanding of art and science and poetry and prose.

I share stories told on such a stage, stories that, like all tales told hereabouts, are courses of weaving dependent on a thousand filaments, spun to a hundred yarns, and knitted and stitched and worked into a tapestry, the narrative of change and transformation. And that stage is an additional character, a plot point, an opportunity for conflict and resolution, living and evolving with time and space and place.

The West is where uncertainty lives, exiled from the East, as there it threatens traditions and customs unexamined but comforting, absolutes and axioms reassuring but irrelevant. And that is the secret, the grand paradox of living and working and growing and raising and dying and remembering in the West. Every day, every moment is a panorama of choice. The choices made yesterday, beyond our reach, and the choices we make tomorrow, beyond our sight—all are subject to mitigation at least and restoration at best, and are affected as well by the ripples of change generated by the choices we make—today.

Uncertainty is an opportunity to exercise hope, employ creativity, expand capacity, strengthen faith, and deepen understanding. One can run from it, and deny the certainty of its return. Or one can embrace it, and harness its natural turbulence to power the sails of one's endeavors.

That's our choice. And sooner or later, we all run out of time.

William Allen

Lander, Wyoming

September 9, 1987

Prologue

Harley Straight swears this is the first and last damn time he takes his brother's call to taxi a train crew. Harley'd never considered it tonight, but it's money, and *ain't it always the damn money*?

Harley's Barbie gave birth to their Joseph ten months past, and *I'll be a sonuvabitch—how the hell did that happen*, Barbie's due to bear Joseph's little brother or sister any day. And Barbie's still working, believe it or not, still a swing-shift operator, taking and writing and giving train orders to crews out of Edgemont, South Dakota, from two in the afternoon until ten at night, lousy Mondays and Tuesdays off. And she won't let up until her water breaks—it's the money.

We had this same damn talk five years ago Harley remembers, his senior year, her junior year, Barbie's knocked up, and Catholic, and sure Harley loves little Emily, but that was supposed to be it, even then, Barb promised.

So Harley sees his choice as no choice, as what kind of a man says no to money, easy money, while his pregnant old lady slaves the night away? *No kind of man.*

If this whole predicament presented itself just two months previous, Harley would have said no to his brother George before the question was finished. Harley's the sole proprietor of Two Moons Motor Lodge, a clean, reputable, dated little motor court, clinging to the north edge of town, where 6th Avenue intersects with U.S. Highway 18, the "money" highway, as it runs north and east to connect to U.S. 385, gateway to all things Black Hills. As a year-round motel operator, Harley's all too aware of the feast-and-famine of the tourist trade. But this year, 1976, the bi-centennial year of America's birth, is the gift that keeps on giving. Every family planning its once-in-two-or-five-or-seven-year vacations, across the nation, has picked this year to investigate the U.S., and most are drawn to explore the mythical American West. And though Edgemont is hardly a destination location, it's most definitely a point of passage for those families on their way to someplace else—headed to South Dakota's Black Hills and Mount Rushmore, Wyoming's Devil Tower and Big Horn Range and Yellowstone, even Montana's Lewis and Clark Trail. So, Harley turned this season, May through August, with three times the numbers of guests as any year before.

But such a windfall goes to maintenance and insurance and roofing and painting, and what's left goes to the bank to pay off short-term loans, and what may still remain, that little bit goes in savings, because waiting out January through April can be cold and dark and hungry.

So, yes, dammit, Harley has used his ninety-minute-warning call wisely. Shaved and showered, watered and fed, carrying a duffel with a change of clothes and toothbrush and his prescription for a "jumpy" heart—ain't no big thing—just in case those train dispatchers down in Alliance decide he's can't just come on home empty, no crew returning. "Deadheading" is something they don't like to see if they can help it. George has told him a hundred times of driving the old taxi van, carrying four crewmen and their grips, their luggage that is, comfortably, and maybe six in a pinch, but it better not be too damn far to go, those old boys be tired and hungry and smell like a dirty grill in a cheap saloon. And George says he'll often get to the little Edgemont depot on a normal, regular old day, the yellow metal building hugging the main line as it dissects the town, and he'll work his way inside between rested crews coming on duty, angry crews coming off duty, fighting to get to the operator's counter where train orders, composed in the Mount Olympus that is the Alliance, Nebraska Dispatcher's Office, and copied and delivered by the operator on duty, he or she telling all and sundry to save their bitching and moaning for their old ladies, as he or she did not write the goddam orders, operators only deliver, so do not be shooting the messenger, and when it comes to that don't be shooting anybody else either.

And although George was told, when receiving his call to duty at home one and a half hours previous, that he was merely picking up a crew out of time at Ardmore, a little siding eight miles down a roller-coaster two-track floating on a sheen of bentonite—a job arduous but fulfilled most often in no more than two hours—this night his job could just as well turn out to be delivering crews all the way to the opposite terminal, Gillette, Wyoming, as there was just a major derailment somewhere, and such emergencies, sadly commonplace, prevail, and George (now Harley in his stead) might see his home and bed in

14

twelve or thirteen hours. Old Harley, a glass-half-empty-type—thanks, Mom—expects the worst as he approaches the midnight operator, Dolly DeGraw, and asks for his formal orders, directions on crew pick-up and drop-off.

"Hey, Dolly, have I still got a Crawford Turn?" Harley knows such is what the railroad folk call driving one engineer and one brakeman from Edgemont to Crawford as a Helper Crew, being that the three crews permanently assigned to Crawford to help coal trains over and past the legendary horseshoe are all yet to achieve their Federally-mandated rest, as a derailment in the coal fields has ripple effects delaying trains for a hundred and fifty miles in all directions.

Dolly's not surprised to see Harley rather than George, for Dolly's George's ex, and George needs off in the first place so that he will be in town bright and early first thing tomorrow as Dolly has successfully challenged George's child-support maximums, and she plans to take George to the cleaners, once and for all.

Dolly's always liked Harley, and Barbie thinks a bit too much. "No change, big boy, one helper crew to Crawford, right back home, you should be tying up right back here as I am getting off work. Wanna get off with me?" Dolly's always kidding, except Dolly's never kidding.

Harley takes the orders from her hand, smiling. "I am literally hours from getting Barbie to the delivery room." And Dolly pats his hand, not letting go. "So after then?"

And Harley pulls away, taking some small comfort in Dolly's consistency, if not her morals. He's back outside and starting up the dented Ford van George drives for the taxi company, based out of Rapid City, getting it warm for the train crew. And an engineer approaches from the parking lot to Harley's left, and a trainman approaches from his right, and peculiar for sure, one additional figure approaches from behind and climbs in the van as well.

Harley turns about to question the figure, a guy maybe, a little guy, hard to see or hear clearly as he or she is sitting pressed to the van's farthest cranny, next to the spare tire and the first aid kit, but the person waves him on, mumbling something about a short call and a just-now-sick brakeman in Crawford.

And Harley gives in—oh well, what the hell—so he can get this show on the road, drop the crew, drive like hell for home, grab Barbie, have a baby, *I still can't believe it, another kid, another dollar.*

Well, Harley's thinking as he pulls away from the depot, the crew already settling in like sleep's the best idea, a short turn out, and a quick return back, weather's fine, and the roads are dry:

What could possibly go wrong with a deadhead home?

Part One

One

There are one million things about retirement I wouldn't trade for the world. Well, okay, I'm working on my problematic relationship with hyperbole. We're co-dependent. Anyway, there are several dozen things I love about irregular employment. As a security guard at eighteen, then administrative clerk for Protection Services at twenty, and a rookie probationary railway agent at twenty-one, leading finally to a series of postings as special agent for the Great Northern, and Northern Pacific, and Colorado & Southern, and the Chicago, Burlington & Quincy—all roads in time merging to this day's Burlington Northern—I always enjoyed *the work*, just never cared much for *the job*.

It's a paradox, I know, and the nature of the West. I'll always cherish a romantic soft-spot for rail history, and I firmly believe that the expansion and development of this country, whether or not you are a fan or critic (and I am both), would have proved physically and emotionally insurmountable without the catalyst our nation's railroads were summoned to be. So, my irregular hours, and my exotic locations, and starting my day with a very rough set of expectations for success, and ending my day, often even the *next* day, exhausted and hungry and sometimes the worse for wear, but exhilarated by the unforeseen turn of events—all these factors I wouldn't trade for anything. But the part that sucked, absolutely and comprehensively sucked in a manner both sucky and suck-a-ditious, was answering to others. And by that, I mean any-damn-body-else, save myself. I have no problem with authority, and when the time comes that I meet with a human being I judge to be wise beyond reason, creative beyond context, and righteous but selfless, I will be the first to recognize her or his natural and valuable superiority, and I will hence forth jump off high cliffs and long bridges and tall buildings at said boss's bidding. Hey, it's a possibility.

The probability? *Ain't gonna happen.*

So, I could've battened-down my hatches, tucked my chin, and ground out forty-two years until a full pension, or do what I *did* do—beat a wretched path through a bureaucratic jungle for twenty years, assuring myself of 75% of a pension upon turning 66, and in the meantime, "hang a shingle." Become a consultant, yeah, that sounds good, a security consultant. A sort of *special* special agent. Cheaper for many small railways as they owe me no benefits, and I can be more discrete, as with experience comes knowing how to pad about the media as if you are one of them, and how to tap-dance round a swollen bureaucracy demanding pointless documentation, and what battles to fight, and when to take a pass.

And—*and*—when to just *quit,* for the lovuh God, because quitting can be a *good* thing, as I can testify, seeing as how I am alive, ambulatory, and reasonably intelligent, and in a handful of limited situations, *astute.* Because I quit the hopeless challenge, and lived to face one *not* insurmountable.

Taking all of this to account, I still wonder why I answered my phone at 3:30 am on the morning of September 9, 1986, my small but snuggly Airstream secure at the edge of Sinks Canyon, just outside of Lander, Wyoming, my adopted hometown town for a host of reasons (yes, a *host*), the first and foremost being it is not on a railway main line to anywhere.

Yeah. But answer the phone I did.

And one week later, I sealed up my trailer and threw two grips in the back of my Bronco.

And I would not see my Airstream again for a month.

Two

Richard "Dicky" Tuttle, Senior Special Agent, Alliance Division, Denver Region speaks on the other end of a bad land line, and it does nothing for his tenor monotone. As I am three-quarters asleep, on slow exit from a world in an alternate galaxy, and one where I was apparently the Lord High Commissioner, I could swear the person on the other end of this line isn't speaking at all, but rather continually honking the old clown horn Clarabell carried about on the Howdy Doody Show. Remember? No? I digress. (But, just for nothing, the first Clarabell—there were three—was Bob Keeshan, who, of course, became our beloved Captain Kangaroo, a well-deserved promotion for all that mandatory honkin'-around.)

I can hear better when I tip my head at a forty-five-degree angle, this true ever since a seasonal track worker in the Nebraska Sand Hills discharged his shotgun just past my left ear, a primitive but effective attempt to communicate his displeasure with my desire to arrest him for cattle rustling. Now I have a tell, signifying my desire to truly listen, unless it is hay fever season, because in an unrelated story, I tend to sneeze at a forty-five-degree angle.

"Hey, Dicky, how's the boy? This line sucks."

"Well, Will, that would be on *your* end, as you are stubborn and insist on living at the end of the world."

"That is rich, as I live in Lander, Wyoming, God's summer home, and you live in Alliance, Nebraska, the land God didn't forget, but sincerely wishes he could." I'm barely into a robe, out my snuggly bed, down the little hall to my tiny kitchen, to hit the brew button on my preloaded coffee maker. Said appliance claims it's now almost a quarter to four, and I wonder how old Dicky is exactly, and what the odds might be of his natural death occurring momentarily. The honking noise returns, I notice my head is no longer tipped, and my disposition no longer sweet.

"Look, Dicky, I really cannot make out a word. But since I'm retired and you are not, if you want to take up my time, climb up on one of your Guernsey-bound trains out of Alliance, don't get off until it gets to Casper, then stay the course, keeping an eye sharp for the Shoshoni siding, where, if you are lucky, the train will slow to twenty for your dismount. Then wait 'til sunrise and catch a ride with ol' Sean McDuff—remember Sean? Signal Supervisor at Bridgeport? He threw up the title and the money, bumped down this way as a Maintainer, except all he's maintaining right now is his fly-fishing technique. He'll drive you into Lander, maybe an hour, an-hour-and-a-half, he drives like a madman, remember to pop for his gas."

The honking sound subsided with my drop of the receiver into its cradle. I could have been nicer. Dicky's not a bad guy, just needing my periodic disabuse of his most fantastical notions. Like what he does on a given day has anything to do with anything in particular. Is that *regret* starting to well up inside me? And the coffee maker goes off signaling it has great good news, and I am distracted, and the world is beautiful once more.

Sidney's in downtown Lander is indescribable. That should do it, right? Okay, great coffee, roasted by Sid her own self, best breakfast ever if you think two eggs and homemade toast *is* the best breakfast ever, best selection of LP's if you believe Tito Puente and Celia Cruz are all one would need to survive the end of the world, and Sid.

Sidney Turner Lowe was born and raised by academics in Lowell, Massachusetts, sent abroad for extended periods by a grandmother-heiress, speaks Spanish, French, Turkish, and Italian, and plays a haunting jazz violin. She speaks little about "the old days," God bless her, but I've pieced together some hints and off-the-cuff remarks suggesting Sidney taught political science at a Boston university, and did some analyst work for the State Department. She wouldn't be specific, but again I gathered odd mentions of dates and times, and her State work coincidentally overlapped with the Bay of Pigs. All this in a body five feet even, maybe, a hundred pounds wet. I've never pinned her down on age. She's the type that was born forty, pre-raised, and self-educated in spite of—not because of—the girls' schools her old-school dad demanded, and a glorious undergrad experience at Cambridge. I'm thinking if I'm 60, she's somewhere thereabouts, but I couldn't tell you why.

Dicky Tuttle woke me way too early two days ago, and I've forgotten the discomfort for the most part. My day starts five times a week here at Sid's, 6:30 on the dot, Tuesday through Saturday. Sid takes Sundays and Mondays off, and so do I. Thankfully, I have less and less to take off *from*.

I walk three blocks down Main St., the original U.S. Highway 287, a senior-statesman-thoroughfare of the American West, and I turn left into Sidney's. The door is painted Santa Fe blue, and it's one of my chores to turn the "Closed" sign around to "Open." Then I start coffee—Farmer Brothers— in two large coffee percolators, and finally I grab an ancient push broom, its handle four feet long and painted yellow. I sweep my way around the main floor, this day through the kitchen, round the storage room, past two tiny restrooms, back to the main room looking out on Main and the morning "rush." Here I finish the job, load the dustpan, dump it in the main garbage, take *that* can to the dumpster in the alley. And for all this, after I wash my hands and return to the front, there is Sid arranging my two scrambled eggs next to two slices of home-baked rye, next to a large orange juice and a steaming cup of coffee. As compensation for my work, I come out far ahead. The deal is further sweetened by getting to wake up to my favorite person (in this specific region), plus a cast of local characters so colorful, you wouldn't buy their descriptions in a *noir* matinee. Suffice to say, Wyoming is a hide-out.

"Had a call, Allen." Sid places one of the last asters of the season in a clear vase by a bottle of green Tabasco, and hands me a fork. I was introduced to Sid years ago by a mutual friend as *Will Allen*. At that specific meeting Sid goes *William?* And I go *Will.* And Sid goes *Billy?* And I, patiently, go *Will.* And Sid goes *Willy A?* And I, not surprisingly, go *Will.* And Sid doesn't miss a beat, and goes *Nice to meet you, Allen.* It's been Allen ever since.

"A call? There's a phone in the Airstream."

Sid pinches a dead leaf from the aster. "Apparently not one anyone answers."

"Got me there." Before I can dig in, Sid's wall phone rings, hanging as it does next to a swinging door between the front counter and the kitchen.

Sid moves like she's thirty, snagging it on the first ring. "Sidney—whatcha need?" Sid still carries a hint of a Boston accent, so this sounds very cool, no nonsense. She gives the poor sucker on the other end three seconds, roll her eyes like a pro, motions me *get your ass over here.*

I do. "Will Allen."

"—is a jerk."

"Little Dicky Tuttle, as I live and breathe."

"Still a jerk."

This doesn't sound right. I'm starting to feel as though I've missed something. "Where are you, Dick?"

"Where you told me to be, you sonuvabitch. I'm freezing my ass off in Shoshoni."

Oh, no. "Dicky, you didn't—"

"I did." Now his tenor was reaching a clown-horn pitch. "You said grab a Guernsey-bound train, I grabbed the local—"

Me: "—worst choice possible."

Dicky: "—which died in Alliance yard, as the midnight switch engineer had a heart attack, the crew had my local split in three sections, two of them blocking the main line—"

Me: "You should have known—"

Dicky: "—shut up, by the time they got the engineer to the hospital and the main line cleared, three eastbound coal trains and four westbound empties ran out of time, died on the vine, crew callers came up short of rested replacements, and I begged a ride with a crew taxi to Guernsey, caught a hot-shot freight out of Guernsey to Casper, and *that sucker* dies enroute as well when one of the oil tanker-cars gets a flat spot on a wheel, derails, calling out Haz-Mat clear the hell from Denver, no one else on duty, nothing moves for four and a half hours, except my bowels, then a new crew shows, we limp into Casper, I beg a ride with a Trainmaster to Shoshoni, where you told me to be, you lousy bastard."

Me, less kind than the situation warrants: "And you're two days late and a dollar short, Dick. Sean McDuff ain't on call as a taxi service for wayward special agents, man's got a job to do as well—"

"Bullshit, Allen. You know as well as I do, he's hiding behind a cottonwood row, casting away on the Big Horn River, doing less than you."

And right damn *here* is where I like to remind my potential clients of the one essential, pivotal, transcendent element to our potential working relationship—*you need me, buddy, ain't the other way round.*

"Senior Special Agent Tuttle, my breakfast is getting cold, my heart colder. And you're tying up Sidney's phone, so—"

"I hate you."

"Poor start."

"All right, dammit, *please* pick me up in Shoshoni. I didn't dress for Wyoming."

"Yes, we are so very different from tropical Alliance—"

"Please—"

"On my way."

Dicky seems *too* relieved. "Wait, where should I wait?"

Sometimes I wonder how many of Dicky's forty railway years have been spent outside his black-leather office.

"Look around, Dick. It's Shoshoni. Stand square on the yellow line, middle of U.S. Highway 20. I'll try not to hit you."

I amble back to my table, apply my Tabasco liberally, and open a copy of the *Casper Tribune*. Sid leaves a copy on every table every morning. She sits at my table now, and the early morning waitress, a high school senior named Juanita Moon, brings her a Denver omelet and sourdough toast.

"Thought you're in a hurry."

"Dicky's in a hurry. Breakfast is the most important meal of the day."

Sid applies Crowheart honey, Wyoming's best, to her toast, signals Juanita for coffee. "You're making him wait. One point for showing him whose got leverage, one point grinding him as a former boss."

I take a refill as Sid gets her first cup of the morning. "Nice work, Juanita." Juanita speaks like words cost money. "Same to ya."

Sidney watches a BN signal maintainer's highrailer, a giant working truck—this truck capable of lowering four steel-wheels to steel-tracks, and riding along where ever a train might, then raising the wheels and driving off into the sunset on a regular road once more. The driver slows as he passes Sid's front window, honks and waves, and I wave back.

Sid arches a grey eyebrow. "Isn't that—"

"—Sean Mc Duff? As *you* live and breathe."

"Allen, you are lucky anybody from North Platte to Moab cares one whit about you, let alone returns your calls."

The toast is to die for. "True, Sidney. 'Lucky' has never been a problem. And how you see me as 'problematic'—I believe that's the word you tend to use—"

Sid stands, as her breakfast is over, and a long work day stands squarely ahead— "*Truculent* is the word I use, and *unapologetically-lazy* works, as does *happily-self-absorbed.*"

And the eggs are perfect. I stand and stretch. "Can't argue those. But I take my time this morning as I'm *helping* my old boss understand how dependent he is on me, and Dicky learns best when he's uncomfortable. His suffering is his learning opportunity."

Sidney shakes her head as if I'm a carny selling my ring-toss game to passing rubes. "How do you know he needs one damn thing? And from you, at that?"

"Oh, Sid." I slide into my insulated barn jacket. "My reasons are two." She rolls her eyes on cue.

"One, Dick Tuttle never leaves his office at the old depot in downtown Alliance as long as he has a probationary agent or an assistant agent to do his bidding. I was that guy for four years before my seniority set me free." I'm to the door, ready to exit.

"And two, Dicky'd never ride an actual train, with an actual crew, go sleepless for the better part of two days, nor spend two seconds in a joint like Shoshoni for any amount of love or money, save for one thing."

Sid's clearing a table, too cheap to hire busboys. "That being?"

"Being," I say, as I exit, "Dick's got a case he doesn't want, or can't solve, or both, and he can't palm it off on Billings or Chicago or Denver."

Sid nods like she's heard the weather report. "You smell a tough case, interesting worst case, fascinating best case, one that buffs the patina of your mythical reputation?"

And just before the door closes, Sid hears me say this:

"I smell that, and I smell money."

Three

I'm headed to Shoshoni at the speed limit. Good citizen? No. I want to make Dicky wait in Shoshoni, deepen his appreciation for the challenges the Northern Arapaho and the Eastern Shoshone face, both tribes "assigned" to Wyoming's Wind River Reservation. I take time to spin past every AM radio station I can pick up, which are few, save for our 50,000-watt, clear-channel station out of Casper, KTWO. If a local happening takes place anywhere from Ravenna, Nebraska, to Sheridan, Wyoming, or from Billings, Montana to Denver, Colorado, and that event can or has or will affect any aspect of the Burlington Northern, I need to know about it. This is who I'm *supposed* to be.

I claim to be a consultant. My card says *Consulting Special Agent,* then lists a number of railways I've worked over the years. Why am I on my own? It usually boils down to a love-hate relationship. I love me, my employers don't. I do have problems with authority, and documentation, and paperwork, and the whole social-emotional canvas upon which "work" in this country is expressed. "Work friends," office romance, the bowling leagues and baby showers and bachelor parties and fund-raisers and raffles, and some idiot's always having a birthday, or the "drink or two" after a tough shift—these all sound harmless, and in some railroad towns, there *is* nothing else to do, and these artifices provide some kind of support system, which, I suppose, is better than nothing, but not *too* damn much better.

Because, work-related friends and romance are based on—work. What happens when one friend or lover is promoted over another? Or has to fire the other? Or hire someone he or she used to date? What happens when work flourishes, and one party's so busy, there's no time for the other? Or work dries up, and people must be let go? The social atmosphere and the work environment can't be unraveled. So, I avoid social relationships with *railroaders* at all costs, and this alone makes me an outlier.

And, I'm not getting any younger. Dawn broke, so to speak, one night when I was sitting in the Stockmen's Café in Edgemont, South Dakota, off-duty, two a.m., alone. Yeah, *hooray* work friends. I realized it was my twenty-year anniversary with the BN (depressing enough as no one hires on a railroad thinking *well, here I go, big money for doing the exact damn thing every lousy day, rain or shine, and—here's the truly super part, I need forty-two years in total before I can retire with 100% of my pension.*

This sudden awareness was just in time, because, and this is *not* an exaggeration, *at that time*, I would have had a hard time choosing between the forty-two-year plan and the one-bullet-to-the-brain option. However, in short order, a close friend, maybe my only friend at that moment, found me and gave me refuge, and I gained strength, and she showed patience and acceptance and no small amount of faith. And we married, and I quit, and I am that consulting special agent ever since.

And ten years after my transition, my wife died, and I'll speak to that in length just as soon as it stops hurting so damn much. Ask me again in ten years.

Traffic's light this morning—sorry, that's a funny joke in Wyoming, we all use it—so I still make good time, and there's Shoshoni over the next rise, lost in the glare of sunrise, lost in time and tragedy. And there, just *lost*, sits Dicky Tuttle, arguing with a little Arapaho kid, a small, beat-up bike between them. I pull up in my Bronco, parking on the wrong side of the street (another traffic joke), and roll down my window.

I can't help smiling. "Who's your little friend?"

Dicky's pissed. "He won't give me a name."

I get out of the truck. "I'm talking to the kid."

The kid loves this, sticks out a hand to shake, says, "Sammy McSqueeze, your honor."

Now Dick's simmering, and I shake the kid's hand. "Clyde Caddidle-hopper, and this is my sidekick, Weak-ass Jones."

I acknowledge Dicky. "What seems to be the problem, officer?"

"The problem, smartass, is this kid's trying to sell me that bike, and he has no proof of ownership whatsoever."

"What kid?"

"*That* kid—" and, of course, Dick looks down to see the kid disappear around the corner, the bike parked at Dick's feet.

I'm already in the Bronco, pulling away slowly. "For somebody in a hurry, you sure love yakkin'." And Dicky swears more violent than I wish to quote, and grabs his grip and tosses it in the back, and barely hauls his butt in and door shut before I punch it and we are off.

I try to soothe. "Look, Dick, we're all of twenty minutes to Riverton, 'less your picky about speed limits, and you look like you could use a lot of coffee, maybe some oatmeal, pre-chewed? Anyway, relax and we'll stop at Speedway Café—you know it, no, I suppose not—you won't be sorry." I end the pitch with my patented big dumb-ass smile, easy to access as it's involuntary and one hundred per cent natural.

Dick pouts, not a good look. "What about your precious *Sidney's?* One you claim is the best in the west?"

"Sorry, Dick, no go. Sidney hates you."

"What the hell? We've never met."

This too easy. "You kind of have. I filled her in."

Now Dick stares out his window, takes a couple of beats off.

"Have I got a choice?"

I floor the Bronco and sit back. "Let's pretend you do."

We listen to KTWO in silence. When I first met Dicky, I had plenty of opportunities to study his patterns of anger display. We are oil and water. Normally, even during my probation, Dick would issue a set of orders, I would question them immediately, and the fire was lit. He did slow burns, maybe it was genetic, I don't know, but I counted on it, as I had no intention of completing an assignment using any of his directives. Let's put it this way— you ask me for change for a buck? I give you four quarters. Dicky? One quarter, six dimes, two nickels, two pennies and a post card. And advice on how to spend it.

We are into Speedway's little parking lot, then to the farthest corner of the sunny dining room. This is where I want Dicky—he's exhausted, half-pissed, but he's about to hire me, and he *has* to hire me, because he wouldn't be here at all, taking my abuse, unless I am the *very last option.*

I love this. I'll try to be kind.

We order. Dicky finally makes eye contact. I am glad to see he isn't holding a weapon.

"Let's do this, Allen. I can't take much more."

"Yeah, fresh air and direct sunlight is a bitch." Ooops.

Dick grits his teeth, produces the mandatory manila folder.

"A taxi van, one driver, one engineer, two brakeman, called to deadhead to Crawford, all three Helper crews are dead-out-of-time, first crew isn't rested for another six hours. For no known reason, the taxi blows past the Crawford depot and the yard, down the road parallel to the Hill, misses a turn, fiery crash, everybody dies—" Dicky consults the folder—"September 9—"

"1976. All due respect, Dick, this *is* 1986—"

"And thank you, I am not a moron, it's a cold case, and one that needs resolution immediately if not sooner." Dick looks different of a sudden, maybe not so angry as scared—that's it, desperate. Maybe this is where I can offer a bit of relief, which will be important, because at some point, Dick will have to see I have the upper hand, and he will be forced to sign off on my contract, *on my terms.*

"Give me the folder, you enjoy your breakfast (Dick ordered the meat-laden rancher's breakfast just because of my 'oatmeal' crack). Then maybe you can answer my questions?"

Dick seems to like this, though he keeps the guard up. Smart move, his part.

And thirty minutes later, I hand the folder back across the table. Dick drains his coffee cup, runs to the restroom, returns. "Ready."

I bet he's not. "Okay, Dick, here's what I'm seeing. And what isn't being said."

I shift on my chair, fix my stare on the old neon clock on the back wall. And—go.

"As you said, this crew is called to perform Helper duty at Crawford. Normally Crawford extra board employees will be called out of Alliance, the main terminal, but they too are completely out of brakeman or engineers that night, at least those that will answer their phones, so here comes the van out of Edgemont." Dick nods. I go on.

"Timmy Nelson, Engineer, and Roger Fointman, Brakeman. Tim's a straight-shooter, a teetotaler, spends his time off at the away-from-home terminal getting his rest at the local library. Roger's lucky to be alive, hippie-dippie, smokes anything he can keep lit, plays high-stakes poker in a "secret" room behind Stockman's, in and out of debt with loan sharks directly connected to the Calderone crime family out of Denver. But here's the sticker, the one swept under the rug—"

"—wait just a minute—" Dicky's defensive.

"—I'll nod your way when it's your turn, Dick. If your initial investigation was any good, you wouldn't be sitting here ten years later and suffering my presence."

Dick shrugs, true enough. I go again.

"A third crew member climbs in the back of the van last second, mumbles a name nobody can hear over the heater fan and diesel roar, he or she just waves at the driver, one Harley Straight, *get movin' and time's a-wastin'*. And here young Harley figures the guy wouldn't be here unless he was supposed to be, who in his right mind'd jump a taxi to Crawford in the middle of the night for kicks?"

Dick nods, I return it. "Yes, sir, I read the part where Harley worked the shift as a favor to his brother-in-law, and he needed money, but he needed back home quick as his wife, an Edgemont operator, was giving birth anytime. Side notes: they got married in high school, and there was a five-year-old girl, Emily, at home this night, plus a ten-month-old surprise named Joseph."

I slip the waiter-guy my credit card, he looks at it like it's the first one he's ever seen—might be the case—and I stand to re-enter my coat. "So, Dick, here's how good your initial investigation was—and this is all in service to you and I cutting out the nonsense, getting down to ground rules and rate of pay." Now Dick's looking like the chorizo he added to the build-it-yourself-omelet (again, I could have told him) is backing up, and note to self *no, he is not riding one more mile in my Bronco, even in the open-air box.*

I sign my credit invoice on the way out, keep moving toward the Bronco in the lot, get to the grill, turn around and lean in. I'm surprised to find Dick *right* behind me, but I did buy his breakfast, so—

"So, Richard Horatio Tuttle, you probably took one look at this ten years back and reckoned. You reckoned, one deadhead crew never touched the Crawford train yard, and they were not traveling in a BN vehicle, and the contracted driver missed a turn on Crawford hill, everybody dies—BN is not responsible, let the taxi company get their ass sued off, who cares? There's a minor-league autopsy performed—no one *officially* requested it, ain't binding—and that only because the first EMT to scene thought something's hinky, calls his GP at the Crawford Clinic, he calls an emeritus-buddy at North Dakota State, they get together and run a handful of unauthorized tests. And that result disappears, as much through disinterest as anything else, because the engineman's family and the brakeman's family bag a hundred grand settlement a piece, no small amount in '76, the Straight family gets next to nothing as the county deputies write up Harley at fault, and nobody comes forth on behalf of the third crew member." Now I nod at Dicky.

"Finally." I smile in response. Dick does not, takes a deep breathe. "An unexpected turn of events has propelled this *matter* back to my desk, and it would be in *both* of *our* best interests if it could quickly be resolved."

"Hold it, hold it, it's coming to me, as if in a dream." Dick looks away. "Yep, I got it. Emily, the five-year-old from the file—I'll be damned, she's fifteen by now, right? Oh, yeah, growing up without a dad in a railroad town, she's smart, she's rebellious,"—Dicky's turning green—"Bingo. Got it, Dicky. She's been digging around, right? Maybe uncovered a name here, a little exchange of cash there? And she's asking *all* the questions, pertinent to her old man or not."

"Goddamit, Allen, I'm retiring on full pension in three years, and I'm up for Regional VP Protective Services in January—"

"Which inflates your pension, plus stock options—"

"Allen—" Dick looks for all the world like his appendix burst.

"Get a hold, Dick. I'll take the case."

Dick doesn't look a whit better. "Really?"

"These conditions. I start now, I end when I say I do, you pay a daily rate plus all expenses unquestioned, and that daily is a number *I* name and I am free to jack it up whenever I please. But—"

"What?" Dicky's white.

"Last condition, you come clean right now. What has Emily Straight, a teen-age girl from Nowhere, South Dakota, got on you and your ten-year-old investigation."

I think Dick's one gag from full-on puke.

He coughs. "Forensics."

"Meaning?"

Dick coughs again. "Harley Straight died on impact. The other three were dead *before* the crash."

"And?"

"And, you relentless bastard, all four had traces of Chloroform in their sinus membranes."

"Shit, Dick, you *are* in a world of hurt."

"Tell me something I *don't* know."

And here is how my main character flaw manifests itself.

"Well, apparently, *how* a *professional conducts an investigation*."

Four

And right on cue, a BN welding truck, driven by a BN welder, pulls into the lot, as I had arranged before leaving Lander.

Arne Birger is driving, and Dicky is struck dumb, or dumber. Imagine the prototypical Viking chieftain. It's Arne. First, his name means *Eagle Keeper.* That's just the start of cool. He stands no more than five-ten, maybe, but he looks like he walked away from the tools of his sculptor-creator all of a piece, perfectly proportioned, classically aligned. Square-face, raptor beak, arctic-river-blue eyes, and a mane to his shoulders, golden-sunlight with harvest highlights, and always seeming to blow back and away from his face by a gentle wind, no matter which way the wind blows.

And the kicker here—Arne's a master-welder. Welders on a railroad are the guns for hire. Tracks are always in need of construction and repair; track beds suffer weather-related and derailment-related damage regularly. Rails and wheels made of steel, these elements interact in a way only a welder can smell and feel and know. I'm envious because I admire any railroad craft that can force the company into a corner, and the company has no choice but to pay. So a welder, a really good welder, shows up when he shows up, goes home when he finishes, and works as much or as little as he chooses.

I grab Dicky's grip and toss it in the back of Arne's truck. Dick climbs in, stunned, and I go *this is Arne Birger, your ride to Alliance,* and Arne goes, with just a twist of an accent, *just an errand or two first,* and I go *take your time, Arne—it's been years since Dicky's seen the Powder River*, and Dicky, waking up, goes *wait just a damn minute, I gotta get back,* and I go *hasta luego!* and slam the door shut, and Arne's off in a cloud of dust, a hearty *Hi-ho, Silver!*

Best part of this, and Dicky'll come to realize it in a few weeks, I started billing him from the second he interrupted my breakfast at Sid's.

At twice my usual rate.

Harley Straight grew up hearing the classic tales of railroaders and their escapades, born and raised in Edgemont, a secondary terminal and crew change point for trains from Alliance, Nebraska and Gillette, Wyoming. All the friends he grew up with were in railroad families, and maybe two of all of them had two parents, and those two being the original two starting that family. The big money made in railroading went to those willing to let the transient lifestyle shape their present and dictate their future—long, irregular hours no one can plan around, dangerous work in the worst weather events, co-workers poorly-trained or working under the influence, and even more money to be made the longer you stay away from home. Young, undereducated boys and men, making more money than anyone in their families had ever made, and this in one year alone. Surpluses spent immediately, and spent on the most impulsive toys and schemes, because another huge check was just another month away.

Harley had none of this. He and his parents were chained at the ankle to their motel during the best months of the year, free only to close it down, maybe travel a bit themselves, when the weather was worst, their money was gone, and they had really no place to go anyway. Harley remembered fondly just one of his "firsts," the first time he got behind the wheel. It was in a friend's two-year-old Corvette, his engineer-daddy buying it as the son had led the local football team to the state championship. Harley and this kid, Aaron-something, were eight miles off the highway, clear the hell back on a ranch two-track, the Vette bouncing and scraping along with its minimal clearance, both boys half-pissed on Annie Greenspring's.

And now, as the glow of lights on the southern horizon signifying Crawford and its train yard appear—slowly, as Harley'd only driven this stretch a few times in a few years, so he drives slow enough now to not miss that turn—a pair of headlights appear out of thin air directly ahead, and they advance on him and the van he is driving. They are in the right lane, Harley's lane.

Harley slows to a stop, as do the oncoming lights. He turns to call over his shoulder, to tell the deadheading crew, to get somebody's opinion—what the hell's going on here? But all three are dead to the world, and Harley knows he's alone in this, whatever the hell this is.

Geesus, I'm making less than minimum wage for this nonsense, and these idiots make more sleeping than I've ever made awake.

The oncoming vehicle makes no move either. Harley puts the van in park, leaves the engine and the heater running—God forbid these morons wake up from their nappies all cold and grouchy—and slips out his door, leaving it open a crack to vent. Well, I wonder who this sonuvabitch is gonna turn out to be, and he approaches the vehicle, and there seems to be a figure approaching him now, backlit in the headlights, a single figure—and Harley stops, as does the figure, and Harley shouts hey as he waves his right arm, the oncoming figure waving his left.

And his reality comes to Harley like waking from a dream, and he picks up a stone off the pavement and tosses it directly at the stranger stopped there. And the stone bounces off the figure, off of Harley—off of a huge panel of mirrored glass.

Here Harley turns at the sound of gravel under feet behind him—finally, those damn trainmen wake up? And a trainman's lantern comes down across his forehead, and everything disappears.

Being as how I'm twenty-five miles from home after I dump Dicky off on Arne, and the same distance from Lander and Sid's, and my Airstream, and it's roughly five hours and three hundred miles to Edgemont, another sixty and an additional hour to Crawford, and then—worst damn part of the trip— another sixty and an hour to Alliance, the *Mordor* of the Middle Earth of Trains. I opt to allow myself what's left of the week (it's still Tuesday) to get the trailer zipped up, make a few calls, call in a few favors, and then plan ahead for an elongated stay on the road.

This kind of lackadaisical logistics is a luxury I enjoy, one I budget for. It sounds simpler than it is, but my twenty years in Protection Services, the fancy name for where you'll find the railroad cops, bought me a pension I'm currently six years from collecting. And it was my great good fortune, in the eyes of some influential transportation executives living in another world in Fort Worth, Texas, to solve a few cases other special agents couldn't or wouldn't crack—a few working in a field they were poorly-suited for, others unconstrained by ethics when unmarked envelopes of cash might be slid under their office doors. I'm not smarter than the average bear, but I'm nosy as hell, easily bored, and way-too-suspicious of coincidences for my own good. And in all honesty, the types of criminals one encounters in railway-related misdemeanors and felonies are the same ones the safety-analysts for appliance companies seek to protect when they require stickers be applied to the tops of new stoves saying *Do Not Touch Hot Surfaces.* Fully half of railway bad guys, I'd wager, have burn-scarred fingertips on their right hands, and half of those identical scars on their lefts.

In short—and it's not—I batted a pretty high average in cases solved, and more importantly, I was adept at keeping politically-explosive incidents out of the papers and off police blotters. So the occasional Sand Hills rancher or Black Hills casino-owner or state senator or house representative might awake to their silver breakfast trays, and see that some sort of skullduggery designed to enrich them or their friends or ruin their enemies had gone south, and these little embarrassments could become major, even career-ending if not solved promptly and quietly.

And it's this dynamic that makes it possible for me to work independently, under my own terms, and make sure that some amount of justice is administered to the guiltiest of the conspirators, be they in three-piece-suits or overalls. I admit it is wildly egocentric on my part to imagine I know who deserves justice, or what constitutes justice, but on more than a few occasions people with more money than sense and more power than integrity were fixing to exercise their lives of privilege, to escape the law and a reckoning, and I found myself in a unique position to toss a monkey-wrench into their works.

I work as often as my rates are paid in full, and the expense account is approved without exception and immediately reimbursed. I love time off, my material existence is inexpensive, and I'm either hanging about Sid's, or spending time with the twins—Joan's at Missoula studying creative writing, Billy's doing an internship for USAID in D.C.

When Wendy died—yes, my wife—the twins were eight, and I was disciplined and scheduled and no-nonsense. Working hard and working harder to balance every hour of time on duty with two hours with the kids was all-consuming, and the sheer intensity of existence helped in my healing process, one I hope to see the end of someday. But when the kids left two years ago— they graduated high school, tied for valedictorian at 16, and couldn't wait for college—a funny thing happened. I drove up to Casper and spent a day hashing out pension promises and savings accounts and a small portfolio Wendy brought into the marriage, and her benefits (she was a shrink at the VA Hospital in Billings until the kids were born) with a really kind man I grew up with (his was the only Mormon family in town) who dedicated his life to managing other peoples' money as if it was his own. That's it. No punchline. He was honest beyond reproach, and as humble as he was talented. Anyway, turns out I am not wealthy, but I am comfortable enough to help the twins through school, and pretty much work whenever I damn well feel like it. So letting the odd railway in question know my financial reality in subtle ways, and pairing it with a pretty damn lucky track record, I get to pick and choose my jobs, further improving my batting average, further buffing up an exaggerated reputation, further justifying my high rates and eccentric work rules.

One of my eccentric rules has been that my consulting contracts will *not* be with employees associated with the former Chicago, Burlington & Quincey, the old CB&Q, one of the old roads making up today's Burlington Northern. And that is because of the four years I spent there as a probationary agent, back in the day, and being broken in by none other than, at *that* *t*ime, Assistant Alliance Division Enforcement Branch Agent, Richard H. (*don't call me Dicky*) Tuttle. But if the case-for-hire is fascinating, or particularly difficult— or if I just *feel* like it, I'll take one from the old Q. But Dick doesn't need to know that.

I'll take my time, now through Sunday night, making some calls, chasing down some railroaders, and those who service them, people I haven't seen in twenty years. I kept Dick's case folder—seriously, *Dick's* folder. When I told Dick I would read it while he finished his breakfast, it certainly didn't *really* take me thirty minutes to read it. It's a police file, for God's sakes, not *Oliver Twist.* I needed Dicky to need the restroom, or I'd had the whole damn thing memorized in seconds. And Dicky finally broke and bolted for the restroom, and I found *his* copy of the file he gave me to read in his briefcase, and switched them out. And of course, Dicky's file contains additional information Dick does not believe it is in my best interests to know.

Interesting information, in the form of personnel files on the Crawford accident's dead engineer, Tim Nelson, and dead brakeman, Riley Fointman, and one more file, this one totally unlike the railroad files, a different font, different template, and no sign of a publisher or printer or collector or administrative aide responsible for typing or printing the file. But it's as interesting as it's puzzling, as this must be *the* file—*the mystery file*— belonging to the brakeman no one knew, no one saw clearly, no one claimed or identified in county morgue, and no one mourned at a public pauper's funeral almost three weeks after the accident.

This file's tag reads: *Maria Teresa Calderone, Denver, Colorado.*

Five

Mid-September in central Wyoming should not be missed. It's a graceful exit from summer, a civil introduction to autumn, and the view of high peaks on almost any horizon, depending on the angle and curve of the highway, begins to include fresh accents of snow at tree line. Lander and Sinks Canyon, of course, and Riverton, the Wind River Canyon, the hot springs at Thermopolis, the southern approaches leading to the Grand Tetons and Yellowstone—these are just a few areas of delightful investigation within a few hours of my home. And I'd rather be at one or all of them than on a lousy telephone connection, returning a call from a senior VP in Protection Services, Fort Worth, Texas, the boss of the boss who bosses Dicky Tuttle. If there is a "tell" a corporation can display that tips you off to a managerial predisposition, the BN's tell is its chain-of-command.

As with most railways, mid-management does the grunt work, providing the buffer upper management needs to insulate itself from the working classes, i.e. the unions. Railway managers historically chose to build transcontinental roads on the backs and bodies of impoverished Asian immigrants, and recently-freed slaves, and dispossessed war vets, and desperate ex-convicts, and those running from the law, as all these groups were powerless, and hungry, and under duress. No limits to working hours, or days worked in succession, or standardized safety rules and procedures, or uniform and certified training—result: people injured, often fatally, people working exhausted and sick, people self-medicating with alcohol and opium to mask the pain and work another day, because *you screw up, you're fired, you plead sick or hurt, you're fired, you speak at all other than to say thanks-boss, you're gone and there's a hundred desperate men waiting in line for your spot.*

And many, many years later the union movements taking place elsewhere in industries throughout the east coast finally worked their way west, and made war on the railways, and embedded themselves in essential occupations, frontline jobs, the tasks that actually make trains move from one spot to another. But even though it's been over a hundred years since those initial skirmishes, management and unions exist in constant opposition. Management contends employees are goldbricks, feather-bedding every job, inventing rules to reduce employee production while increasing employee pay and benefits. Unions contend that, if management had its way, we'd be back in the mid-1800s in a heartbeat, employees in poorly-compensated slavery, used and abused and discarded.

This may or may not be always the case in railroading, but I know that upper-management's aversion to direct communication with the little people is so strong, it creates multiple levels of management beneath, just to assure those at "VP" or above that their blue-serge and grey-flannel and sharkskin suits are safe from the dust and dross of diesel fumes and axle grease, and the attendant sweat and mud and blood.

All this is background to my decision to circumvent any further obstruction or manipulation at the hands of Dicky Tuttle. Now that he is finally knocking on the door of upper-management, he may be perilously close to slipping through those golden doors before I can complete my investigations in a manner I prefer, that is, open and honest and above board, for the most part.

That's where Howard James Humboldt III comes in.

Today H.J. Humboldt is BN's vice-president for regional operations and facilities, sitting in a large corner office, eighth floor of BN headquarters in a standard office park on the outskirts of Fort Worth. Twenty years ago, right around the time I decided to part ways with the BN (again, no such thing as coincidence), Howdy Humboldt was a Trainmaster headquartered in Ravenna, Nebraska, a little town at the far-east end of Alliance's big-money run. There are 238 rail miles separating Alliance, population 9,900, from Ravenna, population 1,300. Alliance, of course, is the main terminal, housing the Superintendent's offices, a major switching yard, a rail car repair facility, a massive roundhouse and its connected storehouse. It is home terminal to three pools of trainmen and enginemen working trains east and northwest and south, into eastern Nebraska and southwest South Dakota and northeast Colorado. The Alliance-Ravenna run is almost two-and-half times the distance of the other routes, and as crews are paid by mileage *and* time, the crews with the most seniority (remember union rules?) win the rights to work East Pool, Alliance-Ravenna. This also gives them the most time off, and that's just great, because what could possibly go wrong when one has a buttload of money and too much free time on one's hands?

Remember the mid-management discussion? Well, "trainmaster" is such a position. On paper this guy is supposed to supervise the crews on duty, make sure rules and regs are followed, keep on-duty intoxication to a minimum (hey, it's the railroad), and try not to piss off the oldest conductors and engineers, because getting crossways with *these* guys can literally bring all traffic to a screaming halt. For one, they can start religiously-following each and every Federal rule and law. No one follows them all, all of the time, lest a train would never get from point A to B in ten days, let alone ten hours. And for two, crews can start getting hungry and sick. They are allotted meal periods, and can wait to ask for them until it is obvious that utilizing their rights to eating would delay traffic across the division. And, in a curious coincidence (?), when a train crew is asked to wait an additional hour or two to eat, said crew often becomes violently ill, and maybe the train needs to be put in a siding, stopped cold, waiting for a new crewman or entire crew to get the train where it was scheduled to go in the first place.

One trainmaster told me his job was akin to herding cats, and another agreed but said it's not cats, it's cobras.

Anyway, Howdy Humboldt would work with the Alliance office when Dicky Tuttle would deign to leave his office and venture out onto actual rails in actual weather. If Dicky was otherwise occupied, a special agent from an adjoining terminal or division might be sent to assist if the situation warranted it.

I was assigned to the Sheridan division at that point in time, and I was summoned to Alliance to undergo periodic training and testing (good ol' t&t) for everything from firearms and hazardous materials to federal and state regulations regarding interstate and intrastate commerce. Although we were issued sidearms, this was hardly Cicero or East St. Louis, for the lovuh God, and our weapons most often lived unloaded in their original carrying case, locked in gun safes in offices or vehicle trunks. And if we were unsure of legal detail while answering a robbery report or an assault allegation, we could make a call to Legal in Fort Worth, or make a courtesy call to our state police, depending on the state, and our relationship with local law enforcement.

I'd bluffed and snoozed through most of the assigned two-day seminar, stopped into the Dispatcher's Office to touch bases with a couple of buddies directing train traffic on the west end and east end, and then started to make for my vehicle and the long ride home, when the east end guy got a call from a trainmaster in Ravenna. He handed it to me, said he had better things to do, and there I was staring at the receiver.

Quick-stop version—it was Howdy, said he needed me in particular, there was a taxi waiting in Alliance, right outside the Dispatcher's office, as we spoke, with crews to deadhead to Ravenna, then he begged—and I mean begged—me to squeeze in the cab, a matter of life and death. *But*, tell *no one*, just between us, right?

Something told me this stunk to high heaven, and something else told me this might pay off in spades, someday, as why is this guy so frantic to get me down to Ravenna, not Dicky, and why should Dicky be kept in the dark? I couldn't resist, and you can never tell when you'll need to cash in a favor.

So, I get to Ravenna, middle of the night, I make Howdy's office, and this guy is trembling like an aspen, as white as ghosts are purported to be. He takes me to a storage office, unlocks two massive padlocks, and there, haphazardly packed in ten-pound sacks of crushed ice is Conductor L.J. Navarro (crewmen are always documented by their initials). Ol' Lance Navarro dead as a dodo, looking much as he did in life, as he was seventy-nine this year, and in railroad years, that's about one hundred and ten.

I shake down Howdy for details, but I can guess most of it. Turns out Lance, a fine family man, church elder, et cetera, purchased himself an early birthday present, a small delight named Veronica, who frequented a rented trailer in an alley behind the depot. Lance could not withstand the sincerity Veronica displayed that evening, twice, and Lance past on, and Veronica freaked out, and she called her landlord—I'll be damned if it ain't Howdy his own self—and Howdy called Alliance, no clue who he was going to ask for, no clue what he would tell whoever answered. Without assigning blame or responsibility, I may have hypothetically facilitated a brief operation in which, when Lance's crew was called on duty, Lance was escorted to the caboose and strapped in at the conductor's desk, the rear brakeman was then ordered by the trainmaster to ride with the head brakeman and engineer in the lead locomotive, a cash incentive was applied to all (Howdy's, for sure), and tragically, it appeared Conductor L.J. Navarro left this world while on duty, a noble employee who died with his boots on. No questions posed by family or co-workers. Family got a death benefit; co-workers were one step closer to working the East Pool.

Yes. Howdy has owed me ever since. And he may have forgotten, but he is about to remember. I called this morning, his secretary said he'd call back, he hasn't, and now we start playing a little hard ball.

Howdy's secretary: "Good afternoon, Vice-President Humboldt's office, may I ask who's calling?"

Me: "Yes, you may."

Secretary: "Excuse me?"

Me: "Okay, you're excused. And you still may ask."

Secretary: "I'm sorry, sir, perhaps we have a poor connection. Who is calling?"

Me: "Don't apologize, young lady. Up to this point, you've done nothing wrong."

Secretary: "Can you hear me, sir?"

Me: "Yes, thank you. Can you hear me?"

Secretary: "Well, yes, of course, I mean—"

Me: "And your name is?"

Secretary: "Well, it's Audrey, but—"

Me: "No last name? Like Cher?"

Audrey: "Well, of course not—"

Me: "No, I shouldn't think so, I mean, what would Cher be doing working for a railroad, right?"

Audrey: "Sir, if you could just give me—"

Me: "My name? Of course, Audrey, and frankly I'm very much surprised you haven't asked until just now. So, please, as I haven't got all day, tell Mr. Humboldt that L.J. Navarro is calling, and I will wait."

Audrey: "Mr. Navarro? I will pass on your message, but—"

Me: "Oh, I'm not L.J. Navarro. No, I'm Will Allen, and please remind him I call on behalf of Veronica as well. Now, Audrey, I'll wait."

And something motivates Audrey to hurdle standard operating procedure, and interrupt Howdy's nap, and in seconds Howdy's on the line.

"Allen?"

"Howdy, you old bastard."

"Oh, my God. Stay at your phone. Give me two minutes."

And I know, he's running not walking to the express elevator, to the ground floor, out to the street, to a row of pay-phone booths. And my phone rings again. Ol' Howdy's fit to be tied, actually convinced—until just this second—time heals all. And in very short order, I disabuse the VP of such a notion, and the call is very short.

But two things are clear.

I have carte blanche in terms of the scope and depth of my investigation, for which I will be compensated in accordance with the terms I previously outlined.

And Dicky Tuttle, or his agents, contemporary or retired, promoted or terminated, will co-operate when required, and in absence of a direct request, will, all and sundry, stay silent and stay the hell out of my way.

Now it's Friday night. Oh, well, what the hell, the sooner I start, the sooner I return.

I rise with the sun Saturday morning. Next stop, Edgemont, South Dakota.

Six

Wendy and I lived for the kind of road trip I embark upon now. We always left home, as I do now, an hour before dawn, black sky, brilliant stars, almost never another car, ahead or behind. We shared a fresh-brewed thermos of strong and bracing coffee, and the background music was classical, almost a theatrical film element as we watched the movie we were making and starring in flash by.

You always keep an eye for animals crossing the road. Already this morning, with only forty-five minutes behind the wheel and the faintest of sunrise-light in the east, and a full moon setting in the west, I've seen antelope and deer and coyote, and fox and a Harris hawk and a Peregrine falcon, not to mention the ubiquitous raven, jack rabbit, and two prairie dogs. Turkey vultures and black-headed vultures alike will be perching on utility poles soon, standing facing east, wings outstretched, seeking warmth and rejuvenation, before spending the next sixteen hours or so gliding the thermal air currents, scanning the high prairie for whatever died the previous evening.

The geology and geography is such that much of what you see, as a homosapien, is all there ever was to be seen by our species. And this scenery *is* to be seen, contemplated, integrated. An eighty-mile-view is commonplace, a hundred and above not out of the question. So, in addition, a sky that size provides a canvas upon which weather systems of magnificent proportions splash and climb and dissipate on and around and between each other, no day's sky is yesterday's, every dusk is unique.

So my atlas tells me Edgemont is about five hours down the road, and Casper is halfway, as I choose the U.S. Highway 26 route, up to Riverton, then Shoshoni, and Powder River, one end of a north-south rail link connecting all the coal mines in the Basin. Sage and mesquite stretch across the panorama like a quilt, and I reduce my speed to ten below the limit. I roll down all the windows, turn off the heater, flip up my collar, pour a thermos-cup-full, and employ cruise-control, punching in a mix tape of Dwight Yoakum and Leonard Bernstein.

I know it might beg belief for the next part, but after twenty years on the road for the company, and another twenty for my own self, certain decisions made, that is choices taken, are arrived at not so much as a means to an end, but as a stick to the hornet's nest. I don't actually consider the BN brass to be behind the deaths of four people, ten years back, for now, as then, the coal and the money flowed so hot and heavy, life was easy to live, why complicate a good thing? Somebody's a problem? Write them up, run them off, heel, run them over, accidents happen. But four at a time? All at once, all together? Even the brass ain't that thick. But I made certain allusions in my brief chat with Howdy, and I know Dicky's pissed, so that's two sticks to the nest, and something should fly out soon.

And that something does, fly, that is, now, over three rises in the highway you can make out behind me in my rearview mirror, and this I see before I hear the low hum morphing to a rumbling, escalating to a whine, and now past me as if my fifty-five was five, going uphill. I would learn later a rider in black drove that Kawasaki Tomcat, slicing through the picture at one hundred plus, and capable if the driver is certifiably nuts, of reaching one-sixty-five.

And I'm too old to be scared, and old enough to know better, because I'm pretty sure this guy just isn't out on a weekend jaunt in the middle of Wyoming. However, I make it a point to know my neighbors, one being the kind and reputable Keith Raven, posted at Shoshoni, in service to the Wyoming Highway Patrol. And ol' Keith should be coming on duty around six, and just ahead is a pull-off with a picnic table, and *eureka*, an emergency telephone, its one-way recipient being the 24-hour-dispatchers desk, WHP.

I figure if I don't drive much over 50, I should come around a long curve east of Shoshoni and be met by a shiny new 1986 Crown Vic—the State of Wyoming spares little when outfitting its lawmen—with its roof bars flashing, the head- and tail-lights pulsing, and Wyoming Highway Patrol Sergeant Keith Raven listening more than talking, and writing while he does.

And I do, and he is. I pull up one side of Keith, my window still down. And next to Keith is a parked Tomcat, steam rising as the sun rises, as the temperature creeps upward. On the bike's other side stands a rider in black, holding a matching helmet, wearing aviator shades. He's speaking in short, rapid bursts, not unlike an automatic weapon, and I can't make out a word. I

47

listen for a few more seconds, no luck, although it's obviously Spanish, peppered with a few English clauses, and several F-bombs. Keith glances up from his ticket-book, catches my eye, and holds his palm up and out at the rider, and the rider is silent.

Non-verbal communication at its best.

"Good to see you, Sergeant." I mean it. Keith rules.

"Good to be seen, William." No one calls me that. Except Wendy. And Keith.

"And this gentleman?" I smile at the rider. He does not return it.

Keith hands me the license the rider handed Keith.

I read aloud. "José Garcia, Ciudad de México. Interesting."

Keith, deadpan as usual, "Mexico's most common first name, most common last name, and from its largest city."

I still smile. José still doesn't. "His crime, Sergeant?"

Keith reads from his citation. "One hundred-twenty in a sixty-five-zone, or as I advised Señor Garcia, one hundred-ninety-three kilometers in a one hundred-and-five kilometer-zone. I wrote the numbers out on the back of his copy, see?"

I walk around to the rider's back, saying, "I think that was very kind." Garcia turns to look at me, and his jacket stretches awkwardly over a bulge under his left arm. He and I see it, then we see the other see it, but Keith steps to Garcia's back, and has both his arms behind him, too, and handcuffs at his wrists.

Keith walks back to his cruiser to call for back-up, as it's a long drive to Casper. Garcia says nothing, and that's a tell. An amateur, or a tourist, either would be raising holy hell in either language. This guy's a pro. He has an assignment, he's been nabbed, he's a Mexican national, and whoever he's working for, he's confident he'll be walking the festive streets of Mexico City in forty-eight hours. I pull a handkerchief from my rear pants pocket, wrap my hand, and remove the nine-mil from his shoulder holster. I walk back around the bike, where a small leather satchel is bungy-corded to the back of the driver's seat. I pop the bungy, the satchel jumps up and out, then down to the ground, its zipper half-open. Keith is back, takes the nine-mil from me, ejects the clip, and one in the chamber, and reaches to snag the satchel.

"What have we here?" Keith opens the zipper the rest of the way, and pulls out three loaded clips, plus a silencer. We both look into the rider's dead eyes.

He finally smiles. *"Cazador de patos."*

Keith smiles as well. "Duck hunter."

"Thanks for hanging around, William." Raven and I are sitting in the cafeteria, WHP's district headquarters on the south edge of Casper, Wyoming's second largest city at a hair past 53,000. As such, it gives me the whim-whams. Three-four hundred folks, up to four or five thousand, that's a town I can wear like a favorite coat.

Keith hands me a copy of my witness statement, and I pretend to read it, and I sign it and hand it back. Keith says. "Don't remember any discussion of the search and seizure laws."

I stand. "Was something search or seized? I remember a stone-cold assassin fixing to pull on either or both of us, and if not now, then soon. And your actions saving us both. Amen. Over and out."

Keith's brewing a fresh pot, and I'm a caffeine junkie, and I sit back down. "What do we make of Señor Garcia?"

Keith pours and distributes. *"I* make a pro, hired by pros, could be to just keep an eye, could be to stalk, and after looking into the business end of his saddle bag, I say somebody somewhere is spending their last days on earth."

"What's the lowdown on dope supply hereabouts?" Through the picture-glass window behind Keith I see a late—as he is running—thin man—as his fat leather briefcase dangles in comic contrast—frantic—as one can only be if worried for one's physical safety—and headed direct for the double-glass front door.

Keith sees my fascination with the newcomer. "Same as anywhere, transient populations, generational poverty, desperation, self-medication. There's a market. And that little nerd you see several minutes late for his client's booking and arraignment, our Latin motor-cyclist is *his* boy in front of the judge today. *That guy*—he's one of the reasons chasing suppliers is like chasing ghosts."

The thin man rushes down the hall past the cafeteria and pushes through the two huge wooden doors into the district court, in session for eight minutes without him.

Keith's matching me cup for cup. He pours once more. "The skinny kid is Walt Whitman. Yeah, seriously. Grew up in Cheyenne, graduated high school in Casper, back down to Laramie for pre-law and law."

I appreciate a kid staying home for school in a state of less than half-a-million. "A Wyoming Cowboy."

"Wouldn't know a cow from a horse without a sign on each." Keith leans back. "But he's diligent, good-hearted, honest-as-permitted to be."

"There's a story there." I love stories.

"Short version, and I can't prove any of it. His old man ran the family appliance store forever, those shopping mall super stores start to bring pressure, the dad starts drinking, things take a nose-dive. Runs into a loan-shark at the kind of bar he didn't know existed until he hit the skids himself. The dad gets neck deep in high interest, even turning the store over won't cover the debt. In a supposedly unrelated incident, every once in a while, we get visits from mean-looking mugs with Denver license plates doing dubious things, or the occasional Hispanic visitor watching other dubious characters delivering large pallets of unmarked materials in the middle of the night to unmarked warehouses, et cetera, you get me, I'm sure."

I do. "So on the rare occasion these dubious characters screw up and the law enforcement community is there to catch them, they go to court—"

Keith's smile is not mirthful. "—and are represented by Walt Whitman, Esquire. Whose father, by the way, has managed to miraculously pull his appliance business out of a very deep hole without any appreciative growth of his customer base."

Keith and I spot a late model Chevy sedan edge into the parking lot as if the driver is unsure of location and function. I've been there. It's frustrating. And I have a hunch. I stand and go *just a sec*, Keith nods, I saunter out (John Wayne *saunters*), and the driver—bald, mid-fifties, white, black hornrims with clip-on sunglasses, and his seat pushed as far forward as possible—waves like a fake salute, then rolls down his window.

I smile like a dumbass, again no choice, and I lean on his car door. "Howdy."

The guy finds this entertaining, as he gets to say *howdy* back, something that doesn't happen often wherever he is from. He pulls a card from his white dress-shirt pocket. I read only long enough to notice *Immigration and Customs Enforcement*, and *Phillip P. Phillips.*

Holy smokes, is it my day for names, or what? "Mr. Phillips, and from ICE. Either you have made a very long drive from the Canadian border, or a very, very long drive from the Mexican border?"

Phillip smiles and visibly relaxes. Oh, boy, he's a small-talker. "Ha, well, yeah, ha, you'd think as much, wouldn't ya? And please, call me Phil?"

Why *Phil,* I wonder? "Sure, Phil. Hope I can remember that. You look lost."

Phil's counting four-four in a three-quarter-time world. "Oh, yeah, ha, yeah, just a bit, well, I'm down here from Shelby, Montana, stationed there, yeah, uh-huh, and there's Federal training going on in Cheyenne for *Deskpro 386,* that's from those boys at *Compaq,* ya know, I guess it's the latest thing, right?"

"I don't care. What are you doing here?" Still smiling like a loon.

"Oh, well, no, why should ya, really, anyways, my guys in Shelby get this call, there's a Mexican national needing to get deported ASAP, somebody official's got to get him to Denver, a government flight, ya know, and wouldn't ya know, I'm the closest thing to anybody official for several hundred miles, so—"

"Wow. That is going to be one interesting road trip for you and—let me guess—José Garcia, lately of Mexico City?"

Phil looks at me like I became John Wayne right before his eyes. "Holy moly, mister, yeah, I mean, yes exactly, Mr. Garcia—he's the guy I'm *transporting*, I believe that's the term."

If I've ever seen something set up to go south *before* it can start going anywhere at all, this is it. But I have other things to do, and I am not, thankfully, a cop, not even kinda. But I can't bear the thought of Phil's carcass showing up somewhere off I-25, coyote-mauled, his little Chevy driven to the nearest truck stop, there exchanged for the first thing Garcia can steal, and Garcia returns to central Wyoming, and *my* stomping grounds, to fulfill his assignment.

I hand Phil my card. "Look, Phil, *before* taking custody of Garcia, please, please, please call a guy I know down in Cheyenne, Department of Criminal Investigation, and a member of the task force that comes and goes with the Fed's interest in our fine state. Tell him you talked with me, and that you're a desk jockey form Shelby—no offense—"

"None taken." Phil's complete attention is focused on my eyeballs.

"—and that ICE has you transporting a Mexican national to Denver all by your lonesome, okay? And tell him—do not forget—Garcia was processed here in Casper on *weapons violations.* Got it?"

Phil's jubilant. "And this call should get me—what?"

"Worst case, one more car buddy on your trip to Denver, but one who can handle Garcia in a pinch. And best case, you won't have to make the trip at all, the Feds will send two to transport."

"Thanks so very very much, uh—" Phil reads my card—"Mr. Allen."

I step away, Phil guides the Chevy into a handicap parking spot, and I'm back sitting down across from Keith just as two uniforms escort Garcia past our vantage point toward what Keith calls the municipal court's holding cell.

Although there is glass between us, Garcia makes eye contact with me, smiles and says—I think—*Te veo pronto.*

I don't have to ask Keith. He looks at me, square on.

"See you soon."

Seven

This particular incident changes my immediate plans. Currently I'm not in danger, but I most definitely do think that the Crawford episode, ten years previous, is not just a botched investigation standing between Dicky Tuttle and his dreams of a corner office and season tickets to the Dallas Cowboys. And although Howard Humboldt's Trainmaster-years are far behind him, the publicity he might have to navigate over a long-deceased conductor and the questionable ethics of renting a trailer exclusively to "working girls" would not likely affect, one way or the other, his remaining years with the Burlington Northern. There are unwritten rules for those achieving senior management. It's very much an old boys club, difficult to enter, almost impossible to exit, even after retirement. Residences, rental cars, vacations, loans, bonuses, golf course memberships, even political introductions leading to power on a national scale as "transportation lobbyists"—these and a host of unseen and undiscussed "ancillary" benefits belong, by right, to the senior management team. A white, male senior management team.

So, if Dicky's behind the Tomcat rider, then Dicky's scared of someone out there more than he's scared of me. And if Humboldt feels I'm putting the screws to his very good thing, his very good thing comes his way as much from the auspices of criminal activities as from his service to the railroad.

Whatever the case, I drive now in a beeline for Crawford, Nebraska. There are two people there with direct and indirect "evidence"—possibly too strong a label, but what each person has may point me in the right direction, and right now that's all I need.

But I also need to find those two folks alive and ambulatory, and I suspect they are for now, as long as I know José Garcia is headed for Nogales, Arizona, ICE processing, and a quick dump on the Nogales, Sonora-side of the border.

Casper, Wyoming to Crawford, Nebraska—two-and-a-half hours, one hundred sixty miles. Now I can take a straight shot east, I-25 to U.S. 18, then

U.S. 20 right into the heart of the Pine Ridge. Seeking radio stations around the dial, music falls into three categories: religious, country, and barely intelligible. The last category has to do with signal scarcity, and the first two have more in common than you might think. Gospel music praises the sinner who perseveres, casts out the devil, and knows the Pearly Gates. Country music testifies to the nobility of such a journey, and would join such an endeavor with alacrity, had a woman not broken a heart, and driven that heart to drink, and then watched that drunken heart break a bottle over a bartender's head, then of course, the heart gets two years' probation and community service, plus AA meetings, where the heart meets the same woman he fell in love with in the first place, and she volunteers to be his sponsor, and they end up in bed, drunk, and—

These long stretches of highway give me too much free time.

I should be concentrating on the beauty of a scenery best described as desolate, but reimagining the implied disparagement as praise. I-25 follows along the North Platte River, a necessary water source for farmers and ranchers from here all the way to where it flows into the Missouri River. For my purposes, I'm watching with particular interest the water levels leaving Casper at around 5,100 feet of elevation, on to Glenrock at 5,000, down to Douglas at 4,800, and finally to Orin Junction at 4,700. This gentle descent allows the secure passage of most of the drainage and rainfall, and that's only sixteen inches a year. But this stretch is also a study in transformation. The scant plant life existing on the highest plains fades and tiny but discernable bluffs begin to appear, first small and delicate. And the closer I get to Crawford, the more the bluffs collect into ridgelines, unevenly covered in short, squat evergreens and scrub oaks, and at the bottom of the ridgelines, washes coalesce, full of the finest gravel and dirt, ready to become mud rivers at the next gully-washer.

Just two miles west of the town of Crawford is Fort Robinson, now a national museum, built and manned originally by the U.S. Army in the early 1870s, designed to protect the Red Cloud Agency and mitigate disturbances between settlers and 13,000 Lakota Sioux. So, history-book bullshit aside, Fort Rob, as the locals call it, was the central point from which to launch the Sioux Wars, those series of battles that in time decimated the Sioux. There are a hundred stories affixed to markers throughout the fort, some true, we think— some false, of course. For instance, there is a cell at the Fort you can visit today, claiming at that very spot on the floor, the great chief Crazy Horse was killed while resisting arrest. Sure. A great chief, thirty-five years old, tired, dehydrated, starving, deprived of weaponry, his greatest fighters dead, surrounded in a garrison—that is exactly the time a captive should think *hey, guys, I think I can escape? And if I'm freakishly-lucky, once free of the cell, I'll just stroll through a heavily-manned garrison, borrow a fed-and-rested horse, and canter into the sunset.* Well, today we are best served by reading our revisionist historians, and studying the personal letters and diaries and transcriptions of oral histories offered by the marginalized rather than the privileged. Then we might turn a critical eye toward our state and national parks and monuments, and the museum labels and panel displays and brochures and guide and docent spiels, so that all voices, and therefore all stories, illuminate our shared narrative, and inform our individual understandings.

I amazed I can cram that much pontificating into the two miles from Fort Rob to the BN depot.

There's one place to start anything in Crawford. Whether looking for a neighbor, or kicking off a fund drive for a good cause, or finding that elusive chief of police, or the even-more elusive mayor, or just wanting to put your fingers on the pulse of the populous, always begin at Daisy's. It's a breakfast and lunch joint with a breakfast and lunch you can easily surpass in your home kitchen, maybe even on a Coleman stove in the back of your Bronco (I'm pretty good), but the counter and tables and booths are arranged in such a way that everyone can hear everybody else, and the result is a sort of audio clearinghouse of Crawford's who's-who doing Crawford's what-what. And—bonus—the coffee's not horrible.

I park the Bronco between two diesel pick-ups, farmers or ranchers no doubt, as their car at home, the one the "missus" drives, that one's called the "sedan," and if it isn't a Buick, it's a Mercury, but never a Caddy, even if you can afford one, as that is "putting on airs." Besides, if the Buick is traded in every two years for the latest Buick, you can send the same message.

I open Daisy's door, and whatya know, there sits Daisy, I bet, at the cash register, filling out the New York Times crossword in pen. So Daisy's no bumpkin, and perseveres, as it is no small trick securing the Times in the middle of nowhere, and this copy is only a day old. Daisy is also perceptive, in that she sees me, the stranger I am, does an initial read, notices my glance to her newspaper, and her smile does not fade one degree.

"The librarian at the college over in Chadron lives on the far side of Fort Rob, she nabs me one of the two copies they get, drops me the copy on her way to work next day," and she starts looking the room over for a table for one.

I don't need isolation this morning. "Counter's fine. You a mind-reader, Miss Daisy?"

She laughs, natural, high-pitched, percussive. I guess she's forty, three kids, and a husband working the railroad in Alliance, or mining out of Gillette, and he gets home when he can. "Maybe I am, sir, or maybe—" she hands me a menu as I take a counter stool, an empty stool on either side—"we ain't as mysterious as we think." With that, she winks, and I think I've made the only contact I'll be needing for the first day or two.

And over the course of the next couple of hours, as Daisy Wenton waits on customers (cousin Debbie runs the little grill-kitchen) and runs the register and buses tables, I start to piece together a small slice of life as lived by the average citizen of Crawford.

Daisy does have three kids, a boy 15 in high school, a girl 13 in middle school, and a baby girl-surprise, in the middle of the terrible twos, Nora, a force of nature. Scotty, the husband and father, is a good man—Daisy's words, as if most men round these parts are not. He's a conductor with enough seniority to be a brakeman on some other conductor's crew on the East Pool, big money, but he likes running the crew, and stays in the West Pool, Alliance to Edgemont, less money, but he's closer to home, even if the closer feeling comes from waving at his wife at the café as he goes pounding by on a loaded coal train.

And Daisy's born and raised local, worked through high school at Fort Rob at the Park's kitchen and dining room, and hotel. She got her teaching degree at Chadron State, just east, just down the road, taught K-3 until she met Scotty at a bar in Chadron, kismet, engaged, married, pregnant and a new mom in one year flat. Her folks died when she was young, probably why she was impatient to get her own family rolling.

"And I never could have made it"—the morning roar has subsided, now she sits at the counter with me, having a coffee herself, gearing up for lunch rush—"if it hadn't been for my mom's dad, our local GP."

I feel like the miner finding that one lonely but gorgeous nugget in the bottom of the pan. "Your grandpa's the local doc?"

"*Was*. Still lives in the same house he and Grandma always have. Retired last year when they rebuilt the old clinic into a little hospital, new rules and regulations, couldn't call his own shots."

My poker face is slipping. "So, I wonder if he was on duty, oh, must have been almost ten years back maybe, a crew taxi accident—"

Daisy laughs, slaps the counter. "Gotcha! Oh, yeah, man you're good." She stands, walks round the counter with our mugs, fills them, returns them, sits back down. This is a good sign. I thought she was fixing to throw me out. "Let me guess. You're a cop? No, no. All due respect, if you are, you're retired." I am mute in my pain. "You're a private investigator? Closer I think, but still, you seem too—I don't know—*I-don't-give-a-da*mn for even a private dick, and you'd charge your client way too much to travel all the way to nowhere and back."

I have to like Daisy. That brain's on overdrive. "You're enjoying this, aren't you? Even enjoying my discomfort, a little bit?"

Daisy nods, one last snort. She gets a breath. "I bet you mostly do what you do without tipping your hand. So I'll give that male ego a chance to heal. Come clean, who and what are you, and why are you here? And why does my old grandpa tip the balance?"

"Will Allen, consulting special agent, working this particular case on behalf of a railroad I am not at liberty to name, but is near and dear to the hearts of those living near a Burlington Northern rail line." Daisy loves this, but I have the feeling she bought into this conversation much earlier. Somehow she knew I was other than I presented, and she knew early in the conversation, before I knew she knew.

"Okay, Will. That's sounds like a bit of a racket you got going there, but something tells me you're pretty much on the up-and-up. And something also tells me if you are 'consulting',"—Daisy makes air quotes—"you were railroading for a considerable stretch before you just couldn't take the baloney anymore and struck out on your own."

Smiling in agreement.

Daisy, too. "Yeah, I thought so. But you know as well as I do, the railroad is the peoples' lifeline. It's a job and benefits and real good money for a high school diploma, and some don't have *that*. Folks might hate the life like hell, but they're going to view you as suspicious, and you may get a cordial schooling about minding your own business, or you might pass the wrong alley up in Edgemont some night, pass out, wake up in the hospital in Rapid, looking at rehab, learning to walk again."

I'm not happy. "Geesus, Daisy, that was a very specific hypothetical, almost like you know somebody such a thing happened to, and how it might have happened ten years back, to someone you know, and I should think twice, think about just turning tail for home, consider myself lucky."

"Will, you do speak in riddles, I'm sure. It's time for the lunch bunch, and it's great knowing you—and in a totally-unrelated situation, my grandpa is Randall Lenore, he's cutting his grass for the last time this fall, right now, at 120 Oak Street, and he has a memory like an elephant."

Daisy stands, shakes my hand, makes for the kitchen to relieve cousin Debbie. She stops in the little doorway to the grill and refrigerators, and turns, still smiling.

"Just sayin', Will Allen."

Eight

Every house in downtown Crawford looks similar, though no two are identical. Boom and bust is written across every little town in the West. A mine might open, or a lumber permit could invigorate a mill, a little pocket of gas or oil not worth thinking twice about might become valuable beyond measure with a declaration of a war, or the invention of a vehicle. But always, the eastern interests with the money to invest encounter a moment unforeseen by locals— the absolute *second* eastern stockholders deem their personal profit-margins to be one-cent less than maximum. And they sell, and prices crumble, and sometimes entire towns—complete with courthouses and churches and stores and train stations and saloons and schools—dry up one day, blow away the next.

Some folks stay, hanging on by a thread, others load the wagons and head on to the next best rumor, and those too old and too poor await their final rewards. Doctor Randall Lenore, *Doc* to everyone, age one to a hundred-and-one, is a stayer. His family was the linchpin of a wagon train of pioneers. And when dispute arose as to where this group should settle, it split. Half of these folks, mostly all from St. Louis, decided to try for Oregon, and Doc's half fell in love with the Pine Ridge.

In time, Crawford came about, and its great good fortune was and is that it is situated at a unique geographical point on the Burlington Northern.

I find Doc right where Daisy said I would, save he's taking a break from the lawn, and he's sitting on his porch, a glass in one hand, a pitcher in the other, and he pours one empty glass full as he watches me park the Bronco. I'm betting Daisy started calling his number the minute I left, and there's nothing wrong with the old man's hearing as he made out the phone bell above the mower, and even had enough time and gumption to produce lemonade for a guest he's never laid eyes on.

Turns out I'm betting correctly. Doc waves me up to the porch. One always waits for the invite. It is only civil, and it is free.

I sit next to him. "Doctor Lenore."

We shake. Doc has Daisy's smile, dead-on. "Mr. Will Allen."

We each take a sip of lemonade, smile and sit back. I look the street over, one way to the other, then begin.

"Sorry to interrupt your last mowing of the season, Doctor, but you seem to have finished and cleaned up in record time." Doc looks a bit at sea, but I persist. "I can't even smell that faint petroleum odor, nor the hint of newly-mown grass." Now Doctor Lenore has feet back under him.

"Oh, yes, well, Daisy is one very busy young lady, easy to get mixed up. My last mow was yesterday, and I'm glad the result pleases you."

Nice try. I don't buy it. "I don't have grandchildren although I'm old enough. My twins are away at school. But when I'm so fortunate as to become a grandpa, I hope for a grandchild like Daisy."

Doc doesn't suffer from false modesty, neither does he milk a compliment.

"You are kind to say so, and she is the best thing ever happened to Loretta and me."

Loretta's not joining us, and I look toward the front door expectantly, but Doc neglects my antics. So I try another slant. "I suspect that young lady was a real handful to raise."

And Doc's laugh rings out, a baritone version of Daisy's. "Oh, hell yes. Oh man, oh man, Mr. Allen. May I call you Will? And I'm Doc, of course." He reaches for a kerchief and wipes one eye. "Maybe somewhere down the pike, if we are fortunate enough to spend more time together, I will tell you the story of the Great Paradox, how it was my responsibility to bail the girl out of our local holding cell on the Friday night before she was scheduled to give the High School's Graduation Valedictorian address."

Now our laughter is relaxed. And I can see in Doc's eyes, like his granddaughter, he'll lend you the shirt off his back, but he doesn't suffer fools gladly.

"It may be my medical training, Will, but how's about we get to business, serious as life can be, then once you are satisfied, we can chat about what warms the cockles of old hearts."

"You're on, Doc." I refill my glass, sip.

Doc says, "I'm glad you enjoy the lemonade."

I smile. I think Doc knows more than he lets on. "I'm an alcoholic, Doc. And recent years have been good to me, and my sponsor has been good to me as well."

Doc smiles again. "You are certainly straight-forward. And I too find my recent years easier to appreciate without alcohol."

I believe in my instincts. Meeting folks like Daisy and Doc is a rare treasure, not just because it's a delight to meet good people, but because I believe I can gauge a person's rate of self-disclosure, compare it to the type and quality of information that person chooses to share, and then dependably determine how far I can trust them—with the information I have, and in some cases, with my personal safety.

I'm also impatient and judgmental, and maybe all that other stuff is rationalization.

Whatever. I decide to tell Doc every step I've taken, every piece of info I have. I know where *I* think I am, but I am dying to know what a central character in the narrative of this case might think of what I have learned. I don't speak quickly, but I'm through in twenty minutes. Doc looks as if he's showed up to a medical convention where the featured speaker claims the Fountain of Youth is real and pumping.

"Well, I'll need a minute or two, Will. Let me try to tell you why. It's been ten years, right? Remember, the taxi driver caught the blame for the wreck, and his family got zip. The brakeman and the engineer, the ones officially called for the job, the taxi company's insurance adjustor rolled in, get this— four days after the wreck, a check for one hundred grand for each family. And that's a damn fortune now for anybody here-abouts, and this was in '76. And nobody's claiming the third body whatsoever. So, not only are there no questions raised—"

"—there's little community support for those folks raising doubts." I've been there before.

Doc smiles. "You get me. But Jimmy Kilroy was one of three EMT's answering the call that night. The other two boys just wanted to get it done, get back to hearth and home."

I smile. I love stories. "But not our Jimmy?"

Doc looks melancholy, shakes it off. "No. Jimmy was my neighbor boy, shoveling my walk, throwing my paper. He'd carry Loretta's groceries every block of the nine from the market, and refuse fifty cents at the end. Never had any intention of leaving this town, save to get the schooling he needed to be the EMT/firefighter he became."

I wish I didn't sense tragedy on-coming. "And Jimmy saw something making no sense, and you are the only one he could trust to share."

"Yes, and I wish to God he'd missed it, or forgotten about it. But it was too damn obvious, whoever set it up thought we're nothing but a bunch of country morons, we'll take the easy way around."

"Which would be?"

"Would be, there's a taxi van down the ravine, probably missing the turn, middle of the night, driver new and tired, maybe falls asleep, who knows? And the other three dead as well."

I stand and stretch, then sit. "And Jimmy sees instead?"

Doc stands and stretches and sits. "Getting old is hell. Anyway, Jimmy's seeing a wreck, no skid marks, so the speed should have been considerable, but it didn't roll side over side, it did one head-over-ass flip, it didn't catch fire"—I start to object—"*until* Jimmy and his buddies pulled the bodies free, almost on cue."

"This is getting good, Doc."

"And by that, you mean it's bad, getting worse."

"Yeah."

"Yeah." Doc gets up, goes in the house to pee, as we've killed one huge pitcher of lemonade. He comes out, gestures I might do the same. "Yeah, just inside the door, a little powder room we fixed for Loretta. You don't have to go a bit a farther—just inside the door."

"Gotcha, just inside the door." *Wow, getting old is hell.* I use the room and return.

Doc looks relieved I managed to make the ten-foot round trip. "Okay, so, we had no place to put bodies that week, power out at the little funeral home, undertakers away at a convention, none of the law enforcement agencies seemed enthusiastic about taking custody of the bodies, doing the paperwork and such. Long and short—all four spend a week in the meat locker over at the processing plant."

"Delicious."

"No kidding. Anyways, Jimmy sees bruising on the bodies, but not in places and intensities making any sense if the bodies were killed by the roll down the ravine."

Now I'm not scared, but I'm sure as hell weary. "That was *not* in my notes, Doc."

"Not surprising, Will. And I bet your notes *do* tell a story about one or more of us doing 'secret' tests with the remains, finding what, nitrous oxide in the corpses' systems?"

"Yeah, exactly."

"Bullshit. Which one of your railroad bosses fed you that?"

I want to kill Dicky. "A divisional supervisory special agent, on the road to a VP job. But he did say the crew was dead before the wreck. So, what gives?"

"Yeah, Will, that's the beauty of it. There's a story for the record—taxi misses turn, crew dies. There's another for the 'conspiracy theorists'—the crew was dead before the van left the road, and they were all screwed up on drugs, alcohol, coke, I heard them all. But there's one more, what we know for sure, and what we got no clue about, but a way this thing might have been made to work—the crew had no drugs in their systems, that we know of, as we did no crazy 'tests', they may have had a few drinks, they are train crews, ya know, but the damage done to these bodies was—"

And here Doc stops. He rises, locks his front door, waves me to follow. I do, and we drive without a word. In five minutes we pull up to the old clinic/new hospital and park Doc's Buick.

He turns to me. "One could imagine those three boys, the trainmen, dying from the injuries they incurred. And one could also imagine that boy driving the van to die of the injuries he incurred as well."

I'm feeling sick. "Meaning?"

"One could imagine all four of those boys dying, but they didn't die in that van, and the driver didn't die in the same circumstance the train crew died in."

"Holy shit."

"Yeah." Doc gets out and heads for a side door.

I follow. "Where we going?"

"I want you to meet Jimmy."

I gulped. "He works here?"

Doc stops at a door marked *Physical Therapy.*

"You could say that, I guess. Jimmy's learning how to walk again."

63

Nine

There're at least two things you can depend on, cruising through the West, encountering a town or village every hundred miles or so, that is, one large enough to support a gas pump and a bar. Or, a bar with a gas pump. Beggars can't be choosers.

One thing is, there will be a late-model 4-wheel drive pickup, the logo of the law enforcement agency-in-charge emblazoned across the side, parked somewhere on the main drag. The purpose here is to slow traffic usually coming into town around sixty, and in slowing, the driver may see just how damn charming the little café or gift shop or—yes, yet another—antique store might be, and he or she will stop, and buy *something*, please oh please.

The second thing is, if the town has around five hundred or more souls— and this qualifies said town to act as a county seat—than there is probably a restaurant, advertised as a "steakhouse," or a "family restaurant," or even "fine dining," all this in neon, at least one letter or word burnt out. And the bigger the town, the better the odds that one of the places to eat and/or drink in town is named *Stockmen's.*

The historical bouquet is obvious. A major component of western development has and will be the narrative of cattle, and those cattlemen need to eat and drink and talk while they're doing it. Not every town has a joint named *Stockman's*, but every town has a joint *like Stockmen's,* and not coincidentally, the joint's got a back room, and the back room has a *game.*

And the game is poker, high stakes, illegal, and the absolute go-to for chronic gamblers and those who would fleece them. The card players come in every flavor: railroaders, miners, drillers, and doctors, lawyers, bankers. They have much in common. They all feel as though the other guy has a real problem, they believe they are plainly better gamblers than most, and that the most curious element of all games played to wager—luck—will ebb and flow, but in due time, always, *always* return, just in time to save them from the yawning pit of financial ruin.

And never in the card room proper, but always in the adjacent bar, on the last stool next to the window, will sit a loan shark. This shark, like his namesake, is patient, as the odds only *really* favor him. Someone will not walk away from the table when all is lost, and someone, drenched in sweat and desperation, will see a possible inside straight, the flush instead of two pair, and someone will see this month's rent check, or his mother-in-law's retirement fund, or a scheme to re-finance a home already second-mortgaged as a *great* idea.

So, really, what's the harm in a quick loan, just a few thousand, just at interest rates starting at 50%, compounded weekly, coming due in a month or two, impossible to pay back all at once, so the remainder rolls over into the next loan, higher rate, shorter turn-around. And here comes the worst part. Turns out the loan shark, once a sort of friend, now informs you he has "sold" your debt to "a gentleman" in Kansas City, or Omaha, or more recently, Denver. So, *this* guy isn't looking so much for full cash repayment, as a favor or two or three, and *those* payments are high stakes.

Maybe you have a flourishing string of fast-food franchises from Miles City, Montana to Sterling, Colorado. A lot of cash turnover, all outlets taken into consideration together, right? Well, now the gentleman needs some money regularly laundered, washed and pressed, please. Or a city or county or state contract for a new highway maintenance facility is up for bid, and the closed-bid system of awards is cramping the gentleman's style, and he needs some inside dope on who is offering what kind of bottom-dollar to plan and build and supply the construction.

Or, and this happens more than one might think, a politician is running for office on the other side of the country, someone you never heard of, someone whose politics make you shudder to even remotely consider—and son-of-a-gun, that guy or gal needs a little contribution, every week for the next fifty-two, come rain or shine. And hey, we don't want to piss off the gentleman, as he has a short temper, a bad memory, and a host of employees with little to do save visit those associates who neglect the gentleman's request for assistance.

The story's as old as the West itself. Back in the 1880s, such a "gentleman" was not tolerated by the likes of the Earps in Kansas, or the same family in Tombstone. *Pure, unadulterated extortion*, the older brothers said, and any other crime or offence paled in comparison. But similar "lawmen" in similar "cow towns" saw this sort of skullduggery as the cost of doing business in the Great American West, and often earned a subsidiary-line of income for their enlightened perspectives.

And today, one hears tales of the Goathorn Tavern in Deadwood, Blackjack's in Gillette, and closer to my present locale, O'Dougherty's, in beautiful downtown Crawford. And I'm not suggesting any of the law enforcement officers in those or other jurisdictions are bent, paid to look away, but rather are limited by funding and staffing and increases in crimes deemed by society-at-large or the microcosm that is the particular rural community, as more likely to endanger their population's well-being.

For instance, I've got a personal file I've been collecting in my spare time for many years, a kind of hobby, dubious as it may be. One night long ago— at that time I still imbibed—I found myself round a table in a bar in Seneca, Nebraska, about halfway between Ravenna and Alliance. Some track equipment on a work train occupying that siding had "been misplaced," and again, as one Agent Tuttle felt averse to moving about outside of the confines of his office, I was dispatched to rectify the situation, *good riddance.*

As booze flowed and tongues loosened, I learned that three of the guys round the table made up a train crew, run out of time on their way to Ravenna, waiting for a taxi to take them down to the terminal to get their rest. Two guys were signal maintainers, and one guy was a maintenance section foreman. More importantly, each had been around long enough to have worked all over the division until their seniority reached the point that they could bid in and keep a job in one town and put down roots. So, of course, "back in the day" stories, and "who can top this?" stories flowed into the wee hours.

Even when I drank, I switched to coffee after the first couple of hours, so maybe I was the only one to notice a pattern. But there seemed, anecdotally at least, to be more than just a few stories of disappearance. That's easily written off, most old-timers claim, by the transient nature of the road, especially amongst the rookies and youngsters and the lawless. Such groups get in trouble sooner, stay in trouble longer, and more often take the easy way out— disappearance.

And within this strange category, the *disappeared*, there are sub-groups. For instance, an eighteen-year-old hires on, in six months he's making three times the money his father's ever made in a year, he buys everything he sees, gets all the credit in the world from the local railway credit union, buys more, develops a habit or two costing yet more money, this in cash—and bankruptcy looms. Stay and seek help and buckle-down and dig your way out? Or run?

Or, a similar pattern presents itself, and is further complicated by marriage, infidelity, alimony, child support, and domestic violence, and even fewer railroaders, young or old, decide to stick it out.

It's the third category, though, that caught my fancy, the same fancy invigorated by stories of space aliens and yetis and Loch Ness and Area 51. Here's where a guy you worked with and around and adjacent to—sometimes for several years—is here today, and *what-the-hell*, gone tomorrow.

Case in point. Just one of the names in my little file is Sebastian Saldonna. "Bast" as he was called in Scottsbluff, was a brakeman on the local switch engine, early forties, father of four, parish church-goer, little league coach. Then one Monday morning, his crew reports to the Scottsbluff depot for their eight o'clock start, and—no Bast. They cover for him until eleven, when the valley Trainmaster shows up unexpectedly, and the jig's up, the yard clerk goes looking for him, his wife's scared to pieces as he went to his "little game" Saturday night as per usual, after Saturday night Mass, and she's clueless. She never asked about his games, he never offered, he always was home by two a.m. Mrs. Saldonna wasn't absolutely sure where the games took place.

I know. Every special agent in the division and throughout the region knows where the one or two "hot" games are held throughout his territory, if for no other reason than schemes of illegal intent most often hatch in close proximity to saloons, cathouses, and high-stakes poker games. And in the North Platte Valley, the only such game at that time was in Scottsbluff, and it was held in a basement underneath a back room, behind a utility room, behind a bar, all of which was east of the switch yard and west of the hide house, and this joint was called *Sweet's.* Irony knows no bounds on the railroad, as a hide house is just that—a creaky lean-to where "green" cow hides, fresh from an adjacent slaughter house, are hung dripping from lines of hooks, and await the arrival of one or two totally-ruined box cars, called "hide" cars, which take this stinking product to factories for processing leather goods.

This disappearance took place before my time, my info coming from "borrowed" files I found in Dicky Tuttle's special file cabinet, the one locked and located behind all the coats and handbooks and rules and regs-folders in his office's personal closest. Dick had eleven other files in there, still does, although he is not aware they have been copied and seized, and yes, it was me.

I brought copies of these with me when I pulled away from my Airstream back in Lander, and I packed them with those files I liberated from Dicky at the coffee shop in Riverton. It wasn't until I watched, and occasionally helped Keith Raven complete his mountain of paperwork in Casper, that I had just a few minutes free to clear my old brainpan, to let the info gathered to this point come and go, a sort of free mediation, *let's see what pops up.*

At one point—Keith needed a coffee and a sandwich, I needed "outside"— I made for the Bronco, kicked the seat back, pulled both sets of files, and just began from the top, no particular order other than a random stack. And it was only fifteen minutes of relative silence, and glorious sunshine, and I was looking at two files. Very different files in terms of styles and typeset and even the most basic of information, but two files with one hair-raising similarity.

Both files in my lap, the file on the left is one of the eleven missing, the ones I'd yanked from Dicky's secret-stash years ago. This file was of BN origin, a Chadron, Nebraska address, an educational record showing high school graduation, Chadron again, and two years majoring in Political Science, University of South Dakota. Then a hiring date, and training, and a first job, switchman, Alliance Yard, midnight shift.

The file on my right is the one Dick still thinks he has, his doctored copy he figured he would use to sell me on the case *is* the copy he has now. My file lists the names and addresses of the dead crewman from the Crawford crew taxi wreck back in '76, immediately recognizable files as standard "BN," typeset and logo and heading for the brakeman and engineer, but the third file, the one *seeming* to indicate the identity of the mystery-brakeman who joined the taxi at the very last minute as it departed Edgemont for Crawford, that is the file from an obviously different source, and no evidence of authorship appears anywhere on those pages.

So, finally, here's the kicker:

The old BN file on my left, the one describing the hiring of a new employee from Chadron, shows a legal name of Stella M. Montenegro.

The file on the right, the one I swapped out with Dicky's, shows a person identified as Maria Teresa Calderone, Denver, Colorado.

And each file sports a poor-quality photo, but not so poor as to cast doubt on a conclusion anyone with vision correctable to 20-20 would draw.

Maria and Stella are one and the same.

Ten

One more reason not to take me home to meet the folks—I hate hospitals. Besides, I'm sixty, and if you are age-appropriate, say between fifty-five and sixty-five, then the folks you'd be taking me home to meet would be between eighty-five and a hundred, and I might *be* meeting them in a *hospital.*

I've had this problem all my life. If I don't follow a distinct and rigid line-of-thought while I am inside a health facility, a sort of self-hypnosis, I'm having an anxiety attack the likes of which makes Jimmy Stewart's turn in *Vertigo* look like a dizzy spell. So, as Doc Lenore has just now pulled up in front of Crawford's new hospital, and he did so without warning, I do not jump out of the car like a jack-in-the-box. Doc notices immediately.

"Yeah, the whim-whams? Me, too. Only mine is the sight of blood."

"Ouch," I say. "Tough considering your line of work."

We edge toward the door to Physical Therapy. Doc nods. "I'd think it would be hard in *your* line of work, considering they call you guys for accidents and derailments, and thefts and assault."

I take a deep breathe before I open the door. "Well, yeah, except I just make it a point to send someone with less seniority in those situations calling for a hospital visit."

Doc leans on the wall. He thinks I need more time. "How about a mandatory visit to the morgue?"

I take another breath and another. "Funny thing, that. No problem at the morgue, or with dead folks in general." And the door is pulled from my hand by a PT tech on the inside. She's all in white scrubs, almost six feet, very strong and very fifty. And the kindest eyes I remember seeing.

"Hey, Doc, howdy Doc's friend. Y'all come visiting?"

Doc gently shoves me forward. "Hey, Betty, this is Will Allen. I wanted him to meet Jimmy, if Jimmy's having a good day."

Betty gestures us inside, and we are walking down an endless hallway. "You kidding? You know Jimmy—*Every day's a good day, some are just better than others.*"

We finally turn and we are on one end of a minor gym, full of PT equipment—weights and ropes and pads and bars, and all types of tortuous and healing equipment. There are two other techs, both busy with clients and their exercises. And at the far end is a young man standing at one end of long parallel bars, waiting for Betty to spot him down the course.

Jimmy Kilroy waves as we approach. "While we're young, Betty."

Betty smacks his arm, albeit not very hard. "While one of us is, Kilroy."

And Doc and I stand back, and I watch one of the most courageous things I've ever seen. Jimmy literally wills himself down the bars, then back again. And again.

Doc whispers to me. "He's so much better than a month ago. The specialists say a pretty-damn-near full recovery is possible, especially with this kid's attitude."

Betty and Jimmy wrap it up. Doc and I escort him to the locker room, and he showers himself, and shaves, and gets dressed, and I pray to God this never happens to me, for I am not made of the right stuff.

Jimmy takes a breather on the bench after he finishes, and we chat until the sun drops below the skylights.

"Yeah," Jimmy starts as if he knows the questions, "whole thing was right out of nowhere. I was on my way back from Edgemont on my bike, I got an Indian, was my dad's, and just south of town, like a bat out of hell, screaming like a banshee comes a Kawasaki—"

I feel sickish. "—a Tomcat?"

"How'd you know?" Jimmy was born smiling, I'm guessing.

"Never mind, I interrupted."

Jimmy looked to the skylight, getting his bearings. "Yeah, it was crazy. This guy, I guess a guy, never seen a girl on a bike like that, this guy's all in black, and he's past me and around a blind corner. Then he's coming back at me, and he pulls the damn bike around, puts it on the ground, sliding right at me. Well, I didn't even think, I couldn't, I over-corrected, off the shoulder, and flipped, and I went one way and my bike the other, and—"

Doc goes. "—and his back and neck took the brunt, but then there were ambulatory issues—"

Jimmy smiling again. "—couldn't walk. *That's* an issue."

Doc finishes. "I still got a connection or two back east, Johns Hopkins, some really nice folks, and we got Jimmy back there and then back here, and he's the luckiest sonuvabitch I have ever known."

I love the story, and I hate where it's going. "Jimmy, time is of the essence, and I cannot at this time tell you why. I'm trading on Doc's credibility here. I need quick and honest answers to three questions, as somebody could be in danger."

Jimmy looks to Doc, Doc nods, Jimmy nods to me. "Shoot."

I shoot. "You said you were in Edgemont, and I take it you were on a visit. Were you visiting Emily Straight?"

Now Jimmy's smile disappears. "Emily? Yeah, I mean, what the hell, hey, we're just friends, geesus, she's not even sixteen."

I hold up one hand. "Relax, I believe you, Jimmy, I'm just putting two and two together, that's all."

Doc shrugs. "Two more questions?"

I nod. "Have you got something going on with Emily's mom?"

Jimmy's almost out of his seat. "Doc, this bastard—"

"—is just trying to keep innocent people safe, Jimmy. Answer the man."

I try to soften the jab. "Jimmy, I know Barbie Straight was pregnant with Emily in high school, so you and Barb aren't that far apart in age. I also know that Barbie and the kids got next to nothing when Harley was killed, and I figure that Emily, growing up dead broke in a hard-luck railroad town, well, she's probably a real tough cookie. So?"

Jimmy's really tired now. "Yes, Barbie and I are together. Third question. I'm wearing thin, Mr. Allen."

"Thanks, Jim, I appreciate it. Third question, which is only important if what I am suspecting is actually happening. And I suspect Emily has quite recently started raising hell again with anyone who will listen about the hinky investigation of her dad's accident, and I think she might have found something, or heard something making her think she has a case."

Jimmy looks to the sky and nods.

Doc sighs. "Oh, no."

I sit forward. "Where is Emily, right now, this moment."

Jimmy's pale. "Barbie, all three kids, in a thirty-year-old station wagon, going to spend the weekend with Barbie's step-sister in Deadwood."

I stand, as does Doc.

"When do they leave?"

And now Jimmy is really and truly spent, and I barely hear him.

"Two hours ago."

Eleven

Apparently I have a new travelling buddy. And he likes the Bronco so much, he buys refreshments every time we stop. And considering my bladder's sixty this year, and I'm betting Doc's is seventy-five or thereabouts, well, breaks are taken. Long ones.

This consideration has immediate effect on the elapsed time to our next destination, Deadwood, South Dakota, a legendary Old West town, once capital of the Dakota Territory. Two and a half hours, 160 miles, but a crap-shoot with the ebb and flow of tourist traffic. And although the kids are back in school across the country, this is when the seniors turn out in record numbers, every third one driving a huge RV, every third RV driver driving an RV for the first time.

Imagine that third of the third's front seat—two huge captain's chairs, each on swivels, the driver stereotypically the old man (it was good enough for Lewis and Clark), his life-love occupying the other chair. He's in the midst of relating the story, for the 117th time, about the day he and his dad were hunting grouse in the Flint Hills of Kansas, and they stopped for a breather, and his dad took a pull on his flask as he was prone to do in those days, and a cloud of grouse jumped out of a cottonwood in a dry stream bed, and by the Good Lord and All the Saints at Sea—there was Bigfoot. And "Mama," as she has come to settle for, ain't listening, but is wrestling with the full, unabridged Rand McNally Road Atlas of the United States, only twelve years old, as who in their right mind'll pop for $5.95 every three years for the cross-country trek from Wichita? But Mama, deep in thought as she is not aware she's combing a map of North rather than South Dakota (why would they have *two*?), is slowly losing consciousness because she has several pairs of glasses (one for reading, one for distance, another for the sun, and a fourth because the rims set off the golden flecks in her chocolate-brown eyes), each pair suspended by a chain around her neck, and as she flits from pair to pair to help "Daddy"

74

navigate this foreign land, the chains intertwine, virtually cutting off her air supply.

Here is where the obligatory passing lanes every twenty miles or so save the day, although the RV's still don't quite get the concept, and half stay in the left lane, while the other half correctly choose the right lane, and the rest of us navigate a slalom course two-and-a-half miles long in order to break free. It's in the middle of one of these challenges that Doc comes out of a reverie.

"Be careful."

I can't help it. "Thanks, Doc. I was seriously considering *not* being careful, but then it occurred to me, slowly mind you, that being reckless might not pay off in the end."

Doc turns away from his window and smiles. "So, you can be a dick."

"The truth will out. I'll try to keep it down, if you'll leave my steering wheel alone."

Doc looks back at the passing RV's. "I'm tense, too. How much trouble might the Straights be in?"

"Well," I sigh, as I swing around the last of the motorized obstacles and break into the open, for the next twenty miles anyway, "we know my Tomcat rider from Mexico is now on the other side of the border, and his record will remain hot, and even if it cools, my friend at the Wyoming Highway Patrol will float the occasional request for status, keeping his file at the forefront with ICE and Border Patrol."

"So we have time, at least from *that* particular direction?"

"That's my guess, and we keep guessing as we have no clue what the Tomcat *hombre* indicates."

"Like?"

"Like, is the taxi tragedy even remotely connected to his interests, or the interests his boss or client represents? Could it even be a cartel connection, all the way up here to hell and back? Is there even a market for dope the big-time players might care about? Or is there a connection with the gambling and loan shark angles? Most crime family influence, of which there was damn little out here until after Korea—most of that was out of Kansas City, a little out of Omaha. But since the mid-sixties, give or take, Denver's a player."

Doc's a quick study. "The Calderones?"

"Yeah." I'm looking for a joint, any joint, with a burger-fry combo to go. I have a feeling we need to make time.

And Doc also reads minds. "I see a place on the right, up there past the truck stop? Looks like it's called *Beary's Burgers?*"

"Thanks, Eagle Eyes." And we are in and parked away from the drive-ups, as I need to make a call, and I'm feeling Doc needs to check in with Loretta sooner or later. There's a pay phone on one side of the kitchen, where I head for, as Doc makes for the front window to get our carry-out burgers.

I make a collect call. Sid answers.

"Collect, Allen? You'll be working this off."

"Couldn't be happier, Sid. Got a bad feeling, thought I'd better check in."

"You have reason, Allen. And give me *somebody's* number up there in Nowhere, will ya? I don't want to be waiting, wondering what the hell's happened."

"Sidney, you care. I knew it, because—"

"Because I have other things to do, all more important than you."

"And we're back. Anyway, call Daisy's in Crawford, Nebraska, she's in the book—"

"Yeah, yeah, just ask for Daisy, I got it."

Doc's got the bag-o-burgers, he's back in the Bronco, digging in.

"And you sound like there's ants in your pants, Sid, why?"

"Why, is because at 6:31 this morning, a Canadian in a full suit, packing a very small weapon, middle of back, climbs out of a brand-new Chrysler, plates out of British Columbia, accent out of Vancouver. This boy's maybe forty, six-four at least, but lanky as lanky knows, thinning blonde hair, straight back, smelling of Vitalis, grey eyes, almost translucent."

"I wish you'd gotten a better look."

"Well, I am a woman of a certain age."

"I'm certain of that. And he wanted?"

"You, Allen. Said he was a provincial agent for the Canadian Pacific, he was in Protection Services, said you two met several years ago at some kind of cross-border training when you were working the Highline in Montana? Something you guys did in Shelby?"

"Well, a nice try on his part."

"He's a hoser?"

"Yes, ma'am. I did do a stint up on the Highline, and we did cross-border training twice. But both times in Havre, never Shelby, and the Canucks we worked with were two Acadians, brothers, listened to nothing but Cajun music, both five-five, maybe, both as square as tall."

"Well, I told him you were in D.C. visiting your Aunt Florrie—"

"*Florrie?*"

"Shut up. As she's got the tremors, you could be gone a few weeks."

"And?"

"And, I kept an eye on the Airstream after he shoves off. And he's back at dusk trying a breaking and entering, but of course—"

"—no go, as my Airstream is Fort Knox—"

"—you and your belief in two redundant locking systems for every one easily picked."

"I, the blind squirrel, finding the occasional nut."

"Well, nuts to you, Allen, I have a lunch rush in progress."

"Thanks Sidney. Really."

"Watch yourself. Nobody else will sweep up the joint for toast."

"And eggs." And Sid hangs up.

Twelve

We're back on the road, Doc's done with lunch and handing me burgers and fries as I need them.

"I'd thought you would have wanted to check in with Loretta, as there were two pay phones back there. I had some change if you needed it."

Doc laughs. "I'm pretty sure you don't have enough change to ring up my girl."

"Oh."

"*Hello, Pearly Gates—a collect call? Forget it.*"

"Doc—"

"Kidding, Will, it's fine. I tend to refer to Loretta like she's still here, and for me, most often, she is. But her sense of humor was great. She would've like you."

I'm trying to pry a foot out my mouth.

Doc hands me another Beary-burger. "Was that your sweetie on the phone?"

"No, not sweetie. It's Sidney back down in Lander. A great friend, the type they don't make anymore."

"Keep 'er, Will, worth her weight in gold."

"Well, that wouldn't be enough for a safe deposit, but yeah, she's the best."

"And she says?"

I'm distracted by the scenery change as we head north. Between the Pine Ridge and the Black Hills, a sort of old west no-man's-land exists. This isn't to mean it can't be reliably traveled, or that it is hiding a host of dangers, waiting for the unsuspecting tenderfoot to stray from the highway, break an axle on red rock, hidden half the year in scrub oak, by now a gorgeous deep red. It is just *relentless*. You can see so far, you can smell so much, and it seems you can hear the raptors and their prey breathe, waiting for the other to make a move. Whether hot as an oven in August, or knee-deep in blowing snow in

March, it's a scenery just as mesmerizing as New Mexico's Land of Enchantment, or Oregon's Craggy Coast. I know it to be a truth—if I weren't living in Lander, my one true home, I would be here.

I realize I've let probably a full minute pass since Doc's question. I look to him and he's obviously enjoying the panorama as much as I am. And he's said nothing.

Man, you gotta like this guy.

"Sidney was just today visited by a CP special agent out of Vancouver, and right at opening—"

"—6:30?"

"Exactly. Like he rolled in just that minute after a long, long drive, or if he took a room last night, he checked out with the sunrise to brace her."

Doc laughs. "*Brace* her? She sounds formidable."

"In a word." My neck hairs are starting to stand, and I can't connect the reflex to reason. "Doc, we need another phone, so let's keep our eyes out."

Doc looks frustrated. "You need to call Sidney again? Can't wait till we make Deadwood?"

"No, it can't, and aren't you a nosy bastard?" I say it with my dumbass smile.

Doc sits back in the bucket seat, regains his smile. "Guilty as charged, Will. Call it the bad habit of an old general practitioner—question everything, accept nothing, dig a little more."

I see the phone booth I need, outside of an out-of-business bar, too far from the Black Hills to make a go of it, too near the big saloons to arouse a tourist's interest. And the last thing to be disconnected and hauled off to another location when a joint goes belly-up is the pay phone and its booth. Or so I hope.

I pull off, approach the booth, dig around for enough change for this idea to work once, and I enter the booth and pull on the door and push it shut behind me. I grab the receiver off its cradle, and there, through the dirty glass, cracked and splashed with graffiti, is Doc. He gives me a wave, then walks off, no particular direction, but *not* back to the Bronco.

First a dime dropped to get the operator, then a request for a collect call to Maggie Connor, Supervising Administrator, Deadwood City Police, then a wait. The operator asks the party in Deadwood if she will accept. The line sucks, it's barely audible.

Then there's a click so loud, it's *clack!* And the line clears.

"Will, you cheap bastard."

"Maggie, you living angel."

"You in town?"

"I will be, and please let's do dinner—I'm on full expenses—"

"—and we will test that theory."

"I'm counting on it, but there's a client—"

"—as usual, what's her name?"

"Glad you asked, it's Emily Straight, fifteen, traveling with two little sibs, mom's driving, and they are headed for the mom's step-sister's house—"

"To hide out?"

"Not initially. Why I'm calling, it might be a good idea. Till I can show. Can you run a couple of your finest by there?"

Maggie laughs. "Oh, don't tell me, *there* is someplace you figure we'll find as we are—"

"—a fine collection of dedicated law enforcement officers, the likes of which—"

"Bullshit, bullshit. Yeah. Got it. Any clue?"

"Just a sec. I open the door," yell *Doc.* Doc appears from around the back of the deserted saloon.

I yell, "Doc, the step-sister's name, address? Anything?"

He looks up and to the side, then, surprised he remembers: "Miller! Yeah, like Janey or Jenny. Oh, yeah, and a block or two from the Goathorn."

Maggie can hear Doc. "Charming. Well, that whittles it down. There's one eight-plex apartment anywhere near the Goat, and one must wonder, considering the occupational choice of at least three of its inhabitants, why this step-sister Miller ain't lookin' up better digs."

"Can you have somebody sit on it?"

"Will, you have *so* much explaining to do—I'll talk to the Captain."

"Maggie, you are an angel, unless you find that condescending, then you are not, but you are something else—"

"Shut up. Swing by the station at six."

I do just that. I introduce Doc to Maggie, and both are curious where and how I made acquaintance with the other. Nosey matches nosey.

I get Doc a room at the Robber's Roost. Every motel and hotel in Deadwood is over-priced until Labor Day, then the competition for a loyal but undersized tourist market heats up as the weather cools down. It's really the best time to be in the Black Hills. The yellows and golds of joe-pie weeds and goldenrod play delightfully off the blue-purple of wild bergamot, all surrounded and protected by stands of Ponderosa Pine. There are no bad views. To paraphrase Jimmy Kilroy, some are just better than others.

Anyway, Doc's winding down, and Maggie and I drop him at his log cabin unit for rest, then we make for the Goathorn, Maggie's favorite pub-for-a-bite. In four minutes, we pull up in front.

"What the hell is a matter with you?" Maggie's *not* chomping at the bit to get out of the Bronco, run up the three wooden steps to the 1890s-fake-front of the Goathorn Grill, and plant a wet-one across the cheek of the proprietor, Wesley Dunhill.

Here's my dumbass smile. "I getting mixed messages, Mags. You love this joint—"

"—I hate this dump."

"You love the food—"

"—which tastes like crap."

"And the very sight of Wes Dunhill makes—"

"—me vomit. Have you got your signals straight now?" Maggie has pointedly *not* unhooked her seatbelt.

"Maggie, I need a favor."

"Will." Maggie's looking out the windshield as if it were a tunnel. "There is a uniform sitting exactly one hundred yards from Emily Straight's step-aunt's apartment, not more than one hundred and fifty yards from this very spot. If you turn to your left, and look up the street, you can see the uniform's tail lights from this very spot—"

"Maggie—"

"Shut up. Further, we have been able to discern—without alarming the family—that Emily and her siblings and her mother and the step-aunt are all inside, munching away on Billy-Boy's pizzas, as the delivery guy was an off-duty cop-friend of mine who owes me a favor, and Billy-Boy's is not the pizza I would have chosen, but nevertheless pizza, and all five are safe, and as happy as any of us might expect to be in such surroundings."

"Maggie—"

"—and *not* finished. *And* all this came to pass because of my personal credibility with my captain, which by the way, was strained, not strengthened, when he found out it's you I want to help. So, Will, *another* favor?"

I wait. She nods. I go.

"Thanks a *million.* Okay, several thousand." I detect a marginal thaw. "Look, Maggie, the last time I was in Deadwood, I admit, things might have gone easier—" Here I stop myself as Maggie's laser-stare locks my eyes, and I sense no love. "Okay, we came very close to blowing up the 1880 train—"

Maggie's turned clear around. "*We*? *We* did not. *You* came within a literal hair's-breadth, of derailing—destroying—our classic, vintage *1880* steam engine and beautifully-renovated passenger cars—and the jobs the train creates, and the money those jobs generate."

Maggie refers to the famous Deadwood 1880 train, one of the Black Hills' most popular summer tourist attractions. Although the concession is one fronted by a private company in partnership with the City of Deadwood, the Hill City to Keystone Turn is actually a formal assignment on the Burlington Northern. Each summer, the day after Memorial Day, the job is bid-in by one Engineer (one still qualified to operate a steam locomotive long after the conclusion of the steam era), one fireman (as one crewman needs to be shoveling coal into the furnace), a formal conductor (dressed in vintage uniform, taking and punching tickets), and one working brakeman (whose only real responsibility is to disconnect the engine and coal car from the leading end of the passenger cars, and reconnect that engine and coal car on the opposite end, so the train can return home, and throw the initial switch and the final switch). It goes without saying in the world of railroaders, that a job working five hours a day, Monday and Tuesday off, working Wednesday through Sunday, and making time-and-a-half for the Saturday, and double-time for the Sunday, and the nature of the job is historical and theatrical, executed in a glorious summer in the Black Hills—such an assignment is manned by crewmen with anywhere from twenty-five to thirty-five years of service.

A younger me, though not too damn much younger, was quietly (secretly) contracted by the Deadwood Tourism Council and the Alliance Division's Dispatcher's Office (bypassing Dicky Tuttle) to run a bit of an op, no one the wiser, as both organizations received extortion letters threatening to derail the 1880 train if a package carrying fifty grand was not discovered by the extortionist at midnight in a bear-proof trash can in the tourist parking lot farthest away from Mount Rushmore, these attractions some thirteen miles and twenty-three minutes apart. The Deadwood Police and BN's official division special agent were officially and publicly charged with arresting the extortionist and saving the train and its riders. And no one save Maggie and her captain and one Protection Services VP in Fort Worth knew I was involved. Long story short, for now—I learned the brakeman on the 1880 train crew was the classic lone wolf thinking he could cut a fat hog, bag the fifty grand for himself, *and* run from his loan shark at the Goathorn, never to be heard from again.

And that brakeman was, actually, never heard from again, save for one scream. His loan shark tipped me of the brakeman's guilt, only because the shark feared never getting his original loan repaid, and the shark would rather see the brakeman go down for hard time, if he couldn't get satisfaction in the conventional manner. Yeah, these bastards are twisted.

I'd caught up with the brakeman while he was on duty on the 1880 train, right at end of day. The train, full of tourists, rolled into the yard, confined on both sides by rows and rows of vehicles, all the way out to a street packed with more tourists and yet more vehicles. The brakeman's last official duty was to throw an old switch, its purpose to guide the train off the main line and into the depot. The switch at the other end of the depot was not lined to permit a train or car to continue on through the station and back on the main.

This was the setting then, when I attempted apprehending the brakeman until Deadwood PD could back me up. Because of my impatience and my ego, I didn't wait for help, the brakeman and I got into a full-blown wrestling match (I still sport his teeth marks on a neck scar), and the train nearly derailed. I pulled my taser free at the penultimate moment, zapped the brakeman, and pulled my back to throw the switch with a second to spare. Extensive loss of life, property, and one-quarter of the tourist industry might have been a tragic reality—but I got lucky.

Not so much the brakeman. My taser caught the back of his right knee. He tried to run, but one leg was useless. Maybe his ability to reason failed him as well, because he thought jumping between passenger cars as they rolled into the depot was his only shot at escape. His right leg failed as he jumped, and the second passenger car rolled over him.

And, as happens with a case to which I am connected, more often than I care to admit, the size and severity of the case needing to be solved is proportionally much larger than the amount of mayhem I *seem* to be generating. In other words, rather than a standing ovation and hearty handshake from the mayor and city council when I have been part or all of solving a case, I have occasionally been driven to a community's city limits in a black and white squad car, pointed in a direction *away* from the little town or village, and the uniform driving me goes *no need comin' back*, and I go *thanks for nothin'*.

Which, pretty much, is exactly what happened in Deadwood. Except that the squad car's driver was the Deadwood PD captain, and he goes *rot in hell,* and I go *have a nice day.*

It's all I had at that moment.

Thirteen

So, it dawns on me as I'm leaning into the Bronco's open window on the driver's side, frantic to convince Maggie I need her inside the Goathorn, then I'll need her over at Emily's step-aunt's, and two things become crystal clear. The first—Maggie isn't really still angry enough to withhold her help from me, although we didn't speak for one full year after that specific screw-up on the tourist train.

This woman is one of the few people I trust implicitly. Think about it a minute. How many people—dead honest—would you not question, just act, if those people suddenly appeared and said *this is life and death, come with me now, no questions, no time to lose.* The correct answer: *damn few people.* And I know I trust Maggie as I trust Sidney. Both never cry over spilt milk, both have unerring faith in *tomorrow,* and neither believe in short-term fixes at the cost of long-term resolutions.

The second issue *is* Wesley Dunhill. And if Maggie has more reasons to despise Dunhill than the Milky Way has stars—well, one more brick in the wall won't matter. I know from way, way back that Wes only recently bought the Goathorn. Word on the street says that Wes and a handful of other business owners bought into upper-Midwest insurance companies, and those companies floundered after covering the cost of a string of freak tornadoes that dismantled a third of Oklahoma. So, it ain't rocket-surgery to figure a couple things out— the boarded-up bar Doc and I stopped at so I could call Maggie, that saloon, out-of-business, belongs to one of Wesley's partners. In stark contrast, Wes just bought the Goathorn. Question here being, Wesley's partner can't keep a two-bit bar open after the insurance company investment went south, but Wes can buy one of the four largest and ornate pub-tavern-restaurants in the Black Hills?

One of these things is not like the other.

I'll take one more shot. "Okay, Maggie, I get it. You are reacting in such a way that indicates Wesley, and probably a truck-load of his buddies, have and are and will cause the Deadwood PD all sorts of problems. And when Wes prospers and his buddies do not, we have an indication of support for Wesley's enterprises coming from outside the Hills. Maybe crime in an *organized* fashion, maybe out of Chicago or Kansas City or Denver."

Maggie, at least, nods and looks my way. "And the case I'm running may have external players at the bottom of it, too. We may be digging out the same varmints, Mags. I don't know who is who in the Hills anymore. You do."

Maggie huffs. "I'm just another clerk, Will, filing and typing and—"

"Maggie, that's bullshit and you know it. You are the hub of a wheel here. You came in young, rebuilt the administrative infrastructure of a failing department, forged a partnership with your captain, and you made yourself indispensable. And you know it. And you're pissed. So, let's put the anger to its best use."

"Smashing your face?"

I'm getting the ghost of a smile. "If you need to, yes, but please wait until *after we are out of the Goathorn.* And please, not the nose. It could not survive another break."

George Straight can't get close enough to his shaving mirror with his glasses on. When he takes them off, he can't see his reflection. Wasn't it Bette Davis—man, now she is a real woman—saying "Old age ain't no place for sissies." With that, George nicks his Adam's apple with his straight razor, and a creamy ridge of shave cream anchored in a crevasse of age turns pink, then red. *Shit.* Sometimes there is no better word.

He reaches for toilet paper to staunch the flow. How old's ol' Bette now? George knows she was born in 1908, same year as his ex-mother-in-law, spittin' image of Dolly, old broad talks about it all the damn time, and if this is '76, then Bette's 68? And although George just turned forty-five, wouldn't kick her out of bed for eatin' crackers. Bette, that is, not the ex-mother-in-law. George stops and stares into the mirror, and the guy staring back is lost. That guy is trying to close-shave under a deadline, even though he has maybe five minutes, if he's lucky, to get on the road and beat feet from his studio apartment over the hair salon in Edgemont, to a roadside rest area just this side of Crawford, Nebraska.

The guy in the mirror just spent another five desperate minutes begging—pleading—with his own baby brother. *I just got called to taxi a crew from the depot to Crawford. And Harley's claiming his old lady's due any damn second. Maybe, maybe not, Harley, but Dolly's got me in court in Rapid at eight sharp tomorrow a-m, I don't show up, my child support goes through the roof, man— I'll be sleeping on your couch, brother.*

And Harley gives in, little brother always does, and Harley'll be leaving Edgemont in about an hour and twenty, but George needs to leave right damn now, Stella just ten minutes back ago calling, just like she warned ol' George she'd have to, she having no choice, and if George really loved Stella the way George claimed, like he's said all those drunk nights in Chadron, well he'd better get moving when she says go.

George runs out the bathroom, stops to tug on a black t-shirt, then a black jacket over that, already wearing black jeans and combat boots. Stella was picky as hell about the details. This guy Stella answers to, this Garcia, he is fearsome, she said. *A strange word to choose*, George thought, *but, ya know— Mexicans.* George'd talk a mile round having to use the term. Growing up hereabouts, the word was a slam. *I mean, they are Mexicans, being from Mexico and all, but man, call a white man Mexican, shit flies.*

Besides, Stella gets all huffy at the subject, about how the language is Spanish, the country is Spain, but only a few Spaniards are Mexicans, and mixing in Indians of all things. George gets a headache at this conversational turn, because Stella's raging on about those little countries on the way down to South America, and how—how's this go?—all those Mexicans are actually Bolivians and Chileans and Argentinians, and she herself, she claims to spend all sorts of time with Colombians, as does that scary little Jose. Well, call y'all what you will, George resolves to dodge this issue in perpetuity, *nothin's worth pissin' off a Mexican.*

George is halfway to the meeting place, Stella says not to worry, she'll be there early, babysitting Jose—man, she talks about that little guy a lot. George is too old to be jealous, and he's secure in his rugged good looks, getting better with age, according to Stella, after a few tequilas. But if George was insecure, ol' Jose's youth—maybe he's thirty, not quite?—and his motor bike—always got a new one, the latest a Ducati maybe, a 900, Stella's always saying how cool—and he's speaking Spanish, too, Stella saying it's the language of love. *Geez—Mexicans.*

George slows, he's catching a series of three flashlight flashes just below the upcoming rise. Stella guides him into a pull-off that becomes a two-track. George stops, his old GMC pick-up coughing when he turns the key. He gets out, grabs Stella and kisses her, she laughs and pushes off, turning the flash light direct in his face.

George is less than happy. "Hey, knock it off, Stella, where the hell's that Jose? I thought we were short on time."

Stella clicks the light off, and she walks back up the two track, stops at a panel van, black as the night. She slides open the side door, a light from within illuminates, and George is staring into a large, window-panel mirror. It's set up on a frame with wide, broad wheels on a rectangular base.

Stella hands George a pair of rawhide gloves and directs him along the path, she pulling on one end of the mirror, he pushing the other. At a distance of about two feet from the white line marking off the highway shoulder, they stop, and Stella swings her end around until the reflective surface is parallel to the highway. George doesn't want to ask any questions. He doesn't want to look confused or weak in front of Stella, and he doesn't want to trip off that famous temper.

Finally, George cannot restrain himself. "Ah, how's this working, again?" Stella laughs, George melts. "Tranquilo, Hor-hay. I didn't tell you yet, so you didn't forget." Stella pulls a large walkie-talkie out of her grip, turns it on, clicks the button twice, waits, hears a two-click back at her. "The next time we hear two clicks over the radio, we roll out this mirror, at a right angle to the highway."

George is now quite confused. "You trying to crash the van with the mirror?"

Stella is patience personified. "We are stopping the van, intact."

George, no better. "We? Wait a minute. Where the hell is your Jose?"

Stella laughs once more, and hands George a bright and shiny brakeman's lantern from her grip. "He is not my Jose—he is our Jose." Stella looks toward the direction the taxi van from Edgemont will soon be approaching.

"And our Jose, mi amigo, is in the taxi van."

George looks at the lantern in his hand, and he feels dizzy, like he's losing blood. "In the van, with my brother?"

Stella still scans the horizon. "Now you're catching on, Hor-hay."
And both Stella and George look to Stella's radio.
"Click-click."

Fourteen

"You know, Mags, it took me all of seventeen full minutes to get you inside the Goathorn." We are sitting at a table by the window, farthest from the door, the bar a distant spectacle. Outside, seniors of every stripe, (white and old, and white and older—*wait, wait, I think that really old cat is Asian, nope, too tall)* are bouncing up and down the wooden-plank sidewalks, each slat giving a different "take" in weight and walking speed. About three out of ten folks are wearing brand new Stetsons, not the *Open Road* or, for half that price, a *Cromwell* or a *Spencer.* These three styles, at least, serve a purpose back home, wherever that might be, at least in the depth of winter, and they look classy—after all it is 1986, not 1886. The three of ten folks, nowadays, are buying for two or three times the price the company's *Rancher* or *Roper*—full-blown, full-size cowboy hats, with serious blocking required, regular cleanings, proper storage. And back home, for most of these well-meaning tourist-rubes, these hats will see the light of day again each Halloween only, the rubes' thinking being a Hollywood cowboy for the office party or the neighborhood Halloween party for the rest of her or his life, well maybe that's makes the exorbitant price *right fair, I reckon.*

Maggie will start chatting when she's ready. And now ain't ready. Since we walked in, she's been preoccupied with shooting laser-knives out her eyeballs at Wesley Dunhill. There is some considerable baggage carried here by Maggie and Wes, and me for that matter. But there should be a whole lot more I do not know about, if Maggie's behavior is a clue. I swear, had she a weapon and a magical ability to kill the houselights, Dunhill's headed for Boot Hill.

Back again to my earlier days in Deadwood, as context is a good thing. Wendy was gone all of three months, and I was hiding in work, job after job on roads from Tuscaloosa to Yakima. I was finally too exhausted to book one more consult, and I found myself on the road to Deadwood. I'm a life-long

Western fanatic, from Tom Mix to this year's remake of *Stagecoach,* third time around. So, too tired to eat, I check into the Bullock Hotel, a virtual Disneyland of old west feeling and flavor.

Shorten this tale up an inch—I run into a couple of retired engineers at breakfast, one has a BN special agent-son with a case he can't crack, time's of the essence, it's the 1880 Train caper I mentioned previously, and I meet Maggie—at my first AA meeting. Alcohol has played more of a role in my life than I'd care to admit, I liked Deadwood and the Hotel, I had a very strong talk with me, and me and I found the meeting in the public library. I'd run into Maggie without formal introduction when I was bumping heads with her captain over how we should handle the extortion case on the tourist train. Maggie was less than impressed (pissed as holy hell) with me coming within a second of burning down her hometown. Anyway, in the crucible that is an AA meeting, bullshit melted away, honesty prevailed, and Maggie offered to be my sponsor, thank God.

However, one other participant in that particular meeting was one Wesley Dunhill. Dunhill and Maggie grew up together, always rivals, often enemies, and Wes positive from puberty to the present, ol' Maggie's just playing hard to get. How worthless is Wes? Well, his short stint in AA was a ruse, one of many over the years, to get close to Maggie, to get himself that eye and ear in the local police department, to get an angle keeping him one step ahead of the law.

Now Mags takes a deep breath, sits back, squares her shoulders, and momentarily places her hands directly on top on mine. This how she gets my attention. What she says, and the way she says it—this is how she keeps my attention.

"Will. Do not turn to look until I say it's clear. While we wait, I will prepare you. Across the room, away over at the bar, right where the end closest to the front door meets the desk with the cash register? Two stools there, I'm pretty sure they can't see us, yet anyway. Wait, wait, ok, here comes the cocktail waitress. And now, look."

And I look, and I see who I expect to see, and the last person I would expect to see. There is Wesley Dunhill, Goathorn proprietor, right where any decent saloon or eatery owner should be, comping drinks for old school buddies, suggesting desserts to a table of Book Club ladies, hyping the special to a bachelor party, none of whom will remember the final bill for the night's festivities.

And Wes this minute sits on the first stool at the bar, waving for his bartender's attention, then holding up two fingers, and pointing those fingers at the gent on the second stool, Doctor Randall Lenore, he who is supposed to be passing his night in his knotty-pine room at the Rooster.

I am taken aback. "Maggie, that's—"

"—Doctor Lenore, *just call him Doc.*" Maggie drains her club soda and lime, signals to a passing waiter for another. "You keep interesting company, Will."

Still aback. "I thought I knew how interesting. Whatcha got on Doc, Maggie?"

"You first. Knowing you too well, you have a few bugs in your bonnet about ol' Doc, don't you?"

I hate it when I'm beaten to the punch. "Okay. Little things, tiny things, but starting to add up." Mags nods, gets her next club soda, sips. "It's quite a list of littles. For instance, can you see Doc's feet from where you're sitting?"

Maggie cranes a bit. "There is a small leather bag, smaller than a suitcase, a little bigger than a backpack."

"It's his go-bag. *Not* his black bag for doctoring. That bag is locked in a cargo space in the Bronco next to my weapon."

Maggie snorts. "Where, by the way, it can do you absolutely no good."

"Unless you are a lousy shot, like me. Then it's good for the general public."

"Sheesh. Go on."

The waiter strolls by to take an order, any order. I wave him off. He says *sheesh.* I am a trend-setter.

"Okay, again, Doc has a grip, what he calls a 'go-bag,' packed to go with me on the spur of the moment when he found out I'd say *Deadwood.* It's one thing to take a medical bag everywhere you go, as you are going all over locally, as a doctor. It's another to have a grip, with toilet articles, a change of clothes, extra coat, watch cap, duplicate personal prescriptions, but why a baton? Doc's excuse *could be* there's a flashlight in the handle, he is seventy-five and fears mugging—in Crawford?"

Maggie's all the way loose, anger gone for now. "And you know how the insides of his bag look, how?"

"Doc and I had to take pee breaks along the way. He never followed me into a restroom, waited for me to leave first, and I did the same. We both had time to search the other's bags. I arrange mine in a certain way. Then I'd check my bag after a pee break. Doc was sifting through it. As I sifted through his when he was otherwise occupied."

Maggie doesn't take notes. In a few hours, she will write an error-free transcript of our conversation. I might as well sign a blank sheet of paper attesting to its accuracy right this second.

"In no particular order, Doc knows Sidney's opening time. He tossed it in a conversation where he's only just learned she exists."

Mags: "Weird."

Me: "In the same conversation, I referred to a visit Sid got from a special agent from the CP. Doc didn't ask what CP means."

Mags: "Because he knows it *Canadian Pacific.* So what?"

Me: "It's hinky. If he knows, and he knows I'm a railroader, he'd make a point of impressing me with his acumen. If he didn't know, and he's a doctor very much still keeping current in his field, his natural curiosity would trigger the question."

Mags: "Maybe, maybe not. What's your read?"

Me: "He didn't know how to play it. He was taken by surprise, he didn't have time to think it through, to figure me out. So he froze, and he let it pass."

Mags: "Next?"

Me: "When you were giving me holy hell on the phone, and I was asking for protection for Emily Straight and family, Doc came up with the name of the step-sister, and a general idea of her apartment location."

Mags: "Things he should have known, or should not have known?"

Me: "Things he never explained knowing."

Mags: "Again, maybe. One more, I hope?"

Me: "I hope, too. Seeing as how we are watching a tête-à-tête 'tween your Wesley and my Doc—"

Mags: "Seeing as how."

Me: "I'm hoping that when I ask you and your colleagues to get a list of all of Wesley Dunhill's incoming calls for this twenty-four-period, the list you get, from a legal tap and legal source, I'm sure, will show one incoming call, probably collect, from one old country doctor, in an abandoned booth, outside a boarded-up saloon, about twenty miles due south of Deadwood."

George Straight is anything but. Straight, that is. He's drunk, and scared out of his mind, and shocked, and puking when he isn't sobbing so hard, he can barely breathe. He's wiping snot and puke and cold sweat from his face and chest and hands. He's used up every paper towel in his studio kitchen, and both rolls of toilet paper, and every single red-white-and-blue-happy-birthday-America cocktail napkin from under the sink. And that's saying something, as his landlady charged into Kmart in Chadron bright and early July 5th, and bought all remaining Bicentennial gear, store-wide, for one nickel on the dollar.

George has spent half the night and half of this day in and out of consciousness. He remembers bits and pieces, beginning with his call to work, then his call to Harley to work the taxi-van trip to Crawford, then driving like a bat out of hell to meet Stella this side of Crawford, like she ordered. *Man, what a bitch.*

What's left of his recollections are terrifying, and if they are true, George doesn't want to live. This second is a rare lucid moment, when the stench of whiskey and its match in regurgitated spirits is battling the sour reek of Lysol and Ajax, the residue of a half-dozen attempts in other rare, lucid moments to clean this small studio if and when the cops show up, if and when George's role in all this becomes clear, if and when just what in sam-hell "all of this" is comes to light—and oh, my God, someone, somewhere is gonna pay. And once more George realizes that he may well turn out to be the one who pays, and the puking begins anew.

George has nothing left to vomit, as the last drop of booze went down almost two hours ago now. And his dry retching is half as loud as his wet heaves, so he hears the knock at the door, down in the garage, the garage upon which his little studio apartment teeters. He looks in the little shaving mirror nailed to the window sill over the sink.

"Oh, my God." He yells, *keep yer shirt on, I'm comin'*, and he grabs a cap, pulls it down over his eyes, grabs a bathrobe out of the laundry hamper, wraps it round his torso, and staggers down shallow concrete steps into complete darkness. He waits. Another hammering from outside the side door, and as it vibrates away from the frame, a brief door-shaped rectangle of light is allowed in, and George can make his way to the door, only banging a knee once, possibly breaking a small toe on his nondominant foot.

George throws the door back, cursing his best, and two police torches blind him.

One torch is wielded by a Dawes County rookie sheriff's deputy, Wally Lemon. His supervising partner, Deputy Sergeant Leo Landy is preoccupied with keeping the rookie from blowing George's head off. Wally is a great kid, but seems to believe no specific or particular police action or strategy is poorly-served by the addition of his service revolver.

George, overwhelmed by the torches, and taken by surprise by two large men in uniform, pukes on Wally's boots, then faints.

Wally reaches for his boots rather than George.

"Can I shoot him now, Sergeant?"

Fifteen

There is always a certain point, sometimes more than one, in every case where it would be easier for me to just kind of leap ahead, blow around a scene or episode, tell you such and such leads to such and such, and *then he confessed to everything, and I'm buyin' the doughnuts!* And twenty years ago, hell, even ten, I did often do just that, because I didn't play squarely by the book then, and I don't now. A buddy of mine, so far away in Montana he's taken on a touch of Canuck accent, says I feel I can do that because I am self-righteous, and oh, if that arrow through the heart is insufficient, I'm an ego-maniac, too.

I get it. He isn't wrong. I'm supposed to see "the book" we hear about throwing at bad guys, or "the keys" we should throw away after using them to lock up a felon, as metaphors for the rules and regs and norms of behavior we, all of us, have hammered together to apply equally to one and all. And this is hardly a new or fresh look at the conundrum as old as civilization itself. Equality under the law can be achieved and protected for people with power and money much more easily and effectively then said equality can be extended to the poor and marginalized. Fining some joker in a Rolls who gets caught throwing his Arby's sack full of greasy wrappers out his car window just as he comes into view of Mount Rushmore, constitutes a one-time payment of one thousand dollars. The poor person, who *is* poor in gold and poor in options, will not have one thousand dollars, will have to work community service all day every Saturday for two months, but his or her job is on Saturday, so she or he gets fired, and when they apply for a new job, they have to tell the littering story again, suffer further humiliation, not get the next job or the next—you see where I'm going here.

So, imagine if you will, criminals with power and money, scooping up desperate and angry and hungry poor people to do their bidding, to shield the bad guys from arrest when and if their dubious business arrangement goes sideways. No long-term successful criminal appears on the front line of his criminal enterprise. He is always insulated by lieutenants, and lawyers, and tax experts, and PR people, and then another layer of the poor, shipping and carrying and receiving and delivering contraband. For next to nothing.

Sometimes a real bad guy, the guy at the top, or maybe his second or third in command can be accessed, if one, being me, is patient and calculating—and lucky. I'm impatient. I hate the time it takes from the quarters going into the vending machine to the second my salted nut roll drops into the tray. I'm not calculating. I'm as surprised when my badly-worn tire blows as I am every other time I have a badly-worn tire blow. But lucky. Yes, I am. Sure, I'm standing right here, aren't I?

And no matter how one goes about solving a case, or grabbing up a villain, no one remembers the lucky aspect as much as they remember your won-loss record. This perspective artificially reinforces your reputation, which is a lucky thing, so you get more work, calling for more luck, et cetera, et cetera. But there is usually a time somewhere just before and just after you close a case that the real bad guy is distracted and therefore open to a direct attack, and those who much care about him have deserted him, and those who are about to institutionalize him for many years to come don't blink twice at an irregularity you suggest indirectly, or propose directly, so a window for some real damage done, and some small justice served—is wide open. And I have been known to watch and wait, sometimes for twenty years and more, and then I'll move, and the bad guy will know *real* bad luck, while I go out a rear window, or fire escape, or disappear completely, reappearing in Lander, snug in the Airstream.

I think about justice more now at sixty than ever at forty. Maybe time is running out. Maybe I've seen so many powerless people, good people, take it in the head and the heart—only because they were in the wrong place, wrong time, and a bad guy needed a shield. But I know sometime in the midpoint of a case, I start to smell something. I mean, literally. Smell something. Not good, not horrible. Sweet, industrial, a little like frying, a little like mildew. Yes, it sure as hell ain't pleasant. But I have come to trust it rather than question it. And when I do that, it works for me. That smell tells me I may not be speaking directly with the central bad guy, or even his confederate, but I'm getting close to the true snakes, sensing a direction, seeing a pattern, formulating a question that leads to a question that leads to the keystone—and the wall goes down.

Maggie and I continue watching Doc and Wesley chatter back and forth at the bar at the Goathorn, draining martinis.

Maggie drains another lime and club, two for her, three for me. "Will, you're looking like that last one was castor oil."

"Doc told me he quit drinking."

"Looks like he does—in between martinis."

I start to stand, sit again. "Should we approach? I don't think he knew we were coming here specifically."

Maggie shakes her head. "He came up with a neighborhood for Emily and family. He's got to think we'll show up sooner or later. If he stinks—your famous smell-test—he isn't trying to hide it."

"You're right. Maybe Doc is a good one, but he's got a separate agenda going, and I'm not positive it parallels mine."

"*Ours,* big boy. *Ours.* Look, I sold the captain on this, but it ends in one second if you hot dog this thing. You cooperate, you share, you back the hell off and let Deadwood PD take it and run, when that time comes." Maggie's half-standing now as two very large men join Doc and Wesley at the bar.

The danger-smell's getting worse. "And I will do all that, Maggie, just as soon as you give me your real story, not that half-ass excuse for buy-in. Y'all have a case you want to make against Wesley, you want to see Wesley hang if you had your way, and you knew Doc the minute you saw him, while he's giving me the impression he's been a lifelong homebody, shufflin' and doctorin' and birthin' up the babies, always in and about Crawford."

Before Maggie can respond, the two large men take an elbow each of Doc's, and the three follow Wesley down the side of the dining room, into a supply room, and disappear.

I touch Maggie's shoulder. "Is there a door out of there?" Maggie hesitates, looks away. "The jig's up, Mags. You're obviously pretty damn comfortable navigating your way around this place, and I buy your hatred for Wesley. I think Deadwood PD has a case against him, one they want to ride home before Feds arrive, as they are prone to do, and you did the work and they get the credit. And there's a couple of dozen other things that don't add up, but I think Doc needs a hand."

Maggie cracks. "There's an additional conference room, kitchen, fridge in there, plus restroom. People go in there, they can be there until the food runs out. But there is also a door up and out to the alley, so Wesley can come and go at will."

"Woof. Right now we better get to that alley. And later we can discuss how you, a simple 'administrator,' can never fail to sway her captain, or have access to all sorts of info you'd think would be classified, like Doc's name and mail, and apparently he spends more time in your parts here about then I would think."

And over the course of the next three minutes or so, I witness just the kind of moves in Maggie that suggest training and instinct, but not necessarily trust.

Maggie and I are out the front door. The car-parker-kid (there goes my word-malfunction again) gets in our way, as I suspect he has been directed to do so. Maggie continues, jogging now around the corner and down the side alley to the back alley. I forcefully suggest to the car-kid he might quickly re-examine his loyalties, as I am a crazy-big tipper, especially if my Bronco appears in ten seconds or less, and more tips to come if and when he feels he can spill on his managers without getting eaten up and spat away.

The Bronco appears, my twenty disappears, I'm around to the alley's mouth and blocking it with my pride and joy. No sign of Mags. No sign of Doc, or Wes, or the goons. And here's another spot where my intractability puts me in a tight space. I own a pair of Colt Official Police .38 Specials, revolvers with the four-inch barrel, a six-round cylinder, primarily chambered for the .38 Special cartridge. And as formidable as that sounds, neither of those puppies will be doing me one bit of good right now. I fashioned a lock box that bolts to the underside of the back seat of the Bronco shortly after I bought the vehicle. Both weapons reside therein, behind a combination lock. Further, they rest there unloaded, although .38 cartridges do also live inside, in a small cardboard box.

I figure Mags either ran the long way around the alley to come back at the other end, or she went to call for back up, or neither, or both. I'm starting to figure she is not the admin she claims to be, maybe never was for all I know, but she's doing something in support of regaining Doc, I'm sure. So, I spin the dial on the safe, hit each number in record time, little door pops open, I grab one of the revolvers and start to load it, and in fact, I get one cartridge into the chamber. I'm stopped by the sight of Maggie walking quickly toward me from the other end of the alley, with her back to the wall. I see no weapon in her hands.

And then everything stops with the opening of a green metal door, marked *Goathorn Loading*. Out steps one large man, then Doc, then the other large

99

man, and then Wesley. All of us pause as if we're about to execute a classic double-take in a Laurel and Hardy movie, although Maggie and I should have suspected some sort of showdown, Wesley and the goons, willing to tempt a kidnap charge, being bad *bad* guys, should not only expect a showdown, they should see it as another day in the life of bandits.

At this point, then, I still see no gun with Maggie, none with Doc, no doubt one gun each with the goons, but those seem deeply lodged in bulges under their armpits. I have one gun out, and in my hand, but it contains one bullet, and that one bullet can be in any one of six chambers. And I feel funny about asking everyone to take a breath, but stand absolutely still, as I need to position my cylinder in such a way as to permit the hammer to drop on and across the flat end, sending the business end of the bullet tearing through space, to throw a real monkey wrench into the escape plans of the bad guys, but not killing Doc, of course.

So, I assume a shooter's position, and yell *freeze, put up your hands,* and Wes runs back to and through the green door, and Doc and the two goons turn my way, away from Maggie. Then, figuring *so far, so good,* I go *Doc, go back to Maggie,* and he tears his arms free of the goons' grip, and moves her way as he if was shot from a cannon.

And right here, I can see a dozen similar situations—show-downs, face downs, one very odd hoe-down, but all scenes in cases where there is no rational pay-off for anyone involved if any one person involved resorts to deadly force. Unfortunately, this doesn't seem to inhibit one or more of this scene's players.

The bigger of the big men digs his weapon free of his coat and holster and takes aim for Doc. The smaller of the big men is confused, then belatedly tries to reach his weapon, too. Now I go *stop, freeze,* with the larger man's back in my sights. He fires once, I fire once. Luck. My bullet was waiting in the correct chamber. The big *big* man is a crap shot. Doc goes down, clutching a calf, the bigger big man goes down on his face, splayed, his weapon dropped aside, as I nailed him center mass. The smaller big man finally frees his weapon, but Maggie's on him in a second. She beats him like a drum, his gun flailing about in his right hand. One last pop to his nose, blood sprays, the small big man drops, out cold, and Mags is leaning against the wall, breathing heavy, eyes glued to me. We watch each other for five full seconds, and even Doc is quiet.

"You're going to give me some dumbass story, Allen, about how that was one bullet, the only one, right?"

I try not to smile, but dumbass is as dumbass does. "Or, *your* story about how that hand-to-hand beat-down you put on bad guy number two was what, admin training?"

Mags is walking away already. Over one shoulder: "—and dinner's on you."

Part Two

Sixteen

I'm sitting in a cubicle, Deadwood PD, set aside for the new guy, or the part-time worker, or somebody's mom or kid showing up early, and the cop she or he is related to isn't ready to go yet—*that* cubicle. Mostly holding dusty files that can't be trashed, waiting for the mandatory fifteen years, and what little room's left is a Mr. Coffee, half a cup of black paste coating the bottom of the carafe, the obligatory store-brand powdered creamer container, empty.

I was told in no uncertain terms by deadwood Police Captain Walter Patterson to *not move one inch.* He speaks with a baritone bordering on bass, he'd easily pass for thirty if he had hair (any), and his five o'clock shadow makes Dick Nixon look clean-shaven. And we have never gotten along, but not just *kinda*. Those I battle with, full voices pounding, there's a reason. In fact, usually years-worth of head-to-head knock-down-drag-outs. Patterson gave me an hour to "get outta Deadwood" the *first* time we met.

But that smell I referred to earlier, it's stepping up, and Maggie's act at our little "shootout" suggests a future for my investigation, especially mixed with the bucket-full of *what-the-hells* dumped on me by *good ol' Doctor Lenore.* Who, by the way, is getting cleared at the hospital as we speak. Doc was grazed, he has a limp, Deadwood PD booked the living specimen of the two large men, the dead specimen taking up space at the morgue. And nobody's seen Wesley, and *there's* a surprise.

I'm good with doing nothing right now. I would never admit it, well, maybe to the kids, but no one else. That is, I've shot a few people. Okay, quite a few people, but few of them died. I didn't go overseas during the Big One. I got a job at 17 as a gofer for the Protection Services Office at the Northern Pacific. I graduated a year early from high school, lied about my age, they took me on officially in forty-four as a probationary agent, then Uncle Sam froze all transportation enforcement positions nationwide, a matter of national security. This led to more than a few occasions, especially along the docks in

Seattle and Tacoma, where bad people, some suspected of working for the very people we were fighting around the world, lived and worked in the shadows. They were confidant, having been placed along the coasts by their respective governments during the "Roaring Twenties," and the good times rolled, and they would last forever—until they didn't, 1929. But now, this handful of "sleeper" agents had been around forever, *haven't they*, and they pulled together with everybody else to make it through, to get by, until *happy days are here again.*

So from forty-four until war's end, I was a junior protection services special agent for the Northern Pacific Railway, if any one asked. And if anyone asked, we'd arrest them, a matter of course. *Loose lips sink ships.* But I was, and to this day I have to be careful how I phrase this—I signed a butt-load of confidentiality agreements—I worked in tandem with representatives of more than one national defense agency, and in that work, I was further delegated to assist the law enforcement agencies attached to the Coast Guard, Navy, and Marines. *Whew.* I don't think that violates much, if anything.

It boiled down to this: we were at war. Territorial and jurisdictional pissing-contests had no place in a context of 24-7-365 winning and losing. There wasn't time to shower, or eat properly, or care for loved ones, or take care of yourself. Everyone had one job, *win the sonuvabitch*—and go home, if home was still there for you.

So, my boss was whoever outranked me on any given day, who got to me first, who said *grab your shit and get in the jeep, here's a case folder.* And since everyone outranked an eighteen-year-old kid (didn't I say twenty-one?), it was my good fortune to work with some of the meanest and kindest, classiest and most vile, honest conmen and cheating holy men, and spies and snipers and cleaners, and women amongst them all, called upon to perform the unthinkable if necessary, to departmentalize the trauma for the sake of their children, and everybody else's.

But a couple of lifetimes later, I lose it when I shoot another human being, and I lose it for much longer if that human being dies. I don't have to know them; I don't care about their life stories. I did what I thought was required at the time. Most often I shot to save or defend others. But that doesn't matter. Dead's dead. And I did it. And I don't have that right.

Just my take. It could change tomorrow. It's good to just sit.

Now Maggie's heading straight for me, looking both ways, I bet, to watch for the Captain, see if she can slide me the hell out of here, *manage the situation* as she refers to it.

"Where's the Bronco?" She taps my shoulder, turns on her heel, and I'm almost running to keep up. *Almost.*

"You hate the Bronco." As we push through the main doors out into the night, wind catches our jackets, and odd refuse flies by at eye-level. I lead to an alley round the block, there my Bronco sits in a restricted zone, two tickets stuffed under the windshield wiper. Maggie gets in the passenger side, and watches me pull the tickets free, letting fly with the wind.

"Goddamit, Will, is it too much to ask for just a little respect?"

I start the Bronco, pull out the alley and into traffic, and head for Maritsa's, Mexican food made by Mexican people, who love to share. For a price, of course.

"Oh, I'm sorry, Mags, thought that was a rhetorical question. Uh, let's see—"

"Do shut it. So, my free meal is at Maritsa's, because it's the one place you can stand—"

"The only people I can stand, Mags, I'm sure you remember." I didn't mention before, as it's not necessary, but Wendy, my Wendy, was Angela Marguerite Verònica LaCosta. As a child she was much taken by Peter Pan, and when she and her seven brothers and sisters played, she was always Wendy.

We pull in, silently agreeing to leave the rest of our business 'til after we're seated. The hostess, Maribel, gives me a hug. She's a senior in high school now, the last time I saw her I was buying boxes of her girl scout cookies.

"Dad in the kitchen?" And I see him waving at me over the warming tray ledge, then Maribel's momma, right next to him. We exchange greetings, I use my horrible Spanish because it makes them laugh so much, and Maribel takes me to the last table in the back, the one with a floor-to-ceiling window, tonight showcasing an orange and red dusk.

Maribel disappears. Mags is tentative, almost like a teenager caught out after curfew. "Menus?"

"Marty knows what to prepare for me, and, in the enchanting tradition of fine Mexican cuisine, he knows what to prepare for you."

"That is—"

"What I'm having."

"You bastard."

"Yeah, free food is a bitch. And you're welcome."

Maribel cuts the tension with a basket of chips, salsa, red and green, plus a frosty virgin Marguerita for Mags, and a bottle of Barbican, British non-alcoholic beer for me. Maribel's dad sends away for it. I owe him much.

"So, since you are still too close to a clean-shoot, maybe—"

"No. No, Mags. You have questions to answer. Time is ticking by."

Maribel is back with two plates of *enchiladas verdes*, chicken prepared exactly right, bathed in tomatillo sauce, wrapped in corn tortillas, rice and refries on the side. Maggie is stunned.

I say, "You are stunned. Therefore, you haven't been eating here in my absence. Your loss."

I wait 'til Maggie gets a mouthful, then my questions begin. "An administrative supervisor doesn't rush a bad guy, one who is armed, then proceed to beat the living crap out of him." Mags takes a swig of the Marguerita, and I hold up a hand to stop her.

"There's a whole line of questions. Next, your history at the Deadwood PD. One day, out of nowhere, in a police department legendary across the west as an administrative train-wreck, an unknown administrative assistant, fresh from business school, so say her transcripts, appears without explanation. The assistant becomes the supervisor in record time, and documentation, filing, cross-referencing, et al, are resurrected. At the same time, her Captain seems to be taking her advice outside of admin, and in time she and the Captain's senior lieutenant butt heads. Son-of-a-gun, good-by lieutenant." Maggie's alternating between sighs of appreciation for her plate and snorty sounds from wanting to interrupt, but wanting rather more to eat more enchilada.

"I have a sack-and-a-half of similar examples, but here's one I like best. Captain Patterson, in every other town throughout the West, would have had me booked and in a holding cell for the kind of dumbass scheme I pulled with the 1880 train. He would have grabbed the DA, and set to dismantling my life, top to bottom. I endangered the prosperity of the entire town. And what do I get. A swat on the butt, and *hit the road, Jack.*"

Mags is deep into the second enchilada, halfway down the marguerita, and playing with the crumbs at the bottom of the chip's basket. "The question?"

My food's cold. I don't care. "No question. A statement. You may well draw a check as chief admin. But you showed up in Deadwood at a time when every tourist town from Ogallala to Manitou Springs, and Estes Park to Moab, every burg with something to look at, and good weather, with good stuff to eat, and plenty to drink—one by one, contraband, as we used to call it, started leaking into the mainstream. In time, first marijuana, and some hash, and coke and hallucinogens, and later any number of prescription uppers and downers and steroids and narcotics become available wherever 'a guy knows a guy who knows a guy.' Tourists across the West have always drunk, and hard at that, but the other crap, if they were into it, they pretty much left home. Why risk transport? It's a tough habit that can't wait a couple of weeks, right?"

Mags nods. Rhetorical.

I smile. "In related developments, Dick Nixon sees to the founding of the Drug Enforcement Administration in '73. Most Fed attention, of course, is focused south, Latin America, South America, cartels, et cetera. And much too late we find our Canadian cousins are quite talented at cannabis husbandry, and harvest, and distribution—probably because they are not brown, so that we thought they were good guys, and that was all the time they needed to get a thriving industry off the ground."

Finally, Mags. "In all fairness, the Canucks have a mostly unpatrolled, unguarded border, if, of course, you fly small planes or captain small boats, or don't mind bushwhacking in four-wheelers."

"And, they are not brown."

"Yeah, yeah."

"Mags, you were, or you are, or you can be—at a moment's notice—DEA."

Maggie waves at Maribel for two more drinks. "We, neither of us are kids, Will. You know, whatever may be true, I won't speak to it."

"Because you can't. And that's fine. If I had to nail it down for some reason—and I wouldn't—I'd call Artie Gleeson, we worked the Great Northern as kids, he's over in South Dakota's Criminal Bureau of Investigation. He rings a bell?" Mags smiles. "That's a bell. Then I'd corroborate drug traffic movements with task force construction—cops of every stripe love to shoot the breeze about that stuff, buy 'em a few beers, off the record. And I'd tie it off with a coffee and doughnut with Bobby Delaine, as he was the regional FBI agent in charge, 'til he wasn't, but he didn't retire, and he wasn't replaced, and he just built a brand-new house over in Hill City, under his wife's name, I believe—what do you suppose old Bobby's up to nowadays?"

Now Maggie's giggling. "Shit, Will Allen, I'm glad you play for my side. Have I taken enough of a beating?"

"One you had coming, Mags. Come on. You could have told me. You *know* that."

"And believe it or not, Will, I almost did, twice at least, and each time you were in a sensitive position, Wendy passes, then the kids move out—anyway, both times you knowing might have put you in harm's way."

I look away. Maggie caught me unaware. "Okay, okay. We care for each other, neither is going to try to spit in the other's punch bowl. But this last question, this one bothers the living hell outta me. Because if I'm right, I'm a goddam fool. And if I'm wrong, how in the hell did I let so much of his crap get by me?"

Maggie's next drink is lasting longer. "His?"

"Doctor Randall Lenore. *Doc.*"

Seventeen

Doctor Randall Lenore feels like a complete idiot whenever he has to wear *patient stuff.* When you cut yourself shaving, and the dot-band-aid. Or you twist an ankle or knee, then struggle with that ace bandage. Or the ice pack for a crack to the head or a split lip. It's then it comes home hard and fast—even a doctor is not beyond the day-to-day mediocrity of mortality.

Doc limps slowly along Rail Street, toward the 1880 Train Depot, sealed off for the season. Several picnic tables under metal rooves are open to pedestrians year-round, and that is where Doc has set up this meet. His injury, the trite "just a graze" across his left calf, is not only embarrassing for a medical man—his opinion—but frustrating as that whole "abduction scene" at the Goathorn should never have happened. Wesley should have not taken offense with Doc's off-hand remark about his heritage—*Dunhill, my ass.* Besides, Wes is the new player, different motivation, different territory, and certainly *not* Doc's boss, whatever he thinks. Doc answers to The Man, grudgingly at that, but the guy plays ball. Wesley, a boss? God forbid—and displaying those two goons for everyone and their uncle to see—amateur hour, really, beneath the owner of a joint as well-known as the Goathorn. Besides, Doc was there when Wes got his marching orders from The Man himself. Guns are never to be displayed in public, worn in any manner visible to the public eye, and the employee or contract agent should suffer arrest before violating these rules, trusting that the one phone call all good Americans are entitled to will produce one Walt Whitman, Attorney-at-Law, licensed in the Dakotas, Montana, Wyoming, Colorado and Nebraska.

And now, that human bulldog, this Will Allen, will not be easily dissuaded, and Doc was on the road to doing exactly that. He had an inside track, and Allen's trust, and Doc could be there as Allen stumbled along, and hide clues or distract attention at the right moments. But Allen, and worse yet, Maggie Connor—*she* is someone Wesley had no clue about, he bought her sweet little admin-act, actually thought one day he would nail her, in his office at the Goathorn no less, now that he's its owner/operator.

What a goddam fool.

Doc scans the red-clay-colored metal tables. All empty, save the one farthest from Doc, the one most hidden from the street and the parking lot. There sits Marcia Fointman, lighting a cigarette for Beverley Moss. A little over ten years ago, Marcia, wife of BN brakeman Riley Fointman, and Beverley, common-law-spouse of BN engineer Tim Nelson, were both awakened in the wee hours with similar phone calls. *Sorry to call at the late hour ma'am. This is Mary Elizabeth James, I'm a radio dispatch, Dawes County Sheriff's—we are sending two deputies to your address right now, and we wanted to give you notice in advance so you could, you know, wake up and dress and all. No, no ma'am, I'll stay on the line til the deputies arrive, should be any minute, why dontcha go ahead and toss on a robe or something? Just put the phone down, I'll stay on, yeah, that's right, sweetie, go ahead, I'll be here.*

And almost immediately red lights shattered the blackness at both houses, and the doors rumbled. Both women answered their doors, both knowing, but sure as hell not wanting to—*they don't send cops in the middle of the night with good news*, and *Oh God is he dead?*

The last similarity was the identical death benefit checks both women received, on the very same day, six months later. Marcia and Emily were talked into a one-time payment of one hundred thousand bucks a piece. But only if both of them agreed to the settlement, as explained by some skinny-ass boy-lawyer named Whitman. And there was a non-disclosure agreement, neither woman too clear on that one, but one more signature and a hundred k was theirs. Well, not so much a hundred, taxes you know, so fifty-five thousand, eight hundred, minus the funeral (they had a joint service and split that cost), and minus another two grand per woman in administrative fees, these straight to the self-same Whitman. Well, almost fifty grand a piece and they sure as hell wouldn't have had that seeing as how there never was two cents in the bank, what with the boys' penchants for ski-doos and snow-doos, and even snow bunnies, those known as well as caboose-chasers, girls who provided the intimacy out there on the road that was a pale substitute for the intimacy at home.

"Marcia, Bev, how are ya?" Doc's got his *ol' country* on "high."

112

Bev looks scared, Marcia looks high.

Bev says, "Good to see you, Doctor. We both just want you to know, we do not aim on 'causing problems,' that's what that rude man in his suit called it, scaring the life out of me—I don't know about Marcia here, but—"

"—scared? Thought I was having a heart attack, really I did. And this man talking funny, asking questions and I don't know what to say, Doc, I swear to God—" Marcia dissolves, Bev trying to poke tissues at her, but keeps missing her hands.

Doc feels like he's trying to settle sheep prior to the slaughter. He hates himself every minute these two are in jeopardy, but they can't know how deep they're in, or sure as hell, like sheep they will bolt, and those called into react won't be kind.

"Bev, Marcia." He pointedly pauses, then takes one hand each in his. "I have been there since the beginning, right?" Both women nod, Marcia finally calming down. "And what was it I said, after you two are at your wits' ends weeks and months after the tragedy? We have to play the long game here, we have to walk a practical path, right? Do we not?" Doc pats and squeezes the hands in his as if his modulation could tell the future. Now both women are calm to the point of groggy, giving into the fatigue anxiety brings to bear.

Bev starts to ramble again, Doc cuts her off. "Bev, Marcia. We have to concentrate. Okay? Number one, okay? Who do you talk to, specially I'm not there?"

They answer in unison, like a joint induction to the girl scouts. "Nobody."

Doc leans farther forward. "Who can you trust with money?"

"Nobody."

"And if somebody presents himself—or herself—claims to know things or wants to help—"

Marcia comes to life. "Shut the goddam door, lock the son of a bitch, call Doc."

Bev looks startled. "Yeah, what she said."

Doc patted hands one more time, released them, sat back, smiling. Inside, Doc's going *Oh, Sweet Mother of God. It's just a matter of time with these two.* And to the women: "You two need to get back to Edgemont, okay? Remember, those kids, they depend on you. This whole thing'll be over in a week, maybe two, tops."

And Bev takes Marcia's arm, and they drift toward an old Jimmy pickup, the license plates expired, and Bev says, "That's what y'all said ten years back, Doc. That is what you said back then."

"Yes, Bev, I did. Now get along home, and you two call me when you get there, I'm going home, too."

And Doc heads back downtown, knowing he has no ride back to Crawford save Will Allen's Bronco, and Will Allen's going to have a shitload of questions, questions Will gracefully did not pose while the EMT's and the Deadwood Police swarmed the aftermath of Wesley's gigantic screw-up. But Doc took advantage of time he should have been "under observation" to deal with the relentless string of messages those two old broads channeled his way, once they got their "visit." And the delivery date for their "medicine."

Doc stops at Mom's Diner, blocks from where he might encounter Will, and God forbid, Maggie—not for hunger, just for thinking. He orders coffee, can't resist a Danish, hauls it back to the last table, back to the wall.

And stops dead.

Somebody sits in shadow, already with *his* back to the wall.

The Canadian, in full suit, no doubt packing a very small weapon, middle of back, no doubt his brand-new Chrysler, BC plates, sits running in the alley, some local juvenile delinquent making fifty or a hundred to make sure no one steals it, and the Vancouver accent guarantees said punk will protect it with his life. This forty-ish tall-drink-of-water, with the grey eyes, almost translucent, Doc believes, because that's where one's soul, if one has one, is supposed to go, supposed to peer out.

He doesn't move. "Doc."

Doc sits across the small table, puts his coffee and Danish in front of him, takes a deep breath, audible in fact, lets it out. "MacAdam, you bastard."

"Doc, settle down—"

"Screw you. It's little ol' housewives you terrorize these days? What, you run outta aliens, no papers, you runnin' 'em and dumpin' 'em just shy of the borders, takin' the cash, and turnin' 'em in to the cops, for a couple bucks extra?"

"Doc." MacAdam shifts, suggesting he might not choose to weather the onslaught much longer.

Doc's in for a penny, in for a pound. "And now what, ya bastard, you gonna shoot an ol' man down in a coffee shop, go out the alley door, put two more in

114

the kid's head you hired to watch your goddam car? And back to Vancouver? To what? Even you gotta boss, ya sonuvabitch." Doc's stopping for air, almost wishing the move would be made, the shot would be taken, and Doc could ask God the next set of questions.

Only MacAdam laughs. Quiet, gentle, brief, but it qualifies. "My, oh my, Lenore, your accent's back in a flash, you get your dander up."

"Well, it's a long way from Edinburgh, another world." Doc's regained his American-Midwest, the medical-professional-approved *patois*.

MacAdam's becoming impatient. Doc remembers all too well the man has the attention span of a fruit fly. *If only he had the same life span.*

Doc jumps in again, maybe stem the flow—it's worth a try. "Listen, it's been ten goddam years, MacAdam. These women, their kids, they have lives to rebuild, then try to make them work. Some are going to get it together, maybe even do great things. And some were screw-ups before that night at Crawford Hill, and they always will be, whether it was a check for fifty grand back then, or a couple a hundred a month right now. They're *little* people, MacAdam, and they can't do that much harm—specially me keeping an eye out for them."

MacAdam looks out to the front of the shop, looks again to the exit to his left, the door to the alley, then to the two doors to his right, the men's and women's rest rooms. Both those doors are slightly ajar, signifying *no occupado.* His gaze returns to Doc's face, one much like the one he remembers looking to when he was a mere lad, his momma having carried him to see his Doc with a fish hook in his thumb, or a three-inch slash across one knee from falling off his bike.

Nostalgia's for suckers.

"Look, Doc. It's you and my dad went through hell together, back in the old days, right? And I heard all the tales, some nights from you both, both you shit-faced, beating that pool-hall upright piano into submission, singing every crap sea chanty either of you knew, or thought you knew." MacAdam pauses, and Doc sees clearly where this will go, today anyway. Pause ends.

"So, Doc, and I mean the best to you and yours, I really goddam-do. But you know my old dad, dead almost nine of those ten years—I promised I'd cut you all the slack I could for as long as I could. And then there'd come a day."

Doc feels almost nothing, save an odd bit of gas. "Today?"

Here MacAdam rises, as does Doc, but MacAdam's right hand reaches for the alley exit door. He smiles, but the effect is not comforting.

"No, Doctor Lenore, not today. But please, remember this. There's a concern from south of your border, and that cannot grow stronger. And there's a greater concern in Vancouver, and *that* one is the more important of the two. So, when I hear of an ICE agent shuttling a Mexican national half-way across our territory, or some goddam-cowboy-railway-cop working for who-knows-who, and stirring up a sleepy DEA, whether he knows it or not—well, my patience, short-lived on the best of days, may resort to the simplest solution, the *elegant* solution."

And Doc knows this exit-line is best left unquestioned, but maybe he's too tired, or too old, or both. "And that solution is?"

"Shoot everybody dead, let God sort them out."

Eighteen

Maggie walks with me to the Bronco. She's a bit unsteady. Three-and-a-half hours of questions from her C-O, then all over again with state investigators, then me barking another particular set of questions with a much more difficult set of answers—a reasonable explanation for her double- or even triple-life tacitly admitted, at least hypothetically—all this is probably one great relief, or a source of out-sized distress. I may know more about her actual occupation or occupations now than her family knows. And this explains, to me at least, why such a strong, intelligent, vibrant woman has never married.

Maggie climbs in the driver's side, even though she can't just now locate the seat belts.

"Where to?" And with a straight face.

Me: "To Dreamland, the only place you are presently capable of taking the wheel."

"Relax, Tex. I'm just warming your seat 'til Doc shows up and the next shit show begins." I climb in the passenger side and turn toward her; glad the keys are in my pocket.

Now she is mock serious. "Unless you'd like me to warm *your* seat, and by that I mean—"

"Everyone in the solar system knows what you mean, and I am flattered and you are quite possibly still in some form of shock, but we'll always have Deadwood."

"Well," and now Mags is playing with the radio to draw attention away, "what happens when Doc surfaces?"

"We have roughly thirty seconds to figure that out." I point past her to Doc, walking up the inclined boardwalk toward us, hunched as though marching into a nor'easter.

The Robber's Roost is just one of many motels of its kind in this part of the country, beginning life in the twenties and thirties as "car camps" and "motor courts." As time and economies progressed, these little mom&pops morphed into "family motels" and "highway hotels," all in competition for the American family's love affair with the open road, subsidized by some of the lowest gasoline prices in the industrialized world. The Roost still has its original free-standing log cabins, each with a separate kitchen, porch and fireplace. Everything inside each one is knotty-pine, ceiling to floor.

By the time the three of us get inside Doc's cabin, freshen up, and scan the gratis snacks and beverages a very smart management has supplied, it's long after midnight. Right this moment, Doc is sawing logs in a redwood rocker, and Mags has fallen asleep in the shower, then born anew in the same shower, and is fighting with a hair dryer whose instructions are written only in Japanese. I'm grinding and brewing coffee (I do this well), throwing together a half-dozen eggs with some salsa verde and frying them up (I do this weller), and peeling three oranges whose existence seems impossible at this time of year in this location.

Mags emerges from the bathroom in a Navajo-patterned robe and rawhide slippers, and if there are other articles of clothing on her person, I cannot attest to that visually, at least from where I am standing. She nudges Doc awake and leads them to our little breakfast table. I'm surprised by the tenderness of her gesture and Doc's appreciation of her effort.

I serve the three of us, complete with toast and steaming coffee mugs. I sit at my place setting, and for a moment I am sad.

Damn Maggie's sensitivity. "Missing someone? Wendy?"

Doc's sipping coffee. "Sidney?"

Maggie speaks before I can. "Naw, Doc, they're just friends. Eleven years difference, ya know."

"Really?" says Doc.

"What the hell?" says me. "Neither of you are supposed to know that much about her—ya know, I'm thinking I can trust either of you less than the distance I could toss your mangey butts."

Doc nods Maggie's way. "He's a sensitive one."

Mags smirks. "Unless he's giving *you* the business, then it's *damn the torpedoes.*"

I butter my toast. I know the correct side to which said butter is most effectively applied. "We've all had our little breaks in the action, but now it's back into the fray. So"—and here I'm done using my butter knife, so I use it to stab the air in two specific directions "—I toss the questions or statements out, either of you takes a shot, I call *bullshit* when I hear it, it goes forward until I no longer find it amusing or useful. Any questions? No? Go."

They seem startled, as I have not asked a question—*just keepin' ya on yer toes!*

So I start.

"Doc, you shifty bastard."

"What's the question?"

"Oh, no question you *are* a shifty bastard. So, let's begin with, oh, I don't know, Sidney's opens at?"

Doc's sensing animosity. "6:30. You needn't be jealous, she advertises it."

"Really?" I ask. "Where?"

Doc thought I'd quit. "Where? What?"

"Where—and before we do a whole Abbott-and-Costello routine—exactly *does* Sid advertise her opening time? And to save you what little face remains, the answer is nowhere, ever, she hates quote-bloody-leeching-Madison Avenue-end-quote, and seriously feels advertising people deserve the chair, that is, the electric one."

Mags is practically chugging hot coffee. "For chrissakes, Doc, do us all a favor—he won't let us go until he's satisfied, and I, for one, have better things to do."

"Better then setting a record straight?" I look pointedly Maggie's way, but Mags is too tired for shame.

Doc's pissed, and I realize he's very rarely *not* in the driver's seat. "All right, I do my digging when I have to. There's always my AMA fraternity, and if I don't recognize any names in a specific town in my directory, I call one at random, apologize for the error, and chat him up. Doctors love to talk about themselves."

I can't resist. "Do tell." Mags looks daggers my way. "Sorry. So, why me and my Lander in the first place?"

Doc's really not looking well. "Dumb luck. About a week before you showed, I was at Daisy's, you know the acoustics, and I hear a welder from down around your parts telling some interesting stories about driving a shanghaied special agent from Alliance in circles for the better part of a day, a deal set up by an ex-special agent down Lander-way. The rest was research."

"And bribery."

"And when *you* do it?"

"Sound investing."

Mags has cleaned her plate, daunting at that, considering she also cleaned the one at Mariska's. Growing girls. Anyway, her patience is no longer with us.

"I'll cut to the chase, Will. You will find, as you did earlier this evening with yours truly, many things can be supposed, and a few things deemed possible, and one or two things even probable. But—I won't testify to this or that for you or anyone else, just as you certainly won't if I get too deep into your early days."

"I blush."

"And you certainly don't expect Doc to give all his tricks away, just because you are so goddam nosy."

Now Doc is looking about the same shade of grey as the only suit I possess. "True, Mags, but the difference here is—I think you work for multiple law enforcement agencies, and I think I have, too." With this I approach Doc and apply my first two fingers to the pulse-point on his neck. "But I can't shake the feeling our good doctor serves multiple masters, and I ain't sure any of 'em is lawful."

Mags stands as I take my fingers away and turn toward her.

"Call an ambulance, Mags, and then call Captain Patterson."

Maggie is at the motel phone by Doc's bed. She dials with her eyes on me.

I'm back with Doc, and his eyes are rolling back in his head.

"Tell them, hurry Mags. Like five-minutes-hurry."

Maggie and I are drinking machine coffee in dime cups in the hospital ER waiting room. Captain Patterson's got the pay phone tied in knots, and two junior officers are running errands in and out, as if their lives depended on it. Their futures as officers most definitely do.

Just because I can't stand a cop, that doesn't make him or her a bad cop. And Patterson's good, in a Broderick Crawford kind of way. Rumor has it he takes Christmas week off for vacation every year, even though he has no family, because someone may catch him smiling when the carolers come calling. But apparently enough skullduggery has come to pass while I was in the immediate company of Maggie, Patterson's secret right-hand-man (or whatever she may *actually* be), he figures I can't possibly be the felon this time around, so, as he is as practical as he is humorless, he figures maybe he can use me. Until he can't. I know where the city limits sign is. He showed me.

Maggie and I react to bad news in similar ways. Busy yourself with solving the case. Get even on your own time.

"Mags, Doc came down the street to where we were parked from the north. If you follow that line straight along, where do you end up?"

"Well, and it doesn't take long, you end up at the 1880 depot, and it's closed for the season. Nobody'd be there"

"Which," I offer, "would be just what you want if—"

"—if you wanted a meeting in confidence." Maggie is up and pacing. Good sign.

"So," I add, "whether Doc was meeting with good ones or bad ones, he didn't feel the need to make a break for it, *then* anyway, as he wasn't running, he hadn't caught a cab, and like that."

"Still, if he was poisoned, which we are just supposing until the surgeon and the internist come back out here—" and here Mags looks down the hallway to the operating theatre, but no joy yet—"when and where did he eat it, drink it, breathe it?"

"I think I'm having a thought."

Maggie ceases pacing. "Like Horton hearing a who?"

"Very similar. Where along that straight line connecting the Bronco and the depot might a doctor grab a pastry, because, when he was riding along with me from Crawford up here, he'd never met a doughnut he didn't like."

Mags is headed to the pay phone booth, still filled with the figure of her captain.

She turns my way to say, "That's got to be *Mom's*" and she's got the captain's full attention. And in short order, Patterson grabs the next junior officer running by, and they are out the door. Maggie approaches with two fresh dime-cup machine coffees.

"Patterson and his sergeant are going to lock down the diner, go through the trash and dishes shy of the washer, see who remembers Doc and what he ordered."

I smile for the first time in a couple of days, that is, sincerely. "But will that be in time?"

Mags doesn't answer, and I look up, and her face is awash with tears.

I hug her. "Maggie, I am so sorry. I had no idea you two are so close." She holds me in place for longer than I thought she might. She hates looking less than formidable, even for a second.

She comes up for air, and steps back, fumbling about with tissues. "It's not so much Doc, it's the kind of thing he represents. I was born and raised on crab cakes in Maryland. And although I've been almost four years on this gig, and ten in the region, I'll always be 'new.'"

We drift back to the waiting room chairs, and she sits. "Doc's a stayer. He was away for school and two wars, stationed on the Olympic Peninsula, and God knows he had a hundred opportunities to be anywhere else, but hell no, back he'd come to Crawford, and he and his old lady would be back on the honeymoon train, everything roses."

The pay phone rings and Mags is on it in two steps. She's silent for longer than she likes to be. Her head turns just a degree or two as she's got a question to pose, but the party on the other end is sucking all the air out of the connection. Then even I can hear the *clack* disconnecting the call.

She turns my way, heading for her seat, but she's obviously taken aback.

I don't do patience. "Informative?"

"On several levels." Mags drains her cup, sets it at her feet, and turns directly my way, eye to eye. "Well, Molly Banda's working overtime, and she's Mom's best waitress, so she had a blow by blow at the tip of her tongue for Patterson. She not only remembered the order, she handed over the food remains, and those are on their way to Rapid. There is a good chance the test results can help save Doc."

"Okay, that's one. And—"

"—and Molly does a full-blown dramatic reading of Doc's meeting with a mysterious stranger."

Can we be so lucky? *I* can, just sayin'. "Great, that's two."

"And Will, we need to talk. I didn't see this coming."

This is not feeling good. "What, who?"

"The stranger waiting for Doc, it appears, was tall, slender, thinning blonde hair, eyes—says Molly—like a zombie's. Wearing a lovely suit, and—"

Not good at all. "—and a BC accent, maybe Vancouver."

"Oh, Will."

"Yeah, Mags. He's visited Sidney as well."

"Geesus. And Molly heard a name." She looks away, then back at me. "MacAdam."

I watch her just long enough. Her tell is a lip bite, left corner, brief but certain. "Oh, Maggie. You're breaking my heart."

"What?"

"I really thought you'd just come clean. I'm a hopeless romantic."

Maggie's looking anywhere else now. "Will—"

"Mags, that's not the first time you've heard the name—'MacAdam.'"

She stands and turns her back. "No, not the first. Or the second, or third."

And my next question, obvious as it may be, is interrupted.

The ER surgeon and internist approach, and neither has removed their masks.

Nineteen

Barbie Straight can't sleep. She doesn't have to look at the fake railroad clock on the wall of her step-sister's kitchen-living room. Ever since the family lost Harley ten, *ten at least*, years back, she wakes at 3:35 on the dot, every God-forsaken morning. The same heart-breaking, gut-wrenching, mind-shattering moment when her pastel princess phone innocently rang and rang and rang.

Barbie used to be a heavy sleeper.

Sorry to call at the late hour ma'am. This is Mary Elizabeth James, I'm a radio dispatch, Dawes County Sheriff's—we are sending two deputies to your address right now, and we wanted to give you notice in advance so you could, you know, wake up and dress and all. No, no ma'am, I'll stay on the line til the deputies arrive, should be any minute, why dontcha go ahead and toss on a robe or something? Just put the phone down, I'll stay on, yeah, that's right, sweetie, go ahead, I'll be here.

Barbie didn't put a robe on. She didn't move. When those deputies arrived, little five-year-old Emily had to let them in, and calm the new baby (Emily always called him *new baby*), and answer the police-men's answers for her momma, and then the ambulance-men's questions.

Because her momma was exactly where the telephone call found her, up on one elbow in bed, receiver still at one ear, her water broken. Barbie kept saying the same thing over and over. *Harley knows the baby's coming. He's coming, he's coming. Any minute.* In a loop. Like a mantra. A mantra ending only when her contractions wouldn't allow an extra breath, an indirect thought.

The deputies called the EMT's, the ambulance got her to the clinic in Edgemont, a doctor was on duty stitching up a bartender who made the mistake of trying to break up a bar fight between cowboys and trainmen without a sawed-off shot gun in his hand—the only real message those ol' boys understand when all and sundry are stinkin' drunk. And one trainman had a knife, and slashing commenced, and nine stitches across the barman's old bald head resulted, but again, important part here, *there was a doctor on duty*, and reasonably sober at that.

There are only two bedrooms in the step-sister's apartment. The *step-sister*. Funny, a lifetime ago, Lizzie walks into Barbie's mother's trailer house, Barbie an only child of five, her father never on the scene. Lizzie, fifteen years older, is to baby-sit Barbie, while Lizzie's dad takes Barbie's mom to dinner and a movie, and the next weekend Lizzie is moving into Barbie's trailer with her dad, and this man is Barbie's dad all of a sudden, and Lizzie's not the baby sitter, she's the step-sister. *Step-sister Lizzie.*

Lizzie's asleep in the master bedroom, sharing it this weekend with her daughter Anita, a freshman at Spearfish State. The other smaller bedroom, and Lizzie's storage room as well, has a double bed wedged in one side, Barbie squeezed in with Emily, now at fifteen, almost sixteen, no longer a child in form or intellect. And the boys—always *the boys* at ten months apart, ten and eleven now, Cooper and Wayne, named for Harley's favorite cowboy stars— wrapped in camo sleeping bags, huddled together for warmth. Barbie reckons Lizzie's behind on the utilities, and Barbie wants to help, but there is no slack in the home budget. Barbie wouldn't have been able to fill the tank on their ancient Falcon station wagon to high-tail it to Deadwood, save for a twenty- dollar bill the boys got in Christmas-mail from that rich old gal down the street who always ask Coop and Wayne to help her with her yard. And the boys gave the twenty up with nary a complaint, as they are quick studies, and good at their hearts. But, by the Blessed Virgin Mother Mary Her Ownself, they are hungry every damn minute of every damn day.

There's a scratching at the apartment door, it opens to the outside like a motel door, so it has a peephole through it, and Barbie takes a look. *I didn't know better, that's an old homeless guy, looking strangely like ol' George, brother-in-law George, fifty-five now if alive, gone like a Christmas goose one year after the accident, right to the day, and not one word, not one since.* And Barbie leaves the door, as these types knock at all the doors, day and night, wanting this and begging that, and for that matter Barbie always shares when she's got it, just been so very, very long since she's had any, let alone extra— and there's the scratch, now a knock, and that old coot going to wake the whole house, and everyone will want to start eating, and where's the money for that?

So, Barbie pulls pepper spray out her purse, and puts one hand on the knob, gives it a hard-right turn, slings open the door and sprays. And the coot goes down, yelling like she stabbed him—silly, as she's never stabbed but one guy, a hundred years ago it seemed, and he had it coming.

Barbie shuts the door behind her. Then she starts kind of rolling him down the porch, then down the steps with her feet, all the time shushing him, 'til he's prone on his back under the spigot in the little yard, there with a garden hose attached. And she makes good use of the set-up, blasting the coot into submission, and cleaning him up a little in the bargain, albeit soaked to the skin. And it's at this point, with the coot only whimpering in complaint, Barbie slides a pulpy-wet billfold out his hip pocket.

One Montana Driver's License. Barbie can barely read without cheaters, so she slides a few feet closer to the one street light for two blocks in any direction. *Jorge Montenegro.* Barbie can read it, no idea how it's supposed to sound. *201 Main St., Libby, MT. And expired five years back.* And Barbie's shoulders sag, because sometimes it's the sheer living itself makes you feel like one more thing, just one more damn thing, and you're going to break for absolutely sure.

And there it is, the thing.

The ID picture, horrible as DMV photos most always are, is George Straight.

George, her missing brother-in-law.

George, the bastard who should have been driving that goddam taxi van, instead of Harley, twice the man George could ever be.

Yeah, it's George, older and thinner and slower.

And Emily's real dad.

Emily and Lizzie and Barbie pull one unspoken collaboration, moving with few words, those whispered—get George off the front lawn, inside, dressed down and showered and shaved, filled up with coffee so black, the spoon stands alone, his wretched clothes washed and dried and wrestled back on him. All this while keeping him quiet, from the kids and the neighbors and innocent passers-by, until, the coffee notwithstanding, George falls dead asleep in the bathtub, the only horizontal expanse unclaimed, and forget Lizzie's bed, Anita sleeps 'til noon.

The sky lightens with the mood, George out of the way for now, Anita and the boys sleeping like nothing out of the ordinary took place. Emily places three little settings at the undersized table, pours much better coffee for three, pours brandy into her mom's and step-aunt's, and tends three store-brand toaster pastries in the toaster oven.

Lizzie comes back in from pulling the last load of rags that man calls clothes out of the dryer in the laundry room all the tenants share in the basement. He has two sets of clothes, they dressed him in the one which underwent a true washing without disintegrating. This second set won't qualify as decent trash. And Barbie comes back from downtown at the little all-night market (thank the Lord for trainmen) with more eggs and cereal and milk and white bread, and paid for with a brand-new fifty-dollar-bill, it slid out of George's work boot when the ladies cut away the heel to remove the boot from the foot. And Barbie's keeping the change, damn right.

The three pastries and the first three coffees are consumed without a word. Each woman stares out in a different direction, no one looking at another. They know as women, keepers-of responsibilities, advocates for justice, that when these exceedingly brief and extraordinarily quiet moments come to pass, usually with no warning, then every second needs appreciation—the next such respite may be years in the making.

But they, better than any man, know time waits for no one. So, Emily begins.

"Uncle George?"

Barbie nods. Lizzie expects Barbie to lead.

Emily: "Jorge Montenegro?"

Barbie: "About nine years or more, when he disappeared, George was keeping company with a lady named Stella Montenegro. She told George she got this far north in the US in an exchange program, some evangelical religion, their church went belly-up, bad investments—I think it was ascension robes—they left her high and dry. George was stupid in love, George and Aunt Dolly—"

Emily: "—a train wreck."

Barbie: "You remember. Well, you were always too far ahead in years. Anyways—"

Lizzie: "I thought I heard he took his *chiquita* to Mexico, lives on a beach, drunk and disorderly."

Barbie: "Yeah, that's one story. Another, more likely, he was in up to his neck in debt, probably cards, couldn't hold his liquor, never did drugs—"

127

Emily: "—then he's spent the last nine years trying his best to learn—"

Barbie: "—Em, we don't know—"

Emily: "—Mom, we sure as hell *do* know, as all three of us just scraped and scrubbed a dozen layers of crap and puke and God-knows-what off him, and it smells like booze and pee and incense, and *way* not enough incense. And we are not doing him or anybody else any damn good politely holding to bullshit stories about George or Daddy or anybody else."

And Lizzie, about to share, backs off. "What are you looking at *me* for, kid?"

Barbie's first line of defense is a set of sniffles, growing to snuffles, then uncontrolled snorts with sobbing. But Emily has become hard this past year, and Barbie doesn't know why, and she can't control her anymore, although she actually never really could.

Emily sees the morning light weaken the overcast, and she sees it as her cue. *Manipulating these two is so easy, it's sad.* Emily goes soft and fem, and her momma and Lizzie—whoever the hell *she* is—are as happy as kittens with yarn balls. Emily shuffles both women off to their bed as their spiked coffees take effect, promising she can clean up, and get the boys and Anita fed, if and when they wake up this day, and within minutes the brandy does its job, and the aunt and the momma sawing logs in harmony from separate rooms.

The snorings give Emily cover, for she has to toss through her aunt's belongings, and some noise must be made to do a proper job. But Emily knows there is a Polaroid camera somewhere on the premises, because dozens of the instant, tacky, dried-up photos are scotch-taped to the refrigerator, most documenting those rare occasions when Anita achieved something somewhere a degree or two above average.

And this takes longer than expected, because Emily would never have guessed the camera lives behind the lettuce crisper in the refrigerator, but Emily takes a break to grab some juice, and *voila!* The camera is out and Emily is in the bathroom, sliding the door gently shut.

George still smells sour, but Emily figures you can't exude in hours all the crap you drank and smoked and snorted for years previous. And there is good fortune, as Emily can only hope. Hours before (it seems like days) the three women were scrubbing George from head to toe, stark-naked in the tub, and because Emily is barely sixteen, Barbie insisted that she and Lizzie would clean the front side (the *dangerous* side) while Emily could scrape off his back.

And there now, unconscious, but lying on his face in his underwear and a Mount Rushmore sweatshirt, is George.

Emily turns on all lights, raises the back of the sweatshirt, and has to get much closer than she prefers. *Where the hell is it? Was I seeing things?* But no, she was not, and to the left of his middle spine, not horizontal but vertical, there lays the tattoo—one Emily would bet money he doesn't even know he has. She takes two snaps, patiently shakes them out, and the pictures develop. She leaves the camera on the toilet seat. It won't matter now. Even if her mom and aunt trip to it, they won't know what they've got. And frankly, Emily feels as though she has done everything she can to protect them—ever since she was five.

And today, this morning, that is over.

Emily pulls her go-bag out of the umbrella rack in the closest, unused as umbrellas cost real money, slips the pictures inside, pulls thirty bucks from her aunt's purse, puts that in her pocket, then pulls forty more and puts it in her mom's purse. There is no sorrow. This plan has been hatching for over four years. But she will miss the boys. They aren't stupid. She hopes they have a chance.

Emily slips out of the front door, slips it closed behind her, and sprints around the corner, headed for uptown Deadwood, to Highway 20 and some heavy-duty hitchhiking—and runs directly into Will Allen, accompanied by a woman Emily's followed twice, but never met officially.

Emily knows her immediate plan is temporarily suspended, but there may be something she can make of these two, now each gently holding her elbow as they move north toward the depot. She hasn't gotten to where she is by pushing the panic button every time something goes hinky. Hinky is life.

The woman is reassuring. "Will's Bronco is just a block over, Emily. We'll swing around over to the PD administration, my office is there, and we will talk, and we will call your mom and—"

Emily stops, and the man and woman underestimate her strength. "We won't need to be calling Barbie. But we will need time alone. Mr. Allen, Ms. Connor."

Will and Mags are taken back, but appreciative, and neither reaches for a weapon when Emily slides her hand in her grip. She pulls out the Polaroids, and hands one each to each.

Maggie is fascinated. "What are we looking at?"

"Two things, equally important, I suspect," says Emily.

And Will, too close to laughing, says, "Is this a tattoo of sorts?"

Emily nods. "And if I miss my guess, it's a car number, a box car number—Q2371."

Maggie bites. "And thing two?"

Emily can't help looking like the cat chomping down on canaries.

"It appears on the back of George Straight."

Will loves lucky when he sees it. "And *not* the singer—the brother of your dad? Your uncle?"

Maggie adds, "And missing, lo these many years?"

"And reappeared," says Emily, seeming twice her age at least, "in my step-aunt's bath tub, much the worse for wear."

Twenty

The sheer size and strength of a diesel locomotive belies the real magic of a freight or passenger train. Commercial American railroad history began, in terms of practical and dependable service, with the B&O Railroad, the legendary Baltimore & Ohio, in 1827. And from then to the present day, communities are enlivened with the scheduled and unscheduled arrivals of freight and passenger trains. There will always be a justifiable fascination with power, and its generation, and its harnessing in order to deliver the train's payload. But ultimately, the expectation and excitement preceding the train's appearance is simply expressed with a question. Who *or* what *does this train bring us?*

And the wrappings, or holders, or containers carrying merchandize and populations are varied and innovative. One of the most recognizable, the most dependable, and the most versatile is the standard freight car—the box car. Everyone's familiar with the box car, most often because we've spent our lives waiting at train crossings as anywhere from a dozen to a hundred or more box cars amble by, usually at restricted speeds if the crossing is in a densely-populated area. Box-shaped, as named, and a hue of colors, and logos, and each with a series of numbers acting as identifiers, the cars are ordered by a customer of the railway when the customer feels she or he can fill the box with goods. Then the sales department quotes a price for the freight. And this is dependent on its weight, its destination, and any state or federal regulations complicating the safe transfer of the car and its cargo.

The box cars come in different lengths and capacities. Generally, car sizes in boxes designated as B-3, B-5, and B7s do much of the work across the nation. The most common boxcars are 50 feet, 6 inches to 60 feet, 9 inches in length, and 9 feet, 4 inches to 9 feet, 6 inches wide. In addition, they average between 10 feet, 10 inches to 11 feet, 8 inches high. If properly maintained, a good box car can carry or rescue almost any other type of freight.

So, one might think, especially if one is a paying customer of a railway, and trusting said railway with safety and delivery and punctuality—all box cars will be ordered and filled and shipped, from Point A to Point B, merchandise intact, paperwork correct, freight costs clear and in line with estimates. No problems, right?

Well, it is extraordinary, considering the sheer numbers of freight and passengers cars moved only one car-length, or from the Florida Keys to Seattle, and everywhere in-between, when most make their journeys as scheduled, product or person safe and sound. Some small numbers of cars are temporarily misplaced or confused with other cars, and smaller numbers yet—very, very small numbers are "lost."

In 1987, there are many ways car numbers are recorded and tracked and transmitted forward. But ten years previous, there were fewer procedures, but procedures that, for the most part, stood the test of time.

For instance, when the deadhead crew from Edgemont was called to deadhead by taxi van to Crawford with one Harley Straight at the wheel, cars coming into a yard or leaving a yard were observed by a human being, classified as a railway clerk. This clerk, often referred to by her or his clerks' union title—outside verifier—wrote down each and every car number as the train past his or her position. So, some trains, those of just a few cars, and cars with a one- or two-letter prefix (say B-N, for example), and a three- or four number suffix (for example, 682), would be relatively easy to verify. And a coal train, with over one hundred coal cars, might well display four-letter prefixes and six-number suffixes (example: ATBX 208791). Such a train, arriving or departing, is more difficult to verify correctly.

Now, add to this erstwhile clerk's work experience the possibility that he or she has already verified ten to twenty trains on an eight-hour shift, and she or he sat in a poorly-sealed car with a crummy heater at two in the morning during a blizzard, and then—when the poor clerk finally made his or her way back to the depot, and gave the list of cars to the chief clerk, and the chief clerk compared the verifier's list to the official manifest every train begins life with and carries forward, and there were too many errors or outright omissions— that poor sucker, that exhausted clerk, would be ordered to locate the sitting train in question somewhere in the train yard, and *walk* the length of the train in the self-same weather conditions, and make another list. And pronto, by the way, because delays cost money.

And finally, one more thing (wait, isn't that what *and finally* means?). Letters and numbers fade, or are covered by snow and ice and grease and oil and dirt and dust and filth and graffiti. I lied. *Two* more things. When two railroads merge, cars are often retired, and buried in long rail spurs acting as car cemeteries, and sometimes cars are completely re-numbered because of duplications, and brought back out to be cleaned and re-built and used again.

So, can you "lose" a car?

Hell, yes. Especially if you put your mind to it.

I am enjoying one of the best parts about being a "consulting special agent." If I was still a regular special agent, plugging away at my forty-two years taking other people's orders, say with the Burlington Northern, my supervisory chief would be tasked with the clarification of this case in terms of the interests and liabilities of the host railway, then sub-dividing those case concerns between junior employees across the division, depending on the agent's location, background, talent, and proximity to the case in terms of historical development or current events.

Woof. So what do *I* get to do? Pretty much whatever I damn please, whenever so. As long as I can justify it. And if I have clearly set my parameters and requirements in my specific contract, running a specific length of time, then my contracting railroad can only, for the most part, hope I call in regularly—and then with more good news than bad.

If I sound spoiled and privileged, I am. But remember this. I put in twenty years at others' beck-and-call just to learn what's what, and none of it would matter if I wasn't pretty good at what I do. And it only takes one major screw-up to discredit forty years of a good track record.

But, yeah, still spoiled.

So, between the reappearance of Doc's surgeon and internist, and our, Maggie and me, that is, our interception of Emily Straight, much has come to pass. Doc's doctors searched about his carcass inside and out, and the pastry samples withstood preliminary tests, and all concerned are surprised, they say, to find Flunitrazepam, a drug only marketed the last twelve years or so, and then overseas for sleeping problems. Just recently reports are surfacing of women in social settings, bars especially, being assaulted after the men they meet slip a form of the drug into a drink. And with a half-life of eighteen to twenty-four hours, the drug will have Doc at its mercy, considering his age, for another couple of days before he's fit to function.

So, it's a short walk from Doc's room at the hospital to the formally-guarded room of George Strait. Ol' George is having some drug-associated complications as well, and those are further entwined with apparent exposure to the elements—days or weeks of sleeping rough, little food and water—and at least one solid beating while captured, and injuries incurred with flight from capture.

This is all conjecture right now. George is rarely awake. When he comes around, he's frantic, as if still running for his life. He's calmed by the floor nurse and the Deadwood uniform on duty or Maggie or me, and he starts to answer very simple questions, and exhaustion sets in, and we wait once more for the next conscious interval.

In the meantime, we have Emily.

This girl is all the clichés, and none of them.

She is head-strong and stubborn. She is rebellious and mercurial. She cares deeply for the well-being of her little brothers, and she's signed off on her mother and aunt, no hard feelings, *adiós.* She seems to tolerate me as long as I don't communicate, even accidently, the least bit of a condescending attitude. She doesn't suffer fools gladly, and she'll point one out, then take him off at the knees in a heartbeat. She's hard to understand if your imagination fails you. If you can't imagine how a railroad town feels, smells, tastes, sounds, and you only wonder what losing your hero-father at five means, growing up with a mom who bought her GED to get hired at the railroad in the first place, works midnights so she can try to make a home for three kids during the day, but still isn't insulted because some moron-deputy cited her husband as the cause of a tragic taxi wreck ten years past, so those assholes running the taxis and scooping up the railroad money in Rapid City had to shell out exactly nothing, not one red cent for the surviving family, her family, and every day since she has been in a desperate struggle to stay barely even with the poverty line.

We've obtained permission to conduct interviews with under-aged Emily from Barbie Straight (*I'm telling you, she doesn't know what the hell you're talking about*), who reassures us whenever she drops by Deadwood PD to bring Emily some food or treat, food Emily always tosses away after her mom leaves. Barbie goes *Em will do whatever you need, she's a real good girl, the right kind, you know what I'm saying?* Each time she walks in and each time she walks away, without fail.

We've made the twelve-hour mark now, fast food wrappers and soda cans littering our table in Conference B, a room so obvious even Emily immediately sized it and said, "*Conference* sounds so much more comforting than *Interrogation*, doesn't it, Mr. Allen?"

Maggie is a big fan. She sees a lot of herself in teenage Emily. Her Connor family-upbringing in Maryland had two parents, problem being they were never the same two. In a bizarre twist, Maggie and two sisters ran home from grade school one afternoon to find out her dad was great, considering, and the "considering" part was her pure and innocent mother got food poisoning from a seafood truck along the Chesapeake that noon, and was dead by four. In six weeks, Maggie's dad had married the lady next door, a widow, and the family merged in her house as it was much nicer, and her dad walked in front of a bus one month after that. And in two months, Maggie's step-mom married the funeral director responsible for providing Maggie's dad with such a nice send-off, and those two waited one whole year to save up for a honeymoon in Sicily, and flew there—well, *almost* there—as the plane landed short of the coast some forty-nine miles, all lost at sea. But the funeral director's parents, two Irish immigrants from Prince Edward Island, knew their Christian duty, adopted the girls, rest being history, how Mags became a Connor.

Maggie's take: *life ain't for the faint of heart.*

So, we three have been passing the current hour debating the relative merits of this year's Academy Awards Best Film category. I'm a fan of *Prizzi's Honor*, Maggie charges it cannot hold a candle to *Out of Africa,* and Emily labeling us both "pedestrian" because we did not understand the inherent superiority of *The Color Purple.*

I'm sipping my eighth cup of machine coffee today. "Okay, kids, back to business, shall we?"

Emily looks away to Maggie. "Do you let men take the lead from weakness, or is it your tactic in service to a greater strategy?"

Maggie looks insulted, then surprised, then thoroughly entertained. "Well, I'm in admin, Emily, so from a transcript-standpoint—"

Emily's over to the coffee machine in two shakes. "And we all three know that's baloney, or why would an admin be in consultation with a guy in a suit and a car with government plates shouting "Fed!" up and down Main St. here, and then the same lady's dressed down, in camo riding shotgun in an Army jeep up and down Crawford Hill just six weeks ago?"

Mags is gobsmacked. I'm considering hiring Emily, save she wouldn't work for someone she doesn't respect. "Yes, Maggie Connor, why would an admin be hanging with—who, Emily?"

Emily's having fun. "—a Navy captain, according to his collar."

I won't let up. "And a captain, indeed, thank-you, Emily."

Mags is to the door and halfway through, shouting *Allen* over one shoulder.

I stand. "Please excuse, me, Emily. I believe you've upset Ms. Connor. Can I get you anything upon my return?"

Emily reaches for a six-month-old *People* magazine. "Good n' Plentys, Mr. Allen, thank you, third row in the candy machine, second from the left. And watch out, there's a peanut M&M stuck just below the Good n' Plentys, put your shoulder into it right after you drop the quarter, you could get lucky."

Twenty-One

Maggie Connor turns on me the second we clear another pair of ears. "What in the hell are you playing at, Will?"

I guess I'm still pissed at Maggie for not being forthright about the "MacAdam" thing. "I have no clue what you mean."

Maggie swears elegantly and marches on down the hallway, hard right into an empty waiting room. "Goddamit, Allen, you may not have one cent's worth of your precious reputation hanging by a thread right now, and I know you have little to no respect for anyone working undercover—"

"—a municipal secretary-implant from the DEA? Really, Mags, how stupid do your D.C. handlers think we are out here?"

"Well to be fair, and other than you, no one really suspected anything—"

"—except for the bad guys, of course, and there lies the tale of the Canuck MacAdam."

"Will—"

"So, let's air this out, then get back to Emily. You knew Dicky Tuttle begged me to take the Crawford Hill case two minutes after I took it. How?"

"Well," Maggie's leaning hard on a row of uncomfortable chairs, "Dicky owes a favor to those involved with what used to be called 'drug intelligence,' before the DEA, and this particular section was associated with the Coast Guard—we, they, bailed out a kid Dicky grew up with, the kid in question deciding he'd sell marijuana from a fishing boat to engineers and trainmen loading containers from the docks onto those mile-long unit-trains up around Seattle."

"Don't tell me, when Dicky botched the Crawford Hill case, he never really knew what it was all about, did he?" Can you wonder why I hate company men? And women?

Mags hits the wall, and sits. "Not then, no he didn't. And not now, really, but he wants his last promotion so bad, he still runs scared when we just even ring once. So, yeah, I knew you'd be along sooner than later."

"Well, thanks so much for the goddam cake you so pointedly did *not* bake, knowing I was coming." I turned to stare out the window, hoping Maggie would either pass out from exhaustion, or excuse herself to the restroom, anything to stop contact with anybody from the human race. Truth be told, one reason I'll always live in my Airstream—no room for two, not really.

"Will, look—"

I'm still at the glass. "Barbie's got an old Ford Falcon station wagon, right?"

"Well—"

"Come on, Connor."

"Okay, yeah, South Dakota plates, 46A-661, almost expired. Why?"

"Because if you can get your shit together by the time I can start up the Bronco and go, then you may join me in the chase."

"Oh, no."

"Oh, yes. Emily's managed to escape *your* conference room, guarded by one of *your* Deadwood uniforms, and hot-wired her own mother's vehicle, and all in the last ten minutes." I'm making for the door as fast as I can.

Maggie's following. "I catch her, I'm throwing away the key."

The Bronco's where I left it, thank goodness. "Not if I hire her, first."

We make the Bronco, and we make the highway, and if I've ever seen those big ol' Falcon tail lights flaring red at dusk, I'm seeing them now, and I back off to let a rise or two come between us.

Maggie doesn't care for the way I tail. "Don't you think you could lose her?"

"Hell, yes, Maggie, if that's all she's thinking, then you bet, she can lose us in a heartbeat. There's a South Dakota state highway taking off in either direction every five miles or so, and county roads, half of those gravel, every mile like clockwork. And that's not to mention every little two-track a ranch or farm will use to access irrigation ditches or feed stock."

Maggie's getting jittery. Too much coffee? I doubt it. She's doesn't share well, especially for having two sisters. "So, then?"

"So, then," I say, "She's on her way to do a little yard work."

Maggie's jittery-*er*. "Mowing the grass?"

"*Train* yard work. She's got herself two box car numbers—George's tattoos—and she's headed to a train yard to check the inventory."

"After all these years."

"Yes." I don't like yet another way Mags takes the conversation, but I'll figure it out later.

"So, we'll head to her hometown—Edgemont—the nearest train yard she knows."

"The uninformed might come to that conclusion." I'll keep taking shots at Mags until she decides to come completely clean. "But I will be taking us to Crawford, the train yard nearest to her daddy's—"

"Accident?" says Maggie.

"Ambush," says me.

Great. A shade over 160 miles, two-and-half hours if I'm lucky. Deadwood to Crawford, South Dakota to Nebraska. Chasing one pistol of a young woman, trusting no one, positive she alone can solve the mystery of her dear departed dad. And riding shotgun with me in pursuit, a woman in her mid-forties, trusting no one, assured she alone can use the teen's so-called murder case as just one more piece, and maybe not *that* important in the overall scheme of things-piece, of a puzzle on the federal level, that level which steamrolls everyone and everything in its path, hiding beneath the sacrosanct shroud of *national security.*

But, I have a plan. As usual. Doesn't mean it'll work out. *Rollin' the dice.*

"Will—" Maggie's trying. My last nerve.

"Don't start." I'm driving with the high-beams, these craggy mini-mesas and bluffs anchored in undulating lifts and drops are just the places free-range cattle, and wandering horses, and turkeys and badgers and deer and coyotes decide *now's the time to cross that highway*, and it's really *not*, and semi-trucks or panel trucks, or sedans or coups—or God forbid, Broncos—collide with the crossers at forty-five to sixty-five miles per hour, and crisis ensues.

There's that. And I can't lose Emily, and I keep hoping against hope Maggie will speak the truth commensurate with the quality of our friendship. I'm a sap.

"Help me watch for animals crossing, and do not speak unless you see one, or you decide to come clean, once and for all. Because you know and I know you know how this Canadian fits into *my* case, and you know how the Mexican motorcyclist fits in as well, and you've known Doc forever, and he's hiding a goddam truckload of info, because for some reason, Doc has proclaimed himself Protector of the Panhandle, but as we have seen this last couple of days, Doc is as expendable as anyone else."

"Can I ask where we're going?" Maggie's not belted in, she's half turned my way, leaning on the door. Memo to self: *rig an ejection seat, front passenger's side.*

"Free country."

"Still a jerk. Okay. Mr. Allen, how are we making our way to Crawford?"

"By vehicle. But as that is as close as you will probably get before you reach over and slap me, the answer is *not* the way Emily is going to take to Edgemont, thence to Crawford." I'm wrestling with an old service station highway map I used to carry in the Bronco, and now in my head, and I'm hoping I'm not far off. "We'll continue to follow her on U.S. 385, but only to Pringle, where I'm betting she'll continue due south on State 89. But I know staying on 385 is longer, but much faster—"

Maggie's trying. "—unless we mow down some innocent Bambi's."

"Right. Then at Hot Springs, I'll head due west back to connect with 89, and hopefully I'll come around in front of Emily's cute but very slow Falcon."

"Because?" Maggie's yawning, still trying to watch for *fauna.*

"Because I want to get to Crawford first. There's a former second-shift operator trying his hand at trapping up and down the hill, and I bet I can catch him out along his trapline as the sun rises."

"And because?"

"Because, Maggie, that guy's got every step and rail and switch in Crawford committed to memory—and especially the cemetery tracks. Some of those cars have been there since before even he hired on."

"He?" I'm thankful she's really starting to hit the wall. This will aid my current plan. Now I'll insure the deal.

"He," I say, "is Richie Convoluto, born and raised on a goat farm three miles north of Marsland, as I met him on Highway 385 north of Alliance years and years ago. And ol' Richie was pulled over on the shoulder, and I thought he might be having tire problems, as he's bent over the trunk of this ancient old coupe, turned out to be a Hudson"—and Mags is nodding off—"and lo and behold, I walk up behind him, and he's got a fresh road-kill, gutting it and skinning it before my eyes. And he senses I'm standing there, totally non-plussed, and he doesn't miss a beat slicing this poor critter out, and goes *sorry, buddy, I saw it first, but I'd be glad to saw ya off a hind-quarter.* And turns out it was a deer, adolescent male, ol' Richie claiming *you stew anything long enough, mister, it'll feed the kids.* Which he had eleven of, between two mothers, one a Sioux lady, a fine woman, she preceded by one of those Russian immigrant-brides, way before it was stylish, and the Russkie, without any warning, became a card-carrying Democrat, so divorce ensued, making way therefore—"

And Mags is sawing logs (nobody looks nice *really* sleeping), and we pull into the only twenty-four-hour gas station in Hot Springs, the first sunrays glinting off the globes atop each gas pump. I run inside, hand the attendant a twenty, a high school kid with a magazine he tried to cover up, and I run out and top off the Bronco. Then I nudge Ms. Connor, already hating myself just a little bit for what I'm about to do. *Wait, wait, okay!* Feeling fine once more, she having several ticks of the odometer to come clean. *You make your choices.*

"Maggie, wake up. I need to gas up. Want to use the ladies'?"

And Mags looks at me like a kid on Christmas morning getting caught for sleeping through Santa, and she stumbles out the Bronco, heads inside the station, grabs the key for the restroom door, and is around the corner. I wait until I hear that metal door slam shut—she is pissed—but not as much as she shall be momentarily.

I turn the Bronco over and slip away, and turn at the fork back onto Highway 89, south, hopeful I am now in front of Emily. I glance in the rearview mirror, and I can clearly make out the teen age attendant, his eyes the size of platters, realizing what I'd done. And what would happen next. He didn't look happy.

And here's another sad clue for those trying to gauge the type of person I am. I'm hoping against hope that when Emily gets to that juncture of highways at Hot Springs, she notices her old Falcon is running on fumes, as her mom never had more than a few bucks to drop in the tank at any given moment, and Emily, in the full innocence and bravado of the typical American teenager, pulls into the gas station—and square into the angry clutches of Maggie Connor, Chief Administrator, Deadwood Police Department. Part-time, at least.

Love to be a fly on *that* wall.

Twenty-Two

The railroad I hired onto as a kid, during the war, bears a passing resemblance to the one I walk through now, this one identified as Crawford station, 30422 on the Burlington Northern route map. It has five tracks in one section. The first two are main lines, east and westbound, and the three others close by act as sidings to park waiting trains, or as staging tracks to switch out cars in need of repair, or switch in other local cars waiting on trains to Chicago, or Seattle. As you cross the tracks, walking west from the depot, you step across the first five, then walk on another ten yards or so to a second set of tracks. These aren't quite as shiny, and the rock ballast caked around the ties is muddy and clustered and cracked. There are spikes missing once in a while, and gaps between rail ends where braces and brackets and welds slowly lose the battle to summer expansion and winter contraction, to weeds and warping.

The first set is called the hide track. Back in the day when cattle were as important to business as coal is today, two medium-sized slaughter houses operated sixteen hours a day, six days a week just fifty yards further north and west. A little pocket track connected the slaughter house sliding doors to the hide track, and the cattle hides collected, wet and steaming in the worst-kept, rejected B-5 box cars, hanging from hooks buried in the ceiling. And each time the hide track collected six to eight cars, those cars would be switched into a local freight train, picking up and setting out freight and empties, a slow journey through the division—from Ravenna, Nebraska at the eastern edge of the Sandhills, to Sheridan, Wyoming, at the feet of the Bighorn Mountains.

The second set past the *hides*, as that track is called, is the hopper track. A *hopper* is an empty gondola car, and gondolas come in many iterations, covered and uncovered, low and long for scrap, tall and square for coal, specialized and generalized as a product demands. The "gonds" here are awaiting a "hospital train," one train made up only of cars-in-need-of-repair, a non-revenue train headed for the car repair facility in Alliance or Gillette,

Wyoming. These have almost no schedule importance in and of themselves, so these cars often collect and rust for weeks if not months, before some industrious station agent accidentally contacts a young and green train dispatcher, and the two rev each other up until the Chief Dispatcher can no longer stand the rah-rah, and he agrees to schedule the hospital train "the next time things are slow." Which is almost never, and even when things *appear* slow, once the hospital train is introduced to the general ebb and flow of trains in either direction, Murphy's Law raises its ugly head, and this slow-pig-of-a-train stops up the works, important trains start to die, and the Chief spends half a shift chewing the green dispatcher's ass—and the industrious station agent, formerly a station operator, never dreaming he'd stay on the job long enough to "bid in" a station agent position with the length of service he's given this railway, gets off scot-free (most often), because Harry Truman's proverbial "buck" always—*always* on the railroad—stops with the train dispatcher. *Why they pay 'em the big bucks.*

And the third track of the second group, the farthest from the depot and lights and concern, is the cemetery spur. All the other tracks in the yard connect, through a series of track switches, to one of the main lines. But a spur is a track, usually short and never maintained, and closed at its far end. A dead end. A cemetery track.

Here cars of every type and description, with prefixes suggesting the car's originating roads, most merged now into a handful of "majors," accumulate and rot. Once in a blue moon of blue moons, a new dead car comes to be "buried" in a string of unknowns—a hand-written list is kept on file in the station agent's safe, and once or twice a year some operator or clerk, normally being hazed as the "new kid," rewrites the lists by hand, then compares the old and new lists, and "when things are slow," the greenest employee is tasked to isolate missing or incorrect car numbers, and solve the mystery—what is the original identity of this car, when was the ID mistake first made, how can this be rectified, and most importantly, which poor bastard draws the short straw and has to report the screw-up to Denver, the regional clearinghouse for car supply and distribution. It's not surprising to know, that onerous call to Denver is rarely made, as long as no one directly asks for a specific car's whereabouts, and the more time elapsed, the lower the probability anyone will ever ask, *ever*.

Those war years saw mail trains, and milk trains, and passenger trains, locals and express, and military trains, and troop trains, and oil and chemical tank car trains run east and west, day and night. Most were shorter than now, lighter than now, steam engines pulling rather than diesel. And each major siding had a track crew dedicated to the station, plus several miles east and west of the yard office, plus a signal maintainer on call day and night. So every major station was a town, a community of railroaders, a village of support, stores and schools and hospitals and churches, and, once the little town accumulated 800 to 1,000 souls, a diner or supper club might be tossed in for good measure.

Today, railroads have and will continue to merge, and minor stations dry up, blow away into unmanned sidings, major stations lucky to re-claim any kind of notoriety. Technology improves communication, and software and hardware, and fewer people are needed to complete more tasks, and those left behind are abandoned to work longer, not smarter. And romance, as manifested in passenger conveyance, has practically become the rose "dying on the vine."

But if you really want to revisit the romance, you need to find a station like Crawford. As long as trains need helpers, as long as a loaded coal train has value, and as long as an elevation gain around a "horseshoe" exists, Crawford will be a village. A home to a station agent, like Little Tony Esposito (and yes, he inherited the job from poppa Big Tony). A home to three engineers and three brakeman, taking turns cutting into and pushing on those massive coal trains. A home to a dedicated track section, four to six track workers also on call 24/7, as any threat of even a minor track malfunction could paralyze a division in a matter of hours. And those arrays of red and green lights and flags acting on signals sent from the dispatchers' control boards, essential to the life-and-death communication amongst and between the trains themselves—permanently-stationed signal maintainers are essential, particularly in case of derailment, blizzard, or the odd tornado or two.

Here, finally, is Crawford, and I'm pulling into Daisy's first, although this might not seem prudent if I desire cover for my actions. I've weighed the credits and costs, and I need information now, not later, so here goes.

Daisy all but drops her receiver on the black desk phone sitting next to the cash register as I pop through the door. Rarely speechless, Daisy is now.

"Table for two, ma'am? As in two, me and you." And I head to the last table against the farthest wall. But I stop and turn for a second. "And Daisy, do me a favor, tell your old grandpa you'll call him back in twenty minutes, would ya?"

I can't translate Daisy's specific countenance other than to say she's definitely off her game, for the moment anyway. So, I sit, and pick up a well-thumbed morning edition of the *Crawford Clipper*, and I start with the obituaries. This way I know who *ain't* in town.

Daisy sits across from me, same look as before. I notice her cousin in the kitchen has been called out to cover the register and phone, so I have Daisy's undivided attention for a few minutes, and with my lead on Emily dwindling, I must make hay while skies are sunny.

"Lighten up, Daisy."

"I didn't expect you back so soon."

I sit back and toss the paper aside. "Yeah, let me help you with that. *You and grandpa* didn't expect me back *at all*. Closer, right?"

"We figured you can take care of yourself." And as if that was too frank, Daisy closes and turns away.

"Yes, thanks. You're a peach. But you didn't figure your ol' grandpa would get between a couple of railroad widows and a seriously bad guy from Vancouver, did you?"

She's back, but strangely composed. "That Connor gal called me, she's been keeping me in the loop about Doc's recovery. I'm guessing she's not who she claims to be?"

Now I'm wishing I'd grabbed a cup on my way back. "That Connor gal—" I use air quotes—"won't be updating you for a while, as she got lost in the metropolis that is Hot Springs, South Dakota. And if you're worried about Emily Straight"—And here Daisy fairly jumps, some tell, I'll tell you—"She'll be here before you know it. But you aren't going to try and find her and hide her from me and the bad guys, whoever they really are."

And Daisy's cycled through to *angry*. "And why am I not?"

"Because, I will, on *my* way out, dial zero, and report a stolen old Falcon, probably in the hands of a minor who may or may not be sixteen, and the locals will contact the county deputies and the state troopers—grand theft auto, you know—and for all we know, she could be a mule on her way to the campus in Chadron, bent on selling the devil's weed to fine Young Republicans and Future Farmers of America."

Daisy's past angry. "You know that's not true."

"I do not *not* know it, even though I'd bet the house against it, as Emily strikes me as the straightest of straight arrows, no pun intended."

145

Daisy tears a paper napkin to shreds, then comes out of her trance. "Sometimes things don't get reported the way they happen, because they don't really happen the way they look. Oh, crap. You know what I mean?"

I can't afford sympathy right now, not right here. "Yes, I do. I get it. Out of context, or misinterpreted, or misquoted. Or the incident causing all hell to break loose appears to have been keyed by one incident or one person, but really, they have nothing to do with each other. Sheer coincidence."

Daisy's relieved. "Yes, exactly. Sheer coincidence."

I stand, and leave a ten on the table for the coffee and doughnut I wasn't offered.

"Bullshit, Daisy. I'm no stranger to coincidence in this job, but I've run into a true one maybe twice since I hired on at eighteen. But neither here nor there, as I'm out of time."

Daisy looks like she just watched a funeral end. No movement, no sound.

"Question one, Doc was keeping his house and property so clean and shiny, especially for a widower, I'd swear he was keeping a guest when he was entertaining me with lemonade."

One tear swells in Daisy's left eye. "George Straight. But George had been gone a week by the time you showed up. Ran away."

"I suspect you won't have to answer this next one, I'll just know." Daisy stands and looks directly into my eyes.

"I've seen file pictures when George was young, and I questioned him in hospital for quite a little bit, though he said little. But I've also seen all the file photos of Harley Straight." Daisy starts blinking.

"Daisy, Emily is a dead ringer for her Uncle George. True or false."

Daisy walks directly into the ladies'.

Twenty-Three

I pull into the gravel parking lot in front of the Crawford depot and stop. I can pull the Bronco right up to the front door, announcing my arrival, or I can park over by the signal maintainers' hut, and gain an additional half an hour so before someone in the railway community spots an old Bronco with Wyoming plates and thinks *well, ain't that somethin'?*

And that somebody will either toddle right on into the station agent's office to report, hoping for free coffee, or sidle on over to Daisy's, thinking he's got himself a news flash he might convert into free pastry. I opt for minimal delay. Besides, I might bump into that station agent myself, as I negotiate the tracks from the mainline out to the cemetery track. Every station agent has a standard time of day where he grabs a clip board and a coffee, and a cigarette or cigar or a pipe, and walks his station—each track, double-checking what's parked on which track and why, comparing what his list says today to what the list said yesterday. Most agents look forward to it. It's twenty minutes to an hour they are legitimately free of any other responsibility. It's a time for peace and quiet.

Big Tony retired and passed on years ago, and Little Tony, it was rumored out in Wyoming, took a one-time early-retirement offer when the BN ate the old SLSF—the St. Louis and San Francisco—in just another of a cascade of mergers nationwide. So, I figure as Richie Convoluto started his career as a midnight extra board operator out this way, until he had the seniority to hold a permanent midnight slot, then the second shift slot (where I met him as he skewered road kill for his kiddies), he'd be first in line seniority-wise to bid in the station agent's golden Monday through Friday, no damn holidays, and six, count them, six weeks of vacation, with another twenty days of sick leave per year, which of course translates to four more weeks of vacation if a fella was so unethical as to call into the Alliance headquarters as sick, but was not.

I get all the way across to the hides track, a rare occasion where no train is using the yard to wait its turn west, while a load has the right of way headed east. The Helpers are also on duty, and in their absence, another train dropped a fresh set of two newly-serviced helper engines. Another set of rejuvenated units will be on their way after midnight when the local roles through.

There are two old B5 hide boxes on the hide track. The slaughter houses, a little mom & pop business, went under years back, so I know the boxes are empty and dry. They still stink. They will always stink. But its manageable, and I walk a wide circle around the boxes, through a gap between old gondolas, and into the cool darkness, the almost-jungle stillness of the cemetery track, sound-proofed with wild red oak. I come around the last car, and I stop, breath held.

The cemetery track is full from one end to the other, thirty-five cars. At the far end I make out an almost Tolkenesque version of a perfectly-square, powerful figure-in-shadows, back turned, and wrestling with a framework of some sort. Over forty years, I've had several opportunities to either sneak up on an individual in a surrounding—giving the person no time to react to my presence, or hide or distort the true purpose of said person's activity—or hail the individual from afar—allowing for a possible action of distraction, or the moments needed for the person warned to arm himself against me. I hail now from the outset, as my chances of living to hail another day are much better. Once I am in close proximity, running is out of the question.

I'm betting on a gut feeling. "Richie! Agent Convoluto!"

The figure freezes. Then there seems to be some minor movement. I head toward who I feel must be Richie, and as I pass down the spur, car by car, I start to wonder why it is exactly I trust gut feelings.

I'm roughly twenty-five cars off, and something is not right. I stop. And almost at a silent count of three, one the rest of the world feels, and I don't, three things happen in almost indiscernible succession.

Four short and ancient cattle cars ahead of where I stand, something startles a great horned owl from a nap, and the huge female tears out of the fourth car from me, all four and a half feet of wingspan, screaming like a banshee, and heads right for me, talons leading. Just before the owl buzzes my position, Emily Straight jumps out from between the two box cars nearest me. And over Emily's shoulder, and beneath the oncoming owl, the shadow-figure-Richie goes into a squat, and both barrels of a shotgun erupt.

Does the world work the way the movies claim? Does everything at a hyper-moment like this go into super-slo-mo? Am I observing and acting in a matrix of transcendent cause and effect? Sadly, no.

Things happen at lightening speeds. I leap forward, hoping that contact with Emily will send her one side of the owl, and away from the shotgun blast. As it turns out, my great horned owl has no more interest in interacting with me than I do with her. This gal pulls straight up when I move ahead. And I catch Emily from behind at her knees, so she folds like a table, forward and down. In less stressful situations, with a clear mind, I'd have weighed the probability that a sawed-off shotgun might have a twenty-five-foot range, with a sixty-degree arc, and we were still well out of danger.

As it is, I'm face down on a ground composed of stuff I *don't* want to know about, with one of Emily's tennis-shod feet in my right eye. Stillness follows the blast. I think I can hear my heartbeat as well as Emily's. And now I definitely hear a slow but steady march of heavy boots crunching through the flotsam. I figure it's been a pretty good life, take the risk, and lift my head. And there stands Richard Robert Convoluto, two dead rabbits in one hand, a smoking sawed-off in the other.

"I will be damned, Will Allen. What in hell are you doing out here?" Emily and I slowly clamber about, purpose being to make our feet before Richie can reload. Then Richie steps a foot forward and squints. "Emily? Girl, are you crazy?" And to this, Emily responds in one of the most surprising and entertaining ways I have ever witnessed.

Emily straightens her jeans and t-shirt, runs a hand through her hair, steps up to Richie, rips one of the dead rabbits from his hand, and proceeds to beat him about the face and neck. All this while yelling *you dumb sonuvabitch!*

Richie drops the other rabbit and the weapon to draw up his hands to protect his eyes, leaving himself clear for Emily's kick to the groin. Richie falls like a sack of feed, on his side, holding his crotch. Emily's now calling him *the dumbest bastard ever lived* while kicking at any part of his torso he can't protect. I've regained my stance, and I'm watching, hands on knees as I get my breath.

Richie's increasingly unhappy. "Allen, goddamit man, pull her off, Allen."

I sense some cosmic scale of justice is being righted. "Doesn't look like she's finished, Richie." Here's where Emily's showing some real athletic chops, alternating kicks with a rhythmic breathing. Girl's got a future, somewhere.

I finally can stand erect. "Emily, Emily please." She stops, hands on hips, taking in a little more air, thank goodness.

"Idiot tried to kill me."

"Kill you?" I smile.

"Okay, kill us, I guess. But he *knows* me. And I guess he knows you, if he can get close enough."

Richie's almost to one knee. I walk over a couple of feet and retrieve his weapon. He decides to stay where he's at, dripping rabbit fur and guts round his shoulders.

"I did not one thing wrong, Allen. I cannot be arrested for protecting me and mine."

I lean against an old beet wagon, once engaged with the Great Western sugar mills to process the harvest. Beet wagons smell about as bad as hide cars.

"If I was a card-carrying member of BN Protection Services, I'd have you in cuffs as we speak, you moron. You're using company property to run your traplines, you're doing it on company time, and you're carrying a weapon. That gets you in front of a judge. Then I swear to His Honor you took a shot at me, a private security operative, and this poor young girl—"

"A minor," Emily inserts. "And you may have killed a perfectly innocent great horned owl. Probably upset the ecological balance around these parts for fifty years to come."

Now I am at Richie's immediate right. "And I'm betting you left some form of eye glasses in your office, as you were always a bit of a vain one, but it doesn't stop you from wielding a weapon, as opposed to a hunting firearm— one more thing I could spin into a third-degree misdemeanor at least, maybe a felony with a push."

Richie makes his feet, one hand still to groin. "I'm listening to all this why?"

"Because you are going to realize I got you by the short hairs, and even if something were to happen to me—" I pointedly lift the sawed-off—"Emily is still in play, and she seems unconstrained by law or statute to chase your ass to the ends of the earth and make you pay."

Emily positions on Richie's left. "What he said."

Richie's fully standing. "What'd ya want?"

Emily's close enough, Richie flinches when she speaks. "Q 2371."

Richie's head jerks her way involuntarily, then he looks down. "Don't know it."

Emily and I both have to laugh. I say, "Please, oh please, when this is all over, play poker with me."

Richie tries again to avert his gaze. "Check 'em yourself, no Q's on the whole damn track."

Emily looks to me. I nod. She takes off, reading car numbers as she goes. I'm feeling good for Emily. I think she's feeling empowered, after years of loneliness and frustration, missing her dad, looking for answers, getting stonewalled by people supposed to be on her side. Maybe that'll make up for getting shot at.

"Richie, you smell like gin. What in God's name happened to you? It's not even close to nine. What do you have for lunch? Boilermakers?"

Richie looks defeated. "Hell, I don't know, Will. I got no reasons. I got excuses. I chose to have more kids than two trailers can hold. I didn't have to play poker in the freight room between incoming trains. And I sure as hell choose to drink when it hurts, and I drink when it doesn't, celebratin', ya know?"

"Let me try a hypothetical, being as how I'm not a real cop. Things got about as dark as you'd ever seen, up past your ass in gambling debts, you were even thinking about using that shotgun on yourself, and out of nowhere, here comes the creepiest drink o' water, walking right into your office in full suit and tie, see-through eyeballs, and he offers you a way out."

Richie's eyes moisten. "And I took it, God help me."

I hear *Allen!* There's Emily at the far end, where we first saw Richie busy with something or other. "Wait here, Richie."

"Where in hell can I go?" He sits flat on open ground, no other position giving him comfort.

I make the last car quickly, considering, and Emily looks triumphant. She points to an old hide-B5-box-car, so deteriorated you can see through it in places, holes the size of your hand.

"Check the number." Emily points with her index, its tip dark and wet.

I draw my finger through the "B" in a freshly sprayed *BN 102371.* I smile.

"So, Ms. Straight, your deduction?"

"It's not like I didn't grow up in a railroad town, but I'm pretty sure when a merger happens, cars are pooled and sometimes renumbered. So a CB&Q, often just a "Q," and its number, 2371, might become a BN car, with a "1-0" leader. Right or wrong?"

"Dead on, sister."

And like a burlesque cue to the sound-effects guy, we hear the shotgun ring out once more.

"Oh, my God, no," and I run, for the first time in years, for the other end of the track.

I can see Richie, prone, on his back, his front steaming, a mess in the early morning.

"Emily, stay back, please." Miraculously, she does as I say.

I kneel down. Richie's eyes are open, seeing nothing. He gurgles, beyond speech.

The shot gun lies beside him. I can hear a car departing the depot, it's pedal to the floor, a whining V-8 winding up.

I put my mouth to Richie's ear. "MacAdam?"

Richie nods, and leaves me.

Twenty-Four

I'm put in mind of one old boy, seeming ancient the day I met him, and I was probably thirty at the time. Conductor Z.P. Walker. "Z.P." for Zebulon Pike. No surprise his daddy was a homesteader in the Nebraska Panhandle, long enough back it was good to know a little something about the Sioux and Pawnee. As a kid-switchman, the "Z.P." degenerated into "Zippy," one of those ironic nicknames, as the man chose to shuffle when called to walk, usually ambled when called to trot, and never, ever ran—the running man, Zip declared, was the man looking forward but planning badly. Zip was a study in efficient slow-motion. He could see ahead in a switch yard, sometimes twenty or even thirty moves. And when several yard tracks, full of single cars destined for disparate destinations, were shuffled like a faro dealer would cut a deck one-handed so fast your eyes hurt to follow—there, standing at the head end of the final collection of cars in perfect order to be cut and dropped along stations throughout the division, there would stand ol' Zip, looking at his fellow switch crew, wondering *what took you guys so long?* The ultimate irony here was that Zip never retired. He died under a runaway box car, not because he didn't see it coming, but because Zip realized he'd finally misjudged a car's speed and distance, and still refused to break into a run. Zip figured *this must be my time.*

I think there was a pinch of that thinking in what happened to ol' Richie. Emily sure as hell roughed him up, but she was a healthy teenager, acting from rage, and he was a half-drunk and desperate station agent, crumbling under the stress of a string of bad choices. I think he might have yelled out to get our attentions when he found himself in danger, or stood with difficulty and put up some resistance. But in conference with the Crawford PD Chief, and the Dawes County Sheriff—and even oh-no-they-had-to-call-him-it's-on-railroad-property Special Agent Dicky Tuttle—all agreed Richie watched his assailant walk to him, load the shotgun, then blow away most of Richie's torso. Said

153

assailant ran like a rabbit, and made a clean getaway. And Richie, faced with overwhelming struggles and challenges, and weakened by sleeplessness and drink, figured *this must be my time.*

I cherish the company of real cops, but I don't care for gatherings of any sort of people, cops or not, in excess of two or three. I can handle four to six for brief periods, and then I slip away, or out, or in. Wherever I can be one-on-one again. I like *persons.* I do not care for *people.* After a shooting like this, even rural locations are awash in village and county and even state investigative agencies, each one fulfilling its own mission statements, and each one duplicating one or more agencies' efforts. This can't be helped, and multiple perspectives from a collection of viewpoints is invaluable. It's also time-consuming. I'm impatient, and I don't mind listening to or telling stories all day long, but I can't stand telling or hearing the same damn story all day long.

All that in service to my short but efficient combined pow-wow with the Sheriff, Chief, and Rally Smith, Panhandle Division Detective Sergeant, Nebraska State Patrol. I wanted to confer with these gentlemen free of Dicky's questionable efforts and agenda, and I wanted to sign off with them, offering my eye-witness testimony, letting them in on what I can about my case without releasing everything in protection of my client. And that's the other complicating construct of a rapidly-changing case: I started this investigation with a nominal client in Dicky Tuttle, and I carry forward the same investigation in service to Emily Straight.

I've officially notified neither Dicky nor Emily, and at this point, neither needs to know. Dicky's bill makes Emily's *pro bono* case possible. Again, a variable justice, but justice nevertheless.

The next bullet point on my mental things-to-do list *is* to talk to Dicky, but one-on-one, where there will not be a record of our conversation, save for the one I will be making, without his knowledge or permission. The recording would never see the light of day in a courtroom. And that fact does serve justice in the broadest sense, especially if you are a felon, and if you have something to hide. But again, not a *real* cop, and I may need this length of tape to wrangle a bad guy or two into a position where an unofficial strain of justice is served. Yes, I rationalize. Yes, I can live with it. So far.

As Emily's with her family once more at their little motel in Edgemont, I shepherd Dicky Tuttle back across Crawford Yard, over tracks and spongy, suspect-surfaces, doing a real number on Dick's hundred-dollar wingtips. We stand amongst a dwindling number of forensics people, and I wait until there are none. I look up at the hide boxcar we stand in front of, BN 102371. A yellow tape reaches from the upper left-hand corner down to the door, there it meets another ascending from the lower right. I reach out and drag a finger across the letters and numbers. I can still smear them.

Dicky's pissed for his shoes, and over-confident being on his own turf, even though he's never walked more than a mile of it combined in forty years.

"So, fake cops, as you call us, we can just smear evidence around? That's okay with the state and county?" Dick reaches for a cigarette and a lighter. I wait until he lights up, draws it down to his toes, then I pluck it out, snap it in half, and stuff it in my jacket pocket. Dicky's pissed again.

"What the hell?"

"No smoking. A crime scene, you know."

"You just—"

"—did what the state investigator did his own self after he heard my story, took prints and pictures of the box inside-out, and every inch of the ground around for fifteen feet. Probably about the time you were sipping your first coffee, watching *Regis and Kathie Lee*."

Dick starts to walk back the way he came.

"Sorry, Dick, that was just a wild guess, stays between us, I promise."

Dick stops.

"And you'll want to come back here, explain a few things about this old hide box, now a crime scene?"

Dick turns, frustrated. "How would I know *anything*?"

"Good point." I leave it at that. "But it's what you haven't done so far. *That's* interesting."

"Like?"

"Like, you didn't go *police tape*? Or, *what's inside*? Or, and I know we attended the same training classes a hundred years back, did you wonder *what's the old hide box got to do with my dead station agent, and whoever killed my dead station agent.*"

Dicky draws and lights another smoke. I do not intercede. "What do you want me to say, Allen?"

I separate the police tapes where they meet, and I pull the sliding cargo door to the right. "Well, other than *I resign*, you can answer one or two of my questions—ones I *know* you know the answers to, or at least can give me a lead, as you have a vested interest, you may remember, in saving your own ass and getting your promotion." I climb up into the car, and turn to gesture him in.

"Not dragging this suit into a hide box."

"It hasn't been wet for ten years, and I think you know that, or suspect it. And Rally Smith found just enough evidentiary anomalies, yet to be tested, I admit, that can be tossed together in some very interesting ways."

Dicky stays outside the car, lighting a new smoke off his last one, then crushing the butt under his wingtip. "Your cockamamie theories, Will. That's why you never made it to Supervisory status, too busy building your own brand, loving the attention every time some bigshot called in asking for you instead of me. And me there to have to clean up the PR, and the politics, doing the *real* work—"

I can't help but laugh. "*That's* the *real* work? Oh, geesus, Dicky, you really believe that, don't you? That, what, sooner or later some blind squirrel will find a nut, and solve a case, maybe put a bad guy away—and what if they never do? Just *oh well, what the hell*? Wives lose their husbands? Kids lose their dads? Shit happens?" I make the mistake of getting angry, and I jump down out of the car. And that is going to hurt tomorrow.

Dick jumps back. "Back off, Will, I'm still the client."

I'm too old for this. I take a deep breath. "You're right, but not about being the client. Howdy Humboldt's going to sign off my bills, whether or not I slap you silly. But that would only feel good for ten or twenty seconds, and at my age, that's a poor ratio of pleasure to pain."

Dick looks relieved, like this might be it, and he can go back to the office.

I almost hate to break his bubble. "But no, your cozy desk will remain vacated until I get some answers."

"All right already."

"Fine. First, what would you say to some clothing remnants found in nooks and crannies inside this old hide box?"

Dick's looking a bit more confident. "Kids doing what kids do, smoking, drinking, making out."

"Yeah, right, and most of *them* wearing the steel-toe work boots, or lined overalls, or safety glasses suggested by the buttons and clasps and shoestring tips and zippers still intact, long after—oh, say ten years after—this box was last used?"

Dick's getting pale. "You can prove that?"

"Ain't up to me, McGee. All the stuff found inside, plus scrapings from everything in view, it's all headed to Lincoln, the lab at the University, then to be forwarded to the FBI—"

"What? Wait a minute, you're bullshitting me now, why—"

I lean back against the door frame. "*Now* you're asking why, Dick. A little late. But again, we trained together, and you know that if for some reason this boxcar was the scene of a felony, or contributed to the transport of those felonious actors, or contraband associated with those actors, and said car crosses state lines—*caramba*! Time for the feds, and *those* labs don't miss a damn thing."

"All true, and still not my problem, not until tests return, and a possibility turns into a probability, and motive is discovered and assigned—"

"Yeah, yeah, yeah." I don't want Dick to go too far afield until I reel him in. "So one last one, Dick, and then you and I go home." He's a little more chipper, poor guy. "Let's just say, for fun, mind you, a taxi cab with a driver and relief Crawford crew, plus a mystery brakeman, does not miss the turn on Crawford Hill, but instead is stopped for some reason."

"And?"

"And, that crew is shanghaied, for some reason, and detained in a box car—"

"Why?"

"Don't know, Dick. Just sayin'. Detained, and bounced around, maybe on purpose with one of the helper units, couple into the box, and slam it, and bounce it, and couple in again, and slam and bounce again. Then those bodies are placed in the taxi, again, but this time the taxi van is pushed over the side on Crawford Hill."

Dick's looking like he has a brand-new lease on life. "Oh, for God's sakes, Allen, who in their right or wrong minds would do something like that? For what possible purpose?" Dick laughs, turns on a heel, starts off.

"That's far enough, Dicky." He detects a measured change in my tone, freezes, turns. "I lied, Dick, about two things. One, is—there *is* one more question." I pull an evidence bag from my barn coat pocket. It contains a cigarette butt. "Why do you suppose, in a box car sporting a seal dated one month after the taxi-van tragedy, and parked on this cemetery track at that day and time, and not moved an inch in ten years according to station agent records—why do you suppose, Dicky, the Dawes County boys would find this relatively new, still moist butt just *inside* the doorway? And one looking, coincidentally, like the brand and style you yourself smokes?"

Dicky's looking, in the eyes, like a spooked fox catching wind of several dozen hunting dogs. Before he can act, smart or otherwise, Rally Smith steps around the corner of the hide box closest to Dicky.

"Special Agent Tuttle, I request the pleasure of your company—we'll need to meet, you and me, with the Chief and Sheriff. You may have a lawyer present, of course. But we'll speak to that formally a bit later."

And Dicky looks to me. *Deflated.* It's the only word that works. "You said you lied about two things. The other?"

"That you and I would be going home. *I* will be, if and when this whole damn case shakes out. But *you*, Dick. That depends on how you can explain away that cigarette butt."

And Rally and Dick walk away toward the depot.

I watch them, thinking *ya know, I would not put it past him.*

Twenty-Five

I'm exhausted. I'm just now realizing that I've yet to check into my own motel room, anywhere along the line. If I've slept at all, I've done it in the Bronco, stopping for a few winks when driving onward became hazardous, or dozing off while sitting outside someone else's digs. It's easier to collapse on the back-bench seat of the Bronco for a few hours than shop for accommodations. And although I'm making some headway, I'm almost as far away from knowing everything I want to know as I was before I left Sidney's. And, in unrelated news, I stink.

I leave the depot behind. The state and county people are gone for now. The BN has called in the second shift operator early and notified her she is, until further notice, the only qualified employee to work the station agent's job. Similarly, the midnight operator is moved to second trick, and an extra board clerk from Alliance (one of the few still qualified to take and pass along train orders) now resides in the midnight slot. Additionally, all three have been instructed to kiss their days-off good-by, as per union rules, all three jobs vacancies have to be advertised for thirty days, and there are no other people on the division qualified and free of other responsibilities. And the trains never stop moving.

I remember one joint from the war years called the Hilltop Motel. I was in the Seattle area then, but a buddy of mine's dad built and ran a little place my friend would rhapsodize about. It was at the highest point in Crawford, he told me, so renting a room there, in small, white clapboard, individual cabins, allowed most tenants a superb sunrise and delightful sunset, both painting the Pine Bluffs every shade of the rainbow. I know, it sounds like the kid ate all the mushrooms he found under dead pine logs up and down the ridges, but he sure enough recommended the Hilltop, the off-chance, of course, somebody like me would ever find themselves in some place like Crawford, Nebraska.

I could stop back in at Daisy's to ask directions, but there I am currently *persona non grata,* and how hard can it be to drive toward the highest point in town?

It's not only *not hard*, I might have done it with my eyes closed. All the streets running north and south go from up to down, and at the top of one—its hilltop—is a white clapboard compound of little units looking more like coastline cottages than mountain cabins. Each one is one large room with the small shower and toilet walled away with a thin door. Each one also contains a small gas stove, refrigerator, and a snack table big enough for two folding chairs. One double-bed and a dresser, holding perhaps the first color portable television ever invented, complete with rabbit-ear antennas, sits at the foot of the bed. Space available for dancing the hootchey-koo is limited.

I get the last, and therefore the highest cottage, number 13. You hear a lot of stories, anecdotes that tend to seed themselves, about how architects and builders and the like avoid using the number 13. Hence the absence of a thirteenth floor, or door, or unit. I've been around this country and a few others, and I have not personally witnessed this classic numeric omission. If anything, at least in the West, it seems an opportunity to grab the classic bad-luck interpretation by its gonads, challenging its power, laughing in its face. And this is true at the Hilltop. Units one through twelve have small signs spelling each number out, and thirteen is, well, *13*.

Courtney "Call me Court" Dancer owns the Hilltop now. On our way walking up to the thirteenth unit—all cars park outside the office at the hill's "bottom"—Court, a man in his late fifties, looking as if he greets each new decade with a naïve joy, beguiles me with origin stories of the motel, its lineage of ownership, and even the requisite ghost story. Thanks to Alfred Hitchcock, every bucolic inn and accommodation in America's countryside has to be spooky to be attractive.

Courtney's halfway through the story of Katie O'Clery (ghosts are always Irish girls or women), taken in her prime (fill in the blank—giving birth, suffering influenza, succumbing to the plague, perishing in a mysterious fire), and because of unrequited love (mother for daughter, daughter for father, fair maiden for bad-boy rebel), is doomed to roam the hallways or attics for eternity, making a sound which renders sleeping problematic (tragic sea chanty, *Amazing Grace*, or anything by Celine Dion).

160

But Court stops before I can find out if I, too, might meet Katie in my little shower.

"What the heck?" Court's messing with the room key and the lock.

"Problem?" I ask. *Let's get back to Katie.*

"I guess not." Court's taking off his trifocals and peering at the door knob, then replacing them and trying everything again. "Well, my cleaning gal, Cindy, she's been with us since forever, and she always locks up after cleaning. I mean, *always.* She has one master key, and I have one, and we both carry them with us everywhere we go—we're kinda crazy that way because, like twenty years back, one of us, me, her, who knows, left a door unlocked, down in unit three I think, doesn't matter—"

"—and it was stripped, right? Cleaned out? Everything stolen, top to bottom?" *Finish, for the lovuh God,* and *what about Katie?*

Court's startled. "Well, yes, that's true."

"So, the door?"

"Oh, yeah, well anyway, I go to unlock it just now, and I pushed the door open, and the key's jammed up, can't get it in—"

"Crap." I pull Court back behind me, and I swing my back pack down and unzip the inner pocket, one I can access through a fake zipper I had sewn in for just this purpose. In a pinch I can access the weapon most special railway agents never have to worry about handling. I ease my hand in and around the grip of an old .38 Police Special, one of two revolvers my father taught me to fire, and I pull it free, and drop the safety, and move slowly to and through the door.

Lucky thing these cottages are so small, one room plus the walled-off shower and toilet. I can see the room in a glance, look under the bed, then bump the door aside to reveal toilet and shower. *No occupado.*

Court is right on my six. I have to peel him off.

"We're good, Court. No intruder, no Katie either."

"Well, still a bit of a problem." Court's new fascination is the two by three window over the little breakfast table. It's as old as the motel, custom-made back in original construction to slide open horizontally.

I'm still holding out for Katie. But I bite. "And that is?"

"That the only way to lock this window is when it's shut, you lay this stick"—he refers to a whittled end of a pool cue—"in the window track, so one window cannot pass the other, and the window is locked."

"And when we came in?"

"The window was open, as I just closed it, and the pool cue was laying on the breakfast table."

I sit on the bed. "Court, I may or may not be a fugitive from a Mexican cartel enforcer, and/or a Canadian single or double-spy-slash-sociopath, and/or North America's finest secretary-slash-intell-Wonder Woman. Oh, and a recently-shot-general-practitioner, and oh again, a kidnapper-slash-saloon-owner on the run from God knows who."

Court sits next to me. "Okay, who?"

"Who? Oh, I mean, like God knows who, a saying, like—"

Court's sincerity is unique among men. "Like rhetorical?"

I smile and stand. "Well, it's certainly becoming that way."

Court's very uncomfortable, showing such by not leaving, not even turning toward my door. "Look, whoever you are and whatever you do for a living, you carry a gun and appear to know how to use it. But it's still my responsibility as your host to protect you. As is stands I recommend you take unit twelve, I'll call the police and Armand."

"Armand's your fixer?"

"Locksmith. I can't guarantee your safety. This isn't right."

I have an idea, that is a thought, once again I hear a *who*. "Court, I know by looking at you, you're the picture of discretion, so let me tell you a bit about me, then I'll tell you my little plan."

So, after Court lends me his little Chevy coupe (I want the Bronco to be front and center for anyone to see as they pass), and I pick up some turkey sands and lemonade, and a few small finds from the hardware store, and return, Court has set my stuff up in unit twelve, and left unit *13* open, still rented to me as is twelve, door unlocked, a smattering of my stuff there as well. And Court takes his share of the lemonade and turkey back down to the office. And I turn on the portable TV, play with the rabbit ears, find only Nebraska Public Television is available, and settle in for a late lunch with Julia Child.

I've done worse. Much worse.

Age and sleep deprivation, lemonade with its sugar-crash, turkey with its tryptophan—these are a few of my favorite things. They are why my lunch with Julia became a six-hour nap. I wake to the static hum of the television, as I lost the picture sometime after I lost consciousness. The sun's been down almost two hours, and it's pitch black in unit twelve.

I stumble over to the bathroom, turn on the little shower, stick my face in the narrow, icy-cold stream, and turn it off. There's some sort of noise outside. It's enough to force me to the window, and peek through louvered-shades. And just as I hoped, but hours ago, and during daylight hours at that, someone might be messing around in *13.*

I'm fortunate ol' Court's as trusting as he seems. He accepted my story, my brief outline of the case, and my request for help. He was happy to keep watch from his office. He would keep track of comings and goings, cars parked in the lot and their license numbers, and those wandering aimlessly about for whatever reason. Each little cottage does have a phone sitting next to the fridge, but I asked Court not to use it unless he perceived a real emergency. I didn't want to spook any visitors.

And now, I think I make out a pen light buzzing around *13* like a wasp looking for freedom. This is another tell, and I'm thinking the intruder is a woman. This is my prejudice, but in my experience, women tend to focus with an alacrity men can never know, and that's reflected in their choice of flashlight. Men, on the other hand, step back for the big picture, disregarding the detail that tells the greater story, and they tend to use the big flashlight, even the trainman's lantern. If I'm right, the chances of a woman being armed are usually less, and I'm always happy to be carrying the only weapon in the room.

So, I ease out of twelve, and walk upward to the buzzing point of light. There is some noise emanating from *13*, but not much, and again I'm betting the intruder is female. I reach in the doorframe, the door slightly ajar. My fingers make the light switch. As I flick the switch, I throw the door in, my revolver already in my left hand, and down at my side.

And I find, to my surprise, I am very right, but simultaneously very wrong.

There, no more than ten feet from me, in a shooter's stance, her nine-mil aimed squarely at my face, is Maggie Connor. And a Maggie with a countenance suggesting she might recognize me all right, but is seriously weighing the pros and cons of blowing my brains out.

Neither of us moves. And then something drops, or clicks, or flips over in Maggie's thought process, and she assumes *at ease,* her weapon dropping to her side.

I'm still moved by how close I came to being a memory. But Maggie goes for the phone, fingers a very-thin phonebook, folds a page back, and tosses it my way.

"Pepperoni and sausage, Will. And lots and lots of beer."

My shoulders drop. I can breathe once more.

"I don't drink."

Maggie starts messing with the antennas on the TV set.

"It's not for you."

Twenty-Six

"You going to eat that?" Maggie's laying across the double bed, her head on my pillows, feet propped up on her rolled-up jacket. Three empty Pabst Blue-Ribbons recline to her right, an empty pizza box to her left. She belches in a manner Marine drill sergeants find delightful, then points to two of the five pizza slices from the second box I've managed to rescue from her clutches. "Those, big boy, you eating *those*?"

"I plan to, if you give me more than two minutes, Hoover."

Maggie jumps up, grabs the slices away, licks each one. "Gonna eat *these*?"

"On second thought, no, Mags, go ahead." There is nothing on the little TV screen except for a crystal-clear picture of a Lawrence Welk re-run, and Maggie's been watching it like it's the first-broadcast airing of *The Ten Commandments*. I'm relieved when Lawrence bids us good-night and waltzes away with the Champagne Lady.

Maggie shakes her head. "Man, they don't make them like that anymore."

I reach over and kill the picture. "Thank God for small favors."

"Elitist."

I drag a chair from the little breakfast table next to the bed. I hand Maggie another Pabst before she can ask for it. She's been easier to deal with per beer.

She reaches out and takes it. "Thanks, dad. Is this where we have *the talk*?"

"This is where I take into account whatever you've been through to get to the place you are now, and I cut you slack, plus respect. And we move on."

Maggie stands, grabs the other chair, still holding the latest beer, and sits within reasoning distance. "And why this from you?"

"Since last I left you marooned in Hot Springs, I've witnessed a man die. This man was a railroader, and most of his career a good one. And like a whole bunch of folks, out here in the *wild*, he lost his way."

Maggie's serious. "And he couldn't get back?"

165

"I sound like the old guy on the park bench, shaking my fist at every kid running by, but it's appropriate here. *Back in the day*, sorry, a guy like Richie stood half a chance of sewing his life back together. He might hit bottom, the company might fire him for a year, no more, hire him back, and his family would never desert him, maybe get him to a twelve-step. Even if his wife divorced him, she'd probably be the one driving him to meetings. And Mrs. Richie, Wanda, partners forever. She'll be running his trap lines."

"Quite a picture."

"It's still the Old West, Mags. Richie left eleven kids behind. Half are grown with their own families, but now they've got to come back and make sure the ones still at home have the support a kid needs, especially now, and especially here."

"And that brings to mind our not-so-little Emily Straight." Maggie stands and starts cleaning up the dinner shrapnel.

"Right. And she is our present-day example, why things are not the way they used to be. Guys like Richie, and Emily's uncle George, they play cards, lose the ranch or the like, then drink or smoke or snort the pain away. Old story. Now, however—"

"Now there's a loan shark at every little high-stakes venue, directly connected to the broken-nose set in K.C. or Denver. And dope in its endless array, not only coming in from the south, quite a distance still, but from the north as well." Now we're getting near sensitive territory once more. I will tip-toe until further notified.

"Yes, Maggie, and I need to know more than I do about two individuals, and I'm going to be asking you, and never divulging my source. Nor do I care who signs your checks, as I know you to be someone who'd never take a dime from a coin return if it wasn't the one you dropped in the phone your own self."

Mags smiles. I'm relieved.

"Thank you. About time. Enough said." The room is straightened, and Maggie goes about putting water in the percolator for coffee. "But I'll be moving on."

"I'm—what? Why?"

"Not your doing, no cause and effect. Got my marching orders." She checks the only real window, satisfied with the nothingness she sees, only the deep dark. "Let's just talk in hypotheticals, knowing we're really not, shall we?"

"Sure." Got to like this person, even when I don't.

"So, trying to stay ahead of organized crime organizations, a specific intelligence agency floats a cooperative venture between two neighboring countries and a select few city and county and state law enforcement agencies—"

"A task force."

"Maybe." We both get it. "But the bad guys are badder than they've ever been, and we've been blind to trouble from the north, as—"

"Brown people are scary, and Canadians are white and polite."

"Maybe. And the bad guys have more intel than ever, buying up good-guys-gone-bad, even placing their own people in-country years before they activate them."

"Sleepers."

"Bingo." Maggi pours two mugs. "Should have tried this with you earlier."

"Coulda, shoulda, woulda—"

"Didn't. I know. Anyways, the reason for the kind of hush-hush directives we haven't seen since Russia and Cuba and missiles and Bays of Pigs. And why you were caught so very unaware—"

"I never would have tipped to Admin-Wonder-Woman being even more than a Deadwood police officer, hypothetically. And I still wonder what set of spook-initials appear at the top of your pay checks."

Maggie drains her mug and refills. "Barter economy. I get two goats and one sheep a month, chickens at Christmas."

I refill, too. "And you're on the move?"

"Maybe. Possibly, too many threads from seemingly-unrelated cases, some as old as—oh, I don't know—say, ten years? May or may not be directly connected to bad actors acting even worse as things progress, but coincidences—"

"—rarely are."

"And those directing someone kind of like me wish to take advantage of a wildcard actor no one saw riding into Dodge and stirring up trouble at every turn—"

"Howdy, ma'am."

"Howdy my ass, cowboy. But my supervisors see value in you, as long as you don't start fires they can't put out. In other words—"

"—I can do things, even troublesome things they wish they could do, but can't take the chance if things go south, as somewhere along the line they and their organization are responsible to the folks up top. Whereas I—"

"—answer to no-damn-body, as far as I can tell." With that, Maggie washes out both our mugs, then heads for my door. She stops and turns. "but know this, Will, those same people calling my shots, if they see you as trouble for them or theirs, you might find yourself in a tight spot, and the cavalry will *not* be riding in for the save."

Neither of us are kids, and even if we were, we know we don't play well together.

We hug, and she punches my shoulder, harder than called for, I believe.

"We'll always have Deadwood," I say, holding open the door.

"Sounds like a personal problem," she says, and disappears into the night.

I rise with the sun and spend an extra five in the steaming-hot shower stream. Two settings, freeze and fire. The little TV tells me the weather in Omaha and Lincoln, more than four hundred miles east of me, but Nebraska is Nebraska. Until you get past North Platte, as Buffalo Bill found, and then you are forever in the Dakota Territory, high plains and pine ridges and black mountains mistakenly named *hills*. I dry and dress and figure. What do bad guys, like ol' Jose Garcia and his bosses, or this slippery MacAdam—what do they make of this region? Is it just another backdrop for their sales and extortion and protection? Is there some hacienda in Jalisco or boathouse in Victoria where either villain just kicks back a few weeks in a year, cleans and stores his weapons, rambles down to a breakfast joint at a park or pier, tips the waiters and waitresses, pats the stray dogs, kisses babies?

And in rinsing the percolator for a pot of coffee of my own, I find a light grey folder, no outside markings, peeking out from under the telephone book from the night last.

"If you can hear me, Mags, thanks a million."

I don't open it until the coffee's in my cup. Then I do.

The inside cover has a faint series of numbers. I'm thinking area code plus seven numbers for the phone number, then three more, probably an extension. And, curiouser and curiouser, three more numbers, then in block letters—*Patagonia*. Geez, spooks. Can't live with 'em, et cetera, et cetera.

Onward. First page blank, I think. I hold it up to the light. Still blank. Turning the page, and there is a younger, meaner (it that is possible) Jose

Garcia, and directly beneath, smaller mugshots of three other men, one young and two old, and here's the kicker—all notated as *Jose Garcia*. If I had to guess, an organized enterprise of bad guys probably needs trained operatives to perform dirty work at the drop of a hat, sombrero or otherwise, and the button man, for lack of a better term, will always claim a generic name if caught or questioned.

Next page, blank again. I hold it to the light again, and still blank. Turn one more, and there is the Ghost of Christmas past. More realistically, the one close-to-decent-picture Maggie's people have of MacAdam, this one taken by an agent on stake-out, I figure, and he or she is snapping pics at a social venue, bigass party, tuxedoes and evening gowns, full tilt. The pictures show an interior not unlike some I've seen in my youth from Seattle to Vancouver, tours of great old houses I'd take in what free time I had in the war years. The exteriors, though, are stunning in their composition. All the shots are candid, of course, and people are obviously drifting from knot to knot of conversations.

And there is a spectacular moon-lit still, next to the beach, where three small groupings of peoples at least one or two sheets to the wind keep the party going. The closest to camera includes a nationally-known U.S. Senator from Washington State, retired just last term. To his right is a gorgeous Hispanic female in little black dress, leaning on a very tall figure, dressed in the formal-wear version of a Canadian naval uniform. It's not a stretch to imagine the identity of this young female, older now, whichever name she might be using in this picture, Montenegro or Calderone. It is, however, a kick in the pants to not only recognize, from all descriptions, a very possible young MacAdam, but to see him comfortably carrying a captain's insignia.

The second grouping holds no surprises. But the third—*ain't it always the third*—gives me much to ponder. Maybe too much.

There is one foolish-looking male, freshening the drink of a younger and chipper Maggie Connor. Here Maggie doesn't seem the least bit unhappy this male looks like a dead-ringer for Wesley Dunhill in his early-thirties. And there's a third person, maybe less effusive, more analytical, watching, her shoulder to the camera, presenting only a profile.

I feel cold, then hot. I drop the file folder and search through the front pocket of my back pack, the real pocket, not the fake one, and pull out a fold-out magnifying glass. I bring the glass and the folder under the kitchen strip of florescent light, and I apply the glass.

169

My cold and heat make way for nausea.

I'm looking at a younger profile of Sidney Turner Lowe.

Twenty-Seven

I look at my watch. I've been standing in the kitchen for roughly three hours. There is sweat across my head and neck. I hope I've been blinking.

I know this. I'm on automatic. I grab my backpack, revolver included, pack in the folder, and head down to the office. I don't bother to lock up unit twelve or *13*. Screw it. It seems anyone and everyone can access my digs whenever they are moved to do so. I make the office door, do not knock, walk around the front counter and up to Court, who is comfortably ensconced at his desk, happily doing his sole-proprietor paperwork—until I come rolling in.

I can see why this guy is successful. He can read body language like a *savant*.

Court jumps up and away from the desk, and angles his chair toward me. "How can I help?"

"You're the best." I sit and grab one of several telephone books stacked in an adjacent knotty-pine shelf. Court makes for his coffee pot with one eye on me. "Well, Mr. Dancer, I need about an hour of your know-how and opinions and sense of the possible versus the probable. Then I need to ask you to lie. So, what do you think?"

Court's already digging through airline schedules and car rental rates with one hand, and washing up coffee mugs with the other. I can't see his feet from here, but I wouldn't be surprised if he was sharpening two pencils with his toes.

"If this helps that Emily girl you spoke of, then no sweat, as long as it's the kind of lying like *I'm hiding Jews in my attic, and the Nazis knock and ask are you hiding Jews in your attic?* type of lying."

He's funny. I'm grateful. "Well, not quite as noble, but yeah, that category of deception."

He pulls up a high stool to use his counter as a desk, and points to his desk phone. "That's an outside line."

"Man, this could get expensive."

"I imagine you will bill some nasty cat with deep-pockets, and I will see recompense."

"Damn right."

Court and I read and research until noon. He's there every time I have a question, and he still never shaves one minute away from any of his customers. I take the yellow legal pad he supplied, now half-spent, and a couple of pockets worth of change for a pay phone in a booth just down the hill about a block. I could have done what I am about to much more easily at his desk, but the less he knows, the more honest he will appear when asked (and he *will* be asked), and I didn't want to spook him—pun intended—but his little joint might be bugged. I know, more than a little paranoid.

It's just me now in a pay booth with a panorama of the Pine Ridge. Other than a stray dog trotting down an alleyway, or the distant ring of the elementary school bell, I'm alone.

Now I can't hide from my gut, and I'm staring at that last picture in the folder again. I don't need to. It is what it is. I'm not a child in one respect, at least. I work in the protection business (the legal, ethical kind), a business flooded with constraints. Laws and statutes, rules and regulations, plus society's addendum of the appropriate, and one's personal sense of fairness— as opposed to justice—are only a few. So, I know people have dual lives, sometimes multiple lives, and they make great domestic and monetary sacrifices for the greater good. An incredibly high number of my associates and colleagues are honest. I'd rank them, you know, one to ten, ten being best, but I hate reducing the value of a human being to the numerical. It's enough to assert that people are mostly good, and those that aren't make it necessary for those in private or public law enforcement to appear to be other than who they really are, sometimes for days or weeks, and in a few cases, forever.

I also assert there's no operative of any stripe who feels absolutely fine upon finding out one's closest friend or relative is not who you believed her or him to be. Intellectually, most of people in enforcement can say, *wow, did* not *see* that *coming*, but deep down, for a millisecond at least, many will think, *but couldn't he have told* me?

I shake myself to the immediate and start dialing the operator. We initiate a series of long-distance calls. A full twenty minutes comes and goes, and I am finally ready for the last call. I place it through the operator, and wait. My pulse is normal, my heart rate the same. No one more surprised than me.

The phone's answered after one-half of a ring.

"Sidney—whatcha need?" Still a hint of a Boston accent. Wonder if *that's* real.

Wow, I thought I was better than that. For the record, *no.*

Sid tries again. "This is Sid, who needs a ride?"

Now I am neither hot nor cold. I activate. No intro. I read from the file.

"Area code 206-501-1173."

"Will?"

"Extension 447."

"Will, what the hell's going on? Are you in trouble, Will? Hello?"

"And what I'm guessing is a code, either for *all's well* or *the shit's hit the fan. Zero-zero-nine.*"

There is a pause on Sid's end. Then I hear the only extended selection of cursing from Sidney I can remember. And then another pause. She sounds tired.

"Will, I am so sorry. I don't catch your drift exactly, but you've run aground on my past somehow or other, and I know you feel like there's sand under your feet, and you're hurt—"

"Patagonia." And now a *very* long pause. I'm jamming in quarters and dimes at the operator's insistence. I speak once more when the bells quit ringing.

"*Patagonia*, goddamit."

"Will—"

"Grab a pencil, I know you're standing next to the order counter."

"Will—"

"Write. 7:09 tomorrow morning. United out of Riverton. You'll get into Rapid City at 10:49. I'll be there. Pack light. We will meet with one or two of my friends who are still, at this moment anyway, who they appear to be. One's FBI, the other's South Dakota CBI. One or both may be officially 'retired,' but everybody knows good agents never do."

"Will, listen, if I could, but I'd have to close the café, or get someone to watch, and we haven't even determined—"

"So time's a wastin', Sidney—I'm not asking. And bring your stuff, and please don't make me spell it out, *what* stuff, I'm running out of change."

"Will, this won't—"

"Pat. A. Gonia."

I hang up.

I'm watching the sun come up over Rapid City Regional Airport. I haven't slept for longer than thirty minutes at a shot, mostly in rest areas along my route. After my call to Lander, to Sid, I needed to go to Edgemont. I needed a conference with Emily Straight. Youth respect truth, I find, and my only real bet to keep her on the right path is to present myself openly, warts and all, then beg her to let me run down her dad's mystery alone. This way, I hope, she keeps her business to herself, keeps her head down, back to school, and somehow, someday knows the truth. Will it set her free? Nothing really does, but I'm open to suggestions.

After Edgemont, I beelined to Deadwood. Although Mags is in the wind for now, her Captain Patterson at Deadwood PD can now see me without wanting to shoot me. Not right away, anyway. We talked off the record. He was never comfortable with the DEA's arrangement to provide cover for one of their agents within a task-target municipal police department, but the South Dakota CBI loved the idea, and Patterson was over-ruled. And he'll always be thankful for the administrative make-over Maggie pushed the department through, and that in what turned out to be her spare time. Now gone, and again, off the record, turns out Maggie rebuilt admin in record time, then successfully handed it off to a first-year HR employee who only has to press the buttons and pull the levers Maggie engineered. So, where was she when she wasn't on property?

Captain Patterson, escorting me out on moderately good terms, said *damned if I know.*

Before I could make for Rapid, I needed to do some footwork. Apropos Wesley Dunhill, owner of the Goathorn, at least until he pulled a major dumb stunt, kidnapping ol' Doc, then hightailing it when one of his crack employees shot ol' Doc.

And, of course, there's ol' Doc himself. When last I saw him, he was shipping off to an ER for treatment of his calf wound, then for an interrogation with Captain Patterson, the very officer who cleared me for killing one of Wesley's goons in defense of Maggie and Doc. I still have to face an official hearing on that situation, and here's hoping I don't get held over on a manslaughter charge. I suspect that will depend on whether the family of said dead goon has been contacted by Walt Whitman, Esquire.

Doc released himself from care and made his way back to Crawford via Edgemont. I imagine he needs to shepherd his sheep, the surviving family members of the Crawford taxi van tragedy. But I've seen him fall off the wagon at least once, and I'm hoping he gets back to his Daisy in one piece. Besides, he knows plenty about what I need to know about, and he's cagey, and I've got to find my way around and past him.

So, I run down anyone in or around the Goathorn that day who might provide some eyewitness testimony if necessary. The two bartenders on duty while Wesley and Doc drank, then argued. Or one or two barflies sitting in close proximity before and after the incident. And the EMTs answering the emergency call when the smoke cleared, and the Deadwood PD officers first to the scene. Front line people, first to the call—these are usually the folks with the most objective and freshest perception of any event. They practice their training, and train for their practice. They are consummate professionals.

I started early enough in the day—still mostly sleeping in the Bronco—to catch many of these people just coming off or on their shifts, and I didn't disrespect them with stupid questions, or leading questions, or questions even a six-year-old would find condescending. I asked who-why-when-where-and-how questions, and then shut up and listened. It was a tight fit, but I made Rapid and the airport just as a United puddle jumper, originating in Riverton and having to go down and back to Denver, touched down with one gentle *thunk!*

I swing the Bronco about so that I am parked in the passenger pick-up lane, two cabs behind me, an extended van in front of me, all waiting for customers booked at any of the local hotels. I'm not parking in the short term, nor going inside to wait with the families and friends and business associates clustered around two ailing coffee machines, speaking about the weather or The Series, or basketball, or football, college and pros. I've said six people are a stretch for me, and I don't want to rain on anyone's parade. Well, maybe Sid's.

Man, this is going to be complicated. Sidney and I have what I'd thought was the textbook platonic relationship. We appreciate the gender differences in communicating, and maintaining a relationship, and all things *trust*—how it's built, and nurtured, and protected. I know Sid's an only child, and I've never used that phrase in conversation with her, and this is because I do not

175

want her thinking I have her pegged with the stereotype. And she knows I have a sister, oldest of my siblings by ten years, about Sid's age, so there may be some overlap in roles there as well. But we've navigated contexts and each other's expectations for quite a while, and it's been a mutually-acclaimed success.

Right up until I opened a little gray folder.

And on cue, out the front revolving door, one leather bag in one hand, a leather purse in the other, dressed as she would be opening the café, but with an addition of a silver watch cap half-covering her ears, walks Sidney. Directly to the Bronco. She tosses her bag and purse in the back, sits down in front, buckles the seat belt, and finally, turns and looks at me.

"Good morning, Allen."

"Good morning, Sid." I pull out and head south. "Thanks for coming."

"Did I have a choice?"

I turn right again at the big illuminated billboard instructing me to *See Mount Rushmore Today!*

"We always have choices."

Sidney adjusts the passenger's bucket forward as far as possible, and now she can see out as well as anyone.

"You asked me to reconstruct my livelihood at a moment's notice, and to do it completely on the basis of trust, no explanation given."

"You're point?"

"Shut up. I need coffee. Why are we headed to Mount Rushmore?"

I target a drive-through coffee window, stop, and order two large, black.

We both finally look each other in the eye, more than a glance. I steer back into traffic.

Sidney sips her coffee, even though it's too hot.

"Now, Allen. Now we're cookin' with gas."

Twenty-Eight

Sidney rides in a bit of a side-saddle. She's belted in but small enough to sit with her legs tucked under her, and utilizing the visibility the Bronco affords, her head is on a swivel.

"First time?" I ask.

"No, actually. It was 1939, I was 24, with a couple of like-minded girlfriends from my grad school cohort. They're burnt out, I'm burnt out, we're about a month from defending our dissertations. Too much wine, and one of the gals just got wired her money for plane fare from her folks in San Francisco, and we rent a car instead, play darts with a map of the U.S.—and we're headed to the Rushmore project."

The aspen stands sprinkled between massive sheets of pines and firs are about half way to full gold. Every few miles, station wagons full of campers, or those damn RV's, are parked in turnouts, designed for photo-bug tourists to stop away from traffic, to snap their brains out.

"Project?" I dodge a station wagon pulling out in front of me, just managing to get around it and miss an oncoming RV. Sid barely reacts.

"Yeah, *project*, back then. The four presidents as we view them today were completed in '41, and—I'm sure you remember—in December of that year most of us became pretty busy with other concerns than tourism, so Mount Rushmore didn't get a lot of play until the early fifties."

We speak not at all now, both watching the scenery slip by, and the station wagon I got around, get back around us in a no passing zone. "Sid, we can clear the air, 'Patagonia,' then maybe I can start to piece together my experiences up here, and then—"

Sid's eyeballing the station wagon again. "Then?"

"I beg your pardon, eternally—I've had another similar experience with someone I thought I knew everything about. But didn't."

177

"So, it's really a 'you' problem, dealing with massive ego, blah, blah, blah."

"I take that as you accepting my apology."

Sid's watching the station wagon with greater interest. "There's a handful of states that don't require license plates on the front bumpers, just the rear."

"Right. Like Arizona."

"And New Mexico, and Pennsylvania."

"But," says Sid, slipping out of her seatbelt, sliding halfway over her seatback to grab her leather bag, "I am not aware of any state that encourages no plate on either bumper." Sid's hand is in and out of the bag like she's quick-drawing on a dirt main street at high noon. Save this time, she pulls a small pair of binoculars.

"What else is in there?" Knowing Sid—or I guess, *not* knowing who I thought I did—there might just about be anything in there.

She puts the glasses to her eyes and spins the focus wheel. "You said 'bring your stuff,' and I brought stuff, so—"

"—shut up. Got it."

"So, I'm thinking we have a stolen vehicle, or a very poor person driving the only car he, yes, he, has and can't afford license, insurance, et cetera."

There is one of those very few passing lanes in the Black Hills coming up in just a sec. "If I've stolen a car, and I want to keep the car, why do I pass like an idiot, drawing attention?"

"Let's find out." Sid nods at the passing lane sign, this one saying we have one-and-a-half miles until the extra lane vanishes. Not a helluva lot of time. But there's more traffic coming the other way right now, and only one other car, a black Crown Vic, about two car-lengths back, waiting to pass us as well.

So, here we go.

Once more, for me time does *not* go fluid, it just becomes complicated exponentially. I floor the Bronco, gears whine, same time the rearview fills with the Vic, coming up on us like a storm, so my pedal remains flat, I whistle past the station wagon. I glance over to see who the driver might be, and I can't as Sid's in the way, but she can see. And whoever it is she sees, her right hand draws a .45 Beretta out of her purse as fast as the binoculars moved previously. She clears the safety but doesn't raise the weapon. Now I'm past the station wagon by five lengths at least. And it seems the wagon's driver is going to respond, but the Vic is still on our tail, and pulls back into the right lane, right behind us.

Before I can say *holy crap*, Sid spins around at the sound of the wagon flooring it, jerking into the other lane as the passing lane is long gone. And this is a poor idea on several levels, as no more than a quarter-mile down the road, there is a tractor-trailer rig pulling a flatbed with two sea-worthy containers stacked one on the other, headed our way at full speed limit, as they have a right to be, being lawful and all.

And if there was no more than an inch-leeway to make the move, the Crown Vic jerks into the left lane, and this holds the station wagon in place. It almost seems the Vic-driver is counting, and then the Vic jerks back into the right lane, directly on our bumper.

The station wagon can suddenly see the road ahead, and there is the oncoming semi, and the right lane is full of our Bronco and the Crown Vic, and there is only one choice for the wagon driver. At the last possible second, the driver veers left, off the road, down the shoulder, through a stock fence, and axle deep into a freshly cultivated alfalfa field. As chance has it, the next pull-out for tourists is clear. We take it, as does the Vic.

I sit still waiting for adrenaline to subside, for my calf cramps to unknot, for my breathing to resume. I look to Sid, and her Beretta is not in sight, nor her binoculars, and she's poking her hair back under the watch cap in the little mirror strapped to the fold-out visor above her. She's also using the mirror to case the figure exiting the Vic, and coming up on her side of the Bronco. She rolls down her window and extends her hand to a man maybe ten years younger than me, similar height and weight, but swarthy in a Mediterranean-bent.

"Bobby Delaine, and you must be Sidney? Sidney Turner Lowe?" He smiles like he loves life, or the early-morning portion, anyway.

Sid smiles, at Bobby, then me, then back to Bobby. "And you're a Fed, and if you are not, put me on an ice floe and kick it out to sea." They're still shaking hands.

I shut off the Bronco, pop the seatbelt, and turn Sid's way. "Once our long-reigning regional FBI Special Agent in Charge."

Sid releases Bobby. "Once?"

Bobby's straight-faced now. "Rumor has it I am retired."

Sid opens her door, moving Bobby over a couple of steps, gets out and stretches like a cat on a divan. "Once a SAC, always a SAC, Bobby Delaine."

I come around the vehicle to meet them, and I get the fish-eye from Sidney. "When did you call for our unofficial backup, this morning before dawn?"

"You got me wrong, Sid. I did not suggest Bobby should ride protection on this segment of travel."

"He's right." Bobby's walking away toward the Vic, motioning us to follow. He opens the front passenger door for Sid, points to the back-passenger door for me, and circles around to his driver's side. Once in, he pulls a thermos from the console with three large Styrofoam cups. He is the rare man who can talk and pour out at the same time.

"Will did, however, ring me up yesterday, much to my surprise, and ask me if he could visit my new Hill City house, and bring a guest. The accompaniment from the airport was just something to fill my time on a beautiful fall morning in the Black Hills."

Sid takes her cups, sniffs it, smiles with approval, and sips, and swallows, and looks Bobby in the eye.

"My ass."

I amazed how that sounds coming from a newcomer to her seventies, and with just enough South Boston spin to give it some heat.

Bobby laughs. "Yeah, mine, too." He hands me my coffee over the seat. "Just as you described her, Will. Which begs the question, why would she possibly be caught dead with the likes of you?"

Sid's still sipping. "I may want to get this stuff for the café." Then to Bobby and me: "I don't buy the 'former' part, the 'used-to-be' part of anybody's story. We all have pasts, we all incurred favors, and we all owe favors, and no one can tell anyone else what the statute of limitations are on integrity. I know what I see, boys."

She holds out her cup to Bobby for a top-off. "I see a young-at-heart and rigorous FBI SAC, one I'm guessing got his start as a beat cop in some east-coast-big-city precinct, and the guy shows promise, makes detective in record time, works through Vice to Robbery to Homicide"—Bobby smiles broadly— "gets itchy for the big time, or gets recruited, and then it's the FBI, or a military branch, or the spooks. All of this, of course, complicated by the extreme effects of a world war, Korea, Viet Nam, plus cold war gigs he just won't play, and others he can't wait to try on."

I stay quiet. Never learned anything while I was talking.

Bobby pours his second. "Who we talking about here, Sidney? Me, you, hell, maybe ol' Will."

"Not finished, Bobby." Bobby shrugs. Sid's on. "So, why would an FBI guy with a solid-gold career appear to retire early, then *not* go back east to his childhood haunts, baseball, hot dogs, apple pie and mama? Instead he hangs out with the little woman, takes up bird watching, maybe a little golf?"

Bobby takes a look around the two cars quickly, then returns his gaze to Sid. "The ring-necked pheasant is our state bird, although not native, as it was introduced by visitors in 1898. I myself favor the common quail. And my handicap is 18, as I am a lefty, and I slice accordingly."

Sid's almost done for the moment. "And the asswipe in the station wagon? I assume a law enforcement officer of some flavor is hunting for the driver as we speak?"

"Absolutely." Bobby's more than mock serious. "That is, I suppose there is."

A thought occurs. "You got a peek inside the wagon, Sidney, at which time you pulled a .45."

"Yes, Allen. This is true. And my reflex wasn't so much based on the driver's ugly mug—though he looked distinctly unhappy about the whole situation—as I was impressed by the second occupant."

Bobby and I in unison: "Second?"

"Yes, and it is gratifying to have your undivided attention. There was a person folding up as tight as possible, in the passenger's floor. And she looked up for only a second, and then we were past."

Again, unison: "She?"

Then Bobby reaches across Sid, pops the glove compartment open, pulls a radio mike out on a long, stretchy cord, and fills two minutes in chatter to a "Unit 6," and "9" and "Home Blue," sharing the joy of the real possibility *two* fugitives might be at large, and one may well be a woman.

When Bobby finishes, Sid turns my way and winks. "When I retired from government service, nobody gave me a gift radio, complete with a bunch of fun friends to play with."

I stretch out across the back seat, still having some trouble with calf-cramps. "Here's a thought. We all know what's official, what's not, who's cold, who's hot—we just talk, all hypothetical, right? No questions digging deeper than one of us can stand, no one wants anybody's covers or ops blown, nobody shot—"

"—if possible," says Bobby. "You in, Sid?"

"I'm not in Lander, am I?"

Twenty-Nine

Bobby bids us follow him to the new house, just north of Hill City, on an acreage in the trees at about five thousand feet, in a setting even God might initially mistake for heaven. We arrive and take up the most comfortable wicker rockers I've ever known. Esther, Bobby's one and only wife, mother of three, with their last kid in high school, is a phenomenal baker, so more coffee and a fresh apple pie appears before our very eyes. We enjoy enough small talk to cover our voracious consumption of bakery goods, and Esther excuses herself. Bobby hears a phone ring, tells us that particular phone is in his office, and he must check it out.

Sid and I sit and regard a conspiracy of ravens debating whatever ravens disagree about. I'm betting it's some fresh roadkill; Sid maintains the alpha raven is telling two adolescents it's time to vacate the nest. I told Sid *my kids couldn't wait to leave the nest*. She said *I get that*.

Bobby's back. He gets a refill and a sliver of pie. We wait. Civility rules.

Bobby chews a bit and sips a little. Ready. "Local law enforcement has an 'all-points' out on our two station wagon lovers, and Artie Gleeson just happens to be doing a little fishing this week in our little town, and he's on his way. Loves pie."

I look to Sid to explain Artie, and she raises a hand to stop me.

"Arturo Luis Gleeson, former Assistant Director, South Dakota Criminal Bureau of Investigation, now emeritus fellow and active consultant to same agency."

My eyebrow, the one still working, raises in surprise.

Sid refills her mug. "I had thirteen hours before my flight left Riverton, Allen, and that's plenty of time for homework." She looks to Bobby. "Well, sir, it looks like most of us in these parts used to be other than we presently are, and to the general public, we appear out of the way, on the shelf, so to speak."

Bobby says, "Don't we?" And he refills. Esther's back with fresh carafes, a cup for Artie, what appears to be banana bread, and four grey folders—same damn grey as Maggie gifted me. Bobby thanks Esther, and there's something in her eyes saying she's as much a part of whatever's going on as any of us.

Bobby continues. "So, the driver, according to information supplied by the Wyoming Highway Patrol, may be one Jose Garcia—"

I'm opening the folder. "—arrested recently by Keith Raven—"

Sid opens hers. "—just outside of Shoshoni."

I reach for the new carafe. "And I will no longer be surprised, about anything."

Sid's on page three already. "Finally."

Bobby's listening to a jazz trio in his head, if his tapping fingers, right hand, are any indication. "Now *that's* quite a story. Seems Will here advised one Phillip Phillips—"

Sid's loving this. "Oh, Allen, tell me you didn't buy that name."

I'm looking for a hole to crawl in. "Bald, mid-fifties, white, black hornrims with clip-on sunglasses—bought it lock and stock."

Bobby's enjoying this almost as much as banana bread. "Yeah, well, this ICE clerk, who we know now is neither with ICE, nor a clerk, picked up Garcia by himself, assured the WHP he would pick up a competent ICE enforcement officer at Casper, and together they would make sure Garcia would find his way to the Sonora side of Nogales, the deportment dump."

I think I *do* feel worse. "Unfortunately—"

Bobby: "Yeah, right. No one has seen either Garcia or Phil since. Well, Phil's vehicle was spotted outside of Fort Collins, Colorado, one of those *Flying J* truck stops, nothing in it except that very pair of horn rims—and the glass in same was just glass, no prescription."

And me: "Okay, now I cannot feel worse than I do."

Sidney, with a straight face. "Treat it as a learning moment, and let's move on, shall we?"

We hear gravel crunch on the long driveway leading from the highway to Bobby's porch. A brand-new four-wheel-drive Ford F-150 leaves a trail of white dust behind, slows, and parks only ten feet away. Out jumps an energetic man, maybe late sixties, not a hair on his head, aviator shades, shirt and jeans and jacket, all denim.

We all shake hands with, and make room for Artie Gleeson. Gleeson's an oddity in these parts. His family is exclusively Mexican for generations, save for one crazy Irishman who came to Mexico on a whim in the twenties, married and stayed, lending his name to a family exclusively Mexican-American ever since. He speaks fluent Spanish of course, long ago married Ana Cisneros, and together they founded a moderately-large branch of the family in South Dakota. He got a job here after spending five years with me as special agents on the Great Northern, right out of a law academy in Las Cruces, New Mexico. Five years as a railroader were five more than Arturo could stand, so he hooked up the with the Spearfish Police Department as a traffic officer, they be thinking (Artie's pretty sure), they were hiring themselves an Irishman, until the interview. So, Artie couldn't do as good a job as his colleagues, he had to do a better job to be average. And he did, from there to departments throughout South Dakota, finally with CBI. Bobby affectionately refers to Artie as *the good Mexican.* Artie calls Bobby *an adequate gringo.*

With a complete cast, things get thick fast. Bobby suggests he leads, as someone must facilitate, and we all agree.

"I'll start at present, work my way back. So, today, we know ol' Jose might be headed back north, with new orders from Jalisco, or to fulfill old orders interrupted by a smart-ass railroad agent—"

"*Special* special agent," I say, but only to clarify. There are chuckles.

"Whatever," Bobby continues, "you set him up in Shoshoni, Will, and queered his play, and I wouldn't be surprised if he desires to make his errand right with his Mexican bosses, and/or seek revenge on that old fart in that old wreck of a Bronco."

Artie slips on cheaters, and takes over. "Agreed. So, we here all know Will, and we all know what I am about to say will be disregarded—*Allen, be careful.*"

Sid's impatient. "Next."

Artie says, "Yes, Sidney. You were involved at one point in one of your careers with Wesley Dunhill, if these photo copies taken several years back are real."

Sidney wants to draw a line in the sand as far as what this boys' club she's surrounded by will figure they can get away with. "You haven't asked a question. But, yes, those copies are accurate. And I'll tell you what I can, as I'm sure all of us are going to share info none of us can cite, or place in real time, at least not without a clearance so high none of us will ever see it in this life. Right?"

All heads nod.

She smiles. "The photo is taken at a shore-side mansion in Washington state, between Tacoma and Seattle."

I'm taking notes on the back of the folder. "No location?"

"Not for you." She doesn't mean to offend. I don't take it as such. "I was on a teaching sabbatical from a Boston university, and I was contacted by a friend I worked for during the war. He was still in *the business,* so to speak, and he knew few folks would recognize me on the west coast, even fewer in the northwest. I posed as a journalist, gained entrance into this particular dinner party, and started interviewing everyone in sight. As the party's winding down, a handful of us migrated to the rear porch, out around the pool and the pier. I didn't know anyone, save one person, and she only by reputation."

I chance it. "Maggie Connor"

Sid begins again. "Yes, well, that night she propositioned the man you see her with, pretty much in front of God and everybody."

I don't want to believe it. "Wesley Dunhill?"

Sid's taken back by my reaction. "Surely he's not on your screen around *here*?"

Artie asks, "Why *not* here?"

Sid sighs. "Okay, look. This Dunhill, when I was paying a favor back to a buddy, that buddy may have been with Interpol, who may or may not have been tailing Dunhill for a money laundering scam they believed he was conducting from Copenhagen—the whole thing turned into guns for more than one African rebel organization."

I'm up. "Then, out of nowhere, Wes disappears from Europe, re-surfaces in Seattle or Tacoma or somewhere in between, and your buddy wants you there pronto, as he knows and trusts your previous work, 'back in the day.'"

Sid nods. "That's pretty much it. I can enter that particular party based on my Boston academic career, and that's me, a studious middle-aged college professor-turned aspiring journalist, appearing to be half-stewed on their open bar."

And Bobby takes a shot. "And you were also acting as a sort of homing device for the clandestine photographer, right? *Get shots of anyone I pause at for more than one minute,* something like that?"

"Yeah, something." Sid scans the porch. "You're saying Dunhill's here? Excuse the following, but what the hell's he doing in the middle of nowhere? I mean, as he sees it."

Artie stands and stretches. "We know what we suspect, and we suspect he started another money laundering set up through an investment scheme in a small but trustworthy insurance company—maybe things in Copenhagen, as you say, got hot, we don't know. But one five-hundred-year hurricane tears up most of Florida, the insurance guys can't spread out the debt with anyone else, all they can do is go under. But in no time, the Goatherd in Deadwood is for sale, then bought, again in no time, and the new sole proprietor is Wesley Dunhill."

And now I'm due again.

"Then I walk in late to the party with a story of my own. A dirty special agent comes to me to save his ass over a botched investigation ten years back, one triggered by the surviving daughter of the taxi van driver, one of four fatalities involved. She and I have two things in common. She has trouble with authority, as do I—news bulletin—especially the kind telling her since she was five that her dad was responsible for the accident, and had her mom so scared she never shared any of the details."

Bobby: "The other thing?"

"The other thing is 'coincidence.' Neither of us entertain them. Why, for instance, does a Doctor Lenore, a GP from Crawford, take such an interest in the entire incident? Why start visiting Emily's family, out of nowhere, six months after the accident, and still doing the visit routine up until about a month ago? And he's developed relationships with the widows of the engineer and the brakeman. Why? And why does he show no interest in the mystery brakeman, the woman climbing aboard the van last, the one whose body no one stepped up to claim?"

Bobby's shaking his head. "It can still sound pretty weak, Will. Ol' Doc's getting along in years, I imagine, maybe he just fancies himself a shepherd of sorts, right? A GP usually has more than enough empathy to go around. Maybe he just takes care of people."

"Maybe," I agree. "But out of nowhere, once more, Maggie's in the middle of things, then taking her leave, then she doesn't know what's going on, but it turns out she knows Wes Dunhill, and not just lately, but years back. And

Doc's no random stranger, that is, someone somewhere briefed her accordingly."

No one speaks to this. And once more I can't help but feel I'm the only one confused about Maggie's role in this case, or any case in particular.

So I launch one, just to see who gets splattered. "And, of course there's good ol' George Straight."

Two interesting things happen. The first is that the last person I figured would or could react is Sid, the Massachusetts academic.

"George Straight? *Amarillo by Morning? All My Exes Live in Texas? That* George Straight?" And Sid is taken by Bobby's look to Artie, and Artie's look to the sky, and even Bobby's Esther, back on the porch to freshen mugs and plates, but frozen in place at the mention of the name.

"The George Straight, Sidney," I say, "who asked his brother to take his shift in Crawford the night that same taxi-van supposedly took the lives of Harley Straight and three trainmen. And the guy, though none of my business, who is far more likely to have fathered Emily Straight—and who just recently turned up at Emily's step-aunt's door in Deadwood, dehydrated and beaten and in shock, after being a missing person for nine years. And last I heard, being held in a Rapid City Hospital under police guard as 'a person of interest' while recuperating."

Bobby's interior phone rings again, Esther's inside to answer, then back in a flash with a *Bobby, it's Edgemont.* And Bobby's gone a minute, maybe, then sits again, looking each of us in the eye before spilling.

"The Edgemont station agent is an old friend—"

Sid rolls eyes. "Of course."

"—and he's just off a call with the new station agent at Crawford, and she reports a fire on property, still going as we speak."

I'm standing already, looking to Sid. "Let me guess. The fire's originated on the cemetery track, probably in a car labelled BN 102371 and sealed as a crime scene, evidence inside."

Bobby's standing with Artie, making it plain they, too, have things to do. "Close, Will. Two cars go up at the same time. Yours, yes, and an old hide box on the hides track, one with a suspiciously fresh letter-number ID—" Bobby consults a fresh note from Esther—"SPS, that's Spokane, Portland and Seattle, right?"

And Sid and I are making for the Bronco in the driveway. I call back to the porch: "and the number is 2371?"

And Bobby hands the note to Artie, and Artie smiles. "2371, sure as hell."

Thirty

I'm bending speed limits on U.S. 385 south, passing RV's, praying the traffic lights are green, or have a very long yellow. Sid's paying little attention to the reckless decisions I make, as long as I pull them off. But she's paying intense attention to her copy of the gray folder, and my auto copy of Rand McNally. Then, so much like Sid, she has a question, or at least a supposition to explore.

"I'm feeling more and more that you have stumbled upon two cases here, one orchestrated by railroaders, and one manipulated by non-railroaders. And both constrained and empowered by police at several levels."

I'm happy but confused. These emotions are not mutually exclusive in men. I suspect Sidney in curious but systematic. "I am happy to hear that, as I feel exactly the same way, but for different reasons."

Sid's deep into the road map. "We can only hope." She takes a straight edge and a Casio pocket-calculator from her bag, and marks a series of lines on the page of South Dakota, then flips back to mark up the page containing Nebraska. Finally she enters numbers from the map into the calculator, plays an etude or two on her keyboard, then tucks her legs beneath her and rolls down the window.

"Golly, we are moving fast."

"When I can, Sid. So, I'm sitting back there at Bobby's watching topics tossed about, and Bobby, then Artie are watching us for reactions—"

"—and we are doing the same with them." Sid sees a mileage sign and takes two more notes.

"Right. But even Esther was surprised by the fire news. And, did you notice, she went back into Bobby's office immediately." There are flashing red lights two rises ahead. I'm in no mood for a slow-down.

Sid sees ahead, too. "I got it." She consults the big map and my old gazetteer. "There's a state highway coming on the left in about a quarter-mile, 89, then about half way to Custer, 87, and we then re-join 385."

I slow. "Upside, little or no traffic to wrestle with."

"Downside, for a little less than an hour, we are on our own."

I glance at Sid, and she looks back direct. "So, you suggest we may have a tail, as our station wagon couple are still at large."

"And why were they in our vicinity in the first place? And why was the woman trying to hide?" I take the left. The state highway is good, if a bit narrow, and the pines and firs are thick to the edge of the shoulders. Even where a gap might exist, ground covers abound circling islands of scrub oak, fiery red. An early fall. "Okay, here's how this seems to sort. Please interject."

"Please try and stop me."

"Right. There is a connection between the railroaders involved. Look at George and Richie. The region is swimming in this kind of hard-luck story. Even Howard Humboldt tries his hand at a low-price cathouse-in-a-trailer, comes back to bite him. He's vulnerable years later. Bad guys could come calling to influence train activity, maybe even individual employees. George wasn't railroad, strictly speaking, but he ran in those crowds as a crew-hauler. Richie didn't have any pull as a fill-in operator, a relief operator, but his gambling problems return as often as his wife has another baby. And sooner or later he is a station agent at a vital intersection, and he is vulnerable to those non-railroading interests."

"So, the Crawford Taxi Tragedy?"

"Could be nothing more than a new driver misses a curb, everybody dies."

Sid's surveying the four directions, as if she expects company to bound from the forests in ambush. "Or somebody saw something they weren't supposed to see, and they got popped."

"Or, and it's just a hunch, the not-railroaders, the bad guys—"

"—cartel, Canuck, the ethnically-defined crime families, or a one-time partnership of two or three local losers—"

"—right, have spent some real time and money doing some outside-the-box thinking, not necessarily organized crime strategy—"

"—because you can always count on greed."

We're coming up on the change in state highways at an intersection marked on both sides by old pine shacks. "Absolutely. Plan and scheme, even rehearse, but somewhere somehow, one of the bad guys is going to let greed feed impatience, and that impatience will spread like a virus, and pretty soon most of the gang or family is ready to move before the planning is complete. And this is such a certainty, law enforcement can get a little too relaxed, a little too certain that the bad guys are going to shoot themselves in the foot, or feet."

The pine shack on the left has one lonely gas pump out front, and a hand-painted sign proclaiming **Beer**. The shack on the right used to be—might still be—a drive-in burger joint. The driveway menus with speakers at each parking space are still there. Neither shack looks like it's open right now. But neither sports a "CLOSED" sign, either. I pull the Bronco off to the right, but ten yards short of the drive-in. I turn off the Bronco and turn to Sid.

She's still surveying. "Is that what you think is going on, maybe with Bobby and Artie and Esther? Group-think? *We wait long enough, the bad ones'll make the big mistake, and we'll nab them, as this is how success has always looked.*"

"Maybe. And maybe Maggie's a part of it, too."

Now, Sidney quits rubber-necking, reaches for her purse, slips out the .45 Beretta, and routinely begins a check of safety and loads, spare clips—

What the—"Sid, there's a second outline in your purse, very much shaped like another Beretta."

Sid's checking immediate terrain, then me. "That would be my second Beretta. And don't tell me that old Police Special is an only child."

"Twins actually. But something else is going on with Maggie. If Bobby and Artie are task-forcing it, and growing complacent, or God-forbid, on the take, they're together in it."

"But Maggie's a lone wolf, you're point-of-view, so she's a player, or getting played?"

And I reach for my backpack just as—*are you kidding me*—a 1976 Buick station wagon, complete with fake wooden body panel, comes around the corner from the south, but rolling at walking speed. I roll down my window, and I can actually hear the engine barely above an idle. It pulls up next to the gas pump at the shack across the highway and goes silent.

Sid's Berettas are next to her on the console, spare clips are in her jacket pocket, and her head is secure in her watch cap. She watches the station wagon, ventures, "Looks like what, twenty-five yards?" Looks to me, staring at her. And laughs. "You said, *bring your stuff.*"

I laugh, even though the station wagon should prevent me from doing so. "I didn't know your stuff would include strategic planning materials and weaponry, plus not just a little bit of attitude."

"Yeah, well, the State Department—"

"My ass."

"And in light of trying to save it, and mine, I think there is a wee bit of a clearing this side of the drive-in, over there by the scrub oak? It looks impervious, but I bet it's shadow there, and better cover if we can get behind the drive-in."

"A couple quick questions, agent," I stall while I check the cylinders in both revolvers, then surprise Sid with an old stun grenade from under my seat, adhered to the back frame.

"Skip explaining the grenade, Allen, it'll make a great story if we live."

"No story. I was new on the docks in Seattle, eighteen, the war, I followed a bull-headed pier sergeant around, some dockworkers were threatening a strike, mostly drunk, the sergeant wanted to lob stunners to break it up. I accidentally cold-cocked him, took both grenades, left him behind a bar in a back alley."

"What happened to the other grenade?"

"Ay, *that's* the story." The wagon's passenger and driver's doors open as one, and a figure emerges from both.

We see. We are given pause. "That's my first question, Sid. So, how do we know they don't just want to talk? And, if this goes south, we know nothing about who is or who isn't in either shack. The station waggoneers could have back up waiting—"

"Or hostages, or no one at all—all things we will find out soon enough. But everything hence forward is best approached by getting cover between us, and a position we choose, not one we are forced to choose."

"And if that little clearing isn't a pathway through the bush?"

"Then," Sid says as she pulls gently on the door handle, "You will have a decision to make, as you, Allen are leading the way." And before I can exhale, she's out the door.

I grab my *stuff*, open the door and run. Straight for that damn shadow, which stills looks exactly like one the closer I get. I hear car doors slam more than once from across the highway, and I'm aware Sid is just behind me and to my left. As I get to the shadowed area, I realize she could have passed me and been around me in two seconds—she's actually laying back a little to cover my six.

Whether I'm frantic or embarrassed over a woman eleven years my senior is keeping me safe, I resolve to make an opening into the dense undergrowth if none exists, even if doing so shreds and breaks skin and bone. But it doesn't come to that. Sid's eyes are better than mine, too, and the shade turns to a small clearing with sawdust in small piles strewn about, and one or two sawhorses folded and leaning against sawn-off pine trunks. Someone's been gathering firewood very much without permits, and I thank them. Our way is clear, Sid is around me, and we're around to the other side of the old drive-inn, still in tree cover, and in position to meet these strangers by surprise whether they come from the same direction, or they come straight on from the gas pump.

Sid says, "Ideas on placement?"

"I defer."

"Cool. So we can both take the backside of that fallen log, maybe ten feet from the highway shoulder, we aren't back-lit, we should be literally in the dark, for them anyway." We move there accordingly. Both of us set upon and around the log, distributing ammo to clean dry placements within arm's reach. I put two flash grenades on the log equidistant between Sid and myself.

Sid glances at the stunners, back to me. "I thought you have one of two, and there was a story."

"Yes, I have one of two, one in the Bronco, one in the backpack, and *that's* the great story. Pretty neat, huh?"

Now the waggoneers move to the back of their wagon, the tail gate is open, and both have their heads inside, prepping something for somebody.

Sid hands me a spotting scope from her backpack, saying nothing. I train it on the wagon.

She pulls another and scans the road between us and the wagon. "First, we still have twenty-five yards between us?"

"Oh, yeah."

"Is the gas pump as old as it looks, and is it currently in operation?"

I see current inspection stickers under the dollars-and-cents rolling numbers on the pump face, but the pump still sports a translucent globe on top, an advertising feature abandoned twenty years ago. The per gallon price is 98 cents a gallon, highway-robbery in Topeka, Kansas, but par for the course in a thriving tourist area.

"The pump's got twenty years on it, minimum. But the inspection's current, and somebody's using it regularly, even paying a buck a gallon. Just a second." It occurs to me then to scan the shack. I'm looking for owners who might be inside and can't get outside, or the odd teen employee, duct-taped to a pop machine with a sock in his mouth.

"And no one inside, all the driveway equipment—windshield cleaners, air hoses, oil cans and the like—all stacked inside. And today is Sunday, so—"

"All clear." Sid takes one knee and asks, "so, to paraphrase Butch Cassidy, *who the hell* are *these guys*?" We both train our spotters. I, for one, wish we had not.

I'm pulling every image from my brainpan at once, and the female, now standing in front of the vehicle, seemingly without care number one, is a dead ringer for Stella Montenegro *aka* Maria Calderone. I, too, would look as confident if I, too, held an assault rifle at my side. And the man—*oh, hell no*—looks just *too* like Jose Garcia, duck hunter. I've told Sid the story, how Keith Raven and I ambushed Jose's Tomcat, then brilliantly shipped him off for deportation with a fake ICE agent I bought hook, line, and sinker.

Sid: "The woman is your Maria/Stella?"

Me: "Yeah."

Sid: "The man?"

Me: "Quack, quack."

Sid: "Oh, shit."

Sid moves to one side with her spotter, then the other.

"New plan, Allen."

Thirty-One

"Seeing as how your boy's probably a killer, I'm thinkin', getting closer, and very much to the right, that would be advantageous."

So Sid directs. We're covered by foliage to the prime point of engagement, says Sid, which she figures is the corner, across the street, the furthest point of the driveway holding the little shack with its gas pump. On the corner itself is an old-style sign, one announcing this shack, I'm guessing, is *Smith's!* It's hand painted, nailed to six-inch by six-inch cedar posts, buried in postholes about a foot, we reckon. If we can make this, we'll have cover, though not the kind that can withstand two assault weapons for a reasonable length of time, as in more than ten seconds. Our two guests decide to start walking across the highway toward our last position, Jose toward the Bronco, Maria/Stella toward the old drive-inn. And, most importantly, with their backs to us.

The rest will depend, as Sid suggests, on my inordinate supply of dumb luck.

And so we begin.

Sid opens fire on the gas pump. I lob a stun grenade, hoping for it to land somewhere this side of Jose and Stella/Maria, and between their aspects of us, in relation to the sign we are behind and their vehicle. Their next avenue of cover is ahead of them, the same distance they would have to travel if they make back for the station wagon. We very much hope they will hesitate for a moment or two before opening up on us.

Jose doesn't hesitate, opens fire, and I'm not surprised. I feel like I am his duck *de jure,* and he won't be returning to Mexico City less than satisfied. Maria/Stella bolts for the drive-in, as Jose opens fire on our sign. Sid stops, takes a knee, ducks—and here is where my luck may show its face any damn second, please. Because now I need to lob the second grenade as close to Jose as possible. I do, and go flat, hoping Jose will just flat out miss.

My placement is not horrible, but the stun doesn't stun until Jose has ripped the top eight inches from the length of the sign. Splinters rain down, and Sid and I must re-commence firing before we hear the explosion, having faith.

Now both of us are firing on the old gas pump, low and as close to where the mechanized pump itself is connected to the gasoline capped off by a spigot, closed and awaiting a trusted consumer to flip the handle on the outside of the casing, allowing the pumping process to begin.

I'm tempted to blast away, fanning-style, knowing Jose won't remain stunned much longer, and sooner or later Maria/Stella is going to see an opening and bring her assault weapon to life. But Sid is my example. Take the time to breathe and aim, then fire, fire, fire, always at the base. Empty both weapons if need be, there is no backup plan.

And in fact, mine are empty. I look to Sid, one .45, empty no doubt, dropped to the ground at her side, her second .45 in proper grip and stance, coming to its end as well.

Sid's perseverance meets dumb luck, same juncture.

Jose's stunned beyond my wildest hopes, but I think it's compounded by the absence of his colleague. In trying to get his bearings, figure the nearest cover, or the optimum result of staying and standing in, one would, of course, consider doing so if, and only if one had the luxury of another shooter on one's side similarly equipped for destruction. But in a matter of seconds, I can see anger and resolution displace the confusion on his face and in his bearing, and he lowers the barrel of his rifle to finish his work. At this point, a familiar Crown Vic comes screaming over the last rise into town. This finally brings Maria/Stella out of her hidey-hole round the corner of the drive-in closest to the Bronco. She begins firing in the general direction of the Vic. This startles Jose, putting it mildly, and he stops firing and turns, seeing the Vic and Stella/Maria where he expected neither to be.

And the coupe de gracie—Sid's second-to-last-round hits pay dirt, the pump ignites, explodes on the leaking fumes, and blasts the side of the station wagon—yes, the side the gas tank lives on. The second blast outweighs the first. And now Jose decides to run, but he doesn't know that we, behind him and blocking one direction of escape, are busy reloading like crazy people, and he sees Maria/Stella was planning to grab the Bronco and run on him all along, and she seems to be keeping the Crown Vic busy for now, and he makes for the Bronco.

This is really hard for us to follow, reloading as previously mentioned, and Sid beats me as I have revolvers and she needs only to jack out and jack in fresh clips. I do see, however, the Crown Vic *not* pull up next to the Bronco, or indeed make any sign of stopping at all. This is when I know Arturo's behind the wheel. Bobby's probably riding shotgun, the better marksman, but Artie's a wheel man through and through.

Artie heads straight for Maria/Stella, hits the brakes just as she throws up the weapon and falls to the ground, her arms covering her head. His skid brings the rear around sharply just catching Jose's knee with the extreme tip of the rear bumper. Jose responds with rounds all over, firing the rifle one-handed. Bobby's firing from the back seat, both windows down, not absolutely sure which direction Artie would choose to skid.

Jose could make a smart move here, I know, because I know Bobby. Make any attempt to drop your weapon, Bobby'll take the chance on you. But for Jose, revenge beats brains, and Jose squares around to get both hands on the assault rifle, and aim—and two shots from Bobby's window puts him down.

That silence after a fire fight always seems to be accompanied by dull, ringing noises. And the air's always redolent with burnt powder. Tension slowly dissipates, and cramps where you didn't know you could cramp take your breath away. Then sound starts to gently return, and the sound of the station wagon burning is eerily similar to that of a gentle brook. The worst of it all is mitigated by checking yourself and those around you for injury.

I find myself sitting behind the wooden sign, back to a post, legs out flat, two revolvers in my lap, loaded and ready and too late. Sid's about six feet south of me, also leaning on post, weapons ready, her head back as if she peers at the sky.

"Sid? Sidney? No, no, no—"

"What?" she yells, pointing at her ears. "Can't hear a damn thing." Although that smile seems as light-hearted as I've ever known her to be.

I grab my chest. "Not funny, dammit. Thought I'd lost you."

Sid jumps up. "Somebody's got a crush."

"Geesus, Sid," as I struggle to my feet, "you sure as hell heard *that*."

"Just screwing with you, Allen. Couldn't be better, seeing as how we just barely escaped being riddled to smithereens."

We walk around the sign and over to the Vic, where dirt and dust still swirl from Artie's skid. Maria/Stella's lying on her back in the back seat, tied at hands and feet, occasionally rolling and kicking and swearing, and in her second language at that. Impressive. Artie and Bobby stand over Jose. He's smaller than I remember when Keith Raven pulled him over for speeding, making quite an impression in his riding leathers.

"Thank you, Arturo, thank you, Bobby." Sid walks like a cat. "And how did Allen's insane luck manifest itself this time out?"

Bobby grabs my shoulder. "Maggie Connor."

I'm as stunned as I'd be had I forgotten to lob the second grenade. "Mags? When did she appear?"

Artie grabs my other shoulder. "She hasn't, that is, we've yet to see her. But you may have seen a couple of sets of red lights up the hill a bit? And we were betting you two would make a left to avoid, even if it left you on your own, in case of a tail."

"What now?" I'm not satisfied with that. "You gambled we would be tailed going back to Crawford?"

"No, no," says Artie, smile broadening. "We *knew* you'd be tailed on your way over to Bobby's house. Maggie tipped us to that as well."

Sid doesn't look angry, but she is certainly confirmed. "You two, three with this Maggie, you used us as running bait. And any damn thing might have gone wrong, either or both of us could have made the wrong move, you could be standing over *us* right now."

Bobby's smile drains away. Artie's looking at the station wagon, only smoldering now. Both men give the slightest shrugs.

"And that, *that* right there, Allen, is why I'm running my breakfast café, and not working for these sanctimonious fools. It's always that goddam shrug—they all do it—that's what gets me in the end." And she walks to the Bronco and gets in the passenger's side.

I'd just as soon move on with Sid this minute. But there are still more questions than answers, and these two need to know where to find me. Neither is looking at me yet.

"I cannot say I wouldn't have done the same damn thing to either of you if I'd stayed in the game as long as you have." Bobby looks like he may start, and Artie's thinking I'm thawing.

"But," I say. "And one big goddam but, I didn't stay in, my choice, and you did hang me out to dry, your choice—and now we're not curious about how far you two will go—we know damn well how far." I sigh involuntarily, and turn and take two steps, and stop, and return.

"And here's the worse part of all. Stringing me out in the middle of nowhere without a net, that is inappropriate. But putting Sidney in harm's way, and in the dark?"

I want to use another word. These are good men.

But no other word fits.

"Unforgivable."

And I turn and walk to the Bronco.

Part Three

Thirty-Two

I head to Pringle, figuring to catch State 89 with the intention of taking it straight into Edgemont, and sooner or later, tie up tonight in Crawford, as Court is holding the fort in the form of my unit *13* at the Hilltop. When we make Pringle, Sid points to the Two Bars Café at the Mercantile. I pull in and park and turn the key.

"You doing a kind of café tour while out and about?"

Sid smiles as she climbs out. "Lemonade out of lemons, Allen. Come on in."

I figure Sidney has a surprise up her sleeve because, well, she's Sidney.

She is, and does.

Sid stands at the counter, and embraces a short, square woman of indeterminate age. The woman is dressed as her idea of a pioneer woman, complete with bonnet. "Allen, this is Mary Derry—Mary, this is Will Allen. He lives in Lander, too."

If Sid thinks she's caught me off guard with her friend's last name, she has another think comin'. "Mary, it's a pleasure. And I'm betting you're related to one or any of the railroad Derrys?"

Mary laughs, open and melodic, and northern Irish. "Ay, lad, my brothers Harry and Larry in train service, Barry and Gary in the roundhouse, and of course Sherry and Terry, secretaries to the Superintendent."

I shake her hand. "Why so few?"

Mary, mock serious, "The rest in junior high and high school, bein' Jerry, Kerry, Perry, and Vera."

"And your hard-working parents?"

"August and Maude." Mary turns on a dime, and we follow her to one of two worn leather booths by the rear window, through which a small herd of deer is visible nibbling the undergrowth, meandering generally south and west.

We sit, Mary disappears, then reappears with coffee and pie, me thinking *what-kinda-pie-who-cares-hallelujah-pie!* Turns out it's gooseberry.

Sid stirs her coffee even though she takes it black. "I met Mary years back when I bought the Lander place, and I planned to start attending all the local and regional tourism conventions, trying to learn best practices, make a few connections."

"I didn't know you're attracted to that type of thing."

"I'm not—that was the first and last one, you know how impatient I am. But I met Mary early on, and we took two seminars together, and then ditched all the rest together, and we both feel we got more out of that particular get-together than most." Mary refills our mugs and heads back to the counter to sell licorice and beef jerky to a carload of Iowans.

I start the talk neither of us want to talk. "I won't make a big deal out of this, but seeing as how you and I could have well died back there, and we seem to be the only ones concerned about such an outcome—I want to thank you and apologize at the same time."

Sid still stirring: "No need."

"Right. Anyway, you wouldn't be here if I hadn't called, and been a rude bastard, and then we both get hung out to dry by men I was vouching for—"

Sid turns her attention to the pie. "—although I've worked jobs in my time where I showed the same lack of respect for other people's safety because I believed I served a 'higher purpose.'"

"Yeah. Me, too. But I had it coming, Sid. You not only came, you had my back, risked your life, and all without one split-second of hesitation. Okay, you look very uncomfortable. Enough. Stopping now. Thanks."

Sid waves at Mary as she winds up counting back change to the Iowan dad-figure. "And thank you for stopping. Frankly, I haven't had a field assignment in years, and it's still exhilarating."

Mary sits on Sid's side. And again, I do not see this one coming.

Sid, getting Mary's direct gaze: "Patagonia."

I look as shocked to Mary as she looks to me. Sid pats her arm. "He's okay."

Mary slumps back against the booth. "When in the name of God will that bloody War be over?"

Sid turns to her coffee, holding the cup in two hands and staring down the liquid. "Can we have you for a few, Mary? Maybe an hour?"

Big sigh. "Sure, kids. Let me get Conrad covering the counter." But instead of getting up, Mary lets go with a *Connie!* that could free a blocked bowel. And out of the kitchen comes a man of indeterminate age, dressed as his idea of a pioneer man, complete with worn and dusty bowler.

"Your mister?" I ask.

"Naw, lad. I'm the big sister served as second mom for the ten children to follow. Different times, different mission." With that, Mary succumbed to a faraway look, and Sidney began on her behalf.

"Will—"

This the first and probably last time Sid uses my first name. I am focused.

"—you were in the Northwest as a kid in '44? And I was there as well for a quick bit, but mostly I was on Prince Edward Island, then Newfoundland, on the behest of State, but not State—blah, blah. Okay, we all signed some form of *official secrets act.* And Mary was in and out of Northern Ireland, working the Troubles, and some German interference, then she was tabbed to follow and join an IRA-splinter escaping to the Tacoma docks about the same time."

"Anyway, you might have been too young to pick this up, let alone know the context, but 'Patagonia' was often used in those parts as a sort of slang term between agents or assets, meaning not so much a safe house as a safe *zone*, a region or district where aid and comfort, or safe shelter or transport might be found. No guarantees. Of course."

Mary's gaze doesn't waver, but she finds voice. "Never guarantees. But always a direction. After I followed the splinter group to Tacoma, a couple of their hotheads—barely kids—got loaded at a dump on the water front. I was doing straight obbo from across the room. Back then, pre-technological wizardry, the powers-who-be would set up a redundant safety—that is, I'm working observation on a subject or two, and there may well be another operative doing the same task, but watching me included, in case something happens to me, or to the one watching me. Well, I'm no wet-behind-the-ears kid at this point, but I should have held my position. The hotheads pissed off a couple of green Army boys on a bender before they shipped out to the Pacific, one of the hotheads and one of the GIs pull knives, this is going to rain down all sorts of MPs and beat cops, and I'm going to learn nothing about who these small fry may take their marching orders from. So as the scuffle passed my table, I sucker-punched the GI and snapped the radical punk's wrist. Unfortunately, the MPs were already halfway in the door and headed for me.

It was a warm Spring, I was out the window, I ran a couple of miles, spotted a booth, dropped a dime to a number not unlike one you've probably seen on certain gray files by now. One ring, one answer: *Patagonia is northeast.*"

Mary looks mentally exhausted, but never quits, I'd bet. "I followed my compass for almost a day, on foot, waiting for another sign, or slip of paper, or the odd street character with a meaningful glance and two or three very odd words. So, I end up that night sleeping under a bridge outside Renton—"

"—north and east of where Seatac is now?" I ask.

Mary's relaxing. "On the nose. And when I wake up, there's a wet and muddy windshield flyer pinned to my jacket, hyping a doughnut joint in Seattle. And I don't have two cents by this time, but legend has it to trust in Patagonia. So I flag a cab, give him the flyer, go *wherever that is, please,* and he laughs, and off we go. We pull up to the doughnut joint, there's this hobo leaning in the doorway, and I'm thinking, he's going to hit me up for a few bucks, and I got exactly nothing for my cab driver. So out I go, and I turn to the driver, and the hobo steps up to the taxi window, hands the driver a twenty, and then shuffles off down the street, no word one. The driver laughs again, takes off. Anyways, I enter the shop, nobody there—I mean nobody— anywhere, save the last booth next to the back door and restrooms, and there sits my 'direct,' same guy I worked with in Belfast, lo and behold."

There is nothing like a good story. "So, your story, in service to me catching the drift of the word Patagonia, keeps the believer moving, which speaks to safety, and speaks to hope, which speaks to faith—perseverance."

Mary smiles at Sid. "Ain't stupid."

Sid smiles at me. "High praise, Allen."

"Thanks, and let me try again, then. So, to extrapolate to present day and context. Patagonia is a word with a meaning to someone who's walked the walk. Someone who's done time in service, public or clandestine, or both. And that someone perceives himself and those he cares about in danger. One or more parties threaten, or promise to threaten those who can't protect themselves. This someone is up in this thing to his neck—"

Sid winks. "—or hers."

I wink. "—or both their necks. And he, she or they aren't so much worried about dealing with bad guys, but they can't always keep everybody, every innocent bystander guaranteed they have a place in Patagonia—in a safe zone."

Mary just nods. No smile. "Keep going."

And I am taken by a most definitive sensation, being my age, looking into the battle-weary faces of two courageous women—none of us spring chickens. That is, *time's a'wastin'.*

So I cut to my chase.

"Doctor Randall Lenore."

And with that, Maggie Connor walks out of the kitchen, and sits beside me in the booth.

"For a sharp cookie, that took you forever."

Thirty-Three

I don't have to react as Maggie sits, next to me and across from Mary and Sid. First, Mary reacts to a smell no one else detects and leaves for the kitchen without a word, no doubt to find the dishwasher or grill cook who thought letting Maggie in the alley door and march through Mary's kitchen was okay. Then Sidney tucks her legs under her, turns to address either of us from one position, and says:

"Maggie Conner. Go to hell."

Maggie's wanting to start the "normalization pitch" too soon. I'm betting she's going to start with the *hey, we've all played hardball back in the day, done things we weren't proud of.* I can tell her that won't work, but I won't, as Maggie's got it coming, and more.

So, Maggie: "Sidney, back in the day—"

Sid: "Screw you, you do not know me, and before you try me on with the *hey, we're both women living in a man's world* pitch, let me save you some time—screw you."

I wished Maggie would look abashed, even for a second. I'm sad for the moment I see in her face, the second or two where she's shopping through old plays she's pulled on agents or assets in the past. And I'm sad Maggie sees so little of the strength and resolution in Sidney, that she's still reading her as just another point of manipulation on Maggie's way to achieving her goal.

In another time and place these two women might get on famously. Not the time, not the place for Sid. "Your little ambush set-up was sheer bullshit, we knew it as it happened, firsthand—and by the way, no-goddam-body has apologized for it—and you and Bobby and Artie knew how it could go down, and y'all pulled the stunt anyway. And just to save a bit a time, here's where you come back with your *greater good* baloney, and once more we say—"

"—screw me. Got it." Maggie looks neither insulted nor repentant. And that's when *I* get it. I turn to Sid, and I catch a similar glint in her eye, as if we caught the same brief glimmer before it faded.

"Maggie's passed it, Sid. And maybe just now, or awfully damned recent, but it's gone. Too late." And Sid nods, resigned, as if she'd just sat through a brief but poignant funeral.

Maggie looks off balance now. "Passed what?"

Sid takes no pleasure in this. She doesn't keep score. "Passed the point of no return, Maggie. It happens to us all, anyone who's done time in protection of the public—cops to spies to private security, county to state to the Feds and the spooks. There are rules and regulations, and laws and statutes, standard operating procedures and Geneva conventions and Miranda warnings. And we try to play by the rules, but the bad guys don't, and justice is served, but not nearly as often as it should be, unless we bend just a little, right place, right time—more than one way to stop a sonuvabitch, right?"

If Mags is getting any of this, I don't see it. She puts the "dead" in deadpan. But I'll be damned if I let it go. There may still be hope.

"It's cognitive dissonance, Maggie," I say, and I hope I see some light return to dead eyes. "We know the right thing to do, and we choose to do the wrong thing, because maybe that'll get us justice. We immediately feel the pain doing wrong, and treat it with the rationale *de jour*. *The greater good—* that's a winner. *And at time of war—*one phrase covers a thousand errors. Or go the other way—*a unique time in history, an unparalleled juncture of events and opportunity.* The politicians crank it out like sausage. But the dissonance builds, and it builds to the point that, at your next opportunity to meet out your particular flavor of "real" justice, nobody's-looking-so-go-ahead—and you realize, shit, this is it. I do this thing one more time, just once more, I'll never get out. I will never quit the job."

Sid stills stirs that coffee, long cold. "And a lot of us quit, like *really* quit. Not like your friends Artie and Bobby, running up the old 'retiree' flag, get seen often enough fishing or golfing, but really some vital part of a task force, or running a deep undercover, maybe even being the 'in-betweens' for domestic and international security agencies who aren't supposed to be mixing domestic and foreign work, but get real, right? Everybody does it, right?"

Maggie cuts in, and she's mad she's been caught, or mad we're right, or both. "No, you mean quit like you and Will have quit? At some point, the going

209

got rough, and you see the light, and your self-righteous bullshit allows you redemption, but then you accept the occasional offer to get back in the game—like you Sid, getting those pictures years ago at that Seattle dinner party? Yeah, I spotted you, checked you out. What, hit a boring spot in your soaring academic career, had a free weekend? And who's running your toy kitchen while you're up here with the big kids? And you, Allen, again, total bullshit. You don't like working for the man? So, you just set up an alternative universe, one in which you still get to play our game, but with your rules, so you always win, unless you don't, then you claim you never cared anyway."

Mags is on a tear. I say, "So, to our 'screw you,' you say—"

"Goddam hypocrites." Maggie looks us both in the eye.

Sid returns the gaze. "And if you can look at hanging Will and I out as bait, no glint of remorse, and you actually believe what you just said, then you *are* passed the point. You're never coming back. Which is fine, Maggie. Just don't kid yourself." And Sid rises, looking to me. "I'm to the restroom, meet you in the Bronco. Do what you need to do." And she leaves the booth.

My last exchange with Maggie put me in mind of the that legal-cliché-moment in every courtroom drama where the defense attorney goes *Your Honor, permission to treat the witness as hostile*? I might as well have been pressing any number of career cops I used for info for my first twenty years on the job, or been cajoling a handful of career cops I'd pissed off in my second twenty. There is a screen now between Maggie and I, one I fear is permanent.

But I asked about facts, about whereabouts, about last sightings. There is little room in those questions for fire and ice. I left for the Bronco after I said "thanks." There was no response.

I'm back to the Bronco, passenger's side, and Sid's in the driver's seat, and I'm aware that at this very moment, neither Sid nor Maggie looks older or younger than the other, but both look younger than me.

Sid says, "I'll drive. *You* will be answering questions, or *we* will be trying to—you know, stuff like that."

"Okay, Sidney Lowe."

Sid slides on sunglasses and says, "We're headed to Crawford via Edgemont, I'm guessing. And we'll touch bases with Emily Straight and kin. And then we'll check in to that Hilltop joint you speak so highly of—and then we sit down hard with Dr. Lenore."

"Exactly," I say, fiddling with the road atlas, checking the rearview mirrors, keeping all upcoming vehicles and those just passed in view long enough to define as friendly or hostile.

Sidney's opted for an additional ten over the speed limit. "The link."

"What link?"

"*The* link. Doc. He's our man, no?"

I'm relaxed now, first time since the shoot-out. "He's our man, yes. Every time I run a conversation he and I've had, back and forth, and very slowly—it just makes sense."

Sid's watching a station wagon behind, but with a smile. "Now every damn wagon's a suspect. Anyway, go ahead. How does Doc fit?"

"Okay, in no particular order. He was born too soon to go to World War One. But he was a superb student, opted for med school instead. So, he's away from Crawford, doing most of his training in the Georgetown area."

Sid nods. "A good neighborhood for spooks and recruitment."

"Could be. And he was old enough to pass on World War Two, and a local doctor to boot, but guess what? He enlists, says he was in Pearl for the duration, no one else in the Nebraska Panhandle in or out of Hawaii over those years remember seeing him out there, *what a coincidence, must've just missed him.*"

Sid's enjoying. "Spookier and spookier. You picked this up at Daisy's?"

"Yep. And—here comes Korea—"

"—and off goes Doc."

I'm enjoying it, too. "Like clockwork. And back to his beloved Crawford after absences that don't quite sync up with everyone else who's involved in the same conflict. Locals wink and say *well, ol'Doc enlists every time Uncle Sam says 'jump,' maybe he has a little extra R&R comin' before a return to the missus.*"

Sid let's an RV pass, one that poorly judged the length of the passing lane. "Your welcome, Minnesota." To me, "So Doc has opportunity throughout his life to run in the same circles as people like Maggie, or this MacAdam, or your ageless but currently dead Jose Garcia. But let's look at this through those lenses we mentioned earlier, the two things happening at the same time, the environments linked by Doctor Randall Lenore."

"Okay," and I'm frantically writing notes as I remember my last tortured conversation with Maggie. I'm half-covering the inside cover of the grey file, and the rest of that page I split in half, labelling one side *Patagonia*, the other

Real World. "So, back at the beginning, Doc doesn't let me in his house, save to use the powder room five feet from where he sat. But he sticks to me like scotch tape when he finds I'm touring his territory, his homeland—"

"—his *Patagonia*, safe harbor. But for who?" Sid steals a glance my way.

"For his flock, almost as if he's a pastor of sorts?"

"For sinners? In pain?"

"Yes. That's it, Sidney. That's it. Pain. Let's roll this back." The fun returns. "Doc's wife dies a long and painful death, ten, maybe fifteen years before the Crawford crash—"

"—he's a doctor, one who's visited foreign ports of call, under several guises for all we know—"

"—and after all the western painkillers fail his wife, he tries out variance cannabis and hashish strains—"

"—which the normal, law-abiding citizen would be hard-pressed to secure abroad and smuggle back home." Sid pulls off the highway into an empty wildlife-viewing-turnout, but backs the Bronco into the parking space, securing the valuable quick-exit position.

I'm comfortable with the spot Sid picked. There's no road coming or going from behind our position, and we can see miles and miles in both directions. It's as good as it gets. "But not difficult if you're freelancing for spooks who will pay you in contraband if such barter greases your gears."

Sid reaches into my glove box for a pencil, but uses it for spinning about like a miniature baton. "Okay, let's jump ahead. Compassionate Doctor Lenore encounters more and more patients with more and more problems. The kids making it home from Nam, in one piece or not, traumatized, battle fatigued. The families losing one or more kids, for any reason. And those boys and girls may have been the lynchpin keeping a family business or ranch or farm together, nobody to work it, nobody to inherit, literally losing the farm."

I'm taking fewer and fewer notes, but things are becoming clearer. "And on the purely domestic scene, the Power River Basin blows up, a bonanza of jobs and wages for miners and drillers and trainmen and every other support-railroader, each occupation with concomitant safety issues and skyrocketing person-injury indexes. And those ranching-farming kids leave the folks for the big money—to help keep the home spread in one piece, at first—and the jig is soon up, and it's just for the money, and rampant materialism, and unconstrained lust—"

"—holy hell, Allen, you're preachin' fire and brimstone."

"Carried away, Sorry. Anyway, we get the point. Bigger and bigger markets for entertainment-by-hallucinogen, more opportunities for self-medication as it serves chronic pain."

"And here," says Sid, reaching behind her past the console for her bag, checking her Berettas and re-positioning the bag at her side, "is where the Real World rubs up against Doc's Patagonia. Doc's not interested in marketing, selling, profit, but he's also sold himself on his special ability to prescribe the right stuff to the right people for the right reasons. But he can't control his mistakes—the patients who abuse his largesse, and use for the sake of using."

"And Doc cuts them off, but they look elsewhere, and a demand, a market grows in our 'middle-of-nowhere.'" I check my backpack now, laying hands on the revolvers for peace of mind, as Sid has spooked me.

"And sooner or later, those neighbors to our south and to our north, both ever-sensitive to the least market vibration in a rich and powerful USA—these fine fellas send out their field folks, to look and watch and see what there is to see."

"And they see, Sidney, an old country doctor, a self-proclaimed benevolent-supplier waging a righteous war on chronic pain, physical and emotional. And doing so smack-dab in the middle of unclaimed territory."

Sid's suddenly upright in her bucket seat, having double-checked the horizon to the north, on our left, and starts the Bronco and floors it, this even though I perceive less than a one-vehicle space between us and an oncoming cattle truck. Sidney's betting on the cattle truck swerving just enough to let her take half a lane from traffic and the other half from the shoulder, and she wins the bet, and we miss a fiery death.

It's then I see in my rear view what prompted Sid to desperate tactics—a set of red and blue emergency lights pulsating from the roof of a low-slung sports coupe, all white, and about a half-mile to our rear, and swerving in and out of tourist-plagued traffic, on a mission.

Sid's busy casing upcoming passing lanes, and no-passing lanes that look promising, and I'm looking the map over for anything passing for a road on the either side of the highway. But Sid walks and chews gum simultaneously.

"You aware of county Mounties or state cops driving Camaros or Mustangs as unmarked patrol vehicles?"

"No, ma'am, I am not."

"And at the risk of sounding like *everything's about us*—"

"Yeah," I agree as I think I've made out a two-track path on the map that a super-hot sports car with almost no clearance would be insane to try. "*They are all about us, and let's check their resolve. One-quarter mile, maybe less, Sidney, on the right, with a one-lane bridge about a hundred feet after the turn.*"

I've never heard Sidney say this before or since.

"Holy Mother of God."

Thirty-Four

And I can hardly blame her. I've given her less than five hundred yards warning for a hard-right turn, then told her please beware of the one-lane bridge a bare hundred feet on a two-track that may be gravel, may be corduroy-ruts, could most definitely be pock-mocked with bentonite craters after a hard rain—and do it all at speed, please.

So, considering she just pulled the "cattle truck maneuver," and we lived and she is at speed-limit-speed once more, but on the bumper of a RV, there is no real visibility accessible forward. Sid is depending on my call to crank a blind hard-right. She says nothing, only glancing out my window.

I say, "on three." My passenger's window is down, and I can just get my right eye focused past the traffic we're sandwiched between. "One. Two—Three."

Sid cranks it hard-right like she was born at Daytona. The rear bumper almost swings around free, save for just a kiss on the right-rear corner by the cattle truck's right-front bumper. Sidney rides the skid and we go three-sixty. The dirt and dust blinds us momentarily, then dissipates long enough to give a full view of the one lane bridge now so close, it wouldn't matter if another vehicle was on it and coming our way—we'd hear only the sound of our respective numbers coming up.

The bridge is open, and we shoot through it like a pinball down a chute, a high-pitched scrape as the Bronco does a shimmy through and out. And news improves as we determine the two-track is maintained, small-coarse-pea-gravel, with sight ahead another full mile-plus until it loops around a baby bluff consumed in scrub oak.

I yell *cover* as we bounce along. I didn't have to. Sidney's making for that turn and refuge as if our lives depend on it. This assumption is the only one we can act on at this time, this place.

The Bronco's doing what it's made for, and earning every second and inch of a stem-to-stern service and assessment the next time I cruise by my mechanic, a guy already amazed by my tendency to abuse my vehicle in the course of my pursuit. I can't wait to introduce him to Sidney.

Things continue to improve for us, although initially we appear to be doomed. We swing around the little bend, and the view opens on a narrow canyon, a rugged drop to a rocky drainage, and a wall climbing steep to the left, the opposite wall gently rising on the right, with a small foot bridge across the barely-running stream. The two track disappears ahead around one more curve, this one at least a full mile on.

Sid stops. "Thoughts?"

I'm looking back. "We have to play it like he, she or they don't give up."

"Agreed." Sid's eyes are closed in focus. "A person owning a car like that, driving around a region where it's the least practical vehicle—that guy's intense."

I get out to stretch away the adrenaline. "And that's reinforced by the type of person carries his own emergency light bar he can whip out when traffic becomes problematic."

Sid stretches now. "And suggests, I think, a guy not giving a good goddam about attracting attention, just figuring he'll shoot his way out of tight spaces."

I look back at the corner we came around, and I know shortly that sports car, bouncing and tearing its under-guard to scrap, will take the same corner. "Element of surprise?"

Sid points to her left, facing back the way we came. "There's very little, save one of us behind that pile of granite rock-fall"—and she points to the right, the steep canyon wall—"and the other behind that small cedar stand."

I agree. "And that only works if there is something ahead which might concentrate his attention long enough for us to come up behind him."

Sid glances at her wrist. "Well, time's well past up. Let's park the Bronco right up to the foot bridge, maybe even just about falling in the stream, but not."

We're both back in the Bronco, doing exactly that. We get out and make for the curve, back the way we came, and our designated hidey-holes, and the roar of an angry and abused V-8 comes our way. And the vehicle, I'm still guessing a Mustang, is making the sounds best affecting us. There is a roar as the driver floors it, then shifts up, then a crash or bang or slap, depending on

216

what the almost-no-clearance underbelly is coming into contact with, then gearing-down, and the cycle begins again.

I'm behind the cedar clump at the steep wall, Sid's behind the granite pile, and I'm wishing we both had granite piles, as they sound impenetrable as regards gunfire. But if wishes were fishes, there'd be tuna for lunch, and they ain't, and there isn't. And now that long white hood precedes the rest of the vehicle into the corner, and here comes a car nearly twenty years old, but looking like it just rolled off the show room floor.

A 1969 Ford Mustang Shelby Cobra GT 500 / 428 Cobra Jet. Looking like a twelve-year-old had smoked his first joint on a Halloween night, then was dared to take this little number on a joyride, and lost the main road, and went totally paranoid, and lost his way, but getting picked up for Grand Theft-Auto scares him more than being lost, which fuels the foot-to-the-floor-gear-up-gear-down cycle of destruction. But however it looks to me, I'm pretty sure we're going to find out a full-grown, less-than-pleased-adult is behind the wheel, with weapons close at hand.

The driver must almost immediately spot my Bronco ahead. The Mustang skids to a stop. The driver's window drops quickly, then the door opens and closes, releasing a figure training a pair of binoculars on the Bronco. I see no weapon in a holster or stuck in a belt at the back, anyway. I wave at Sid, and we converge on the Mustang from the rear, trying to balance speed and sound.

The driver hears me before Sid, and he swings around with the binoculars still at his eyes. I'm standing at the left rear tail light, with one revolver trained at the driver's head. Sid is at the Mustangs right headlight with her Beretta trained on the driver's back. And she's looking puzzled because she can see the look of recognition on my face, and the look is not one of reunion and joy.

The driver drops the binoculars, secured to his neck with strap, and smiles. And I say, "Son of a bitch."

And Sidney says, "Who is he?"

And as he turns toward Sidney, I say, "Sidney, this is Phillip P. Phillips, Lately of Shelby, Montana, and quite a liar, as it turns out."

Bald, mid-fifties, white, black hornrims with clip-on sunglasses, Phillip is delighted to say, "Howdy, Miss Sidney. A pleasure to meet you, and see Mr. Allen once more." And Phillip turns to open his car door, and I notice two items on his console—a nine-mil and a grey folder.

"Please don't move, Phil, cuz I'll shoot, and I aim main-body-mass, because I'm not fancy enough to 'wing' you, as they say in the movies." Phil smiles and steps away from the door.

"Sid," I say not taking my eyes or sights off Phillip, "please grab that gun and file as you find them."

Sid does so, and Phillips says, "I didn't lie about Shelby, Mr. Allen. It's a grand little town."

Sidney's deep into the grey file, the nine-mil relieved of its rounds and lying at her feet, and her Beretta tucked in the back of her jeans. "Grand little town, maybe. Grand little border crossing, definitely. You need to see this file, Allen. And I'm betting Phil's console is also holding a couple of sets of cuffs, and those cuffs are meant for you and me."

I whistle This Land is Your Land as I gesture to Phil a clear reach in and retrieve the cuffs, and he gestures back *who me?*, and I gesture in return it's now or kneecaps. This is enough, as the cuffs appear, and I secure his hands behind his back, Sid secures his ankles, and I pop open the trunk. Now Phil seems less an interesting acquaintance, and more a potential road hazard. "You're kidding, Allen. It could be hours before I'm found."

Sid has dog-eared a couple of pages in the grey file and placed a large paper clip on the last two addendums. She hands me the file and takes my .38 to ease my perusing. Before I can start, she walks up next to Phil, still not pleased by the way, and gives him a hip. He's off balanced enough by his constraints to topple over into the trunk, and neatly at that. But before dropping the lid, and ignoring a colorful string of epithets ol' Phil did not seem to have in him, Sid's got one last question.

"You can ride in the back, still trussed of course, if you can answer this to my satisfaction: does the name Maggie Connor mean anything to you?"

I can see as clearly as Sid that Phil wasn't expecting the question, nor the name. It was a brief tell, and Phil knows his stuff, but the jaw muscle on his left side flexed, just a second in duration. Then, "Never heard of her."

Sid smiles and drops the lid, and the cursing resumes. We walk around and sit on the Mustang's hood. Sid hands back my Police Special. "Quite a liar. And I bet you thought I was going to say *MacAdam*."

"I did, and the overall exchange was jarring. Apparently I still can't trust myself to be objective about the real Maggie. Thanks, Sidney."

"That's what friends are for," Sid says and points to the inside cover of the file. "And before you start whistling Dion Warwick, check out that set of numbers, and the last photo."

The inside cover has a faint series of numbers, just like the grey file Maggie left me when she departed my room at the Hilltop. Again, area code plus seven numbers for the phone number, then three more, probably an extension. And, three more numbers, then in block letters—*Patagonia.*

It's hard to breathe. "I'll be damned."

Sid says, "As will I. The last picture?"

I guess I'll just give up breathing altogether.

The last photo is Sidney and me, sharing breakfast, not that long ago.

"What do you notice, Allen? Something strange?"

And I don't have to study it very long. Just long enough to realize the picture was taken from *inside* Sidney's Cafe.

Thirty-Five

I'm back in the driver's seat, and I suggest a straight shot to Crawford, to ol' Doc's. Sidney concurs and continues combing the file.

"There's got to be something in here besides the photo Maggie included for Phil's eyes only, not for ours."

"Well, the numbers and Patagonia, and the picture is disturbing at many levels." I'm still checking the rear views regularly, but sooner or later those who wish us harm must be running out of bad guys.

"There's something else. I just can't isolate it." Sid looks up smiling. "By the way, isn't this where we look for a phone booth along the way, call up one of your buddies—you know, Mags or Bobby or Artie. Let them know the location of a Mustang, and the special guest in the trunk?"

"Yes, this is where I would start looking, and here is me looking, and here is me not seeing a damn thing. Too bad. Why? You notice the nine-mil you removed from Phil's console? I think it played a major role in his Plan A for us. Plan B was handcuffs, but only if something unforeseen came about."

"And I forgot to return the nine-mil," says Sid, and she opens the glove compartment and sets it in gently, though still bereft of ammunition.

"And I threw the key to the cuffs as far down that little creek as I could," say I.

"That's my boy." And Sid is back to scouring the grey file.

The light is stunning, the scenery so comforting, I'm tempted to relax and enjoy. Sidney has not lost one degree of vigilance, and her reflex default to an earlier training, wherever and from whomever she secured it, is inspiring. She's keeping me going. And this line of thought leads me to my continued disappointment with all things Maggie. Every time I think I can concoct a reasonable rationale for Maggie's actions, she not only fails to defend herself, she manages to act one more time as if she is rooting for those bad guys.

Light dawns, I hope. "Sid, I can argue Maggie is misinformed, or that she *is* beyond the point of no return, or she has put her confidence in the wrong people—whatever—but I cannot imagine Maggie's 'bent.'"

Sid looks up long enough to say, "Beware 'I can't imagine.' That very failure of imagination works in favor of some very bad people."

"And?"

"And," and she returns her gaze to the file, "having said that, I can't believe Maggie Conner, at least the one I've seen, the one I've watched, is dirty."

"Aha. So 'back in the day' you two *did* work together?"

"Geez, Allen, you know people take oaths about secrecy and keeping those oaths a lifetime, and—no, I never worked *with* Maggie, but once or twice, maybe, I was in the immediate vicinity, concerned about activities of my own."

"If I'm working from any other vantage than 'bent,' then Maggie's not DEA either, which leaves the spooks—"

"Which places her time with the Deadwood PD in a very bad light."

"Right, so she is with the DEA, or shared among one or more of the military security agencies, and that being the case, let's pretend, she's doing her best to take down a big guy or two at the top of the heap, while keeping a well-meaning little local hero safe from the type of wolf she hunts."

Now Sid closes the file, and studies the horizon. "Like the late Jose Garcia, a rep of one of the cartels, or anyone else sent in his stead, probably named Jose Garcia—"

"—and MacAdam. You met him at your café. You spoke for some length of time, right? But you didn't recognize each other from that big social-do in the Seattle vicinity all those years ago?"

Sid sits back, slumping just a little. "It might have been fifteen years back—no, twenty? Oh, my God—and it might have been at a Canadian financier's mansion on Bainbridge Island, off of Elliot Bay, due west of the Capitol Hill neighborhood, downtown Seattle. And no, no bells ringing back in Lander, not until you showed me the photo in *your* grey file. Looks like ol' Mags put one file together for several actors in this little matinee, each file customized to trip specific triggers at certain times."

I am weary. "Seems to have worked."

So is Sid. "And again, I am not in Lander, am I?"

"No." And I see a large Phillips 66 sign rise up on the right as we approach, and I hit the blinkers, turn, slide in between gas pumps, and ask the teenager walking out of the office to greet us to *fill 'er up*. Sidney's out as well, and follows me to the phone booth on the other side of the service bay. She has her bag and the grey file.

"What's our play?"

"Every grey file we've been privy to, each has had a series of numbers and 'Patagonia' at the end, right?" I start digging for phone change.

Sid does, too, and hands me several quarters. "That's right, thus far."

"Just a sec." I dial zero, get the operator, ask her to hold up. "Read the number off for me, Sid."

"206-524-3387 and 097. And 309, plus Patagonia."

I repeat the number to the operator, pausing after "3387," saying "extension 097."

I put my hand over the phone to whisper to Sid. "She says 206 is Bainbridge Island. Your Bainbridge?" Sid's eyebrows raise. I bend down in order for Sid to listen in first hand.

The line rings fully four times, stops, and a mid-range masculine voice says, "Number?"

I have only one left. "309."

There is a pause long enough that Sid motions for me to hang up. I almost do so, and then the voice returns.

"Patagonia. *Daisy's.*" This followed by a *click*.

I look Sid straight on. "The voice?"

"MacAdam."

Stunned, but getting used it, I start for the Bronco.

Sid does not. "Wait, wait. Let's review. MacAdam comes all the way to Lander, feeds me a story about your shared railroad history, then attempts a breaking and entering on the Airstream. And had he been successful, and knowing you were not there, he may have well left you a present of sorts, the kind you might trigger on your return."

"Right, maybe. Okay, likely. And?"

"And you are the length of a thirty-five-car cemetery-track in Crawford Yard from each other when MacAdam loads Richie Convoluto's shotgun and kills him, right there, in the moment, without a second thought."

I'm catching her drift. "Yes, according to Richie."

"And finally," Sid says, and starts walking toward a Coke machine flanking the gas station's front door, where also leans the teenager who filled the Bronco with gas and is awaiting payment, "and this same MacAdam coincidentally runs into Doc at a café in Deadwood, and slips Doc a mickey, then, once again—poof—disappears."

The drift grows. "Yes, according to Doc."

"And finally-plus-one, if that was MacAdam's voice, it must be recorded, otherwise he's back in Victoria, or wherever he calls home. But—"

"—but, no, he's here. Gotta be. Why leave it to someone else now?"

I hand the teen some cash, and Sid drops a quarter in the machine. She pulls a bottle, pops the cap, hands me the soda, and gets one more. "I advocate for *not* making for Daisy's like a swallow returning to Capistrano. Especially considering MacAdam himself named 'Patagonia' to be *Daisy's.*"

"Yeah, that bothers me. According to you and Mary, that 'Patagonia' tradition was a regional understanding, the Northwest, and the descriptor supplied was a direction, not a specific town or even location. Right?"

"Right." Sid's always watching the highway. "So, either MacAdam wants you and/or us at Daisy's, or he wants us to do something very much the opposite, us thinking we're out-smarting him."

"Okay, but if that's the case, then he believes he's in a position to know what we're doing before we do it."

Sid finally looks away from the highway. "So he's got eyes and ears out here. Can we get around that?"

And now I head for the Bronco again, and Sid is right with me. "I think so, and I believe the answer is Courtney Dancer."

We stay southbound through Hot Springs, rather than to jog west over to Edgemont, then south to Crawford. We resolve to get in touch with Emily Straight and family as soon as possible, but right now "Patagonia" calls. We don't leave Hot Springs, however, before stopping into the library. There Sidney makes for the reference librarian's desk, and tells her a poignant tale of traveling all the way from Wyoming to surprise her nephew with his own official library card, so that he, now thirteen, can begin his own, independent exploration of the classics. Unfortunately, Sid can't precisely remember her nephew's exact street address, although she can drive right there, *ya know*, and can she use the librarian's phone to place a call, maybe two, if his mom's at work—single mom, yes, very noble.

And of course, the librarian says Sid should make as many calls as she deems necessary, and in the meantime, the librarian will get started making a card, and finding a copy of all the Twain-worlds of Tom and Huck and Becky, just give her a few minutes. So Sid calls Court, gives him a quick low-down, explains our situation, and they formulate a plan. No plan is foolproof, and this one depends on being under the cover of night, but Court is delighted to meet the challenge. And a by-the-way from Court, says Sid, there are a couple of very standard black or charcoal gray sedans, one a Crown Vic, the other a Buick, passing by and cruising the parking lot, every three hours like clockwork, amen.

"I figured," I say, minding the speed limit, as we are still a couple hours from sunset. "Court got plate numbers, I'll bet the farm."

Sid sits back, one foot on the dash. "You win. The Crown Vic, South Dakota. And the Buick? A twist. Alberta. Canada nevertheless."

Our time until sighting Crawford has been just enough to devise a "sort of" plan—one vague enough to free us from reflexive responses to negative stimuli. Stimuli, like—oh, I don't know—guns pointed at us, or pointed at us and firing, or even pointed at us and firing and accurately, at that. But our pencil-plan's beginning and end is designed to take into account what we think we know, and that part in the middle where we really can't find our butts with both hands? Well, hope springs eternal.

So, as to the beginning.

We try to drive a very recognizable Bronco into Crawford alerting as few locals as possible. There's no way to tell how many citizens think of themselves as Crawfordians, and how many consider themselves Patigonians. The latter may feel a duty to feed our whereabouts into the local grapevine, and this could bode poorly. Considering this, we come into Crawford from the north on State 71, avoiding the busier U.S. 20, and take the first exit possible, this being Beech Street. We are still north of the depot and yards, and we can skirt most folks headed east and north, crossing the White River, and find safety in a heavily-treed city park. When we exit the park on the south end, we merge immediately onto an east-west-running Main Street. And again, two-thirds of the little town still lies south of us.

The wait for sunset is minimal. Still both of us seem wired, even though as "not-cops," we have no worries about physically detaining or arresting anyone. But to this point, I watched Doc take a bullet, I killed a man, I heard another man killed with a shotgun, a station wagon with two people and their bad intentions tried to kill both Sid and me with assault rifles, and Phillip Phillips chased us down in a vehicle suggesting his assignment was of the highest importance, and he packed a gun for his picnic.

So, legal responsibilities aside, we have reason to be on high alert.

Sid seems distracted, watching a lovely sunset, dabbing designs on the car window in the steam her breath leaves. "We are here, Allen. And if I relayed your requests to Courtney Dancer correctly, and he followed them correctly, we are about to meet up with Doc, and unbeknownst to a new Jose Garcia, or an old Macadam, or any of the police agencies we have managed to work with or alienate."

"Yep. And as soon as we get a bit more darkness, we take Main two blocks over to Second Street, and there we'll find the celebrated O'Dougherty's."

Sid's head is on a swivel as the time to begin draws near. Some reflexes. And she's interested in a figure in the playground here at the south end of City Park. "And this O'Dougherty's joint is Crawford's version of Deadwood's Goathorn?"

And now I'm straining to make out a boy near the playground equipment, I think, on one of those low-slung bikes, and he seems to have a particular interest in us. "It once was similar to the Goathorn, at least in purpose. The weekend place to be, great steaks, lots of booze for that audience, but most importantly for old soldiers like me, a backroom with a high-stakes game, and a handy-dandy loan shark warming the last booth by the alley door."

Sid says, "Cover me," and slips out the Bronco without a sound. Of course I don't think she needs me to jump behind my driver's door, a .38 Special in either hand, just to make sure she can walk over to Opie at the swingsets. There is a danger she can spook him, but she's banking on her small frame and warm smile. And she banks well. The kid doesn't move. She engages him, they chat, and she reaches into a pocket and hands him something. They shake hands, and he's off like a rocket.

Sid returns with a big smile. "Great kid. I'm thinking about Doc, the benevolent protector of all things small town-precious, and I think of the Pied Piper, and if I wanted to keep a pulse on my little town, who better to use as eyes and ears than—"

"—rodents?"

"Ha-ha. Kids. All the kids know Doc, he delivered most of them, and he might be 'medicating' a serious number of their parents."

I check my watch against the times Court should expect our arrival at the restaurant. "Brilliant. And this kid?"

"Brian Bollinger, mom's the post-mistress, dad's one of two plumbers in town. I told him we are friends of Doc's, waiting to meet him here at the park, then we're headed for Deadwood. And I risked the kid would take a twenty for his efforts—small risk—and grab a movie with his buddies, as we can check in with Doc on his behalf."

"Therefore keeping the young lad away from Daisy's and whoever is watching for us there." I slip out of the Bronco with my backpack, as does Sidney, and we take the short walk two blocks and change, but to the alley behind O'Dougherty's, and the infamous alley-door, and its infamous last booth.

Sid stops about a yard from the door. It appears to be locked. "And how do we know that if we can get in, instead of using the front door like normal people, there might well be a certified member of the 'broken-nose' crowd resting his big ol' ass in that specific booth?"

And here's where things always begin, usually a might shaky, and adrenalin's all you really have to trust. "We *don't* know, Sid."

Her left shoulder drops, as does her the right corner of her mouth, and this often makes for her "wearily-entertained" mode. "Oh, so *that's* where we're at. Super."

We both take one last check of where our weapons are stored, and our access to those weapons, and I check my watch again, and wait about twenty seconds, and it's time.

I knock twice, wait three beats, knock once. The door isn't locked on the other side, and slowly swings open.

Courtney Dancer fills the doorframe. "Will. And Sidney? You look like you sound." And Court leads us inside, just a few steps, and there is a worn-leather booth, smelling faintly of grill-grease and malt. And sitting watching us walk in, and not too damn happy, is Doctor Randall Lenore.

Doc starts to shift his weight out of the booth bench to stand, but Court sits at his side, and puts one hand on Doc's arm.

"I'm sorry, Uncle, but this thing has got to come to an end."

Thirty-Six

Sid and I return stares. Doc collapses back into the upholstery. And Court gestures toward the opposite seating. "Sorry, Will. Sidney. I just didn't want to tip my hand. I mean, you could have been anyone, maybe wanting to hurt Doc, and I had to be sure you two have his best interests at heart."

Doc comes around. "I'll be the judge of that, goddamit."

Court stands. "Let me get Doc some coffee, and you guys?"

Sid smiles to both our hosts. "Sure, black. And should we have, uh, security concerns?" Sid nods toward the back door, and glances to the front of the house.

"No problems. That door locks from the inside when it closes, and its Monday, so the restaurant's closed, and the help is way up front doing some training with management."

I'm catching on. "And you know this because?"

Court's signature smile. "Because the manager is Cousin Hannah."

"And Cousin Hannah?"

"Is Daisy's sister. Back in a flash."

Since last I've seen Doc, things have deteriorated. I imagine the pressure from trying to keep his patients and clients happy and quiet, and the vice-pressure he's endured living between the law on one side and his Canada-Mexico overlords on the other, has built to the point of breaking. I'm hoping the presence of Doc's nephew, in my opinion a special human being, will serve as comfort, and create an atmosphere in which we can bring about a safe and lawful conclusion to this episode. And which, in my experience, can just as likely implode, taking us all along to oblivion.

Hope springs.

Sid reads Doc a tad differently. She accepts a steaming mug from Court, waits until he sits once more, then gently touches Doc's forearm. He starts, but doesn't pull away.

"Doc, you look tired, and you deserve to. Your twenty-four-seven vigilance would tax a squad of younger men." Doc looks vaguely appreciative. "But that's not it, is it? You look scared, the real-thing-scared." Doc looks down and away, and a tear fills one eye. Sid waits, then says, "When, Doc? When and where did you last see him? MacAdam?"

Court is alert once again, and less than gentle. "Uncle? I just asked you this very afternoon, I said I'll pick you up down the street from your house, I said we were going to Fort Rob for dinner, you needed a rest, and I asked, are you okay, anybody causing you grief?" Court looks to us, frustrated, and not pleased.

Doc comes about enough to turn toward his nephew. "Yes, and we do not go to Fort Rob, do we, as you said we would, but we come here, even though it's closed, and you almost carry me in, and won't tell me why, and you may just have gotten us all in a world of trouble, thank you." Before we, anyone of us can respond, Doc holds up one hand, and sips at the coffee mug in the other. It seems a lifetime, but he probably finishes half the cup, and seems to improve just short of a miracle. He says, "Okay. Just start. If MacAdam or his troops are in or around Daisy's, that's a fifteen-minute walk, or a two-minute car ride. Let's get to it."

I've been waiting, not knowing how to phrase most of this, but Doc's right. Time's a'wastin'.

"Great. I'll start. In no particular order. Jimmy Kilroy, EMT, Crawford-crash trauma and motorcycle-assault trauma. Tim Nelson and Riley Fointman, Crawford-crash engineer and brakeman. I'm betting they were not there coincidentally. I'm betting both had long histories of the most common PI's on the railroad—back strain leading to a myriad of surgeries and treatments. Those histories meant chronic pain, and it also meant two railroad employees who might easily be 'bent' if a bad guy needed a favor." Sid's scratching a few notes in the grey folder, Court's gaze is squarely on me, but Doc seems to be in and out.

But I get his attention with this.

"Daisy Wenton—"

"You bastard—" and Court has to holdback a hand headed for my throat.

"Daisy Wenton—respectfully, Doc—mentioned the first time we chatted about how close everybody in a rural area gets, where economic interests are few but essential, and everybody's connected somehow. Like how Daisy's a cousin on her dad's side to Tim Nelson's widow, and how Riley Fointman's sister was Daisy's best school friend from kindergarten to graduation. And how much pain both women were suffering, single moms since the Crawford crash, the settlement money long gone, their kids finding trouble instead of work."

Sid gives me a glance, so I stop. She starts. "Did it start with your wife, Doc? The chronic pain, the medical establishment's blind eye to suffering?"

This does the trick. Doc's gaze is up and to the left, but he isn't here right now. "I've had many foreign experiences since I was a kid. You know, folks in other parts of the world don't look down on those struggling in pain in a bad way, call them weak or immoral for using a little of the stuff God made for us all. Look at all the aboriginal populations. Not one looks to the old or sick or emotionally tortured and says, too bad. It's your cross to bear. There are teas and gums and tars and smokes—and no, you don't do it every day or week. There's a shaman in every village, and the shaman keeps you on the right path. When you need the help, you get it, and only in moderation."

Sid says softly, "And you are a shaman, Doc, for Crawford, for the Panhandle."

But Doc doesn't hear. "And once I was recruited the first time—not supposed to be in Shanghai, but there I was—I had access to methods to bring a little of this or a little of that into the country. I took it in compensation, my handler knew my purposes, he understood my mission. I know they believed in me, you know, the government fellas, they let it go at that. And after that, any old war or a 'police action,' or a 'regional conflict' as they like to call their shootouts, I read the papers and before you knew it, there comes my handler, and I'd tell the folks hereabouts, we all gotta do our parts, and the government fellas would get a special nurse to watch Loretta—you know she was never really well, even when we first courted, but she was as special as she was delicate."

I wait a beat. "Those special assignments, Doc. I'm thinking you were posted as a medico to the regional commands at the fronts, even sometimes behind the front? I can tell you're a past master at the 'comforting physician' routine, and if there was an officer soon to crack from the pressure, or one who had cracked and gone rogue or double agent, you'd spot the signals, gain their confidence, and sooner or later they'd spill everything to ol' Doc, their 'safe harbor.' You assured them of their 'doctor-patient' confidentiality, you were a lockbox of disclosure, of discretion. But—"

229

Doc's eyes are out of focus, and tears run down both cheeks. "—there's a war on, the greater good, and I'd rat those poor bastards up to command without a second thought. And some would get shipped home, but only for a show trial in the States, keeps everybody in line. Most of them, wasn't a lot really, they'd just get sent out to the worst-case active battle on tap, drive them or drop them in, no help, no support, bodies and medals sent home for a hero's burial. Nobody loses, nobody wins."

Court is holding his uncle's hand throughout. "Is this what fueled your chronic-pain relief-crusade, Uncle? Was it the guilt? For every kid or man or woman making the wrong choice, for your betrayal, this buying and supplying contraband like it was aspirin or Epsom salts, this was supposed to earn you redemption?"

Doc was still overseas somewhere, many years ago, looking into a tragic pair of young eyes.

Court looks to Sid and I, and takes a deep breath. "I left town after high school, couldn't wait to blow Nebraska forever. Then after a few spins round the world, my great-aunt writes me, says the Hilltop's up for sale, come on home and cease your foolishness, and she gets Daisy and Doc and half my high school class to turn up the fire, and I come back for a reunion, and the rest is history. But it didn't take long to pick up on a pattern or two. And those poor folks suffering a righteous discomfort—no fault of their own and victims of a cold, cruel world—those folks found themselves comfort with Doc. But he wasn't peddling. A soul in torment—he or she and Doc became a unit of sorts. Doc's like a sponsor, a supporter, a counselor. And God spare you if you try to sell Doc a line of bullshit to get high. You'll find yourself in deep water, no boat, and Doc'll let you tread until you can't. But I sensed things were getting out of hand."

I look to Sid. She nods. I address Court, as Doc seems semiconscious. "We figure at some point things got 'commercial,' for lack of a better word. Doc couldn't control junkies, they reached further and further away for their needs, word spread about Doc's little domain. Maybe a loan shark or two saw a pressure point to take advantage, stories spread, and here comes a cartel scout to feel out the situation, then a cousin or two from north of the border, and before Doc knows it, he has to cut them in to play ball. He can't risk the big boys cutting him off from all supplies, and he can't risk his people getting hurt to keep him in line."

Sid's kept Court under a magnifying glass, watching every twitch. The "nephew" thing keeps her at arm's-length, I'm guessing. She says, "And two worlds accidentally collide ten years back, don't they?" Court's taken off-guard by the switch in questioners. "George Straight was always one of Doc's, wasn't he? But no one knew but Doc, no clue at all. Because George had to keep his chauffers' license, he had to stay on the road in the taxi-van, hauling crews at all times of the day and night, as he's in a relentless struggle to pay Dolly's alimony and ever-increasing child support. So Doc's got him buzzed enough to stay awake on a delivery, then he's got to get him sleeping quick to be ready eight hours later, and here comes another crew order."

Court seems to have made a decision of some kind, and it deflates him. "Look, on those rare occasions ol' George got a day off, he started spending them at the college bars in Chadron. Hiding, I guess, but looking for some sort of support or understanding from a woman who wasn't Dolly. And he got wound up with this Stella gal, and he thought it was true love, but that Jose guy was never far away—I kept telling him there is going to be an "ask" sooner or later, these young, hot girls have better things to do, and she's going to have a deal for him, and he'll be between a rock and a hard spot." This part of the story arouses Doc a bit, and he moans, and Court's that much closer to breaking down. But he manages. "And when it came, it was viscous."

And Court pauses again. Then, "It's a helluva lot easier to show than tell, right?"

"Let's walk down to the 'hides' track, the depot's only a couple blocks from here."

I look to Sid, but she seems unaffected. I feel less than confident. "Is that a real good idea? We're not really sure how good our good guys are, and where the hell our bad guys are, and we just got word when we were in Hill City that there was a fire, two cars on two tracks in fact, and in Crawford yard. Aside from all the normal rail traffic in and out, aren't there still a boatload of investigators crawling over every track?"

"Well," and Court has the grace to blush, "it's second trick now, things are slower in and out the office, and I know the second-trick operator a little—"

Sid's still watching closely. "—don't tell me, your aunt, your cousin, your half-sister once removed by marriage?"

Court's still good-natured. "He—Chuck Ponson—is my *friend*." And Court puts just enough emphasis on the word to send the message. "The investigators are returning at sun-up, and we can walk in from the opposite end of the yard without raising any eyebrows. But I need you to see this for George. He was in a very bad spot, and a very bad place, and he's never lived a peaceful moment since. You got to see it to understand."

Doc looks marginal once more. I say, "Get Doc in the restroom, Court, see if he can come with. Let me talk with Sid." They make for the men's, and Sis and I stop at the alley door.

Sid's smiling, and I'm at sea. She says, "Why are you in this, Allen?"

I say, "What do you mean?"

"You've said Dicky Tuttle hired you to save his ass. Then you transferred your loyalty to Emily Straight. You probably have enough with this set of stories to spin one for Howdy Humboldt down in Ft. Worth. And Tuttle gets his promotion, and Humboldt pays your absurdly-high bill—"

"—and nobody pays for four dead folks in a taxi, another dead railroader in his own damn station yard, and the only person in the whole bloody scenario most likely to look like a bad guy to local authorities is the only guy that gives a goddam about the little people, the folks he lives to serve."

"Doc." Sid cracks open the door, then looks up and down the alley. We both step out.

I'm exhausted, visions of my Airstream dance in my head. "I'd love to drive us back to Lander, Sid. Right now. But as it stands, Doc won't run, nor hide, nor lie about his actions, and somebody, somewhere is going to see him as an easy mark, and a quick close to a cold case. They will screw him to death, rack up a few political points, and throw away the key."

Sid's peeking back in the alley door. "Gotcha, Allen. We're here until we aren't. And right now I suggest we aren't—let's go."

I peek over her head. "Good idea, and *sonuvabitch.*"

Because I make out the other end of the restaurant, the front counter, where Court and Doc seem to be in earnest conversation with two familiar faces.

One's Maggie Connor.

The other—the mysterious MacAdam.

Thirty-Seven

Either I am pulling Sid back, or she's pulling me, or both—but we are away from the alley way door, and sprinting the two blocks back to the park and the Bronco. We're in our seats and out the park, hard left on First, north onto a county road, and we don't care as long as it isn't blocked. In a mile it narrows into one lane, and we have obviously made our way into a working ranch. We see no signs of life.

Sid points to a feed silo about a hundred yards on from the initial main barn and adjacent equipment enclosures. "Good a place as any." And she is right. I circle around the silo once before I park on the far side, the silo between us and anyone moved to follow.

I turn the key, get out and open my lock box. The second .38 Special presents itself, and I grab the half-empty ammo box. I take these around to the tail gate, drop it, and use it as a table to load one revolver and double-check the other. Sid takes advantage of one half the lowered tail gate, easing Beretta one and two from her bag with the necessary ammo.

I don't know what to say. "I don't know what to say."

Sid nods at my preparations. "Miss this type of thing?"

"Absolutely not. Outside the war, I must've prepped for possible action a hundred times in forty years, and followed through *maybe* a half dozen times." The dust trail we set off has settled, no signs of any followers, no sign of ranch life. "And that includes our escapades to this point."

Sid's binoculars are busy with a three-sixty. "Similar for me. I've had a lot fewer preps, and my so-called 'active career' began and ended rather quickly, but I never minded getting ready, always hoping it would come to nothing. Usually did." She stops her sweep at about two o'clock, north by northeast. "Allen, you know we have one very real option."

"Let me guess. You've deduced this ranch road probably swings about to re-connect with State 71, which can take us straight north to Straight's in

Edgemont. Give Emily what we know, counsel her to take the Edgemont Chief of Police into her confidence, he'll go to CBI, the family'll get protection, Artie'll have to earn his 'pension.'"

Sid's fixed on the northern-most point of our foreshortened horizon. "Yep. Or we can stick, get to the hides track and the cemetery track, and find therein the answers to our quandary."

Sid's super-awareness in invaluable, and it gives me a permanent case of the whim-whams. "Or just another set of questions, guarded by a bad guy with no sense of humor. Questions like how does Doc stay safe with neighbors on both borders in his business? Can he stay safe from local and federal prosecution if he can solve the cartel-slash-MacAdam problem? How did Emily Straight decide there was more to her dad's story than she was hearing? And so is she part of the solution, or another problem?"

Sid's getting antsy. "And the one thing, the one part of your little narrative that just seems wildly out of place in an already-complicated tableau—Wesley Dunhill. Ol' Wes, more lucky than smart, still at-large, and my choice for the unknowing match to this particular powder keg."

I pick up the binoculars and sweep around. "And not for nothin', what the hell are Maggie and MacAdam doing together? And why are Court and Doc chatting away with those two like it's old home week?"

"We do seem the odd men out." Sid smiles. "So to speak. But whatever their motives, isn't anyone aware of our general location figuring we're headed to the depot? Where else would anyone go?"

And here, this second, two really bad ideas come to mind. And I advance them because I have absolutely no other ideas.

"Sid, let's do two things. One, let's take the Bronco back to the park, but leave it in the most obvious spot possible, somewhere anybody can see it, bold and brassy."

"Okay, that sounds dumb."

"Then you will love the second thing."

"And that is?"

"We steal a car."

The last time I hotwired a car it wasn't a car. It was an Army jeep parked in a public lot next to crappy bar, a Seattle honky-tonk, 1944, maybe May, or June. Whatever. My commanding officer *de jure* was a Navy security second lieutenant named Brand who needed a hand following a couple of young lovers throughout downtown, hoping sooner or later to catch them red-handed in a "drop," picking up or leaving information for their handlers, or for a set of assets they themselves had cultivated. Either way, there was a war on, most people were green at international conflict, and the youngest screwed up the most often. No surprises there.

The surprise was that the lovers were Russian. The Russians were supposed to be U.S. Allies, yet these two, cleared by the State Department, and naturalized as "specialty shopkeepers," way back in '39, seemed unable to live without frequent visits to unguarded and unpopulated stretches of shoreline in and around the Washington and Oregon coasts. And especially in the middle of the night.

Lieutenant Brand told me he'd been chasing them all over the Puget Sound for months, but just lately the lovers became night owls in Downtown Portland, then Tacoma, and that very week, Seattle. We lost them in a busy market block, and then Brand got a glance of the male headed down an alleyway. He ordered me to get our vehicle, an unmarked Ford he brought to town himself, and meet him where the alley flushed out onto a state highway about a mile east of where we stood. I started to object, and he reminded me which of us was an officer, and he left me standing there. I remember watching him disappear in a crowd with a .45 in one hand.

I found the Ford where we'd left it in public parking. The battery was dead. I searched for jumper cables, even jimmied the trunk—no luck. I panicked, thinking of that poor guy, couldn't have been more than twenty-seven or eight, in a very bad spot and waiting for me to rescue him. An Army jeep pulled into our lot, two MPs climbed out and ran into a bar across the street. I didn't hesitate. Hoping they were called to break up a fight, I went to work hotwiring the jeep, using only what I'd seen in movies as a guide. It shouldn't have worked.

It did. I spun out of the lot, floored it and tore down the street with the market, flew past one more block, then put everything the jeep had into covering that one mile east and the alleyway's end. I didn't stop when the intersection presented itself. I cranked the jeep left as hard as I could, I'm went up on two wheels, and as I'm came down I saw the Russian man and woman in the middle of the street, firing guns in the direction Brand should be coming. I could see no farther than their backs, and again, no hesitation. I floored the jeep and targeted the Russian lovers in the windshield over the steering wheel like it was a rifle sight. Both turned at the same time to face me, both brought their weapons up to fire, and both disappeared under the front of the jeep. The collision almost threw me out of the jeep, but I brought it about some twenty yards past the collision point, and sat there with the headlights fully illuminating two bodies, bloody ragdolls, steam rising from open wounds.

If that wasn't sufficient trauma, Lieutenant Brand came up from behind me, the last place I should have found him. He said he got lost trying to jump a fence and runaround the two Russians, figuring I'd show up sooner or later and we'd stop them together. Both Russians bled out before help arrived. Brand abruptly ran when help did appear, and I never saw him again. I was told later that day no one named Brand, second lieutenant, existed. I was nineteen years old.

And this time I'm hotwiring a car, it's not a car. It's a Burlington Northern Signal Maintainer's high rail, much like the one Arne Birger, master-welder, drove all over the Powder River with Dicky Tuttle as prisoner—a large pick-up filled to overflowing with the appropriate tools and parts to fix malfunctioning train signals for hundreds of miles in every direction. These high rails have large metal wheels, like small train wheels, that will drop down on a rail so that the pickup moves over the tracks just like a train. That's not in a plan at this time, but one can never be too prepared.

This vehicle is sitting alone in the city park we used previously. It's not uncommon for two or more employees working the same territory or assignment to go to lunch or dinner together, and leave one of their company vehicles parked. Sid accused me of choosing this particular vehicle to steal because it just happened to be the first one we ran across. I would not totally discount that motive. But I also saw this pickup as the easy was to get close to Crawford yard, across the tracks, and all the way over to the site of the recently-torched railcars, all without arousing attention. One more company vehicle shouldn't matter, I hope. And as far as "hot-wiring" goes, I'd rather not admit I found the keys over the driver's visor, but there you are.

It's a *Twilight Zone* scenario becoming all too real as we slowly progress the three blocks from the park to the depot and yard. It *is* twilight, a grey-silver dusk grotesquely illuminated every thirty feet or so by red and green track signals, and by tall mercury lights, randomly popping on across the yard as each independent light-pole's sensors measure the declining ambient light. Occasionally a brakeman will wander by on his way from helper engine to depot, or a track worker will chat up a welder fixing to begin repairs to a switch on the back tracks. All this is accompanied by the syncopated rhythms of portable radios, clicking on and clicking off, before and after sharp questions and commands. You can easily imagine this scene repeated across the country, around the world in metroplexes and hamlets alike. But by the time we've crossed the main tracks, just in time before a loaded coal train is given permission to enter on the main and run to and through to the first siding, sound is muffled, and then gone save for our vehicle. Or that's what one would expect if one thought no one else stalks the hide tracks, or paces along the cemetery track.

Both our windows are down, the headlights are off, and I pull up behind an equipment shed just large enough to hide our vehicle's considerable bulk, and turn off the engine. Neither of us speak until what few noises we can make out are identified.

"Listen." Sid points out the window, generally west, mostly in the direction of the first hide track. I feel like I'm undergoing the company-mandated hearing exam, alone in an isolation booth with ill-fitting earphones screwed to my head. And just as those first test-beeps are barely discernible, I catch a hint of syllable, at first thinking someone's radio is playing a commercial.

Sid holds up to fingers, exactly when I make out the second speaker, possibly a male voice, but not one lower than tenor, for sure. I nod in agreement, then shrug. Sid returns the shrug. There is no good time to begin this move, but every second we delay increases the chances we are discovered by those least enamored with us. So uncharacteristically, I lead.

I hit the kill-switch on the dome light, and I open and shut the truck door as quietly as possible. I have just the one revolver in my left hand, because this somehow does *not* feel like the prelude to the Gunfight at the OK Corral, that a conclusion to this event, bloody or otherwise won't be predicated on gross firepower, but on instinctual recognition of the best chance. Sid agrees in that she duplicates my actions, bringing one of the two .45s in her bag, and we stand together in the shadow farthest west of the shed's corner. From here, the last car in the hide track is visible, and bizarrely illuminated by a single worker's fixed spotlight. The smell of old fire and it's fighting hangs in the air, and I am distracted by Sid's ability to focus.

She squeezes my arm, and whispers. "Someone's about midway along that first car, the one somebody lit up, I think it's a woman's voice. And there is another voice, the man's maybe, far enough away I can't make out words—and he is not pleased."

We listen another few moments, and I have to agree with Sid. I whisper. "Got a guess? How many car lengths away?" This catches us both off-guard, and it's all we can do not to giggle.

Sid sobers first. "What am I, a bat?" We listen again as the give-and-take becomes more intense. We start naturally drifting down the line of cars on our side, the side away from those holding court. And two shots—*pop pop*—freeze us in place. We paste ourselves as flat as possible to the ground on our side, and peer under the car into the lane's width between the hide track and hopper track. We can make out a form pressed between the first two broken and bent old hopper cars. Two more shots ring out from further down the lane between the hides and hopper tracks, and they ricochet off the car immediately in front of the hiding human form, showering the crouching person with sparks.

"Who the hell's that?" I say to Sid, no longer in whisper per unwritten rule seventeen, *once a gunfight breaks out, the participants can speak as loudly and often as they deem necessary.*

Sid's actually thinking, as I am not, weighing possibilities. "Emily Straight? Wouldn't be the first time."

"Doesn't feel right. Maggie?" Then the form gathers herself, turns and ducks down and fires three rounds. She stands, and is definitely a "she," and runs down one car length to hide once more.

Sid and I say together, "No, not Maggie." Maggie does nothing by half-steps, and Sid feels the same. Then hostile fire is returned once more from farther down the lane, and the woman or girl spins around ready to run forward again, and I catch a profile, one that I think is remarkable, one that I thought previously was remarkable as I observed her tied and trussed in the back seat of Bobby Delaine's Crown Vic.

"It's Stella Montenegro."

Sid looks at me like I'm speaking Swahili. "What? No. Bobby and Artie had her tied up like a prize pig after our ambush. So they couldn't have—oh, shit. I guess they could have let her walk, for their task force, for their master plan—"

"—for the greater good. *Their* greater good." I'm moving on down our side of the hides, Sid close. "How about we cut it in half. There's supposed to be about thirty or so cars here. We drop down a dozen more, try to cross over?"

Sid's with me. "See if we can get behind whoever's laying fire Stella's way?"

"It's all we got."

"It is all we have."

I lead.

Thirty-Eight

It is right about here, right about now.

Over the years you translate moments and contexts and rhythms, and you transpose scenes and scenarios and formats. It's beyond a verbal description, unless you count the silences between beats of a working heart as music. And in those moments recorded in the aftermaths of dreams, one particular, singular feeling clicks. It's the sensation the very tips of your fingers register when you have slowly and confidently turned the dial on a combination lock toward that third number, knowing in your bones as you approach it, the tumbler has to drop, the lock must be released.

That's the *click!*

And you know that you are in the best place you can be, and at the penultimate moment, or fate has conspired, as they say, and you are about to step backward off the edge of a cliff, with only the time from launch to impact to consider what went wrong.

And, unbidden, the adrenaline kicks, and you are *off*.

I choose to cross between two old tank cars, doing all I can to keep from touching the rusting surface areas. These two tanks smell as though they always carried petroleum products, but every poisonous chemical devised to improve our standards of living have probably crossed the country at least once in a tank car. The remnants sit for decades in some cases, deteriorating the container, combining to form new, unintended concoctions—you got it, it would ruin a decent pair of jeans.

And climbing over the couplers connecting one car to another is a chore itself. The coupler is a huge metal, two-finger claw. It's pushed toward a similar claw in the next car until, like shaking hands, each clicks into the other and locks. The stories of safety failures through misjudgment by switchmen as cars are pushed together are beyond number. Loss of a leg or arm, or even a life result. And though I know there is no engine pulling or pushing on this particular string of cars, and that the couplers I'm climbing over are secure in place, I can't but help run the file of personal injuries and fatalities in memory. Each victim no doubt felt as secure in his moment as I do in mine.

I'm over the couplers and giving Sid a hand as she mounts them, and she is over and down, and we stand holding our breath, waiting, waiting for some hint, some further clue as to who is where. Shooting has paused. Thank God for small favors.

I whisper so low I'm not sure Sid can hear. "I'm going to cross to the track directly, between those two old beet wagons." I pause while Sidney stares into the darkness, makes out my tentative destination, and nods. She puts her back as flat to the tank as possible, .45 held like a pro. It only just now dawns on me. She is a pro, retired or otherwise.

I peek out to the left, toward the end of the track with the burnt-out SP&S box car, then to the right, to the other end closest to the main yard and the depot. If there is still a figure or figures to the left, they've taken cover as Sid and I have, between cars. I feel a slight prod in the back from Sid, and she's right, there *is* no time like the present, and I run across. It's the sort of thing that feels like a lifetime, and then I'm safe between the beet wagons. I'm almost jubilant I'm not leaking blood.

I look back the way I came. Sid is down on a knee, pointing to her left, now my right, and signaling *five.* I go prone and count five cars. I can't see the cars on my track, of course, but five ahead of Sid, someone is carrying a pen light of sorts, using it to signal across to someone, I presume, positioned in a similar manner to Sid and me. We manage to wave and point in a style communicating what we see and our understanding of what we think the other sees, so I stand, but I do so with the help of a chain hanging from the coupler assembly between the beet wagons, and a corroded link snaps, and the chain falls to the ground. It isn't the loud clang of metal to metal or metal to asphalt, but it's enough of a clunk that the two figures five cars ahead start playing pen lights down the tracks, trying to determine the sound's source. And this is immediately helpful to Stella Montenegro in that she now has a general direction to concentrate her fire, and she fires two rounds on each track about midway between Sid and me and our mystery twins five cars closer to Stella.

The most unnerving facet of this particular get-together is uncertainty. There seem to be five of us involved here, although we can't be sure there aren't fifty. We know we think two are between Stella and our location, but there may be more, and we don't know who they are, good or bad. And we know Stella and the mystery twins are exchanging live fire in general directions at irregular rates, a sure recipe for the wrong people to catch the wrong round at the least auspicious moment.

What better moment, after two full minutes of total silence now, for a wildcard to fly from the deck and change the order and parameters in manners unforeseen? I hadn't noticed two mercury lights secured to thirty-foot utility polls on either side of the tracks two cars further back from Sid and me. And the dusk finally embraces a full conversion to night, and the lights' sensors take command, and the mercury lights explode.

This part of the yard becomes day, almost high noon. Sid and I are backlit to the other three, invisible for all practical purposes. And the scene in front of us would be hilarious on a summertime playhouse stage. The two minutes between shots was put to good use by Stella and the mystery twins to rearrange their relative positions to each other, and unbeknownst to them—to us.

Stella got by her pursuers in the dark shadows, and apparently after she'd passed by them, they moved farther toward her original position. So Sid and I remain unseen midway down the track, Stella's pursuers assume a position roughly three car-lengths away from Stella, headed toward the burnt-out SP&S car, and Stella is almost three cars away from us, heading our way.

The lights freeze the players in mid-step. Then Stella turns just as the mystery twin do, and the three are facing each other once more, all in shooter's pose. I look to Sid, and she is training her .45 on someone, and I can only guess without speaking, as that would put our security in danger. And she looks my way, and I am doing the same, and she is under the same constraint. And I'm sure if I could freeze time, and Sid and I could chat over a nice coffee, we'd be exchanging our impressions of discovering the figure on our left, past and left of Stella, is Maggie Connor. But that discovery would pale in comparison to discovering the other shooter is Wesley Dunhill.

So, in the nanoseconds in which these types of things occur, I know Sid and I are running our brainpans on overdrive. If a firefight breaks out now that the three see each other and closer than ever, giving each confidence in the accuracy of their shots, do Sid and I take cover and pray? Do I shoot Wesley before he can shoot Stella, and how do I know—as he doesn't know Sid and I are behind him—he won't then turn his weapon on Maggie? And since my loss of confidence in Maggie, how do I know she might not shoot Stella, then

Wesley, then herself or us as well, once she discovers we are here and learning much of what she's been hiding from us, and possibly from her contacts and assets, and possibly from her boss or bosses, depending on how many outfits she pledges allegiance to.

Oh, what a tangled web we weave.

And I am moved. I look over to Sid, and she can read my face, and there is that look saying *oh my God, the boy's had another idea, and he's drunk on his own luck, and he's gonna do what just came to him, and now I can only get ready to rock'n'roll, I don't wanna die, oh, well, it's been a good life.*

"Nobody moves." That seemed to go over. Nobody did. "Sid has you sighted in, Maggie, and I have Wesley the very same, and Stella, either one of us can swing over to you and probably make the shot."

And that's all I've got. I hope Sid notes that clipped final couple of words.

She does. "Please know, people, I could shoot Maggie right now and feel bad for the rest of the night, but one night only. And I really don't know you other two, so actually that makes it easier for me, being as how I wouldn't care one way or the other."

Now that was not how I thought Sid would respond. I figured she'd be short and cold and mean to overcompensate for her small frame. And it would make up for me sounding like the perennial white guy on a walk through a Marrakesh bazaar, acting as if he knows what's happening, and never really having a clue.

Stella's first: "No."

Let me rephrase that. "Sorry, Stella, that was not a yes-or-no question. See, I said *freeze*, and everyone did, so at least to that point, we are in agreement."

Maggie's fit to be tied. "For the love of God, Allen, shut up."

And finally, Wesley Dunhill. "Connor, what the hell is *this*? You brought me out here, you said we had a deal."

You gotta love Sid. "Deal? What deal's that, Maggie? With the Deadwood PD? Or are you NCIS, or maybe ICE?"

I'm trying not to lose my sight on Wesley, but there is some quick fun to be had.

Stella's back. "ICE? You coming after me—ICE? You trade me out, Connor?"

Maggie's losing her midwestern accent. "Wait a minute, everybody shut up—" while she has her gun trained somewhere between Wes and Stella, feigning neutrality, yet her barrel, like a needle on a lie detector, wavers one way, then the other—"Wesley, we have the deal we have always had. And Stella, do not listen to these two idiots. We can relax, and come together, we can fix the little problem here, and take up where we left off."

I'm up. "And where you left off, Maggie? Excuse me, but it seemed for all the world like you and Wesley left off trying to shoot holes through Stella, and in large numbers."

And Sid. "So, Stella, that can't be good for you, and we have no idea, really, what you may or may not have done, and—bonus—we are not cops—"

Me. "—well, technically I *am* a cop, but only if you travel to railway property, and then decide to commit a criminal act on that property, and I see you, or I don't see you, but someone else does—"

Sid. "—but only on the railroad he's contracted to at the time, because, see, he's a private investigator, sort of—"

Me. "—what do you mean, *sort of*? That's *exactly* what I do—" And Sid and I have combined to distract and confuse and frustrate our three guests long enough to take a couple of steps closer to Stella, and to each other, sharpening our angles to Wesley and Maggie, if good guys have to shoot bad guys, or good guys have to shoot once-good guys, now confused guys. But I'm feeling both Sid and I know Maggie's temperament on a good day is one marginally-equipped to undergo high stress in fluid situations, unless those situations are of her design.

In other words, Maggie's due to snap.

Thirty-Nine

I need a last straw. "Cool off, Wesley, ol' Mags is still your DEA girl—"

Maggie's barrel swings undeniably my way. "—I don't know what the hell you're up to, Allen—"

Wesley's losing it, and his weapon drifts toward Maggie. "DEA? You bitch. You said you're the new CSIS bunch, you said you could get me to Ottawa—"

I see Stella's scanning the site for the quickest exit once the shooting begins, and I'm thinking she may be considering starting the fire to cover her exit. Her attention tangentially considers Sid and me, and she immediately writes us off by age, gender, and her quick contempt for my bringing a revolver to the party. That leaves her maybe shooting Wes, and I get the feeling he was doing most of the firing in her direction just minutes ago, and she might stand a better chance with even a furious Maggie, depending on what *their* beef is all about.

And Maggie's made a decision. I see it in the set of her jaw.

But Sid makes one last stab at derailing her, at mitigating the angle of her weapon.

"*CSIS*? Oh, Maggie, you didn't—"

"Shut up, Sidney. Please don't make me—"

"—but that explains so much—"

And the straw lands on the camel's back. Maggie's weapon swings toward Sid in anger. My revolver trains itself, it seems, on Maggie in response. But when Maggie turns toward Sidney, her angle must pass through Stella—standing between Sid and I on one side, and Maggie and Wesley on the other—and Stella moves down and away to clear her shot. And in these nanoseconds, Wesley has considered his risks and rewards, and he misreads Stella's dive to the ground as a play to get a clear shot at Wesley. He panics, takes a knee to decrease his target area, and fires toward Stella. And in one unique alignment

245

of four reflex actions, each patterned by separate histories and trainings—Stella and Maggie and Sidney and I aim and fire. And Wesley drops over like a bookend pushed from a shelf, two rounds to the head, and two to the chest.

The next bit is as unexpected as it is efficient. The four remaining actors stay in place, telling each other much without speaking. Maggie's weapon is trained on Stella, and Stella's on Maggie. And Sid's is on Maggie. And mine is on Maggie.

Maggie reads this, and lays her gun at her feet, now looking only to Stella. "You're making a grave mistake, Stella. You don't know these people."

"I will take that chance, Connor. I know who's aiming at who." With that, Stella hands me her weapon butt first, then picks up Maggie's and hands it to Sidney. And, placid beyond imagination, Stella Montenegro sits down next to the body of Wesley Dunhill, steam rising from his wounds.

Stella Montenegro lights a cigarette within spitting distance of the no smoking sign in a cinder block conference room one floor above the Crawford Police Department main office, two floors above the basement holding cells. The Assistant Police Chief, Clark Rasmussen, is waiting for the county's public defender to appear in service to Stella's right to due process. Stella actually waived her right verbally, wanting to get on with this so she can re-establish contact with someone within a federal agency—someone who could do for her what she *thought* Maggie Connor was doing for her.

Taking into account three of the people in this room were only three hours ago pointing loaded weapons at, and in close proximity to each other, the mood is cordial. Clark explains the Chief would most definitely be here normally, all events being so out of the ordinary for little ol' Crawford, but Estes Monfort, Acting Chief, is away at one of those darn FBI things, and the Crawford PD got itself a grant, but one earmarked for federal training only, and it's dead come first of the year, so you know how that goes.

Stella expresses a curiosity for the established federal hierarchy "out here" in the "outback," and Clark thinks that is "high-larious," and reminds himself to tell ol' Estes when he returns, as the Chief sure doesn't see the Panhandle that way. And I'm surprised when Sidney offers Stella, unbidden, to make a couple of calls on her behalf before she signs anything, now or forever, because it's very important to be very sure of who is who, not just who says who is.

Stella thanks Sidney. "Yes. I thought the Connor lady was my, what do you call it—handler, yes. She said, years ago you know, she was DEA on a special assignment, and I was special, and I cooperate and give information, and I feel, especially when my handler, she points a gun at me, well, I am not special, not special at all."

Which brings about my first question in this little session. "So, what the hell is CSIS?"

Sidney leans back to take us all in. "The Canadian Security Intelligence Service. It's been up and running a couple of years now, but it's been on a super-secret planning-board for much longer, so who knows how long Maggie's been playing both sides of the street, and with whose knowledge—and better yet—with whose permission." Clark refills our Styrofoam cops with better-than-most precinct-blend, and Sid continues.

"The Mounties have served a foreign and domestic purpose since the advent of Canada. It would be like if the FBI and CIA worked out of the same house, one name, one mandate. And the seventies brought severe challenges in terms of corruption and rumors of foreign double-dealing, which finally lead to '84 and the McDonald Commission. The chief recommendation being the split of domestic and foreign intelligence gathering, with an obvious commitment on both sides for full transparency."

I see. "High-larious." Clark smiles. "I imagine it doesn't work any better or worse than the friction between the CIA and FBI."

"And another fourteen intelligence agencies in the U.S. alone." Sid leans forward, elbows on the table. "But anyway, I can only figure that Maggie's ultimate loyalty is to Canada. Maybe a birth parent was Canadian, she was delivered in Canada, or maybe she forges records for other reasons, who knows? And it explains a lot. She's been in close proximity to MacAdam on more than one occasion without explanation, and MacAdam has appeared on and off cameras in military dress from both countries—"

"—except when he tours the American West in Italian suits, and openly attracting attention with B.C. plates," I say. And now Clark, really past serious interest in other than crimes provable in and about the Crawford city limits, stands and excuses himself, as the search for the public defender must have stalled.

With this, Stella visibly deflates, head and shoulders committing to a similar pitch and yaw. "Man, that guy, I thought he never leave." Her eyes still hold the fire of the shootout, and she focuses on Sidney. "Okay, lady, are you good to your word? My time is running out here."

Sid, as always, earnest and honest. "Look, Stella, I have maybe two people still in the game who I trust without question, and I can still contact both, and I can tell you the names of neither one. That's where the trust comes in. If we can manage to get you put in the custody of an honest cop, federal level now, there will be little opportunity for those that fear you to act against you."

Stella smiles like a woman with multiple past lives, each ending tragically. "Well, Sidney, I would say the same thing if I am you and you are me. And you are right. And I believe you are good, or I would not have handed my weapon to you. But even here—this Nebraska—it is not Mexico City, it is not Vancouver. And yet, danger is here. People die."

I need more than this if I am going to plead Stella's case. "Talk about Wesley."

Stella's eyes fixate on the lighting. "This comes from Connor, and she says it comes from MacAdam, too. Dunhill was the sort of asset MacAdam wanted and Maggie wanted. They found him after a bust for transporting marijuana in Alberta. MacAdam was one of the trouble-makers in the Mounties, so he might have planned to go bad, and use Dunhill to get there. But Connor tells me early and often, she might look like she works for many agencies, no matter. I stick with her; she will end up high up in this CSIS."

I finally accept I know less than nothing about Maggie Connor. "And you are in trouble, or could be in trouble with—who—the Mexicans, the Colombians? Or the Calderones, a little closer to home, right? So that's when you reach out for protection, and you turn double-operative for Maggie? And, let me guess, right around the time of the Crawford tragedy."

Stella is coy. "All good guesses, and I will fill in the answers with somebody with power. But yes. I was sent here in 1975. Two reasons. My family was on the bad side of a cartel. And I am—what do you say—dead ringer for Maria Calderone. Maybe, maybe I say, if Calderone family needs a presence to make people think Maria is in one place, not another, somebody like me is valuable."

I say, "Up to a point."

Stella says, "Up to a point. As you say. And this Wesley, he hustles every angle, no thinking. He hears of the Doctor, feels there should be profit involved. And he tries to impress my boss, not lucky at that, and tries to make a direct deal with Doc, and he threatens him."

I'm catching on. "So Doc feels threatened by Wes, and about this time MacAdam hears more and more stories of Doc—but MacAdam is like a male Maggie, only bent enough to take advantage of a side-hustle when he sees it. He doesn't see Doc as a savior, or Wes as a small-time screw-up, but he sees the whole setting—the big picture—as one Big Idea. Railroads as transport for drugs."

Sidney nods as if entertaining the notion of an automatic transmission over a straight stick. "Makes sense from one end to the other. Someone else has built and paid for the transport system. And that system connects every market with every other. And how tough is it to recruit a handful of trainmen here and there, already suffering the pressures and demands of a transient life style, and promise them a cut of product each time they deliver. I mean, how often are cabooses—"

"—way cars."

"—whatever. How often are they searched?"

I see it working. "About as often as they are thoroughly cleaned. Which is not very damn often."

Stella laughs. "Maybe you are right, maybe. And think about it, you sit up high in the caboose, way car yes, if someone comes you see them first, throw your load out of the window, make a note of location. Who will know? And specially here in your 'outback.'"

Clark Rasmussen re-enters with a lanky white guy, maybe old enough to drive, in khakis and a polo shirt, dragging along an oversize leather satchel. Clark starts, "Well, folks, this ain't a public defender, but Miss Montenegro might be happy to hear—"

I reach in to shake the boy's hand. "Walt Whitman as I live and breathe. And how was the drive from Casper?"

"Oh hell, no," says Clark, and you can tell this will be yet another story for his boss, Chief Estes. "This ol' boy flew right up to the city park in a big black helicopter."

And I look to Stella, trying to read her take on her new position in all of this. And frankly, her look could be one of fascination for the random way the world works. Or just as easily, her countenance might be a pleasant mask behind which, those big, brown eyes are searching for an exit.

Or looking for the odd, closed door or sealed window that could be turned into an exit.

Forty

Sid and I are walking away on our own recognizance, for no good reason other than Doc's nephew, Court, told Assistant Chief Clark we are "good ones." We'll have to return to Dawes County once a grand jury is summoned and selected and sat—an annual event often taking several months to prepare. And the evening is gentle, not nearly as cold as it should be, here "in the middle of nowhere."

We are silent until the Bronco is in sight, sleeping it appears, in the city park lot, right where I recently stole a railroad high-railer. This Sid finds entertaining. "What do you get for grand theft auto in Nebraska these days?"

"I get a light scolding, if you can call it that, from Clark Rasmussen, who was more interested in how one hotwires a truck than my purpose for utilizing a company vehicle in advancement of my railroad-sanctioned investigation."

Sid's incredulous. "You are shitting me."

"Language, young lady."

"Are you *ever* held responsible for what you do?"

"Rarely. And on those occasions, I plead senility."

"That works?"

"What works?"

And we have made the Bronco, and there are weapons to tend to, and to relocate into secure storage and carrying-accoutrements, and we meet again in the front seats, me in the driver's, Sid in passenger's.

I say, "Where to?"

Sid says, "I wish you hadn't asked."

"Because?"

"Because," she says, rolling down her window, letting in the cold, "you might have just reflexively headed for Lander without a thought, and by the time we made, oh I don't know, Lusk, maybe? Maybe then you would think of a question so far unanswered, but, hey, it's too late to turn around."

251

"And this won't happen now why?"

"Because, goddamit, your dumbass curiosity might be viral, because I think I've caught it."

I'm idling at the entrance to the city park, left is north to Edgemont, and a meet with Emily Straight. Right is south to U.S. 20 and home—and also maybe five whole minutes to Daisy's. "Need a coffee for the road?"

Sid rolls the window back up. "What the hell."

Daisy, according to her "hours" sign in her doorway, says the door is locked at midnight. It's almost 1:30 now, and there are at least four cars in the lot, plus walk-ins, no doubt. But the twenty or so pie-eating-coffee-guzzling patrons manage to go mute as one being when Sis and I come through the door.

Sid whispers, "Don't."

I say, with mock importance, "As you were."

We take a table way, way back. Sid sits, and while reading the one-page menu, says, "Have I ever once asked you about your wife?"

I have to think. "No. No, you haven't. I bring her up on occasion, but you've never asked, nor have you posed a follow-up question."

Sid waves at a busboy, lifting her clean but empty cup his way. "Was she a saint?"

The busboy is good-natured, and brings a carafe, fills both our cups, and leaves the carafe. He knows a good tipper when he sees one. "She wasn't at first."

Sid spots someone on the other side of the restroom-doors enclosure. She is up and off, and as she goes, she says, "Well, she sure as hell is one now."

I can't argue that. And this is one of those times, when a case is cleared, this is when my first thought is still *wait 'til I tell Wendy about*—and my heart still drops, and it gets better though, anywhere from a couple weeks to a couple of months. But hey, it's only been ten years.

Sid returns without a gleeful smile so much as a resolute smirk. And she is followed by Daisy, who is followed by a handsome—like Old West handsome—man dressed clean, clean-shaven, smelling of *Brut*. And at this time of the morning, he's got to be a trainman freshly rested and called back to duty, to drive to Alliance, and conduct a train and its crew to Edgemont, and when he rides through Crawford, wave from his seat high in the cupola of his way car, wave at his frantically-busy wife serving the fine people of Crawford, and taking notes for her uncle as regards those that seek his comfort.

Sid and I are introduced to Daisy's husband, and Daisy kisses him, and he is off to work. And Daisy sits, but isn't angry, and maybe is a little bit sheepish.

I feel for her, but I know she is a strong, competent adult who has made her choices and stands by the results. So I get straight to it.

"Without having to squeeze Jimmy Kilroy, and the Edgemont widows, or George Straight if he hasn't just drifted away—or especially your grandpa, as he's looking mighty poor just lately—"

Daisy's no longer sheepish. "—yeah, thanks for that."

"Save me the accusatory stare, young lady. You and yours have created this weird hybrid Shangri-La, free from pain at first, until everybody and their sister starts qualifying for treatment, no pain too small. And Doc's line between benevolent healer and small-time dealer is razor-thin. Who do you suppose is going to show up? A sequence of Jose Garcias until you start playing ball, right? But who swings in then to fight your fights, MacAdam? And in and out, depending on her need for you—and not the other way around—comes ol' Maggie, always hinting at working in secret for those-who-shall-go-unnamed, always ready to help you bend the rules for one of yours, if you can clue her in on what the boys from the south and the Canucks from the north are up to in these parts."

Daisy starting to stand. "That is a horrible mischaracterization of our town, and our people, and Doc—for the lovuh God, you think he's rolling in dough, getting his own folks hooked?"

Sid motions for her to sit. "Look, Daisy, if things were going so damn well, then tell me about Crawford. Tell us about the taxi van." Daisy is angry, on the verge of tears, but some things have been kept closed too long.

She stands. "Office." And she is away.

I look to Sid. "Safe?"

"Safe enough for now. For us."

"But keep an eye?"

"Oh, yes."

We make the short hall past the restrooms into a room no larger than a utility closet, and then I realize that is what this enclosure used to be. So, although Sidney and I are in chairs on one side of Daisy's desk and Daisy's on the other, shelves begin on all four walls about five feet from the floor and extend to the ceiling. Add no windows whatsoever, and my claustrophobia, normally dormant in the West, starts crawling up my spine.

Daisy is working tissues into shreds. "Nobody thought much about it, I mean, a huge tragedy, and everybody who railroads knows everybody else. Huge funerals. Bigger wakes. But little Jimmy Kilroy, the All-American boy, he sees too much. Keeps camping out on Doc's porch with *inconsistent bruising-this,* and *taxi location in relation to speed-that,* even *why did it blow up when it did?*"

"Well," I say, not wanting to strain Daisy dry in one sitting, "let me take a guess or two." And Sid looks like she has a couple up her sleeve as well.

I try to get comfortable, pretend the walls aren't closing in. "I'm betting the taxi was slowed and taken over when some sort of large reflective surface, a mirror on wheels if you please, was rolled into place that night, probably by Stella with George's very hesitant cooperation, and at the direction of the current 'Jose Garcia,' the muscle-of-the-minute supervising from Jalisco, or wherever."

Sid's having better luck with Daisy, Daisy showing just a touch more sincerity when Sid speaks. I glance over. She takes over.

"But word has it Doc did some illegal forensics-testing at Jimmy's prodding, then Doc claims it didn't happen."

"It didn't, but Doc thought if Jalisco thought he had something on them, they would back off." Daisy looks like there's a thaw in progress, and I plan to stay clear.

Sid says, "But the engineman and brakemen, they *were* dead before the crash of the taxi."

"Yes." Daisy looks each of us in the eye in turn. "This is my fault. I helped choreograph this set-up—my idea, Doc's blessing. Stella wanted free of her old pals in Mexico, and we needed an incident demonstrating to the cartels, well, we just weren't worth their time and trouble. When George and Stella stopped the taxi with the mirror, and George's brother, Harley, got out, they had only a second to act. George was supposed to hit Harley, but he couldn't, and Stella grabbed the lantern from him, and hit Harley. And they go to the taxi, and the trainmen are still sleeping, except for Jose, who never was, just pretending."

Now I'm in. "Okay, wait. I'm sorry to interrupt, Daisy, but with Harley out of the taxi, that left the engineman, Timmy Nelson, and Roger Fointman, the brakeman. And the mystery trainman no one identified until after the burials, and then I only know because I got a hold of an *eyes-only* file I wasn't supposed to see—that mystery brakeman was ID'd as one Maria Calderone. In other words, no Jose Garcia."

Daisy's still thawing. "Yes. And this is why you people are so easy to fool. You think you know what you do not know."

Sid smiles. "That puts it rather well. Don't you think, Allen?"

"Apparently I do not—*think*, that is. So, Daisy, please teach me."

"I hope you are listening. The name *Jose Garcia* is just a handle for whatever thug is sent from south of the border to do reconnaissance, or make deals, or just plain extort us for more money and less product. That night the so-called mystery brakeman was the current *Jose*, but this time a female. The body found after the wreck was an unfortunate illegal who had crossed a cartel-financed mule, didn't pay up the money for the trip, and threatened to go to the law. The cartel-in-question—and before you ask, hell no, I am not naming names—had an opportunity to make an example of the no-pay-gal, and tag her with the *Maria Calderone* name, and the real Maria, who loves to have virtually no one know exactly where she is or how long she's been there, *that* Maria was delighted."

Sid's on a roll. "And Nelson and Fointman?"

Daisy's developing dark circles beneath her eyes. "That particular Jose Garcia, she greased a few railway clerks' palms—their eyes practically fall out of their heads when they see crisp hundreds in multiple amounts—and Fointman and another engineer, both owing some important loan sharks more than either man was worth, were called to work out of turn. As luck would have it, the engineer missed his call, as he was losing even more borrowed money at the game behind Stockmen's, and Nelson, being the truly nice guy he was, took the call last minute, thinking he could pull down a day's pay in short order, than surprise his wife with something nice for their anniversary."

Now Daisy can't stop the tears. "Ten years, I still see his wife's face at the funerals."

The worse moment possible for me to interject. "And I am sorry again, Daisy, but where did they die?"

"In the BN 102371, the hide car on the cemetery track. The female Jose Garcia took Nelson and Fointman there, and the body Stella was entrusted with—the dead migrant. And she inflicted injuries, still hoping to bring some money back home again. Stella won't give any details, as she had to stay with Jose and watch and pretend she didn't care. Nelson couldn't talk about what he didn't know, and Fointman had nothing to give, dead broke as usual, so they put the taxi occupants back in the taxi, now quite dead, and they rolled it off the curve, but not before Jose straps a pipe bomb to the frame. It doesn't explode on impact, and Jose takes off, long trip back home—*que sera, sera.*"

"But it *did* go off later, just as the EMT's got the occupants clear," says Sidney.

Daisy shrugs. "Random chance."

I've got one last question, and Sid's looking at me like *it's one too many.* "So Harley was out cold all this time, I imagine waiting with George while Stella and Jose did their business. And again, Daisy, I am very truly sorry—"

"Go on, goddamit."

"Someone put Harley back in the taxi. I assume you were nowhere in proximity, and Doc probably didn't know,"—Daisy shrugs—"and you say Jose, the gal, hightailed it down Mexico way, so either Stella or—"

Daisy spits out "George."

Sid gives it a beat or two. "I'm assuming the brothers' relationship was always difficult? At least for George?"

Daisy stands. This is coming to an end. "George had spent five years watching the only child he would probably ever father—and not be sabotaged by Dolly—grow into a delightful little girl. And George would never have her, and George would never have Barbie, because Harley got her first, and his parents willed the motel to Harley when the brothers were just kids, and on and on and on."

I say, "And George disappeared and reappeared, and his life was crap."

Daisy flares. "Oh, please. He could put an end to it any time. The gutless bastard. He could blow his brains out. I'll lend him a gun."

Daisy's to the door. "We all, *all* of us, have choices." She points to the diner's front room.

"Now get the hell out of here. We're closed."

Epilogue

"So, we're deadheading home?"

Sid's driving, it's sunrise over the Pine Ridge, and Lander is a mere four hours and forty-five minutes, or 306 miles due west, for the most part. My mom and dad, whenever we were on a road trip, loved to get up at the crack of dawn and drive about a hundred miles before stopping at a mom & pop for breakfast. Roads are mostly deserted, the sunrise is all yours, and then breakfast and a full carafe of Farmer Brothers is a real treat.

Sid doesn't share the tradition, but is up for anything, or so the last couple of days have proven. We pass through Fort Robinson at what railroaders would call "restricted speed," ten to fifteen files and hour, not because traffic is an issue in the dying light of a Fall tourist season, but because there seems to be something strangely reverential in passing the old fort, and the officers' quarters, and the parade grounds. And here Sid poses the question.

"Well, yeah, I guess you could say we are—" I begin.

"Because we ran out of time, so to speak?"

"And we need to get home and get our rest. Yeah."

And between the Fort and Harrison, we don't speak again, taking advantage of what I'm told is called a "companionable silence." I'm also told I would know what that meant if I took the time to *be* companionable.

Sid waits at the one and only traffic light in Sioux County, the one at the intersection of the highway and Sioux County High School. School buses are just now starting to warm up engines. "I have questions." She glances my way. I am staring at the school buses.

"Same," I say.

"Same questions?" Sid asks.

"We'll find out. You first."

Sid accelerates as we leave town. "Okay. Do you feel your contract is fulfilled?"

"*Not* the same questions. But, all right. No, not entirely." I wonder what they pay school bus drivers out here. "With Dicky Tuttle? Sure. That little scum ball was lucky to get me at twice the price, and by the way, we are still on his dime, so when we stop at Orin Junction for that delicious convenience-store cuisine, load-up."

"Roger." Sid's doing eighty in a sixty-five. "And Emily Straight?"

"Not so much." And this does bother me. "I'm sure she knows George is her birth-father, and she's a bulldog. She's got the guts to tail people like Maggie and get away with it, she has a place in the game someday."

"I pray not," says Sidney.

"Same. Anyway, I can't help but think that MacAdam is a very bad guy, so bad that he can continue working for domestic and foreign intelligence service, all the time padding his nest with the odd nefarious caper."

Sid nods. "He has too much on too many people up top. He is his own insurance policy."

"Right." And we are out into very subtle hills, rising and falling, even at speed, like a kiddie-carnival ride. "And Maggie aside, whatever the hell's she's up to, this MacAdam is above—"

"—the law?"

"Justice." And I smirk as I say it, and Sidney laughs.

I say, "Yeah, I get it. I set up my work to be all my own way, my decisions, my responsibilities, and I meet out justice to my liking. I'm a hypocrite, I get it."

Sid's eyes are straight ahead. "Just checkin'."

"But MacAdam works *too* easily. He drives through the middle of rural America almost unnoticed, killing people—"

"—allegedly."

"Whatever, and slipping ol' Doc a mickey that almost kills him? For what? Was Doc or Richie so insignificant to MacAdam, he can swat them like mosquitoes? And MacAdam's courted by the mighty and powerful, as you saw first-hand your own self."

"I'm trying to forget."

"Well, don't. I may need your memories."

"Allen." Sid is slowing down.

"Orin is still another half an hour, at least."

Sid isn't listening. One of those ubiquitous "historical markers" is a quarter-mile, and there is always a shallow turn-off where any of America's three history grads over the last fifty years can indulge their love of the dead.

Sid pulls in. And turns to me. "You are not."

"Not what?" I'm pretty sure most of this doesn't have to be said.

"You don't like MacAdam, who does, and whether it's jealousy, or resentment, or that tortured scale-of-justice thing you go on about, you're developing a vendetta."

"Scrabble points."

Sid turns off the radio rather than compete with the farm report. "A vendetta demands a feud, and your family is the good guys, you figure—and MacAdam's is the bad guys, no matter who they are. This is dangerous. And a vendetta by default is vengeful, that is the killer of the one killed must be killed himself, and by one of the victim's family members. And again, this is dangerous."

I want to speak, to vent, to challenge every word. I can't. She's right.

Sis restarts the Bronco, eases back onto the highway. "And I know your twins as well as any maiden aunt might—"

"They love you."

"How could they not? And they lost a world-class mom, and the least you can do, you selfish bastard, is protect their dad." A mileage sign for Orin passes, but I can't read it in time.

"Okay." I think I see a grain elevator on the horizon.

"Okay, what?"

"Okay, Sidney Lowe, I will protect myself as I have but one true purpose, and that is supporting my college kids in the level of comfort to which they have become accustomed."

"Damn straight." Sid smiles and shares this one with me. "You said we are breakfasting at a convenience store?"

"Frozen breakfast burritos, I remember. It ain't no *Sidney's.*"

"What is, Allen? What *is*?"

THERE'S ALWAYS ONE MORE THING

A real spring won't grace Sinks Canyon until mid-April at best, and then a hard freeze is still on the table. But it's April 1, and my travel to town, and my walk to Sidney's is inspired by chinook winds from the west, ruffling the trees and bushes and elevating the normal 6:30 temperature to mid-morning levels. I turn the corner halfway through the downtown main drag, and there, two parking spaces from Sidney's café entrance is a Crown Vic, eerily familiar, idling, all windows steamed over.

I start to enter the café to get my sweeping started and my breakfast earned, when I spot the South Dakota license plate at the same time as the passenger's window buzzes down. And a face that's hard to dislike smiles and says, *"Buenas dias, Señor Allen. Cómo estás?"*

"Todo está bien, Artie Gleason, unless it's not." I swing around the front of the Vic and climb in the passenger's side. It's roasty-toasty.

Artie's ever-present smile works; it's magic, and I have trouble remembering exactly why I'd ever considered throttling him. "So, Arturo Luís Gleason, former Assistant Director, South Dakota Criminal Bureau of Investigation, now emeritus fellow—you're a long way from home, brother."

"I am, and right now I count this a small victory as you have neither broken my nose nor shot off my kneecap." The defrosters are doing their job, and I can see Sidney peering through the café's front door window wondering why I would be late on a regular weekday.

"Sid's going to roll out here and do either or both to you if I don't show up in a couple minutes."

Artie's smile drops a lumen or two. "How would she know it's me?"

Maybe I'm in control here. "She's recognized your plates from the little ambush you set up for us in September."

Artie's demeanor stiffens. "That was Maggie Conner's, but very well. Okay. I'm here to share a couple of pieces of information, stuff I figured you care to know."

My demeanor lightens. "Very well, and you could have used a phone, and this is no Sunday drive for you, but please, continue."

Artie glances at Sid in the window. "So, we're feeling the growing presence of our neighbors from the north in terms of new infusions of premium product, so to speak—"

"—and our neighbors from the south?"

Artie's eye-to-eye now. "A tactical retreat for the moment. Mexico figures Colombia is proving a handful, and matters close to home are essential to regular supply. We are just too far away."

"But MacAdam?" I don't like saying the Canuck's name aloud.

"*Or*, someone very much like him seems to be openly experimenting with trains as transport—"

"They're running pot and hash and coke on way cars, cabooses, across state lines, across national borders."

"Yeah."

"And?" I tap my watch. "Tick-tock."

"And, in an unrelated development" Artie says, looking away again, "Emily Straight, recently turning sixteen and gaining a driver's license, borrowed her mother's car—you remember Barbie."

My hands on the door handle. "As kids will do. And?"

Now Artie's back is to me, as he sounds every day of his age. "And that was three days ago, and we think she was headed for Sheridan, Wyoming."

Okay. Day officially ruined. "Wyoming's Jewel? Was she alone?"

"Good news, bad news. She was not alone."

"Bad news?"

"She was accompanied, as far as we can tell, by her Uncle George."

I'm out of the car and into Sid's. My broom is not where it's supposed to be, but Sidney is sitting at the front counter with two plates of eggs and toast and two coffees and the carafe. I sit next to her and we start to rid our plates of their treasure. In between bites I brief Sid on our visitor. She says nothing until the end.

"So a sixteen-year-old girl is on a mission to clear the name of a dead father, and she enlists the uncle complicit in that death to travel with her, and travel all the way to the Bighorn Mountains, and, oh yeah, that uncle is actually her biological father, which she may or may not know. Is that about it?" Sid drains her mug.

I'm refilling the mugs. "Other than a quick reference to a possible real or imagined sighting of MacAdam—"

"—what now?" Sid is standing. So, I do, too.

"Seems the Canadian may be testing American coal routes for dope transport."

261

Sid clears our plates in record time. "When do we leave?"

I look hard at her, something I rarely do. We hold for about ten seconds. And Sid breaks it. "When?"

I pick her up in the Bronco one hour later.

Four hours, sixteen minutes. 238 miles to Sheridan, Wyoming.

Deadhead Sheridan.

THE END